THE SPITFIRE GIRLS

Jenny Holmes

CORGI BOOKS

TRANSWORLD PUBLISHERS
61–63 Uxbridge Road, London W5 5SA
www.penguin.co.uk

Transworld is part of the Penguin Random House group of companies
whose addresses can be found at global.penguinrandomhouse.com

Penguin
Random House
UK

First published in Great Britain in 2019 by Corgi Books
an imprint of Transworld Publishers

A CIP catalogue record for this book
is available from the British Library.

ISBN
9780552175821

Typeset in 11.5/14 pt New Baskerville ITC by Jouve (UK), Milton Keynes
Printed and bound in Great Britain by Clays Ltd, Elcograf S.p.A.

Penguin Random House is committed to a sustainable
future for our business, our readers and our planet. This book is made
from Forest Stewardship Council® certified paper.

MIX
Paper from
responsible sources
FSC® C018179

5 7 9 10 8 6 4

For my daughters, Kate and Eve.
And in memory of my Land Girl mother, Barbara,
and my father, Jim, who served in the Royal Navy
during the Second World War.

CHAPTER ONE

September 1943

'Hold on to your hat!' Lilian Watkins yelled at Mary Holland as the merry-go-round at Highcliff fair eased forward.

Sitting side-saddle on her gaily painted horse, Mary jammed her forage cap more firmly over her forehead. She held tight to the pole with her left hand and grinned over her shoulder at her fellow ATA driver who had failed to take her own advice and now squealed with dismay as her hat was dislodged by a sudden rise into the air. The cap fell to the floor beneath Lilian's prancing stallion's hooves. Her carefully curled fair hair blew into her eyes as she leaned sideways to retrieve it.

'Here, let me.' A lad in Navy ratings uniform beat Lilian to it. Jumping from his horse, he nipped underneath her rising mount and rescued her hat then handed it to her with a wink and a mock salute.

'Lilian Watkins, you did that on purpose!' Mary challenged her friend above the hurdy-gurdy music and the low rumble of the engine that propelled them forward. 'I know you did.'

Lilian grinned. On they soared astride their lacquered, wild-eyed chargers, high in the air then dipping low, with the laughing sailor back on his horse and stretching out to offer Lilian a cigarette. Observers on the ground smiled and waved at the riders, eager for their own turns, while the stony-faced operator in her pay booth cast a disapproving eye over the sailor's and Lilian's shenanigans.

'Is that it?' the nimble Navy man cried as, all too soon, the ride slowed and came to an end. 'That's never worth threepence!'

'Hear, hear!' Lilian agreed. She let her skirt slide up to within an inch of her stocking tops as she slipped from her mount.

The operator's take-it-or-leave-it shrug told them there was no point arguing. Before they knew it, fresh riders had swarmed on to the platform to take their places and Mary, Lilian and her new acquaintance stood aimlessly on the muddy grass.

'Tom Robbins,' the sailor introduced himself. He seemed a cocksure chap, with shoulders back and chest out. 'But it's Spanner to my friends. I'm a mechanic on board one of His Majesty's merchant ships,' he explained. 'I've got twelve hours' shore leave and I'm ready and willing to make the most of every minute.'

'Pleased to meet you, Spanner.' Lilian leaned in for a light for her cigarette. 'Mary and I belong to the ATA, in case you were wondering. But you can already tell by our uniform.' She ran a hand lightly down her front, over her dark blue jacket, tightly belted at the waist, and her matching skirt. Then she ostentatiously straightened her black tie.

'Like a Woodbine?' Spanner asked Mary, who shook her head. It was obvious that three was a crowd. Lilian and her sailor boy had already linked arms and were sauntering past the dodgems towards the shooting gallery.

'Anything to Anywhere; that's what ATA stands for, isn't it?' Spanner quipped as they walked along.

Lilian jabbed him with her elbow. 'Air Transport Auxiliary, I'll have you know.'

'Is that right? You mean you two Atta girls do your bit for the war effort by hurtling through the air in Spitfires and the like?' Spanner was clearly impressed as he anchored Lilian's arm around his waist.

'I should cocoa!' Lilian exclaimed. 'We leave that to the Lucinda Cholmondley-Smythes of this world, don't we, Mary? We're just drivers who taxi the pilots back to the ferry pool at Rixley. We let the toffee-nosed daredevils of this world do the flying, ta very much.'

For a while Mary listened to their chatter then chose to lag behind. Soon the brash music and the stallholders' cries drowned out Lilian and her brand-new beau's teasing voices. This was the last Mary would see of her friend all evening, she forecast, as she watched their back views disappear under the red and white striped awning of the shooting gallery. She breathed in the sweet, earthy smell of trampled grass, heard the dull thump of dodgem cars colliding and watched sparks fly from the overhead mesh.

'Got a light, love?' a man asked as she walked on towards the Moonrocket ride. He was a fisherman type, dressed in cable-knit sweater and rubber boots, holding the stub of a cigarette between nicotine-stained fingers. His face was in shadow, eyes gleaming, and his tone implied that he expected more than a light if she stopped to oblige.

So Mary shook her head and concentrated on the huge sign ahead: 'Moonrocket – Thrill Ride of the Year', with a metal dome rising high behind it. Under the brightly lit canopy there were a dozen or so rocket-shaped cars ready to whirl passengers around a central pillar to which they were attached by long steel arms.

Why not give it a go? Mary thought. She handed over her coppers and chose an empty space rocket. As she waited for the ride to fill up, she began to think about the drive home from the Yorkshire fishing port of Highcliff to Rixley. *Shall I wait for Lilian or leave her to find her own way?* she wondered as the final door clicked shut and the Moonrocket shot into action. There was an excited yelp from a pair of lads in the car in front and Mary just had time to snatch her cap from her head before she was thrust backwards against the wooden backrest and the lights of the fairground became a blur.

Her rocket rose and tilted on its steel arm. Music thumped through a loudspeaker. The wind caught her hair. *I'm flying!* High in the air, with pale blobs of faces staring up at her – tilting inwards, speeding on. *If only, if only!*

Still, Mary's heart lifted with the thrill of it – the surge of exhilaration at being airborne that ended all too soon as the machine slowed and her space rocket dipped to the ground.

Suddenly her mood changed. She was sick of the

4

funfair – the gaudiness and shallowness, the whipping up of excitement, the false thrills. It had been a long day: driving two pilots to a ferry pool in the north-east where she had met up with fellow driver Lilian for the return journey. They'd taken in the travelling fair at Highcliff en route because it happened to be there and because they were two girls at a loose end on their Friday night off and why not ride the helter-skelter and pick up a couple of chaps while they were there? It had seemed a good idea at the time.

'No need to wait for me!' Lilian caught up with Mary beside the entrance to the Ghost Train. She still had her sailor boy in tow and a teddy bear prize tucked under her arm. 'Spanner here rides a motorbike. He's promised to give me a lift home.'

Mary nodded and smiled.

'Don't worry, I'll look after her.' Spanner slipped an arm round Lilian's waist. The Ghost Train doors flew open and three laden carriages rattled to a stop. Breathless passengers tumbled out.

Mary understood that the rides provided moments of escape for fishermen's wives whose homes had been flattened by *Luftwaffe* bombs, for sailors on leave like Spanner and for drivers like themselves who dutifully ferried pilots to aerodromes scattered along the east coast of England and across the Yorkshire Wolds and Moors. She accepted all that but for the moment she'd had her fill.

'Have a grand time,' she told Lilian with a faint smile.

'We will,' Lilian and Spanner chimed as they joined the queue for the Ghost Train.

For Mary there was a dark, solitary drive ahead, followed by a night in the narrow bed in her Nissen hut billet, a new chit to pick up in the morning and no doubt another long, arduous day tomorrow. Meanwhile, the night-time journey to Rixley proved to be a ghost train of sorts, peopled with RAF airmen Mary knew who had never returned from sorties over the North Sea, and with school friends missing in Burma, North Africa and now Sicily where the Allies scrapped it out with Mussolini. Their faint, echoing voices accompanied her along narrow lanes with high hedges, past silent farmhouses and the church of St Wilfred in Rixley, overlooking the village green and row of cottages; past officers' quarters at stately Burton Grange until at last Mary reached the row of long, low huts at the edge of the woods bordering the base that she now called home.

There was the usual jumble of chairs and tables and a strong smell of bacon sizzling under the grill when Mary entered the canteen the next morning. A couple of girl pilots from the ferry pool had pushed aside the furniture to do their exercises while a third had dragged two tables together to lay out a paper pattern over the tweed fabric she'd chosen for her winter skirt. The ops-room typist pinned and snipped, all the while humming along to the music blaring from the loudspeaker. Various members of the ground crew sat around smoking thin roll-ups and wolfing down platefuls of bacon and eggs with lashings of HP sauce; among them was Stan Green, who gave Mary a wave as she crossed the room to line up at the counter.

'Where's your pal?' he called to her.

Lilian's bunk bed hadn't been slept in. Mary had noticed this without surprise as she'd headed for the wash house first thing that morning. 'Last seen heading for the Ghost Train in Highcliff,' she reported with a straight face.

The spit and crackle of bacon drew her attention and when she'd been served and she turned around again, she almost bumped into pilots Angela Browne and Bobbie Fraser, fresh from their callisthenics in the corner of the room.

'Oh, I say!' A breathless Angela eyed Mary's full plate: sausages were heaped on top of the bacon and there was fried bread to mop up the sauce from the baked beans. 'If I ate all that lot I'd never squeeze into my uniform. How do you do it, Mary? How do you stay so slim?'

'I expect it runs in the family,' Bobbie surmised. 'Mary comes from a line of women without an ounce of spare fat between them. Am I right?'

'Something like that,' Mary mumbled as she headed for Stan's table. 'Give me strength,' she muttered crossly as she sat down.

'What's up?' Stan asked when he saw the frown and pursed lips. 'Has First Officer Browne been getting up your nose again?'

'No more than usual.'

'Take no notice.' Stan was an RAF mechanic seconded to the ferry pool. A broad-featured, good-humoured chap, his boyhood love of Meccano models had led to a job in a motorcycle workshop – 'Royal Enfield Bullets are my speciality'. From there, at the age of twenty-one, he'd joined the Royal Air

Force and trained to service fighter aircraft – 'Spitfires mainly; there's nothing to beat the sound of that Merlin engine at full throttle'. He and Mary had arrived at Rixley together at the start of the second week in May and had immediately hit it off, though she was the shy, thin-skinned type while nothing ever got Stan down. 'What did Lilian get up to exactly?'

Mary shrugged. 'Don't ask me. But I expect she'll be here soon.'

'Say no more.' Stan winked. 'Talk of the devil,' he added as a bedraggled Lilian put in a bleary-eyed appearance, jacket unbuttoned and black tie askew.

She was immediately spotted and seized upon by Flight Lieutenant Cameron Ainslie. Rixley's strict second in command took Lilian by the arm and hustled her out of the door, heading across the small square of mowed lawn and out of sight into the office at the foot of the control tower.

Mary's stomach tightened and her frown deepened.

'What's this? Lilian's second warning?' Stan asked as he pushed aside his empty plate.

'Third,' Mary said.

Stan sucked his teeth. 'Tut-tut. This is Flight Lieutenant Cameron Ainslie we're talking about; you don't want to get on the wrong side of him.'

'On the other hand, he won't want to lose one of his drivers if he can help it.' Mary pointed out the obvious. Air Transport Auxiliary personnel didn't grow on trees, despite a recent War Office push to recruit new ground staff and pilots under the proud Latin motto *Aetheris Avidi*, which few took the trouble to learn the meaning of. However, last year's advertisement featuring the latest Spit Mark IX had succeeded in pulling in more wounded ex-pilots from the Great War and the usual smattering of socialite women eager to follow in the footsteps of Amy Johnson and Pauline Gower. But there was still more work to be done before supply met an ever increasing demand, a fact that Ainslie would be all too well aware of as he disciplined Lilian.

Mary glanced anxiously out of the window in time to see her friend emerge from the flight lieutenant's office. Clattering her knife and fork on to her plate and asking Stan to keep an eye on her food, she rushed to the door.

'Don't ask,' Lilian said before Mary could speak, making a slashing gesture across her throat. 'That's me; I've had my marching orders.'

'Really and truly?' Mary spotted Ainslie in his office, standing with his back to the window and speaking into the telephone. She followed Lilian along the narrow asphalt path towards their bunk-room, shaded by the boughs of ancient oak trees at the edge of Burton Wood.

'As of right this moment,' Lilian confirmed. Her chin was up and her heavily made-up face had taken on a defiant expression. 'For bringing the organization into disrepute, whatever that means. See if I care. They can put their Hurricanes and their Lancasters and their yes-sir-no-sirs in their pipes and smoke them!' Like Mary, Lilian had harboured dreams of learning to fly when she'd joined the ATA, only to find that lack of previous flying experience would keep her confined to duties on the ground. 'Typist or canteen worker; that's what to aim for,' the prune-faced recruitment officer had informed her. Lilian had proved her wrong by training as a driver but that wasn't exactly flying, was it?

'I'm sorry you're leaving.' Mary watched her friend take shirts and skirts from her locker and fling them into a battered brown suitcase. 'So what now?'

'Who cares?' Lilian couldn't wait to be gone. 'Don't worry about me, Mary. I'll land on my feet.'

'I don't doubt it.'

'I will. There's a big world out there, don't you know.' She snapped her suitcase shut then glanced at her reflection in the mottled mirror on the inside of her locker door. Her fair curls had drooped and her lipstick was smudged. 'Shall I tell you what Spanner said to me last night? He said I should try for a job as a fashion model; I was better-looking than a lot you see on the covers of magazines.' That had been before the couple's heated fumblings in a bus shelter overlooking Highcliff harbour and the rest that had gone on in the grounds of the ruined church perched on the clifftop half a mile outside town. And before Spanner had looked at his watch and beaten a hasty retreat, pleading curfew and leaving Lilian to hitch a lift back to Rixley in the grey dawn light. No motorbike ride home after all; no address, nothing.

'Write to me, let me know how you get on,' Mary urged.

'I will,' Lilian promised.

She won't. Mary sighed as she headed back to the canteen to finish her breakfast. Girls like Lilian never did.

*

10

'It's my birthday next month.' In the noisy melee of the canteen Bobbie watched Angela polish off her second cup of tea of the morning. 'October the fifth, to be exact.'

Angela swallowed before she spoke. 'May one ask?'

'How old? Yes, one may. I'll be twenty-two and I've got my heart set on being promoted to first officer before then, if I can clock up the five hundred hours in time. Then I'll be able to fly Wellingtons and Whitleys as well as Spits.'

Angela smiled at the idea of Bobbie, all five foot three of her, taking charge of the big, twin-engine bombers. With her wavy, sandy-coloured hair, pale skin and eager smile, she had the gleeful look of a schoolgirl on a day's outing to the seaside. 'If you don't clock up the five hundred, I'm sure your mama can have a word in the sainted Pauline's shell-like ear.' Although they'd known each other for less than a year, Angela was aware that Bobbie's family was well connected; so much so that in the years leading up to the war, their big estate in the Scottish Highlands had often hosted shooting parties from south of the border, comprising politicians, titled lords and close friends of the ATA commander herself.

Bobbie, however, took nothing for granted. 'I'd rather do it on merit.' She frowned and shook her head as she tucked into her breakfast. 'Anyway, enough about me. I hear congratulations are in order.'

'They are?' Angela seemed puzzled and then amused. 'Oh Lord, don't tell me: I've gone and got myself engaged to dear Lionel without realizing!'

'Very funny.' Feeling a twinge of sympathy towards Angela's long-suffering beau, Bobbie pressed on. 'No, as a matter of fact I'm talking about the recruitment poster.'

'Oh, that!' Angela waved her hand dismissively.

'It's true, then?' Bobbie persisted. 'You're destined to be our next Atta poster girl? Fame and fortune beckons?'

'Apparently.' Angela seemed unconcerned. Certainly some chap with a professional-looking camera had shown up one day in late August to snap her sitting on the wing of a Spit and climbing into the cockpit dressed in zip-up Sidcot suit and carrying her helmet, allowing her dark hair to blow freely in the wind. She hadn't thought much of it until a letter had arrived two days earlier, informing her that she had the honour of being selected to be the latest ATA poster girl.

'"Eager for the Air", eh?' Bobbie quoted the English translation of the Air Transport Auxiliary motto. She recalled as if it were yesterday the precious moment when her own flying instructor had told her, 'It's all yours, lassie!', before sending her off on her first solo flight in a Gypsy Moth. Bobbie had taken off and risen high above the green aerodrome, leaving the land behind and heading out over the sea buffeted by her own slipstream. She'd felt no fear, only the thrill of flying; a thrill like no other before or since.

'Oh yes, you know me; always ready for the next mission,' Angela confirmed as the background music stopped and a voice blared at them through the loudspeaker system.

The tinny voice on the Tannoy issued the first orders of the day: 'Will all pilots report to the operations room for their chits. Repeat: all pilots to the operations room!'

'Here we go!' Quick as a flash Bobbie was out of her seat and racing for the door, ahead of Angela and half a dozen male pilots. They scrambled for the operations room on the first floor of the control tower where they formed a disorderly queue under a sign saying 'Pilots Report Here', waiting to be issued with a slip of paper detailing their destination for the day.

'Let's hope the rain holds off.' A second officer at the rear of the queue glanced up at serious clouds gathering in the east. Having to fly through low cloud was an ATA pilot's worst nightmare, forcing them down to unsafe heights and making it almost impossible to spot landmarks such as rivers, roads and railways.

Bobbie reached through the hatch to take her chit then pushed free of the crowd. 'Lossiemouth!' she announced with a victorious wave of her slip of paper. 'Hurrah, home from home!'

Angela received her chit and read that she was to head a hundred miles north-west in her favourite aircraft, the glorious Spitfire Mark IX. She raced across the grass to the locker room to pick up her flying helmet and map then upstairs again to the met room for a full weather report before pulling her vital blue book out of her top pocket. Each page of the small spiral-bound notebook contained the basic dos and don'ts for piloting a plane, whether Hawker Hurricane, Spitfire or Lancaster. Angela devoured the page devoted to the latest Spit – speeds for take-off, climbing and cruising, the handling of the throttle and so on – then checked her chit again to note that her particular plane was adapted for photo reconnaissance, having cameras fitted to each wing and an extra-large fuel tank concealed under the cowling in front of the cockpit. 'To take her out across the Atlantic,' she said out loud as she sprinted across the airfield lugging her parachute pack with her.

She found Stan and a young apprentice waiting on the runway next to her aircraft and watched the youngster wipe the Perspex canopy with a clean, soft cloth while Stan made a final check of the propeller speed unit. The experienced mechanic had already changed the plugs and topped up the fuel tanks before breakfast.

'Over to you, First Officer Browne,' Stan commented as Angela stepped in spritely fashion on to the port wing and climbed into the cockpit. She felt her heart rate quicken as she lowered the new bubble-type canopy over her head and settled into the narrow seat. Then she strapped herself in and adjusted her goggles before giving a thumbs-up to Stan.

Chocks away. She opened the throttle and the Merlin engine emitted its throaty roar. Angela was all set to taxi to her take-off point, one eye on the ever-darkening clouds (were the met boys certain it wasn't going to throw it down?), heart racing now as she picked up speed and felt the rise of the Spit's nose, the surge forward as she left the ground. *Like a kick up the backside*, Angela thought. The new Spit was powerful, fast, utterly beautiful. Perfect; love at first sight.

Later that day, as First Officer Jean Dobson approached Runway 2 at Rixley, she flew into a thick bank of cloud.

'Damn!' She couldn't see a blasted thing, only wet, grey mist billowing past her cockpit. Less than twenty miles to landing and now this!

As the aircraft shuddered and tilted off course, Jean remembered the drill for dealing with sudden cloud: straighten up first then climb to a safe height of ten or twelve hundred feet and return to the original course. Don't fiddle with the throttle. Attempt a shallow dive to the safety break-off height of eight hundred feet.

That's all very well, she thought as her Spit Mark V lurched in the turbulence and her altimeter jerked down to six hundred. She was ferrying the four-year-old aircraft from Walsall in the West Midlands back to Rixley after some major repair work to the propeller shaft and undercarriage. *It would help if they taught us how to read the blinking instruments instead of forcing us to rely on what we can see with our own eyes!* The lights on the indicator panel winked at her without her having a clue what they were telling her. On top of which, the Spit had no working radio.

Jean swore hard then climbed again. She would make one more dive and if she still had zero visibility she would have to admit defeat by climbing fast to a height of 1,500 feet then bailing out and relying on her parachute to bring her safely down. Otherwise she was in imminent danger of flying slap-bang into a hidden hillside. *If in doubt, bail out* – that was what the manual said. Save your own skin and leave the pilotless plane to crash to the ground.

Jean's mouth felt dry as she dived a second time. The plane jerked and shuddered then suddenly emerged from the cloud at not much more than treetop height, with the rain pelting down. By some miracle she found herself only half a mile away from her destination. But she wasn't out of danger yet, for she knew that her nose-heavy Spit could easily flip over on a puddled landing strip and, lo and behold, Jean made out that much of the runway stood in water.

She reminded herself that her stark choice was to climb again then bail out or else attempt to land. Swallowing hard, she chose the latter. *Let's risk it*, she thought. Every single aircraft the RAF could lay their hands on was vital at this stage of the war and it was her job to deliver this Spitfire in one piece. So she flew in low over Burton Wood, keeping the aerodrome control tower in her sights, bracing herself for the impact of landing. Sure enough, there was a sudden bounce when the tyres hit the ground then the aircraft slewed to one side as mud and water spewed everywhere, covering the cockpit with mucky spray. *Jam on the brakes, keep the plane upright. Pray.*

The Spit didn't flip. Instead, it skidded down the waterlogged runway before squealing to a halt and allowing Jean to heave a sigh of relief. She sat for a few seconds without moving, listening to the rain pelt down. Then she released her harness and raised the cockpit roof.

'That was a close shave,' Stan shouted from under

his sou'wester as he ran from a hangar and offered Jean a hand to jump down to the ground. A black oilskin cape protected the mechanic from the worst of the downpour. 'You cleared those trees by thirty feet at the most.'

'Thanks, Stan.' Jean's heart still battered against her ribs but she wouldn't show how scared she'd been. 'What's the met office playing at, giving us the go-ahead to fly in this filthy weather?'

'Search me. I'm only the engine wallah.' Stan was mightily glad to see Jean step out of that cockpit. She was one of the best and bravest, was Jean. And with her long, silky fair hair and wide grey eyes she was better-looking than Angela Browne any day of the week. In fact, in Stan's humble opinion, if anyone deserved to be on a recruitment poster for the Atta girls, it was Jean.

Not that he would tell her this and not that she would invite him to. Jean was the type who kept herself to herself and concentrated on her flying. And by God, she was an ace of the skies. Stan didn't know any other pilot, man or woman, who could have landed that Spit in these conditions – mud and water everywhere, engine whining, tyres squealing. And then she'd stepped out of the cockpit cool as a cucumber, as if she'd taken a joyride in a Fox Moth at a flying circus: *roll-up, roll-up, a half-crown a go!* Stan had to hand it to Jean Dobson, she'd come up the hard way and risen to the very top. The *crème de la crème*, as the Angelas and Bobbies of this world might have said. *The cat's whiskers* was Stan's version. And a bloody knockout in the looks department. He watched Jean walk slowly through the downpour towards the operations room where she would report the Spitfire's safe arrival then clock off for the day.

It was a Saturday. For a second or two Stan thought of asking Jean to go to the flicks with him. He pictured it: a mumbled invitation from him, a cool glance from her then a quick, apologetic shake of her head. The idea flitted away again. Come to think of it, Stan couldn't imagine Jean Dobson settling into a cinema seat with an ice cream in her hand and the light from the screen flickering across her beautiful face. No chance. So Stan would put on his raincoat and stroll down to the Fox and Hounds in Rixley instead. He'd throw a few darts, down a few pints – enjoy a normal Saturday night. Then, come Sunday, it would be business as usual.

CHAPTER TWO

'Apparently Jean flew into a freak storm.' Later the following evening Angela sat with Bobbie, whisky glass in hand, in the officers' mess at Burton Grange. 'The usual problem: cold air blew in off the North Sea sooner than forecast. The met boys were caught with their trousers down.'

'Don't they have eyes in their heads?' Bobbie protested after she'd listened to Angela's account of Jean's emergency landing in the middle of a downpour. Bobbie had recently got back from Lossiemouth after an overnight stay and a long train journey home that had involved many diversions and delays. Now all she wanted to do was to settle into a leather armchair and relax in the lounge bar of the stately home requisitioned two years earlier. One wing currently served as a convalescent hospital and the other as ATA officers' quarters. 'Anyone could see that there was bound to be a storm.'

'It was the timing they got wrong,' Angela emphasized. Her own weekend had been all work and no play too – flying the reconnaissance Spit over to the Lancashire–Cumberland border to drop it off in Whitehaven ready for service over the Irish Sea and beyond. She'd then stayed overnight in a down-at-heel bed and breakfast before being picked up and driven home by that mouse Mary Holland, who never had a word to say for herself unless absolutely pushed. 'You know, I sometimes wonder about Mary,' she mused as Bobbie put her dainty feet up on a padded stool and took a sip of her whisky. 'What goes on inside that head of hers?'

'Mary who?' Bobbie's attention was partly on Squadron Leader Hilary Stevens, the commanding officer of the ferry pool, and Cameron Ainslie; the two officers were ensconced in the far corner of the room, close to the bar. Shrouded in cigarette smoke, they were talking to a third man whom she'd never clapped eyes on before. The newcomer was slight and long-limbed, clean-shaven and with a neat side parting in his strikingly fair hair. His legs were crossed and he jiggled his right foot as he listened attentively to the other two men. 'Who's that?' she remarked casually when Angela paused to draw breath.

'I haven't a clue. Mary Holland; that's who I'm talking about. Do pay attention, Bobbie. You know: the driver with those enormous grey eyes and dark lashes, chin-length brown hair, never wears a scrap of make-up. Quiet as a mouse. You do know her!'

'Oh yes. And why are we talking about her, pray?' Bobbie felt the whisky burn her throat. There was a comforting glow from a log fire and a low table lamp cast long shadows over the intricate pattern of the Turkish rug. *Breathe in oak and leather, polish and woodsmoke – close your eyes and for a few moments imagine you're at home with springer spaniels Captain and Rufus at your feet and the war a million miles away.*

'Because Mary is an enigma,' Angela insisted. 'I've just spent several hours cooped up in a car with her and I don't know any more about her than I did before we set off – which is almost nothing, by the way.'

'She's a pretty girl, though. I've heard she worked as a carder in a woollen mill before the war.'

'Which one?' Angela's family owned several big woollen mills in West Yorkshire. They'd been founded by her grandfather in the late eighteen hundreds and made him pots of money: enough to buy up half the county and to build an entire town – street after street of respectable terraced housing, complete with shops and a children's playground, for workers who agreed to sign the pledge and attend church every Sunday.

'No idea.' Refusing to be drawn on the uninspiring topic of Mary Holland, Bobbie's gaze wandered around the oak-panelled room until she noticed Jean sitting by herself in a window seat, quietly reading a book. 'Look over there; the heroine of the hour,' she told Angela. 'Now we can get the tale straight from the horse's mouth.'

Jean's sleek blonde head was buried in *Great Expectations*, a gift from her mother on winning her Flying Scholarship at the age of seventeen. The book went everywhere with her, through Women's Air Reserve flying school where she received fifty hours of instruction and clocked up two hundred hours' flying time. From there, with no money behind her, Jean had been forced to drop out of the flying game for a while and find work as an usherette in the local fleapit and as a waitress in a Lyons tea shop, saving her wages, biding her time and dreaming.

There was trouble at home: Jean's mother had had to give up her job as a librarian to look after her ailing father, but Jean had never let go of her ambition to keep on flying and one evening, during a shift at the cinema, an item about the ATA on Pathé News had caught her attention. The civilian organization, officially set up at the start of 1940 but only fully operational in late 1941, needed more pilots and they needed them quickly. Jean had stored the information but not acted upon it until a chance meeting in a pub with a certain First Officer Douglas Thornton had kicked her into action. At his bidding she'd filled in an application form and been accepted on the training course at Thame. Here she'd buckled down to pass exams in maths, geometry, grammar and composition, besides going back to square one in a dummy cockpit, forced to relearn the basics despite her earlier experience. However, an instructor there had picked up on Jean's unusual ability and taken her to one side.

'You know you'll be doing a man's job without getting a man's pay if you join the ATA?' he'd reminded her. 'You'll get twenty per cent less than the men.'

'Not if the push for equal pay gets through.' The dispute had been going on for a while now. 'It could happen at any moment,' Jean had reminded her instructor. 'Anyway, is that the only downside?' she'd asked with a raised eyebrow and a direct stare.

'Besides risking your life every time you take to the air, you mean?' He was teaching his grandmother to suck eggs with this one, he'd quickly realized.

Jean had nodded to acknowledge the danger. She'd heard of a recent near miss when an ATA pilot flying a Spit from one ferry pool to another in poor visibility had been mistaken for the enemy by British anti-aircraft artillery. The plane had come under attack and only the pilot's skill and the Spitfire's supreme handling had averted disaster.

The instructor had left it at that. Jean would soon find out for herself the other pitfalls of joining the hundred or so female pilots currently ferrying fighters and bombers around the country. For the time being, he would let her follow her dream.

Now, sitting in the lounge bar of the converted mansion, with the equal pay fight won and six months in to what Jean regarded as the best job in the world, she reached the part in the book where Pip discovers the shocking truth about Magwitch, his convict-patron. *Terrific name for a jailbird*, she thought with a shudder. *Magwitch – part maggot, part sorcerer.* And that harrowing scene in the churchyard near the beginning where the graves of Pip's dead brothers and sisters are laid out like lozenges in a row – well, that was unforgettable. The surprise of the book was that in the end Pip's savage benefactor turned out to be more honourable than many of his betters. Dickens was clever that way.

'Hello there, Jean. What are you reading?' Bobbie came across the room with a spring in her step.

Jean looked up with a guilty start then held up the book for Bobbie to read the title on the spine, only to feel the volume snatched from her hands.

'Forget that old dull-as-ditch-water stuff. Let me drag you over to have a good old chat with Angela and me.'

Reluctantly Jean stood up and smoothed the creases out of her skirt, a navy blue, slim-fitting one that she teamed with a crisp white blouse. She felt distinctly prim and proper next to diminutive Bobbie in her soft cashmere sweater and high-waisted black trousers and Angela who sat by the fire in an embroidered satin blouse with a plunging neckline and a gathered crimson skirt that gave her a gypsy air.

While Bobbie darted to the bar to fetch Jean an unasked-for glass of whisky, Angela drew her fellow pilot down into an empty armchair. 'We demand the lowdown on yesterday,' she informed her with one of her glittering smiles. 'But we were meant to wait for Bobbie and it seems she's been held up.'

Diverted on her way to the bar, Bobbie was deep in conversation with Cameron, Hilary and their as yet unnamed companion. The three men had stood up in gentlemanly fashion and Angela and Jean could see that introductions were being made.

'Heigh-ho.' Angela sighed as she saw the new airman lean in towards Bobbie, smiling and laughing, giving her his full attention. 'Like a wasp around a honey pot, eh? Or should that be a bee? Anyway, fire away, Jean; tell me how you managed to land that old Spit in yesterday's downpour. I'm all ears.'

'Edward Simpson; Teddy to my friends.' The newest arrival at Burton Grange immediately took to the tiny, vivacious girl in sweater and slacks. He'd deliberately mirrored her opening salvo of 'Roberta Fraser; Bobbie to my friends'; breathily delivered and with a charming grin.

'Hello, Teddy, very good to meet you. I'm a member

of the Anything to Anywhere brigade, aiming for my five hundred hours. You're RAF, I see.'

'Yes; Flight Lieutenant, at your service.' Teddy quickly overcame his first impression that Bobbie wasn't old enough or tall enough to fly anything bigger than a kite.

'Uh-oh, I've seen that look before!' she said with a light laugh. '"The hand that rocks the cradle wrecks the crate", eh?'

He silently cursed himself for blushing. This was not going as well as he'd hoped. 'Not at all. I'm sure . . . that is to say . . .' He looked towards his fellow officers for reassurance.

'Take no notice; she's kidding,' Hilary said in his clipped, narrow voice. He produced his words from far back in his throat and his hooded eyes suggested suspicion.

'It's not that you're a woman,' Teddy stammered, digging himself in deeper. 'I'm sure women are perfectly capable . . . I mean, it's just that . . .'

Hilary put a warning hand on Teddy's arm. 'Bobbie joined the National Women's Air Reserve straight out of finishing school, like her friend Angela over there.' He nodded in the direction of Angela and Jean who seemed deep in earnest conversation by the fire. 'The ATA practically snapped their hands off when they applied to join early this year.'

Teddy cleared his throat. He didn't like women teasing him but he had to remember his manners. 'Of course. No offence intended.'

'None taken.' Bobbie's eyes sparkled as she cheekily stole a cigarette from the packet laid out on the men's table, next to an unopened pack of cards. 'If you really wanted to insult us, try this for size, from an article I read recently in *Aeroplane* magazine – here it is verbatim.' She cleared her throat then declaimed the words slowly. '"The menace is the woman who thinks she ought to be flying in a high-speed bomber when she really has not the intelligence to scrub the floor of a hospital properly."' Bobbie challenged Teddy with a direct, unblinking stare. 'Honestly; without a word of a lie.'

'Shocking.' Cameron intervened as he tipped his glasses to sit more firmly above the prominent bridge of his nose. Taller than both Hilary and Teddy, he wore his fair hair in a similar style to the newcomer's: with a side parting, slicked back with Brylcreem. Even when dressed in civvies, as he was now, he looked immaculate – always closely shaven and well groomed, down to the tiniest detail. Seeing Teddy Simpson's flushed cheeks, Cameron realized that Bobbie was pushing her luck and wished she would return promptly to her fireside chair.

'Of course, Bobbie and Angela set out to prove the opposite,' Hilary pointed out urbanely. 'And Jean, too, for that matter.'

'At which point . . .' With a last bright smile followed by an alluring puff on her cigarette and a swish of her wide, silky trousers, Bobbie moved on. 'Scotch on the rocks,' she told the bartender in her best Joan Crawford drawl. 'And make it a double, baby.'

'So, Jean, where did you learn to fly?' Angela and Jean had moved on from events of the previous day by the time Bobbie arrived with Jean's drink. 'Who was your instructor? When did you first realize that flying was for you?'

'Steady on,' Bobbie protested as she curled up in her chair. 'Give the poor girl a chance.' Angela's questions had obviously flustered Jean, whose cheeks had coloured up and whose forehead bore a slight frown.

'It's all right, I don't mind,' Jean said. Flying was one subject she was happy to expand on. 'I first started on this road three years ago, with a scholarship.'

'For the Women's Air Reserve? Good for you.' *So far, so normal*, Angela thought. Many of her friends had attended the school, having grown bored with ballet dancing, horse riding and swanning around the London clubs. Getting there on a scholarship meant that Jean must be exceptionally bright, however.

Jean went on in a low, calm voice. 'But my first time in the air was earlier than that – on my twelfth birthday, in fact. My uncle gave me half a crown for a ride in a Fox Moth.'

'You don't say.' For Angela this altered the picture a little. 'Where was that?'

'At a flying circus near where I lived.' Jean picked up the new inflexion in her interrogator's voice. Angela had evidently been expecting to hear of a rich papa with his own private plane. When Jean spoke again it was with more reserve. 'It was such a thrill to be airborne for the first time. I'll never forget it.'

'Quite.' Bobbie had missed the nuances of this exchange and bounded on through the conversation. 'I couldn't get enough of it after my first go. I pestered and pestered for Father to let me take the controls of his Gypsy Moth until finally he gave way. Likewise, when the war started – I had a big battle to convince him that flying for the ATA was the best way to keep me out of the way of bombs and so on. No front-line action for me, I'm afraid.'

'From what I gather, Bobbie is a daddy's girl,' Angela explained. 'An only child, you see. What was it exactly that brought you to Rixley, Jean?'

Jean thought before she answered. She tried not to be nettled by her companions' superior manner; after all, they'd started life at the top of the pile so could have no notion of what it meant to scrimp and save to work from the bottom up. Perhaps it was time they learned. 'To Rixley?' she repeated. 'Actually, the trigger for it was First Officer Thornton.'

'Was it, by Jove?' The unlikely connection between the older ex-RAF man and elegant, cool-as-ice Jean puzzled Bobbie. After all, Douglas was by no means the inspiring type; quite the opposite. His desk-bound job at Rixley was vital but hardly exciting, allocating pilots their planes and destinations for the day, taking into account weather conditions and so forth. Besides, he was older than many at the base – pushing forty, by Bobbie's reckoning. He was rather thickset and hampered by a serious leg injury sustained when he ditched his Wellington bomber into the sea during the evacuation of Dunkirk. Douglas had been left with a pronounced limp and a fixed resentment of the fact that he could no longer fly anything more challenging than lumbering Avro Ansons, the airborne taxis used by the ATA.

'Yes. I'd finished my shift in the Highcliff Gaumont,' Jean continued in her clear, determined voice. Let Angela and Bobbie draw their own conclusions. 'Selling ice creams, and so on. It was late but I decided to call in at the Harbour Inn on my way home—'

'You mean the Harbour Inn in Highcliff?' Angela cut in. Things were getting distinctly interesting so she leaned forward in her chair.

'The very one. Highcliff is my home town. My dad worked on the fishing trawlers all his life, until his boat was caught in a storm and went down with all hands except for him. He lost three fingers on his right hand to frostbite. Anyway, on this particular night I wasn't keen to go straight home after work. It was a Monday so I knew the pub would be quiet. In fact, the only other person in there was a man in Air Transport Auxiliary uniform who turned out to be none other than . . .'

'Douglas.' Bobbie got the picture – a drab, empty bar with uncomfortable wooden settles, pictures of fishing vessels on the walls, maybe a few grimy horse brasses over the mantelpiece, Douglas looking morose as usual.

Jean nodded. 'We got talking. He told me what he did and where he was based and then I mentioned that I'd thought of joining the ATA but hadn't got any further than that. One thing led to another. First Officer Thornton promised to put in a good word for me if I applied – I honestly believe that's what got me past the interviewing panel.'

'And lo, here we all are!' This was definitely something that Angela would have a natter with Bobbie about later: how the war threw you together with all different types. Actually, Angela was warming to Jean, having thought her too cool and distant until now. 'And you're the star of the show, bringing that Spit in the way you did. I admire your nerve.'

'But you and Douglas – tell us more!' Whisky had brought out the gossip in Bobbie. With one eye still on Teddy Simpson and with curiosity bubbling up inside her, she risked another personal question.

But the ice maiden in Jean resurfaced. She stood up and smoothed down her skirt once more. 'There's nothing more to tell,' she insisted, picking up her copy of *Great Expectations*, which Bobbie had plonked down on the arm of her chair. 'That's it; The End.'

Exactly a week after Lilian had been unceremoniously dismissed from the service, a new driver arrived at Rixley to take her place.

'What's her name and what's she like?' Stan asked Mary as they took an evening walk together through Burton Wood. There was a chill in the air and they'd both remarked on how rapidly the days were shortening. The leaves on the oak trees had curled at the edges and were yellowing, while fallen acorns and beech nuts carpeted the damp ground.

Mary enjoyed the crunch underfoot and the smell of decay. 'Olive Pearson is her name. I've only just met her so how should I know what she's like?'

'Blimey, Mary.' Stan laughed at her tendency to take things too literally. 'I'm only asking for your first impression.'

'Tallish, plumpish, wears glasses . . .'

Stan threw up his hands in protest. 'I can see that

for myself. I thought you'd had tea with her in the canteen.'

'I did – with your pal Gordon Mason and young Harry Wood. Gordon did most of the talking, as per usual. Why don't you ask him what Olive is like?'

'I will when I get a chance.' Stan sauntered ahead with his hands in his pockets, whistling a tune he'd heard on the wireless and couldn't get out of his head.

Mary stopped to pick up a handful of acorns and turn them over on her palm. Gordon was Stan's fellow mechanic, just back from home leave and full of stories about the family fruit and veg stall and his father's complaints about not being able to get hold of citrus fruits and pineapples. 'I told him, he should be so lucky,' Gordon had announced to anyone in the canteen who would listen. 'Where does Dad think he is – back in Jamaica? Pineapples, I ask you!'

After a few more paces, Stan stopped and turned. 'What's up? What's eating you now?' he asked Mary.

She threw down the acorns. 'Nothing.'

'Something is; I can tell.' Something was always eating Mary if only she would admit it. 'Come on; you can tell your Uncle Stanley.'

Mary laughed in spite of herself. Stan was a mere two years older than her: twenty-one to her nineteen. 'The fact is some people don't know how lucky they are.'

'Like who, for example?'

'Name any officer billeted at the Grange for a start.' The Angelas and the Bobbies, Hilarys and Camerons. She knew she didn't need to spell it out.

'Ah yes; soft mattresses, hot water on tap, toasting

their tootsies by a big log fire. Whereas we have to make do with bunk beds in a freezing Nissen hut and ice-cold water in a communal wash house, eh?'

'Yes, but it's more than that.' In the shadows of the wood and in Stan's easy company, Mary's tongue was slowly loosened. 'It's not fair – they get all the chances.'

'True.' He looked long and hard at Mary's expression. She seemed sad and wary behind those big grey eyes. 'But thank your lucky stars you don't have to put up with them, day in, day out.'

'Yes, I only have to drive them from one ferry pool to another,' she agreed. 'But that's bad enough.'

'Still; think of poor Jean.' Thinking of Jean was something that Stan did often – her soft hair and long, slim fingers, the determined set of her jaw, the watchful look in her eyes. 'She has to put up with Angela and Co. looking down their noses at her at close quarters, worse luck.'

'She does?' Mary was surprised. 'They do?'

'Yes, Jean's not like them. Haven't you noticed?'

'I can't say I have.'

'No, you wouldn't.' Being shy and keeping yourself to yourself was one thing, but not noticing what was going on under your nose was another. That was one aspect of Mary's personality that annoyed Stan. 'Wake up, girl.'

'All right then, I suppose you're right.'

'You bet I am.' He walked ahead again, between thick silver-grey trunks and low overhanging boughs.

Mary softened her manner. 'I'm sorry. I didn't mean to upset you. Anyway, I didn't know you cared so much about Jean.'

'I don't,' he shot back at her before abruptly changing the subject. 'By the way, did you listen to the news on the wireless today? They say Hitler's planning to evacuate civilians from Berlin, thanks to the hiding we've given them lately.'

'Poor devils.' Mary recalled watching the newsreels of the London Blitz soon after the war had started: the bombed-out houses and burning buildings, children playing in the rubble. Now the boot seemed to be on the other foot.

'It's them or us,' Stan said matter-of-factly. 'Mussolini's on his way out too so we must be doing something right. I should think so too, since we've got over half the men and women of this country involved in the war effort.'

'Stan.' Mary stepped in front of him and began to walk slowly backwards until she bumped into a solid tree trunk. 'Can you please stop talking and listen for a moment?'

For a split second he thought that Mary was going to fling her arms around his neck and kiss him, here in the woods, in the gathering dusk.

'I went on the Moonrocket ride at Highcliff funfair,' she blurted out, colour flooding her pale cheeks.

He drew his chin towards his neck and took his hands from his pockets. 'Come again?'

'The Moonrocket,' she repeated. 'It sounds daft, doesn't it?'

'And . . . ?' he prompted. He should have known better; Mary wasn't the type to invite a quick kiss and a cuddle.

'For a moment I closed my eyes and blocked out all the noise. It felt as if I was really flying; up in the

33

clouds in a Spit, looking down on everything.' Tears welled up and she fell silent.

'I see,' he said slowly.

'I wasn't, though. I was just on a silly fairground ride.'

'But you could if you wanted to. I mean, do it for real.'

Mary shook her head.

'Why not?'

'Flying Spitfires isn't for me.'

'Why not?' Stan said again, feeling bold enough to link arms with her and walk on. 'If you really want to, why not corner Squadron Leader Stevens and ask him for an application form?'

'No, I couldn't.'

'Yes, you could. You just have to open your mouth and say the words: "I'd like to put my name down for a conversion course and train as a pilot, please." Nice and clear, looking him straight in the eye.'

'And he wouldn't laugh at me?'

'Why should he? There's a new ATA campaign on the go. They need recruits and they need them fast.'

'I know – they're putting Angela Browne on the posters.'

'That means they will say yes to you, Mary. You and girls like you, who know how to read a map and follow orders to the letter.'

She drank in his words thirstily. 'Oh,' she said softly and with a dawning realization that what Stan said might be true.

'Yes; "Oh"!' They approached the far edge of the wood and glimpsed the landscaped grounds of Burton Grange. At the same time they noticed the faint drone of aeroplane engines high above. 'Do it, Mary, if you really want to.'

'I do,' she murmured. To fly a new Spitfire from factory to ferry pool; the easy-on-the-eye little aircraft with its elegant, elliptical wings and smooth lines, its azure camouflage. Mary saw in her mind's eye the Spit Mark IX's effortless rise from the ground, the elegant dip of the starboard wing as it banked and disappeared into the clouds.

The sound of approaching engines grew louder as Mary and Stan walked clear of the wood. They spotted six planes in the east, silhouetted against a darkening sky.

'Boche!' Stan yelped. He dragged her to the ground, face down. 'Messerschmitts and Heinkels!'

At that moment the German gunners unleashed ribbons of machine-gun bullets – *ack-ack-ack!* The deadly ammunition tore into the smooth lawns of the stately home and shattered windows. *Ack-ack!* It ricocheted off stone walls and set fire to a line of cars parked outside the main entrance to the house, their petrol tanks exploding in a sheet of yellow flames.

'Keep your head down!' Stan yelled as Mary dared to look up.

She pressed her face into the earth. There was the heavy thud of a bomb landing forty feet away, followed by an enormous, ear-splitting explosion. The ground opened up. There was a shower of earth and rubble. A second thud and another deafening explosion. Trees splintered and crashed down. There were flames everywhere. Mary closed her eyes and held her breath until it was over. *Don't breathe. Don't look up. Pray to God to come out of this in one piece.*

CHAPTER THREE

The distant bells of St Wilfred's broke the early-morning silence as Jean, Bobbie and Angela stood in the main doorway of Burton Grange and looked out over the bombed grounds.

No one spoke as they took in the havoc wreaked by the German bombers the night before.

Smoke still rose from burnt-out vehicles and deep, jagged craters scarred the once-smooth lawns. Tall redwoods at the edge of the estate had toppled and their straight trunks lay criss-crossed on the ground. Closer to where they stood, a pile of rubble from the remains of the stone portico prevented the three young women from walking down the broad steps.

Angela sighed then turned away. As she went back inside, she was forced to step over shards of broken glass and noticed for the first time that the banister to the main staircase had collapsed and that a huge portrait of a Lady somebody or other in powdered wig and wide crinoline hung in tatters, slashed by shrapnel from top to bottom.

Bobbie and Jean lingered in the doorway. They had been awake all night, helping nurses and porters from the convalescent wing to stretcher their patients to the relative safety of waiting field ambulances that would transport them to hospital in Highcliff. A direct hit on the sprawling mansion had destroyed the roof of two of the wards and it had been immediately apparent that a full evacuation was necessary. It was only when some of the rubble had been cleared that two bodies had been found underneath: one in pyjamas, one in a nurse's uniform but otherwise unidentifiable. Bobbie had been the one to discover the nurse. She'd seen a hand amongst the dust and debris and started to scrabble at the loose stones, uncovering an arm and then a bloodied female torso, hoping against hope that the person buried beneath would still be alive. Douglas had helped her by scraping away the grey plaster dust from the nurse's face and trying to breathe air into her lungs. In the end Bobbie had pulled him away and told him it was no good. The woman's skull had been crushed. There was nothing to be done.

'At least they missed their main target.' In the grim, grey dawn Jean was the first to relay the news she'd just received from Stan about the state of play at the airfield. 'All three runways are still in one piece. So are the two hangars. None of the aircraft were damaged.'

Bobbie nodded. 'That's something, I suppose.' Both women felt crushed by the horror of last night's events, unable to decide what to do next until Angela returned with urgent news.

'Hilary has ordered a roll-call. We're to assemble in the stable yard. Come quickly.'

So they dashed through the house, out on to the back terrace and then down a flight of narrow steps and round a corner into a courtyard flanked by rows of stables, all still intact. Bobbie and Angela joined one end of a line of officers standing nervously under the clock tower while Jean inserted herself in the middle of the row.

'Where's Douglas?' Bobbie whispered, having failed to spot him in the line-up.

'Coming now.' Angela pointed to where he emerged from a side door of the main house, limping heavily as usual, without his glasses and covered in dust.

'What about Cameron?' Bobbie looked up and down the line to find there was no sign of their second in command.

Angela's and Bobbie's hearts sank. Hours had passed since the bombs had dropped. Had anyone seen Cameron since then? Perhaps he'd been unlucky enough to have been strolling in the grounds when the Germans began their attack. He might, even now, be lying wounded in the parkland or in the woods beyond.

New boy Teddy came along the row with clipboard and pen, calling names and ticking them off as he went but not making eye contact. He kept his expression businesslike – tick, tick, tick.

Spotting Hilary standing under the arched entrance into the courtyard, Angela broke ranks. She sprinted down the line and almost crashed into her commanding officer, letting Cameron's name tumble from her lips.

Hilary paused to give her time to pull herself together. There was not a hair out of place or a speck of dirt on his uniform. 'Yes, First Officer Browne; what is it?'

'No one knows what's happened to Cameron,' she gasped.

'Sir,' he prompted with a touch of impatience.

'Sir,' she echoed faintly. How could Hilary be so unmoved? Two peas in a pod, he and Cameron had been at Oxford together, had played rugby on the college playing fields and joined the RAF at the same time. They were part of the crowd that had inhabited the London clubs in the early years of the war.

'For your information, Flight Lieutenant Ainslie elected to help drive three badly wounded patients to the King Edward Hospital in Highcliff. There was some urgency in the situation. He himself was unhurt.'

Hilary's formal reply was intended to put Angela in her place. She inhaled sharply then lowered her head to let out a long, slow breath. As Teddy joined them with his clipboard, she withdrew silently and looked so crestfallen that at first Bobbie imagined that she brought bad news.

'Cameron's all right, thank heavens. He drove injured men to the hospital,' Angela reported. 'And I've made a proper charlie of myself.'

'Cameron's safe?' Bobbie asked for confirmation as the orderly line disintegrated and Jean rejoined them. Feet shuffled off over the cobbles and voices expressed murmured opinions as to whether or not the Rixley officers would be allowed to remain in the undamaged wing of the Grange.

'Yes, panic over.' Angela ran a trembling hand through her hair and repeated the good news. She reached automatically for a cigarette, slipped it between her lips then left it unlit.

'Mary Holland went with him,' Jean informed them.

Bobbie and Angela looked at her in astonishment. 'You knew!' Bobbie gasped.

Jean nodded. Every bone in her body ached and her hands bled from tearing at the rubble. 'Stan told me. He happened to be walking in the wood with Mary when the bombs dropped. Mary saw she was needed to help drive the wounded to hospital. Cameron volunteered to go with her.'

'So all's well.' Bobbie's sigh of relief was loud and heartfelt.

'Until the next time,' Angela said with uncharacteristic solemnity, eyes glazed, cigarette forgotten.

Silence descended on the empty courtyard once more. Rooks rose from the clock tower, borne on the wind high over the ruined wing of Burton Grange.

Mary had driven the only available vehicle – a kitchen supplies lorry – at breakneck speed along roads without street lamps, her headlights dimmed and dipped as required by wartime regulations, tyres squealing as she braked for hairpin bends then speeding helter-skelter down a one-in-four hill on the final descent into Highcliff.

In the back of the Tilly truck, which was still loaded with sacks of potatoes, Cameron had done what he could for the patients from the convalescent wing. He started by stemming the flow of blood from a corporal's leg wound with an improvised tourniquet – a strip of cloth fashioned from the man's pyjama jacket. He'd propped the poor blighter up against the sacks and instructed him to keep both hands pressed firmly on the wound. A second man, a petty officer in the Royal Navy, had been in a worse state. He had burns to his face and chest and had cried out in agony during the ten-mile journey. The third had no evident injuries but lay unresponsive on the floor of the truck, flung like a wooden puppet this way and that as the lorry careered around bends.

On the outskirts of town, close to where the funfair had been set up a week before, Mary had been unsure of the way and had stopped to ask for directions from two fishermen emerging from a pub in black oilskins.

'Carry straight on until you can't go any further,' one had instructed. 'You'll see the harbour ahead of you. King Edward's is the big building on your left.'

Inside the lorry the burned man had carried on screaming. Cameron had thumped on the cab partition and yelled for Mary to get a move on. The noise had jerked her into action and she'd driven on, hands gripping the wheel and sitting forward in her seat until the stark hospital building came into view. She'd parked as close to the main entrance as possible then sprinted to find help.

Inside the hospital she'd been met by chaos: patients lying on stretchers or on the floor, nurses and porters running in all directions, doctors yelling orders. Apparently there'd been a second direct hit on Maltby Bay, a tiny fishing village three miles away. Several of the terraced cottages lining its narrow main street had been demolished and rescuers were still pulling survivors out of the rubble. Mary had seen a mother lying on a stretcher clutching a very young child and had been unable to tell if either was still alive. An old man had wandered down the corridor calling out in a thin, lost voice for Rhoda – over and over again; the name and nothing else. Sick at heart, Mary had dashed outside and told Cameron that they must do their best to carry their three injured men inside unaided.

Nodding, Cameron had spoken to the patient with the leg wound. 'You hear that, Keith? Do you think you can make it by yourself? Good chap. Mary, join me up here.' He had offered his hand to pull her inside then arranged how they would carry the burns victim into the building. 'Too late for him, worse luck,' Cameron had said, indicating their third patient lying motionless on the floor.

The screams of the burned man had subsided by this time but he'd groaned loudly as Mary and Cameron had stood to either side of him, slung his arms around their shoulders and hauled him out of the lorry. They'd dragged him into the building where a nurse had assessed the situation and immediately taken charge. 'Is either of you injured?' she'd asked Mary and Cameron as porters arrived with yet another stretcher.

'No, but we've a dead man outside,' Cameron had replied calmly.

Mary had felt herself shoved to one side as more of the injured Maltby villagers had been carried in. She'd watched with her head spinning as Cameron and the nurse continued to organize then suddenly, without knowing how it had happened, she'd sunk to her knees then fainted. She'd regained consciousness to find herself sitting on a bench outside the hospital entrance, drinking water from a tin mug that Cameron had offered her. The night sky was pitch black and full of noises: car engines whining, doors slamming, feet crunching over gravel, men crying, women and children wailing – but all happening as if at a distance.

'You passed out,' Cameron had explained. His tie was undone and his shirt open at the collar. His jacket was around Mary's shoulders. He'd cut her off before she could speak. 'No need to apologize. Your driving was first class, by the way. But we have a problem.' He'd explained that their vehicle was practically out of petrol.

'So we're stuck here?'

'It looks like it. There's probably enough juice left in the tank to get us a short distance so I suggest we drive a little way out of town then park up overnight. It'll be morning before we can find a garage that's open.'

Still woozy, Mary had climbed into the passenger seat of the kitchen lorry while Cameron had taken the wheel. They'd made it up the hill to the church ruins overlooking the harbour before the engine had pinked then stalled. He'd free-wheeled off the road and into the churchyard at the edge of the cliff.

'You stretch out in the cab; I'll sleep in the back.' Before she'd had time to argue, Cameron had left her with his jacket for warmth.

She'd opened the window and gazed down at the dark, glittering sea. Then she had fallen asleep and woken to gulls crying and the sight of Cameron's lithe, loose-limbed figure approaching between the weather-worn graves carrying a jerrycan full of petrol.

'Don't worry; that's one of our boys.' He pointed to a plane passing overhead before unscrewing the petrol cap and filling the tank. 'A Lancaster, by the look of it.'

The sky was blue and cloudless. A small speck crawled from east to west.

'No; on second thoughts, a Wellington,' Cameron remarked as he climbed into the cab. He took off his glasses and wiped them fastidiously with a clean rag stored under the dashboard.

'How can you tell from this distance?'

'Easy. Aircraft identification – it's one of the first things you learn at Torquay, along with swimming and dinghy training. Here; I managed to scrounge this off the bloke at the petrol pump.' He handed Mary a thick slice of bread and dripping and kept one for himself.

She took it and continued to watch the plane as she ate. The pilot was approaching land and making a gradual descent, most likely heading for the nearest RAF station. 'Why is he by himself?' she asked.

'Probably returning from overnight reconnaissance – taking pictures, and so on. How are you feeling? Did you get any sleep?'

Mary chewed and nodded. For the first time since she'd arrived at Rixley she recognized that there was a real person behind Cameron Ainslie's uniform. Until now all she'd seen was a cardboard cut-out: a typical clean-shaven, short-back-and-sides officer with a nasal voice and a way of looking a few inches over a person's head whenever he deigned to speak – someone to be wary of.

'Good show.' Swallowing the last of his bread, he

turned on the engine and reversed between the graves. 'You'll be able to have a shower and change your things as soon as we get back. I'll fill in all the paperwork and so on; no need for you to worry about that.'

'Thank you.' Cameron's remark made Mary wonder what they would find back in Rixley. There was a great deal of damage to Burton Grange for a start. But what about the ferry pool and the people she knew at the base?

'It hasn't been too much for you, has it?' Cameron glanced sideways at her as he steered the Tilly through the church gates on to the road. Mary appeared to be exhausted; she had a look in her eyes that could only be described as faraway, as if removed from the present situation.

'No; I'm fine.'

'Good; that's all right then.' Natural curiosity made him want to learn more about Mary's circumstances but he held back as he worked up through the gears until they crested the hill and began a long descent into the next valley, hugging the coast as they went. 'Remind me; how long have you been at Rixley?'

'Four and a half months.'

'Longer than me, then.' Cameron had arrived midway through June, after a gruelling tour of duty over Belgium and France. 'The powers that be made it clear that I was living on borrowed time. Officially we're only supposed to fly six missions before we can expect to cop it.'

'Why? How many missions did you fly?' Taken aback by his familiar tone, Mary turned her head to study her companion's profile with its high forehead, long, straight nose and clean, square jaw.

'Thirty, not counting gardening sorties and nick-elling raids.'

'What are they?'

'Leaflet drops over enemy territory. Propaganda and such like.'

'Is that why they posted you here? To take you away from the main action for a while?'

'That's it; I'm officially "resting". After this, they'll probably send me on to RAF Training Command to pass on my so-called expertise. "Make the RAF supreme", and all that.'

'"Never in the field of human conflict . . ."' Mary reacted to Cameron's breezy bravado by quoting a memorable speech given by the prime minister during the Battle of Britain.

Cameron picked up the thread. '"Was so much owed by so many . . ."'

'"To so few,"' she concluded, then smiled.

They were deep in a valley, with glimpses of the sea's flat horizon to the left and expanses of stubble fields to the right. 'You do have plenty to say for yourself after all.'

Shifting in her seat so that she looked out of the side window, Mary frowned and fell silent.

He noticed the sudden change in her demeanour. 'I'm sorry. I didn't mean to sound as if I was talking down to you.'

He had, though. Men of his class couldn't bloody well help it, when all was said and done. Her brief conversation with the second in command had been like a sudden gleam of sunlight through thick clouds, vanishing almost as soon as it had appeared.

Mary stared out of the window, hands tightly

clasped in her lap and lips pressed together as the Tilly turned away from the coast and they drove inland in awkward silence.

In the officers' quarters at Burton Grange the big clean-up had begun. Members of Rixley ground staff had arrived with mops and buckets, brooms and dusters and had spent the whole morning putting things to rights.

'Bloody stone dust gets everywhere,' Gordon Mason complained to Harry and Stan when they stepped outside for a cigarette.

New recruit Harry, looking all of twelve years old, with his mop of curly brown hair and freckled face, coughed into his handkerchief then blew his nose vigorously.

He too had breathed in clouds of muck as he'd swept and dusted. He was covered from head to foot in a pale grey powder. It clogged his nostrils and caught at the back of his throat but at least he felt they'd dealt with the worst of it and could soon expect to be let off the hook and sent back to base.

Stan eyed them both with amusement; the innocent recruit who looked fed up to the teeth and the older mechanic. He was about to make a joke about Gordon's dark skin being lightened by the thick layer of dust (along the lines of, 'Blimey, mate – you look like one of us!') but then thought better of it. Knowing Gordon, it would have led to a sock in the jaw and a scuffle; probably quite right, too. So Stan stubbed out his cigarette then picked up his mop and bucket and returned to the lounge where he found a few of the officers with their sleeves rolled up, doing their bit to get the bar back in working order in time for the normal evening gathering.

'Hilary has informed the top brass that he wants us to stay where we are.' As usual, Angela was the one in the know. She was dressed in dark green slacks and an oversized white shirt, with her shiny dark hair concealed beneath a crimson scarf tied neatly around her head. Alongside her, Bobbie polished and buffed the bar top, kitted out in a borrowed beret and navy blue overalls with the trouser bottoms rolled up.

'I don't see why we shouldn't.' Bobbie was also in favour of staying on at the Grange, or what was left of it. After all, her first-floor room – a light and airy space with a view over the grounds – was undamaged. She had her gramophone and a stack of jazz records, plenty of reading material to be going on with and space in her wardrobe for dresses, skirts, slacks and so on. 'We're only five minutes from the ferry pool as the crow flies. Besides, if we had to change our billets, the chances are we'd be scattered all over the countryside, tucked away in a poky little farmhouse or living above the village shop.'

'Yes, it'll take more than a few bombs for Jerry to force us out of Burton Grange.' Angela swept up broken glass behind the counter. 'What do you think, Teddy? Can we knock the place back into shape?'

'Most definitely.' Eager to show willing, Teddy had been hard at work all morning, taping up cracked window panes and setting doors back on their hinges. He was a decent handyman, having been taught how to mend things by his grandfather, a joiner by trade – much to his widowed mother's disapproval.

'Dad, Edward doesn't have time to mess about with chisels and screwdrivers,' she would complain to the old man. 'He has to do his homework. And afterwards he must revise for his scholarship exam.' And so it had gone on through much of Teddy's childhood: the tussle between the generations, until he'd landed fairly and squarely in his mother's camp by gaining entry to the grammar school with top marks for his year. Thereafter it had been mostly books and brainwork, prizes in mathematics combined with significant successes on the county athletics tracks and a growing awareness that the sky was the limit if only he, Teddy Simpson, applied himself and was careful to mix with the right people.

'That's right, never say die.' Angela bustled past him carrying a dustpan full of broken glass. She took it out of the back door into the cobbled mews where she spotted Cameron stepping down from the cab of a worse-for-wear Tilly, his jacket slung over his shoulder. For once he looked in need of a good wash and a shave. With a delighted cry, she put down her dustpan and ran to greet him, flinging her arms around his neck. 'Thank heavens; the wanderer returns!'

'Careful. Don't strangle me,' he warned as he straightened his glasses then extricated himself.

'Cameron, I was desperately worried about you. I imagined all sorts of disasters. Excuse the Mrs Mopp get-up, by the way.' Angela's cheeks reddened slightly as she stepped back then walked with him into the house.

'You smell of whisky,' he remarked. 'Isn't it a bit early for that?'

She laughed self-consciously. 'It's not how it seems. I've been a busy bee, clearing up behind the bar. I swear, hand on heart. Anyway, darling, I need you to give me a blow-by-blow account.'

'Not now,' he said wearily. He'd come from dropping the intriguing Mary Holland at her barracks at the airfield and at present all he wanted to do was sleep. 'Perhaps later.'

Angela's disappointment was evident. The corners of her full mouth turned down and a frown appeared. 'This evening then,' she murmured.

But an exhausted Cameron disappeared into his room and slept through the afternoon and evening, forcing Angela to wait in vain for him to show up in the lounge and share his experiences over a glass of the hard stuff.

Instead, she sat at the newly restored bar and twiddled her thumbs, only half listening to Teddy's anecdote about how once, when still with the Initial Training Wing, he'd flown his Spit over the house in Manchester where his mother lived and put on a flamboyant display of aerobatics for her benefit. The inevitable reprimand from Training Command had followed but Teddy hadn't regretted it. It was only high spirits, after all, and it showed pride in his achievements. He'd won his wings soon after and had quickly achieved his present rank of flight lieutenant.

'I reckon I can make wing commander with a fair wind behind me,' he concluded as he drained his glass.

'And good luck to you,' she replied absent-mindedly. Though Teddy was handsome in a trim, clean-cut way – tall and slim (maybe a little too angular) – it turned out he wasn't the most entertaining of companions. He was too earnest and Angela thought she detected insecurity beneath the bravado. She yawned delicately and excused herself. 'An early night beckons.' She slipped from her stool and quietly made her exit. As she left the room she glanced over her shoulder to see Douglas and Hilary having a pow-wow in their usual corner and Teddy swiftly moving on to chat with Bobbie. Angela crossed the hall and passed under the torn portrait, up the staircase minus its banister, along the landing to the women's quarters and her room next door to Bobbie's overlooking the lawn and the road beyond.

CHAPTER FOUR

Sometimes sleep refused to come.

Angela lay awake until after midnight, listening to every creak of floorboard and sigh of wind against her window panes. She heard footsteps in the corridor, the turn of a door knob then the sound of water splashing into a bowl in Bobbie's room. After a while the flick of a switch told her that her neighbour's light was off. Silence then except for the tick of Angela's alarm clock, accompanied by much tossing and turning and pummelling of pillows.

Then there was a light tap on her door and, without waiting to be invited, Bobbie crept into the room.

'Are you awake?' she whispered.

Angela sat up. 'Wide awake,' she assured her. 'Come in.'

'I couldn't sleep,' Bobbie confessed.

'Me neither.' Angela patted her cream satin counterpane. 'Come and sit.'

'I've tried counting sheep but it was no good.' Bobbie cut a dejected figure as she padded barefoot across the room. She wore boys' pyjamas and bedsocks for extra warmth and her unruly waves were held in place by a pale blue silk scarf tied gypsy-style around her head. 'Are you sure I haven't woken you?'

'Quite sure.' Reaching over to switch on her bed-side lamp, Angela admitted she was glad to see Bobbie. 'What does this remind you of?' she asked as she made room for her friend on the side of her bed then drew her knees up under her chin.

'Hmm. Midnight feasts in a school dorm, but without the hot chocolate and marshmallows?'

'Quite. And without Matron eavesdropping outside the door.' Angela's mind skimmed back through the years to a more innocent time. 'I don't know about you in your school in Edinburgh, but all I needed to worry about in those days was the danger of forgetting the past tense of a French verb or the date for the Battle of Malplaquet.'

'1709,' Bobbie recited automatically. 'Blenheim: 1704, Ramillies: 1706, Oudenarde: 1708 . . .'

'Malplaquet: 1709,' Angela chimed in. 'We were mere babes in arms back then. Battles were what we learned about from musty tomes. Now we know they're bullets and bombs, blood and Lord knows what else.'

'Is that why you couldn't sleep? You were thinking about yesterday evening?'

'Partly. And I was giving myself a good ticking-off.'

'Whatever for?' In Bobbie's eyes Angela was well-nigh perfect: her film-star looks went alongside an unflappable, breezy manner that she managed to maintain in the face of all dangers.

Angela tutted and studied the backs of her hands in the yellow lamplight. 'It's difficult to put my finger on. I suppose I'm annoyed with myself for losing my composure when Cameron didn't show up at roll-call.'

'That was understandable.' Bobbie suspected that there was more.

'And then when he did come back to the Grange, do you know what I did?'

Bobbie shook her head.

'I threw my arms around his neck and almost knocked his glasses off! I know, I know; it's bad form. He's one of Lionel's best friends, for goodness sake.'

'But you didn't . . . ? You don't . . . ?'

'Have any serious feelings for Cameron?' Angela inspected a bruise on her knuckles and several raw scratches on her wrist. 'I didn't think I did.'

'But now you're not so sure?' Bobbie didn't say so but she thought that there might be something in this. She'd noticed that Angela came alive whenever she talked to Cameron. There was a special sparkle in her eyes and an intimacy in her movements – touching and stroking, smiling and tilting her head.

'I was until this morning,' Angela said hesitantly. She recalled the knot in her stomach when she'd noticed her old friend was missing from the line-up and the way her imagination had run riot with various tragic possibilities. 'I've always tried to think of him as my superior officer and a good pal from the old days; never anything more. But oh dear me, when I saw him step down from the Tilly without a mark on him, I felt my heart beat so fast that it practically jumped out of my chest.'

'What about Cameron? Did he say anything?'

Angela gave an embarrassed laugh. 'You know

what he's like: stiff upper lip and all that. He asked me to stop strangling him so I did.'

'Typical. But that doesn't tell us what was going on beneath the surface,' Bobbie reasoned. 'The fact is he knows that you and Lionel are practically engaged. He would do his best to respect that.'

'True.' Angela tried hard to sort out the muddle going on inside her head. 'Oh, don't ask me, Bobbie; I don't know what to think. I suspect I'm an awfully fickle girl, that's all. But that's enough about me. What's the matter with you? Why can't you sleep?'

'No particular reason. I read through my last letter from Mummy before I hit the hay and it must have set me thinking more than usual.'

'It made you homesick for all that Scottish heather and fresh air.'

'In a way. But I'm in my element here at Rixley, flying Spits and so on. The letter didn't make me want to rush home and do the Highland Fling.'

'With a chap in a kilt waiting in the wings.'

'There's no chap in a kilt,' Bobbie insisted. 'I was too busy riding ponies and learning to fly when I was growing up to take much notice of boys.'

'But I bet they took notice of you,' Angela guessed. 'Every eligible bachelor north of the border must have beaten a path to your door at some time or another.'

'Not that I noticed.' Bobbie grimaced. 'But that rather brings me to the point.'

'The reason why you're here, sitting on my bed and robbing me of my beauty sleep?'

'Yes, it turns out you're not the only one whose heart has been going pitter-patter of late.'

'No, wait – let me guess!' *Of course!* 'Teddy Simpson,' Angela murmured after the briefest of pauses. There had been that flirting episode at the bar on the evening of the handsome flight lieutenant's arrival, and again tonight as Angela had made her early exit.

Bobbie's pale colouring was suffused with crimson. 'Oh Lord,' she groaned. 'Was it blindingly obvious?'

'To me it was,' Angela said with a nod, 'because I know you so well, my dear. But rest assured, no one else will have noticed.'

Desperate not to be seen as one of those louche girls who flings herself at anything in trousers, Bobbie took comfort in Angela's opinion. 'Don't worry; I'll have got over it by tomorrow morning,' she insisted firmly. 'My mind will be back on altimeters and wind direction. I'll be thousands of feet up in my Spit and I won't be giving Teddy Simpson another thought.'

On the Wednesday after the bombing raid, Jean stood at the end of the single runway at Seddon aerodrome and looked at her watch. First Officer Douglas Thornton was running late. The nearby canteen looked a more inviting prospect than standing here in the drizzle waiting for him to pick her up so she thought she might as well snatch a quick cup of tea.

'That was a first-class landing.' The mechanic whose job it was to run out to jam the chocks under her wheels caught up with her and held open the canteen door to a burst of loud chatter, a hiss of steam from the tea urn and a clatter of knives and forks. 'I've watched many an aircraft land on this airfield in my time; it's awkward and not one in twenty manages it the way you did.'

'It's easy in the latest Spit,' Jean replied modestly. Since the disastrous events of the previous Saturday the squadron leader had been keen to move out as many aircraft as possible in case Jerry decided to strike again, which meant that Jean and her co-pilots had flown out of Rixley at least twice a day, distributing planes to nearby airfields but rarely ferrying new ones back in. 'The Mark IX handles so well you feel you've sprouted wings like an actual bird.'

The mechanic was having none of it; he went on praising Jean as they queued for their tea and he refused to let her pay for hers. 'It's on me,' he insisted.

So she sat with him and the ground crew, allowing her new admirer to breeze through a few introductions – 'Colin, Arnold; this is Jean Dobson. Jean, meet Colin and Arnold. My name's Jimmy, by the way.'

Occasionally she glanced out of the window to see if Douglas's Anson was anywhere in sight and as it got to seven o'clock she realized they would have all-on to make it home before dark so she drummed her fingers lightly on the table, scarcely listening to the chatter going on around her.

'Are you wondering what's keeping him?' Jimmy picked up on Jean's fidgety behaviour.

'You mean my taxi ride home?'

'Yes. If it happens to be First Officer Thornton you're waiting for, he's been held up back at Rixley.

57

There was a problem with his Anson's instrument panel, by all accounts.'

Jean's heart sank. Her hopes of a long hot soak in the bath followed by an early night were fading fast.

But then the slow drone of the Anson's engine told her that her lift home had arrived at last and, hastily thanking Jimmy for the tea and snatching her leather helmet and parachute pack from the table, she ran out to the end of the runway to watch Douglas land the lumbering giant then taxi to a halt.

'Sorry I'm late,' he called to her from his cockpit.

'It doesn't matter; I'm sure it couldn't be helped.' She scrambled in beside him, strapped herself in then waited for him to execute a slow U-turn.

He completed the manoeuvre then tapped the glass cover of his temperamental climb-and-descent indicator to check that the needle was still operating as it should. Once satisfied, he opened the throttle and built up the revs before hurtling down the runway, back the way he'd come.

Safely airborne, Jean relaxed in the passenger seat for the thirty-minute flight back to base. 'To what do I owe the honour?' she remarked as they rose through a thin layer of wispy white cloud to be greeted by the marvellous sight of the sun setting over a western hill. As the ATA officer in charge of masterminding each day's operations, it wasn't often that Douglas flew between ferry pools himself.

'Everyone's busy. There was no one else I could send,' he answered, checking his dials and opening the throttle to its maximum. 'I take it you're enjoying the Mark IX?'

'You can say that again.' Below them, between the

clouds, autumn fields were a pale, straw-coloured patchwork dissected by the silver ribbon of a river that gleamed in the dusk light. 'Have you ever flown one?'

'No, worse luck. I flew one of the early Spits for the RAF, though.' He recalled his glory days with a rueful smile.

Jean looked with new interest at her companion. How old might Douglas be? Between thirty-five and forty, she guessed, though his tight-fitting flying helmet and goggles hid his greying hair and the wrinkles around his eyes. He wore his leather pilot's jacket with the collar turned up and sheepskin gauntlets to protect his hands from the cold. 'When was that?' she asked with eager curiosity.

'Nineteen forty-one. They designed her to fly low and fast and to turn on a sixpence. I knew the second I climbed into her cockpit for the very first time that she was streets ahead of anything I'd ever flown before. I couldn't wait to get into combat in her, which I did for a few months but then I ran into a spot of bother over Dunkirk – in a Wellington, as it happens.' Douglas slapped the side of his injured left leg impatiently. 'This put paid to my front-line action once and for all.'

'I'm sorry to hear that.'

'Not half as sorry as I was.'

Jean watched Douglas lean forward to tap the instrument dials – seemingly a nervous habit with him. She hadn't expected to get so much out of her normally reserved companion during this rare shared flight but now that he'd started talking there seemed to be no stopping him.

'It was no go for me after that; the RAF didn't

want to know. The only way for me to keep on flying was to join the ATA. But I still carry my old dog tags with me.' He dipped his left hand into his top pocket and drew out two octagonal Bakelite discs threaded on to a thick cotton cord. One was red, the other green, and each was stamped with: *Thornton, D W, 43792.*

'I'm sorry,' she said again, trying to imagine what it must have been like for Douglas to have had his hopes and ambitions so cruelly dashed.

'Yes. A chap reads in the official pamphlets all the uplifting guff about mighty engines roaring a symphony of power and speed, and so on. That kind of thing really inspired me. I was already mad about driving sports cars.' Douglas's voice slowed and he gazed out of the side window through the thin layer of cloud at the land below, following the course of a canal and counting off the locks before veering east to pick up the line of a railway track that would see them safely home – and not a moment too soon to judge by the fading light. 'The day I won my wings and took up my duties as aircraftsman second class was the best day of my life bar none.'

'A dream come true,' Jean murmured, thinking that fate was full of twists and turns. For instance, if she'd gone straight home from work on the night when she'd run into Douglas drowning his sorrows in the pub, she might never have had the confidence she'd needed to send off the application form for the job she was doing now. 'Your bad luck turned out nicely for me,' she reminded him gently.

He looked keenly at her without saying anything.

'That night in the Harbour Inn,' she explained

him. 'We wouldn't have met if you'd still been flying your Spits, et cetera. It's you I have to thank for all this.' Jean gestured towards the windscreen and the thin clouds below, glowing red and gold in the setting sun. 'I still have to pinch myself sometimes to know that it's true.'

'Four missions in eighty hours,' Douglas continued as if she hadn't spoken. 'All with the 74 "Tiger" Squadron. Four kills and seven other hits for me, each one chalked up on my fuselage. Two more kills and I'd have won my Distinguished Flying Cross. But it wasn't to be.'

Jean watched him tap the dials again. Their change of direction had increased the force of the headwind and she heard the engine falter and felt the aircraft shudder with the effort of holding its course. For a few seconds they were in danger of stalling until Douglas opened up the throttle to boost the revs and they flew safely on. When he made out Rixley station at the end of the railway line he slowly began his descent. The momentary lapse of concentration bothered Jean but she said nothing about it. Soon she recognized the dark area of Burton Wood and its three adjoining runways. They descended fast and low, preparing for landing in the dying light. Once again Jean's reactions were quicker than the pilot's; he was a few seconds late in pressing the overhead lever to lower and lock the undercarriage. Two green lights appeared with moments to spare then the wheels hit the ground and the plane squealed to an undignified halt.

'Sorry about that,' Douglas said as the Anson slewed sideways. 'It's been a long day.'

Jean noticed the stern, closed look on Stan's face as he and Gordon ran from the nearest hangar to slide the chocks in place. 'For you and me both,' she said as she unstrapped her seat harness. 'But thanks anyway; you got us back before dark.'

She and her pilot climbed out of the cockpit together, took off their helmets and goggles then walked to the operations room to clock off for the day. The small, cream-painted room was deserted, with maps, a typewriter and files cluttering the desk and two messages for Douglas left on a spike on the window sill.

'I hope you didn't mind my rabbiting on,' he said quietly as Jean filled in the necessary form and he read his messages. 'I don't normally do that.'

'Not at all,' she assured him with a smile. She had a sense of them both hovering over the paperwork, unsure of what to say or do next.

'Can I give you a lift to the Grange?' Douglas offered with a feigned casualness that didn't deceive Jean.

She caught her breath. 'I was planning to walk back,' she began then changed her mind. 'But yes – why not? It'll be dark in ten minutes. Ta; a ride back would be most welcome.'

They went out to Douglas's Ford and he opened the passenger door for Jean before swiftly taking his place behind the wheel. Gordon and Stan watched them from the shelter of the Anson's starboard wing, a strong smell of burnt rubber in their nostrils. Gordon grinned and tipped his head knowingly in the direction of Douglas's car but Stan didn't react. 'We'll have to change these tyres first thing tomorrow,' he muttered through gritted teeth.

Bobbie hadn't been so lucky in her attempt to get back to Rixley before dark. She'd flown south to a maintenance unit in West Bromwich to drop off an aircraft that she didn't much enjoy flying: a P-40 Tomahawk whose throttle had to be pushed forwards rather than backwards, much to her surprise. It would teach her to read her Ferry Pilots' Notes more thoroughly in future, she decided. In any case, she'd delivered the Tomahawk successfully then taken a train to Crewe, expecting to make a north-bound connection and arrive home in time for a much-needed bath. However, her first train had been delayed and then diverted and she'd ended up in the back of beyond, in a country station called Harkness with rosebay willow herb going to seed between the wooden sleepers and no sign of the stationmaster in the small cottage at the end of the platform.

Stranded! Bobbie put her bag on the station bench then slumped down beside it. It seemed like a dismal end to a frustrating day until a long-legged figure hove into view and loped towards her.

'Hello, Bobbie, fancy meeting you here!' Teddy laughed at her astonished expression. He was wearing his pilot's jacket and carrying a canvas hold-all which he dumped beside hers on the bench.

She jumped up with a smile, trying to control the tell-tale pitter-patter. *What luck! Teddy of all people!* 'I say, this is a nice surprise,' she burbled.

'Likewise – although, to be honest, I did expect to find you here. There's a telephone box in the village and I got on the blower to Rixley. They told me that my train wasn't the only one to have been diverted.'

'Yours too?' The broad smile gave way to a more arch expression. After all, she really must not make her liking for Teddy too obvious.

He nodded. 'Would you like the bad news first or the good?'

'The bad, please. No, don't tell me – we've missed the last train of the day?'

'Quite.' Teddy pulled out a packet of Player's and offered her one. 'But the good news is: there's a handy bed and breakfast less than five minutes' walk from here.'

'Excellent.' Things were looking up, Bobbie thought as she picked up her bag. 'Does there also happen to be a decent hostelry nearby, by any chance?'

'There's a place called the Rose and Crown in the centre of the village. We could call in there once we've got settled in our digs.' Teddy could tell that Bobbie was trying but failing to maintain a sophisticated air. He noticed her fingers tremble as she put the cigarette to her lips and accepted a light before they walked under the station clock then out on to a road with a narrow pavement, bordered by a rough grass verge and a deep ditch.

He smiled to himself as they set off at a rapid pace towards what passed for a hub of activity around here; in other words, the old-fashioned pub and a single row of houses, one of which was to be their billet for the night. In spite of having privately set his sights on poster-girl Angela on the day he'd arrived at the Grange, Teddy found himself once more appreciating Bobbie's slight build and pale complexion. She reminded him of an old girlfriend from his home town, though Nancy Jennings hadn't had anything like Bobbie's gilded start in life.

'Is this it?' Bobbie asked as they passed the Rose and Crown and Teddy came to a halt outside number 6 Station Row. The humble house fronted straight on to the pavement. It had a low door with a stone lintel and a single room to the right. The window had no net curtains so that any passer-by might glance inside at the shabby armchairs to either side of an old-fashioned fireplace complete with brass fender and worn hearthrug.

'Yes. Were you hoping for something better?' Another smile played over Teddy's lips.

Bobbie pretended otherwise. 'Good Lord above, no. We all have to make sacrifices.' But where on earth were they to sleep? she wondered. Surely there were two bedrooms at most in this tiny house, and one of those must be occupied by the owner. To hide her confusion she lowered her head and slowly ground out the stub of her cigarette.

Teddy knocked on the door. It was answered by an elderly, stooping woman in carpet slippers and flowered overall, her white hair neatly waved and her thin face heavily lined. 'Hello, Mrs Evans; it's me again – Flight Lieutenant Simpson. And this is Second Officer Fraser: the other pilot I mentioned.'

'Follow me.' With a quick glance at Bobbie but without further ado the old woman turned down the narrow corridor and indicated a flight of stairs ending in a small landing with a door to either side. 'Room on the left,' she said shortly before disappearing into the living room at the foot of the stairs.

'Good Lord above!' Bobbie murmured. She looked at Teddy in alarm. 'Mrs Evans surely doesn't expect . . . ?'

Teddy was enjoying the moment. It seemed that Bobbie had only one expression of surprise and he liked the way she rolled the 'r' in 'Lord' with a true Scots burr. 'Heavens; no.'

'What then? Do you propose to sleep on the floor?' Silently kicking herself for her gaucheness, she raised one eyebrow before setting foot on the bottom stair. Angela would have behaved differently, she was sure. There would have been more aplomb and a sharp witticism to put Teddy in his place.

'If you prefer,' he began. 'Or else I could . . .'

'I think not!' she said with a flash of her grey eyes.

'. . . pull the armchairs together in the living room and sleep on those,' he proposed calmly.

'Ah.'

'Why, what did you think I was going to say?'

Bobbie saw that he'd been deliberately toying with her. 'Teddy Simpson, you're an awful tease!' She turned away and took the stairs two at a time while he followed Mrs Evans into the living room. Bobbie opened her door to find a single bed of the old-fashioned iron variety, complete with lumpy horsehair mattress and a chipped chamber pot underneath. There was a jug and basin on a washstand with a mirror on the wall above and a mahogany wardrobe taking up too much floor space beside it. It would have to do. Bobbie ran back downstairs without even combing her hair. She opened the living-room door to find Teddy alone and the landlady nowhere to be seen. 'Come along, Flight

Lieutenant Simpson, you owe me a Dubonnet and lemonade!'

'Right you are, Second Officer Fraser.' He'd played it correctly, he thought. It turned out that Bobbie could indeed take a joke and who knew what might happen later that night, after a couple of drinks at the Rose and Crown? After all, these were free and easy times and Atta girls had a racy reputation amongst the RAF pilots he'd known in previous postings. He linked arms with her and stepped out on to the pavement. 'A Dubonnet and lemonade it is.'

The rain came down in earnest soon after Douglas had driven off with Jean in his gleaming black Ford, its blackout-adapted headlights glimmering through the gloom.

'Wouldn't it be better to refuel the Anson now?' Gordon asked Stan. It would entail one of them venturing from under the wing to run and fetch the petrol tanker from its parking place next to Hangar 2 – a sprint of two hundred yards through the downpour.

'No, the morning will do.' Stan kicked the nearest worn tyre with uncalled-for vehemence. 'Bloody idiot,' he grumbled under his breath.

'Who – me?' Gordon shot back.

'No, First Officer Douglas bloody Thornton! Did you see the way he came in to land?'

Gordon shrugged. It was easy to work out what was really eating his companion but now was not the time to kid Stan about the soft spot he'd obviously developed for Jean Dobson.

'What the hell was he playing at?' Stan went on. 'He nearly overshot the runway and landed belly-up in Burton Wood.'

Gordon turned up his collar and hunched his shoulders, ready to make a dash for it. 'See you over in the canteen?' he prompted.

'No, not right now. I'm off to check the Spit in Hangar One that limped in yesterday afternoon with a damaged prop.'

'Please yourself,' Gordon called over his shoulder as he ran across the grass and disappeared into the canteen hut.

Stan grunted. He ignored the rain and walked slowly towards the hangar, through the wide doors into a cavernous space where two small Corsairs were lined up next to a Lancaster and beyond that the Spit. As he approached the fighter plane it was obvious from a glance that the propeller blades had been badly bent out of shape by enemy fire and that the pilot had been lucky to have limped back to base. It couldn't be fixed in a hurry, Stan decided. Better wait until morning. Still, he was in no rush to call it a day so he decided to refuel the Anson after all. He walked back to the doorway to spot Mary parking her car next to the petrol tanker close to Hangar 2. She looked worn out and seemed to have no coat or umbrella with her so Stan grabbed an oilskin cape from a nearby hook and hurried towards her.

'Here; put this on.' He slung the cape around her shoulders. 'Can't have you catching your death, can we?'

'Ta, Stan, I appreciate it.' It was nice to see a friendly face after a long drive all the way back from

Oxfordshire and especially kind of Stan to bring the cape. He was a decent, brotherly sort – good-looking in a sturdy, deep-chested way, built like a middle-weight boxer, she thought. 'Come on; why not let me treat you to a nice, hot cup of tea?' She veered towards the lights of the canteen and before he could say no she'd steered him inside and sat him down at a table beside one of the misted-up windows overlooking the square of neatly mown lawn. 'With or without?' she asked.

'Without, ta.' Ignoring a knowing look from Gordon, who sat on the opposite side of the room with Harry and newcomer Olive Pearson, he wiped the window pane with the side of his hand then stared out into the dark. 'Why so late back?' he asked Mary when she returned with the tea.

She told him about her day: how she'd had to drop off two RAF men – one a wireless operator, one a gunner – at a training centre more than two hundred miles away and then drive back again.

'Blimey, no wonder you look all-in.' There were dark circles under her eyes and her face was pale and drawn. 'Will you be able to have a lie-in tomorrow?'

'I doubt it. First Officer Thornton wants me to cover for Olive. She's got forty-eight hours' home leave.'

'What for? She's only just got here.'

'The family's had bad news – her brother's gone missing in action.'

'Fair enough.' Though Stan had no immediate family to worry about, he could see why Olive might need her couple of days off to support her grieving mother. 'Have you got brothers?' he asked Mary.

'Two,' she replied. 'Tom's in North Africa – Tunisia when I last heard. I don't have a clue where Frank is. He's the oldest. I lost track of him before the war started so it's anyone's guess what he's up to now.'

'You don't know and you don't want to know, eh?'

Mary nodded. *If only you knew the half of it*, she thought. Black sheep didn't cover it as far as her brother Frank was concerned. His antics had seen him thrown out of the house by their father by the time he was eighteen. 'I'd rather not talk about it if you don't mind.'

Stan wrinkled his nose. There she went again, bringing down the shutters with a single bat of her long dark lashes, retreating into her own world of shadows and ghosts. Mary Holland was one dissatisfied girl, he decided. 'Did you fill in that application form yet?' he demanded with a quick tap of the table to draw her attention.

'What application form?'

'For the Class Two conversion course. Come on, Mary; you know what I'm talking about.'

She raised her mug and sipped her tea, giving him that same guarded look.

'You haven't, have you?'

'Not yet,' she admitted.

Stan tapped the table a second time. 'You want to know what I think?'

'Not really.'

'Well, pin back your lugholes and I'll tell you anyway.' Someone had to, or else Mary would drift on from week to week without pursuing her dream of flying. 'I think that the chip on your shoulder is the only thing that's stopping you from going ahead.'

'What chip?' Stan had a cheek; assuming that he had the right to talk to her in this way. She frowned, looked down at the table and muttered sulkily.

'I'm talking about the grudge you carry around with you. You're always comparing yourself with girls like Bobbie and Angela and feeling sorry for yourself that you didn't have their leg-up in life.'

Mary resisted the urge to storm off, a move that would draw unwanted attention. Instead, she leaned across the table to hiss at Stan: 'I'm not sorry for myself!'

'Yes, you are, and I don't altogether blame you. But you don't need to carry on as you are, hating life's golden girls and not doing anything about it; not when you could take the conversion course and join them.'

'I don't hate them,' she argued weakly.

'Then fill in the form and go to Thame,' he insisted, as if it was the most natural thing in the world. 'Once you get rid of that nasty chip there'll be no stopping you.'

Mary glanced up at him, her eyes flashing with a mixture of resentment and determination. 'All right, I will,' she muttered, rising to the challenge at last.

'Tomorrow first thing, when you go to the ops room to collect your chit. March right up to the squadron leader and tell him you want to learn to fly.'

She studied her hands splayed palms down on the table. 'No, not him,' she said thoughtfully. There was someone else she would rather ask. 'I will do it but in my own way in my own time.'

'Promise?'

'I promise,' she agreed, looking straight at Stan without blinking.

He drained his mug then smiled. 'That's more like it. You'll be up and at 'em before you know it – on the posters alongside Angela, hopping into that cockpit with your compass and stopwatch and taking to the skies with the best of them. And good luck to you, Mary. You deserve it.'

The Rose and Crown in Harkness had seen better days. The yellowing plaster on the walls of the low-ceilinged Snug was cracked and a thick layer of dust coated the window sills and the rows of mostly empty shelves behind the bar. Still, Bobbie found the atmosphere convivial enough, especially with Teddy at her side.

'The problem with Jerry,' he opined to the portly, middle-aged landlord, who provided them with the third round of the evening, 'is that he flies strictly according to the rules. Always the same formation, always regimented; that makes it easy for our lads to work out his next move in advance, which is a great advantage when you think about it.'

The landlord nodded and smiled as he pulled Teddy's pint. John Hughes didn't object to the young airman's exaggerated swagger; in fact, he saw that it formed a necessary shield to protect these RAF boys from the perils involved in fighting for King and country. *Rather him than me*, he thought as he carried on serving.

'Believe me, I've seen it with my own eyes,' Teddy sailed on confidently. 'I ran into a bunch of them off the Essex coast late last year. My squadron was scrambled to intercept them head-on at twenty thousand feet. I took a decision to split off from the others and come at Jerry from port side. The closest Messerschmitt was a sitting duck; you could hear bullets pinging off his fuselage as I hit my target. Jerry's canopy was smashed to pieces. I reckon his oxygen tube was cut clean through as well.'

Aware that three or four other men at the bar were listening, Teddy paused to let the full impact sink in. The landlord nodded again as he pushed the glass of beer across the counter. 'What about you, young lady?' he asked Bobbie. 'Will it be another Dubonnet? We've run out of lemonade.'

'A straight Dubonnet is fine,' she assured him, though her head was already spinning and she felt a little unsteady on her feet.

She and Teddy took their drinks to a quiet corner.

'Rixley must seem awfully tame after the action you've seen.' Bobbie did her best to ignore the curious stares of the other customers, which she put down to the fact that the locals rarely saw outsiders in their pub. She pushed back her mane of light brown hair then raised her glass and took a small sip.

'Oops,' Teddy commented, reaching forward to rescue her glass when she put it down close to the edge of the table. He saved it from overbalancing and spilling on to her lap. 'I'm glad of a change of scene, to tell you the truth. I'm expecting a new posting any time now.'

'That's a pity.' Bobbie's unguarded comment slipped

out. She blushed and took another sip. 'Where will they send you – do you know?'

'To America, all being well; to train their pilots and test their new aircraft. That's what I'd like to do next. You never know; it might even bring that promotion to wing commander before the Yanks and Mr Churchill wind things up with Herr Hitler.'

Bobbie did her best not to be distracted by the immaculate parting in Teddy's fair hair. It must take practice to get it so straight and to make the hair lie sleek and flat to either side. There was one rebellious lock at the crown, though. She thought of pointing it out but decided against it. 'I have a target of my own to aim for,' she confided. 'I hope to clock up enough hours to make first officer by the time my birthday comes round.'

Teddy's early impression of Bobbie had been confirmed by their evening together: she was a bright, shiny little thing with more than a touch of the tomboy about her. And he was increasingly certain that she was keen on yours truly. 'And when will that be?' he asked.

'In a couple of weeks' time.' Hoping that he would ask for precise details and then offer to help her celebrate the occasion, Bobbie was disappointed when Teddy started to quiz her about her family and life before the ATA.

'So where exactly is this country pile of yours?' He shuffled along the wooden bench to sit closer to her and rest his arms along the back of the settle.

She could practically feel his breath on her cheek and smell the shaving soap he used. 'Up in the Highlands, north of Glencoe.'

'And is it a castle or more like a shooting lodge?'

'It's a Victorian idea of a castle, I suppose. You know: a rambling old place, with turrets and so on.'

'Stags' heads on the walls? Suits of armour in the banqueting hall?'

Bobbie nodded. 'You must come and see for yourself when all this is over.'

'I'd like that.' Teddy's arm edged down on to her shoulder and he let his hand dangle forward. 'I expect you had ponies and so forth?'

'You expect right, Flight Lieutenant Simpson.' She made a show of removing his hand. 'And you? Might I have come across you in the showjumping world in your youth?'

'Not on your nelly. If I wanted to jump anything, I preferred to do it on my own two feet, thank you very much. Hurdles, high jump – you name it.'

Everything in the room had taken on an unusual tilt, Bobbie noticed. 'Why are those men at the bar staring at us?' she enquired with genuine puzzlement.

'It's you they're staring at, Second Officer Fraser. They're bewitched by your beauty.'

Dismissing the onlookers, she used her elbow to dig him in the ribs. The room tilted the other way as the landlord came across to sweep their empty glasses from the table then call time on his remaining customers.

'Time for bed.' Teddy stood up and offered Bobbie his hand. He slipped it through the crook of his elbow then steered her towards the door. When he found that it had started to rain, he whipped off his jacket and hung it around her shoulders to walk her back to their cramped billet, chatting as they went.

'About time too.' Mrs Evans's sour face greeted them on the doorstep. 'I've been waiting up for you so I could lock the door.' No sooner said than the landlady had ushered them in and turned the key. 'I'm off up to my room,' she informed them. 'I'd appreciate it if you two kept the noise down.'

'And thar she blows!' Teddy whispered conspiratorially as the landlady mounted the stairs. As Bobbie giggled, he slipped his hand into the pocket of his jacket, pulled out a hip flask and waved it in tantalizing fashion in front of her. 'Nightcap?'

Woozy – that was the word for how she felt when she shook her head, as if her brain was loose and knocking against her skull. 'No, ta. Better not.'

'Sure?' He lured her from the narrow hallway into the living room by continuing to wave the metal flask.

She followed him with a laugh. Then, before she knew it, the flask had vanished, the jacket had slipped from her shoulders and Teddy's hands were around her waist, his lips pressing against hers. She pulled back from the embrace.

'Better not,' she said again.

'Sure?' he repeated.

His lips tasted of tobacco and Bobbie wasn't certain whether or not she liked that. But the kiss had felt nice once she'd got over the surprise. So she leaned in and initiated another, softer one. It went on for longer and she floated into it, enjoying the feel of Teddy's hands on her hips and her arms around his neck. Tobacco and soap, the scratch of stubble against her cheek.

At last, after what felt like an eternity, he stepped

back. 'These walls have ears,' he warned as footsteps sounded on the bare wooden stairs and the landlady reappeared at the door, hot-water bottle in hand.

'I forgot to fill this,' she muttered at the guilty-looking pair. 'And just as well, by the look of things.'

'And I'll say goodnight!' Bobbie said gaily, stumbling over the hearthrug as she left the room and faintly aware that she didn't want to give the landlady any more cause for gossip. 'Goodnight, Teddy,' she mumbled as she leaned heavily on the banister and fumbled her way up to her room.

'The first train to Rixley leaves at eight,' he called after her. 'With luck we'll be back in time for elevenses.'

'Champion. I'll be down for breakfast, seven on the dot,' she said from the landing. At least that's what she'd attempted to say. It might not have come out of her mouth with crystal clarity but Teddy had probably got the drift. Bobbie opened her bedroom door, stumbled forward and within two steps she was flat on her back on the lumpy bed, fully dressed, teeth unbrushed, and already sinking deep into oblivion.

CHAPTER FIVE

The note from Lionel lay open on Angela's dressing table as she chose her silvery-grey silk dress for their first evening together since June.

'Dearest Angela,' it began. 'Write down this date in your diary: Saturday, the 25th of September. My ship is in dock for repairs. I've been granted shore leave for twenty-four hours and will come and pick you up as soon as ever I can. Where shall we go? Shall I take you dancing or would you prefer to find a quiet spot to sit and catch up? It's entirely up to you. The main thing is that we'll spend a few precious hours together. I can hardly wait, my darling. Until then – with love and kisses, Lionel.'

Grey silk – close-fitting with a gored skirt and a halter neck. Black patent shoes. A corsage of pink silk roses.

After she'd received Lionel's note on the previous Wednesday, Angela had scribbled a hasty reply – 'What a lovely surprise – too exciting – missing you dreadfully – all love, Angie xx'. Their reunion had been bound to happen eventually so she might as well settle her mind to the visit.

'Better here or here?' she asked Bobbie as she

moved the corsage to various positions along the neckline of her gown.

'High on the shoulder,' was Bobbie's advice.

'This lipstick or this?'

'The coral pink.' Angela had shared her news about Lionel a few moments earlier, when Bobbie had walked into her room to find her in petticoat and stockings, wondering what to wear. 'Where will he take you?' she asked enviously.

'To the Mount Hotel in Highcliff, overlooking the harbour. But the arrangement is that he'll pick me up here. I'm to meet him downstairs in the bar at half past seven.' A glance at her watch told Angela that she had a mere twenty minutes to get dressed. 'Now, darling, if you don't mind . . .'

Bobbie felt herself being whisked out into the corridor, almost bumping into Jean who was dressed in a pale blue twin-set and her dark blue skirt, with a double string of cultured pearls around her neck. Flustered apologies were exchanged and it became obvious that both girls were heading in the same direction: down the damaged main staircase and into the lounge bar overlooking the front terrace.

'The days are closing in already,' Bobbie commented, casting a glance through a long, low window, still taped up after the German attack. 'Autumn is really setting in.'

'"Season of mists and mellow fruitfulness".' Struggling for something to say in response, Jean threw in the tired quotation.

'Shelley?' Bobbie hazarded a guess.

'Keats.'

'I was close!' Laughing off her mistake, Bobbie

noticed Douglas catch Jean's attention so she headed on alone to the bar where she broke up a cosy gathering of Cameron, Teddy and Hilary. 'Guess who's due here any minute to meet Angela. Lovely Lionel; that's who.'

Hilary and Cameron greeted the news enthusiastically while Teddy asked Bobbie what she would like to drink.

'Orange juice if there is any,' she replied.

'Staying away from the Dubonnet tonight, eh?'

'Yes; after Wednesday I've signed the pledge,' she declared, one eye on the door so that she was the first to spot Lionel enter through the main door in his navy blue mess jacket, white waistcoat and trousers. 'Wait there; I'll be back,' she told Teddy before sprinting across the room to greet the new arrival.

Lionel wasn't prepared for the whirlwind that was Bobbie Fraser. In fact, he was feeling nervous about the evening ahead, tugging at the hem of his jacket and clearing his throat, glancing behind him at his MG sports car parked outside the door. 'Steady on,' he told Bobbie as she took both hands and tugged him towards the bar. 'I'm a little early. Oughtn't I to wait here in the hall for Angie to appear?'

'Oh, don't worry – she's still trying on frocks, you know what she's like. Hilary and Cameron are here in the bar. And you look as if you could do with some Dutch courage.'

So they went in together, Lionel in the dress uniform of a Royal Navy captain and Bobbie in a swirl of emerald-green chiffon, to warm handshakes and a barrage of questions as to where Lionel's ship was docked and demands for a detailed account of his latest naval adventures.

'It's good to see your ugly face again,' Cameron told him with a friendly nudge. 'How long has it been?'

'Too long,' Hilary broke in, relaxing for once and falling into their old familiar way. 'Knowing Angela, she won't be down for ages yet, Lionel. So what'll you have to drink – your usual Scotch?'

Amid the buzz of conversation Teddy approached Bobbie with her glass of orange cordial. 'Why the glad rags?' he asked, admiring her tiny waist and bare shoulders while trying to steer her clear of the crowd.

'This old thing!' she teased, adjusting her straps. 'No particular reason.'

'You look nice anyway.' Now that Teddy had succeeded in cornering Bobbie, he was scarcely paying her any attention. From what he could pick up from overheard snatches, it seemed that the Royal Navy visitor belonged to Angela. He was a substantially built chap whose white waistcoat and starched white shirt emphasized his healthy tan but whose nicotine-stained fingers showed a heavy smoking habit – one of the inevitable side effects of being a Navy man. His thick brown hair and bushy eyebrows made him seem less refined than his old school chums, Hilary and Cameron, and on the whole Teddy thought that the naval man looked and sounded unremarkable. If it ever came to a contest for Angela's favours between this steady-as-you-go sea captain and himself, Teddy was pretty sure who would come out on top.

'Teddy?' Bobbie tugged at his sleeve.

'Hmm?' Here came Angela now, swanning down the stairs in a slim, silver evening dress, in full war paint. Her dark hair was swept up and she glided into the room.

'I said, I'm organizing a soirée to celebrate my birthday next month so please keep the evening of the fifth free.'

'I will, provided Herr Hitler lets us,' Teddy said with a smile. 'Unless I'm already winging my way across the pond to teach the Yanks how to fly, that is.'

Bobbie caught Hilary's stern glance and smiled uneasily at him. Across the room, sitting together in a window seat, Jean and Douglas seemed sealed in their own world of earnest and no doubt clever conversation, while at that moment Lionel turned to see Angela make her entrance and was instantly oblivious to everyone else there. What must it be like, Bobbie wondered, to be as enraptured as Lionel Cawthorn obviously was? So blind, some might say.

'Now, how about a real drink?' Teddy prompted, taking the glass of cordial from Bobbie without waiting for a reply.

In the women's billet at Rixley, Mary packed her suitcase. She looked back over the day's events with a flutter of excitement mixed with strong apprehension, remembering how, at midday, she'd chosen her moment to knock on the office door next to the control tower then entered to find Flight Lieutenant Cameron Ainslie sitting at his desk, up to his eyes in paperwork as usual. This had been her plan: to catch him alone, with no other officer around.

'Yes?' he'd enquired in his abrupt way, a pencil tucked behind his ear and with a distracted air. But when he'd seen that it was Mary hovering nervously by the door, he'd taken off his glasses, closed the buff-coloured file that he'd been working on and encouraged her to take a seat. 'Now, what can I do for you?'

'Sir, I'd like an application form for the pilots' conversion course, please.' The carefully rehearsed sentence had emerged stiffly and she'd resisted the urge to flee from the room.

Cameron's eyes had widened for a moment.

He's about to send me packing. Mary had been convinced that her request would be turned down point-blank.

'Yes; very good.' Rapidly overcoming his surprise, he'd stood up and pulled open the appropriate drawer in the steel filing cabinet behind him. 'Good idea, Mary.' He'd dispensed with formalities as he handed her the form and given her an encouraging smile. 'I'm sure you'll get on very well.'

'If they decide to accept me.' Taking the paperwork from him, she'd scraped back her chair and stood up.

'No, no; stay here and fill it in,' Cameron had suggested, handing her his fountain pen and making it clear that he would leave her in peace to get on with it. 'Might as well, eh? There's a blotting pad there, under that pile of papers. I'll be back in five minutes,' he'd said as he'd departed. 'I'll vouch for you, by the way,' he'd added as though delivering an afterthought.

When he'd returned, he'd taken the completed

form from her. 'I've been on the blower to an associate of Commander Gower and put in a good word for you,' he'd informed her.

'Already?' With Cameron's backing, things were obviously moving much faster than Mary had anticipated. The pace of events had unsettled her but she'd tried not to let it show.

'Yes. I emphasized how efficient you've always been as a driver and how calm you are in an emergency. They're obviously keen to have you – that goes without saying.'

Lost for words, she'd taken a deep breath to compose herself.

Typical Mary – silent and hard to read. Cameron had watched her struggle to take things in. Recalling how touchy she could be, he'd steered away from any comment that might sound condescending and stuck with the practical instead. 'It'll mean a couple of weeks down in Thame, learning the ropes – aircraft and engine theory in the classroom to start with. But it shouldn't be long before an instructor takes you up in a dual-control Corsair or the old Gypsy Moth and before you know it you'll be flying solo.'

He'd made it sound straightforward – something that Mary could actually achieve. 'Thank you, sir.' She'd breathed the words of gratitude. 'I mean it; thank you very much.'

'No need for the sir; we're off duty.' He'd smiled briefly and held the door open for her. She'd left the office, her cheeks burning and her head in a whirl – even more so when half an hour later, she'd encountered Stan sitting with Jean in the canteen.

'So, you finally plucked up courage,' he'd said as she'd sat next to him and watched him tuck into bully beef and mash. 'Congratulations, Mary; you're on your way.'

'How did you find out?' Instinctively she'd batted away Stan's warm words.

'A little bird told me,' Stan had said with a wink over the hiss of the tea urn and the rattle of cutlery.

'What does he mean, "you're on your way"?' Jean had asked. 'What have I missed?'

'Mary here has only gone and applied for the pilot conversion course and been accepted,' he informed her. 'What do you make of that?'

Jean had studied Mary's flushed cheeks. 'I think that's a marvellous idea,' she'd said calmly. 'Don't worry; you'll sail through with flying colours.'

'Do you think so?' Mary had a sneaking admiration for Jean and valued her opinion. 'Am I cut out to be a pilot, though? That's what I wonder.'

Jean had smiled warmly. 'It's natural to be nervous. But yes, I'd say you're exactly what they're looking for. And good for you for plucking up the courage – I know what it takes to fill in that form.'

Mary had nodded then let out a loud sigh. 'It's thanks to Stan. He gave me the kick I needed.'

'You're welcome.' Pleased that Mary had seen fit to confide in Jean, Stan's smile was broad. 'And here's another bit of news: Flight Lieutenant Ainslie has ordered me to drive you to Highcliff first thing tomorrow morning, to put you on the train to Thame. They'll bring in another driver pronto to fill your shoes, but we know there's no shortage of volunteers in that department.'

So I didn't dream it, Mary had thought. *I really am signed up for the course!*

'Early to bed for you tonight,' Stan had advised as Jean had cleared his empty plate and carried it with hers to the trolley stacked with dirty crockery. 'We'll have to be up with the lark to get to Highcliff by seven.'

Which was why now, as dusk fell and rain swept across the airfield, Mary was folding her civvy clothes – two skirts, three blouses, one maroon woollen dress, a pair of court shoes, two sets of underclothes – and leaving her washbag and hair-brush handy on top of her bedside locker for an early start. The room was silent except for the hiss of the paraffin stove at the far end of the hut and the erratic gusting of raindrops against the dark window panes. It was to be Mary's last Saturday night at Rixley for a while at least and she felt an unexpected twinge of regret. Despite the new world of opportunities open-ing up before her, there was no doubt in her mind that she would miss the familiar faces – Stan, Gor-don, Harry, Jean and the rest – and the safety of her old routine.

Lionel had whisked Angela off in his sports car and Teddy had unaccountably vanished when Hilary approached Bobbie at the bar. 'Good to see Lionel again, albeit briefly,' he remarked as he perched on the stool next to hers.

Bobbie was on edge, wondering where on earth Teddy had sloped off to. 'Yes, lovely Lionel. I've only met him twice before but I took to him from the off.' She swilled her drink around her glass then took a small sip.

'He's a good chap; decent through and through,' Hilary agreed. Despite his off-duty rig of fawn and brown knitted cardigan teamed with twill slacks and polished brogues, his abrupt military air remained. 'We go back a long way, Lionel and I.'

'So I gather.' Angela had told Bobbie vivid stories about what the small gang of Oxford graduates – Angela's brother Hugh plus Cameron, Hilary and Lionel – used to get up to in the London clubs a couple of years earlier. 'I hear it was great fun. The good old days, eh?'

Hilary downed the last of his drink. 'Yes, but a word of advice – don't believe everything Angela tells you. She has a tendency to exaggerate.'

'So the rumours are false – you didn't go from theatre to dance hall every night then off to a club to drink into the wee small hours?'

'Not every night.'

'Just once in a while, eh? I still say it must have been fun.'

'Yes, it was.' Hilary had approached Bobbie with a more serious purpose. 'Which brings me to a matter concerning you and Teddy Simpson.'

Bobbie was startled by the apparent switch in direction. 'What on earth do you mean?' she asked defensively.

'First of all, Bobbie, I'm sorry about your overnight stay in Harkness earlier this week.'

'Why are you sorry?' she enquired with assumed nonchalance. 'It's not the first time that I've been stranded and I'm sure it won't be the last.'

Hilary's mouth twitched in irritation. 'I hear that the only bed and breakfast available proved unsatisfactory.' He raised his hand to stop her from interrupting. 'It's all written down in the report that Teddy lodged with Douglas; the lack of a separate room and so on.'

Bobbie blinked then shook her head violently. 'Teddy and I didn't have to share . . . I took the bedroom and he slept in the living room. I hope he made that clear.'

'I'm pleased to hear it. Still, it was unfortunate that you two were thrown together in that way.' Rapping his empty glass down on the bar, Hilary forged on. 'Obviously, from a professional point of view, it's preferable for male and female personnel to observe a certain distance.'

'Who says so?' Bobbie's heart lurched.

'I do. At least until they've had the time to form a proper acquaintance,' her commanding officer insisted. 'It's early days – Teddy Simpson has only just got here.'

'Listen to me, Hilary: nothing improper happened at Harkness.' She spoke with heavy emphasis on the word 'improper'.

'I'm not suggesting that it did.'

'Yes, you are; that's exactly what you're suggesting. And while we're on the subject, let me point out that it would be none of your business even if it had.' Bobbie's heart continued to thump as she put her glass on the bar and slid down from her stool. 'It's not against the law, so far as I know.'

'Quite. But it's my job to maintain discipline in this ferry pool and in my view it's best not to risk muddying the waters with the ups and downs of personal relationships.' Though Hilary had failed to anticipate Bobbie's irate reaction to his well-meaning advice, he knew that it was too late to backtrack. 'Please don't take offence. All I'm saying is that a girl needs to know a good deal more about a chap before she jumps in with both feet.'

'And I thank you for your advice.' Bobbie fought back tears of embarrassment and fury. For the first time in her life her morals had been called into question and she was left with a very unpleasant feeling in the pit of her stomach. 'Now if you don't mind, Hilary, I'll say goodnight.'

He watched her flounce away in a cloud of bright green chiffon, nose in the air and looking straight ahead.

Cameron sidled up to him, pipe in hand. 'What's got into our wee Scottish lassie tonight?' He assumed, rightly, that Hilary had been heavy-handed over some minor matter of discipline – after all, subtlety had never been his strong suit.

'Lord knows,' Hilary said with a shrug. He hadn't had to deal with women pilots until he'd been posted to Rixley and the truth was he was a little out of his depth. He'd been warned in advance that women didn't always like taking orders and privately suspected that aviation would never be their field of expertise. But he didn't expect them to fly off the handle the way Bobbie had just done. 'Never mind, old thing; she'll get over it,' he told a puzzled Cameron. 'It's my round. What can I get you?'

'I'm sorry; this place isn't up to much.' Lionel glanced around the Lounge Bar of the Mount Hotel. It was a stuffy room with faded wallpaper and shapeless armchairs with worn chintz covers. A dingy oil painting of a sailing ship adorned the chimney breast and the only other occupant of the room was an elderly man in tweeds who smoked a pipe in his fireside chair.

'Never mind – beggars can't be choosers.' Determined to make the best of things, Angela chose a corner as far away from the old man as possible. 'My goodness; that's quite a cough,' she whispered as the pipe smoker's chest rattled and he spat into the grate.

'We could try somewhere else?' Lionel suggested.

'No, darling – not before we've raised a glass or two.' She settled into one of the armchairs, legs elegantly crossed.

'You're sure?' He hovered next to her chair, reflecting that he'd imagined a better place than this for their reunion. But the only alternative to the Mount had been one of the poky harbour-side pubs filled with rowdy fishermen and their sharp-tongued wives.

'Quite sure. Sit down, darling; do.' Angela leaned forward to pat the seat of the chair opposite. 'Look, here comes someone to take our order.'

A woman with crimped grey hair, wearing a mustard-coloured dress that gave her complexion a sallow tinge, listened to their requests then went away without speaking. She quickly returned with their drinks on a stained wooden tray and deposited them on a low table, again without saying a word. The man by the fire continued to cough and spit.

Lionel's grimace made Angela laugh. 'Please don't worry; I'm perfectly happy here and I'm all ears, waiting to hear the low-down – the top-secret things they won't allow you to write in your letters. Whose ships have you been sinking and what heroic tales do you have to tell?'

Same old Angela, Lionel thought, *making light of the most awful events*. He understood that this was how she got through: by refusing to think too deeply or seriously. 'Lately we've been in the Aegean. My ship sailed from Malta earlier this month. We ran into trouble off Corfu; hence we're currently in dry dock awaiting repairs.' He stopped short of relating any more details and sat uncomfortably with his drink.

'Why so cagey? No, of course; you're not allowed even to speak about it. It's all hush-hush. I quite understand.' She smiled at him to hide her disappointment at how the evening was going, though the distance between them yawned as wide and deep as the Grand Canyon. 'What news of the family?' she prompted cheerily.

'Father's still hard at it in the War Office, working with Montgomery on God knows what fresh tactics for North Africa. Mother is well and living quietly in the house in Dorset. What about yours?'

'Still at the mill with slaves,' Angela quipped. 'Father can't keep up with the never-ending orders for worsted for army uniforms. He's put the women in the spinning and weaving sheds on overtime and keeps the looms running seven days a week but it's impossible to keep up with the demand. The men have mostly been conscripted, of course.'

The pleasantries continued for several more minutes, exasperating Angela and puzzling Lionel. Neither seemed able to break through the polite veneer until she stood up suddenly and suggested a walk in the hotel grounds.

'But it's raining,' he objected. 'You'll get wet.'

'I don't mind; I'm wearing a decent winter coat. Come along; let's get a breath of fresh air.' She led the way, turning up her fur collar then pausing in the front entrance to test for raindrops. 'See, it's easing off.'

So they stepped outside into a damp mist that rolled in off the sea, deciding to leave the hotel grounds and venture a short way along a cliff path to the sound of waves crashing on to the rocks below.

'It's single file, I'm afraid.' Angela picked her way carefully while Lionel followed. She felt the wind raise the hem of her skirt and blow her hair in all directions. Straight ahead, the dark outline of a ruined church loomed. 'It's blowing a gale. What do you say we seek shelter for a while?'

Again Lionel followed without saying anything. Angela had always been full of surprises. It was one of the aspects of her character that had first fascinated him: the way she would take it into her head to leave a smoky club on the Strand to roam the broad streets and end up paddling in the fountain in Trafalgar Square, not minding if she attracted comments from strangers. There was one time when she'd dared him and her brother Hugh to climb one of the plinths and sit astride the lion to sing 'Rule Britannia', which they'd done to her great delight. Such light-hearted fun had suited the times. But now, with the world turned upside down, it seemed out of kilter with the prevailing mood. As they approached the churchyard in the thick darkness, Lionel took out his cigarette case and quietly lit up.

'There, that's better.' She found a sheltered spot out of the wind. 'Smell the salt in the air. Isn't it glorious? On second thoughts, you've probably had enough of the old briny to last a lifetime.'

'Angela.' He drew smoke deep into his lungs.

'What is it, darling?' It was chillier than expected so she wrapped her coat more closely across her chest, feeling the cold smoothness of its satin lining.

'We must talk,' Lionel insisted. 'It's been so long since we had the opportunity.'

'I know; ages and ages.' She could scarcely see his features but his tone of voice told her that he was building up to the serious topic that she'd been doing her best to avoid.

'About our future,' he continued doggedly. 'I'd like to know one way or the other where we're going with all this.'

'Oh.' She sighed, leaning back against a rough stone arch. 'Why must we be going anywhere? Why can't we forget about tomorrow and live in the moment – now especially?'

'Because of the war?'

'Yes. None of us knows if there'll even be a tomorrow. Take me, for instance. I'm up in my Spit at ten thousand feet, never knowing what I'll find – a sudden thunderstorm or Jerry coming at me out of nowhere and me unarmed, with only a simple compass and a stopwatch to get me out of trouble. And there's you on your captain's bridge, watching out for the next torpedo or squadron of Heinkels flying at you out of nowhere. You see?'

Her face was a pale disc against the stone, her dark eyes wider than ever. Lionel leaned in and kissed her. 'That's why,' he murmured as he drew back. 'If there isn't to be a tomorrow, well, at least let me know if you feel for me what I feel for you. That would be something to be going on with.'

Angela felt her heartbeat quicken. They'd been in this situation several times before: Lionel seeking the reassurance of a formal engagement, her feeling the pressure of making a commitment. Previously she'd been able to fudge it by returning his kisses in a light-hearted way, saying that she was truly fond of him and didn't want their relationship to end. Which was true. But she'd wanted them to go on in an open-ended way, sharing good times, not looking too far ahead. They were still young, after all.

'Well?'

'I'm fond of you,' she whispered.

'But do you love me? Will you marry me?'

The cold mist surrounded them, the sea roared. Danger crowded in on them from all sides, and with this feeling of life running out of control Angela drew Lionel close. What answer should she give? Should she say the words he longed to hear?

CHAPTER SIX

'Will all pilots report to the operations room for their chits!'

The call over the Tannoy system broke the early-morning silence of the airfield as Mary set off with Stan for Highcliff station.

'Repeat: all pilots to the operations room!'

'That'll be you in no time at all,' Stan assured her as he drove through the gates.

Mary twisted round in her seat to return Jean's hasty wave as she sprinted out of the canteen ahead of Angela Browne and Bobbie Fraser. The three women pilots wore their sheepskin jackets unzipped over their Sidcot suits and carried their helmets as they rushed across the lawn to be first into the ops room to receive their orders for the day. The idea that she would soon be joining them gave Mary butterflies in her stomach.

Stan settled in to enjoy the drive past Burton Grange, through Rixley village with its church and row of cottages then on towards the coast. 'You certainly made a good impression on someone,' he teased Mary, who had slung her suitcase on the back seat of the car and now looked nervously ahead. 'I'm talking about Flight Lieutenant Ainslie. I overheard him singing your praises on the phone yesterday – he couldn't say enough in your favour.'

'Lord knows why,' she murmured as they entered a green and gold tunnel formed by overhanging branches of closely planted trees. Glimpses of a bright blue sky between the autumn leaves promised a fine day ahead. 'The only time he's had anything to do with me was when we ferried those patients from the convalescent wing to the hospital on that dreadful night and I ended up in a dead faint on the floor.'

'He didn't mention that,' Stan said with a smile. 'It was all: "Mary Holland is an excellent driver . . . In my experience Mary Holland is extremely dependable . . . She may not have many qualifications but she has a darned good head on her shoulders."'

Mary laughed at Stan's accurate impression of their superior officer's accent. She blushed nonetheless. 'I've got a lot to live up to, then.'

'You can do it.' The car emerged from the trees on to a sunlit scene of rolling hills broken up by small copses and the occasional rocky outcrop. 'Make sure to drop me a line telling me how you're getting on.'

'I will,' she promised. She swayed against Stan as the car rounded a bend at top speed, her face still flushed.

'Oops!' He grinned.

'Stan Green, you did that on purpose!'

'As if I would.'

She flicked his arm with her fingers; a 'take that!' gesture that didn't need words.

'Mind you don't take on any fancy airs down there in Thame,' he warned. 'We don't want you coming back to Yorkshire all la-di-da.'

'As if!' She wished that all men were as easy to get on with as Stan. 'Haven't you thought of applying for the conversion course yourself?' she mentioned as they passed between high hawthorn hedges. Was it her imagination or was the sky already lightening the way it did when you approached the coast?

'Not likely,' he protested. 'I prefer to keep both feet firmly on the ground.'

'You mean you're afraid of heights?'

'Scared stiff; always have been. I'll go like a bat out of hell on two wheels or four but you won't find me going within half a mile of an aeroplane, unless it's to mend the fuel pump or what have you. If you ask me, a man would be born with a pair of wings if he was meant to fly.'

'Or she,' Mary corrected. She spied her first glimpse of a glittering watery horizon straight ahead. 'So why push me into doing what you would never do yourself?'

'Fair point.' Stan always enjoyed chipping away at Mary's brittle reticence and regretted that their journey was coming to an end. 'I hope you realize that I'll miss our little chats.'

'Yes and likewise. But I hope I'll be back.'

'It depends on where you get posted.'

They approached the outskirts of town then drove through narrow streets until they came to the railway station perched on flat ground overlooking the harbour. Stan parked the car close to the ticket office and waited while Mary retrieved her suitcase from the back seat. 'Good luck,' he told her, his strong forearms resting on the rim of the steering wheel.

She nodded and thanked him. This was it; there

was no turning back. The train waiting on the platform would carry her along its gleaming tracks, steam hissing and billowing from the funnel, whistle screeching – away from a narrow life that had had its fair share of deprivation and misery, widening out to new horizons. 'Goodbye, Stan.'

He smiled and nodded then pulled away from the kerb. In his rear-view mirror he saw Mary still standing there in her smart navy blue uniform, clutching her suitcase. She looked young, he thought, and a bit lonely and lost.

'You said yes?' Bobbie could scarcely believe what Angela was telling her as they waited outside Hangar 2 for Gordon and Stan to taxi their Spits on to the runway. The two women stood well clear of the wide doors, shouting above the whine of the powerful Merlin engines. 'Lionel proposed marriage and you accepted!'

'I did indeed.' Angela had waited from the Sunday until Wednesday to impart her news, hoping to adjust to her new status before sharing it with others.

'Why didn't you tell me straight away? You must be over the moon. Oh, I say!'

Angela gave Bobbie a wry smile. 'Lionel has proposed to me before, of course, and I've asked him to wait. This time I felt it would be too cruel.'

'But you do want to marry him?'

'Do I?' Angela turned over the question in her mind. 'I don't want to marry anyone else, let's put it that way.'

The half-hearted answer didn't satisfy Bobbie, who felt a surge of sympathy towards lovelorn Lionel.

Sometimes Angela was a cold fish. It was as if she didn't have any real heart. Then again, perhaps she simply kept her emotions carefully hidden beneath that glossy, glamorous surface. 'Congratulations. I'm very pleased for you both. Do you have a ring? Have you told your papa?'

Stan sat behind the wheel of a heavy Amazon lorry, towing Angela's plane towards Runway 1. Its wingtips barely cleared the doorway so he steered carefully.

'Not yet,' Angela answered. 'I've left it to Lionel to ask Pa's permission before he buys the ring and we broadcast the news.' She remembered the moment in the dark grounds of the ruined church when Lionel had pressed her to tell him how she felt. *Truthfully?* she should have replied. *I feel confused. I have no idea what's really going on between us. We're comfortable together and I know I can depend on you. But is that enough?* But when it came to it she hadn't had the heart to confess her doubts and so had agreed to the engagement. 'Keep it under your hat for now,' she told Bobbie before following her Spit on to the runway.

'Drat!' Bobbie realized that she'd come on to the airfield without her goggles and gauntlets. She sprinted back to the ops room where she'd left them, still amazed by Angela's news and by the casual way in which she'd announced it. 'I shan't be a minute!' she called up to Gordon as he towed her plane towards Runway 3. At the bottom of the stairs leading up to the control tower, she ran into Teddy, who was still waiting for his chit. 'Goggles,' she explained hastily before dashing up to the ops room.

He was still there when she came down again.

'I wrote down the fifth in my diary,' he told her casually. 'For your birthday soirée.'

'Super. Sorry, I must dash.'

He caught her by the wrist and swung her towards him. 'I thought you'd be pleased.'

'I am; thrilled.'

'Where will it be held? Who else will be there?'

Bobbie tried to pull away but found that Teddy's grip was too strong. 'I haven't decided on the venue yet. I'll invite the usual crowd – Hilary, Cameron, et cetera.'

'Angela?' Teddy prompted.

'Of course. Now I really must dash.'

He released her at last and watched her scamper away, like a little red squirrel in her zip-up suit and brown leather jacket, helmet strapped firmly under her chin. Hearing someone approach from behind, he stepped aside to let Cameron emerge from the office he shared with Hilary and Douglas.

Cameron had been irritated to see the blatant way Teddy had held Bobbie back. He'd spotted it through the window and decided that it showed a lack of respect so had come out to tick him off. But Teddy was already on the move, up the stairs and into the ops room to learn from Douglas that his job for the day was to fly a lumbering four-engine Stirling to a ferry pool in Leicestershire: a mundane task that Teddy didn't relish.

From behind his desk Douglas studied the young pilot's scowl as he picked up his chit and departed. *There's something not quite right about Teddy Simpson*, he thought. *Surely I can't be the only one who wonders why a top-notch fighter pilot has been posted to Rixley to do lowly ferry pool work with the ATA.* Perhaps he would mention his doubts to Cameron or Hilary. *Is our new boy as good as he says he is? Or is there something we haven't been told?*

The morning ticked on without Douglas being able to raise his concern and it soon slipped from his mind. Running his hand through his thick hair, he switched his attention to cross-checking conflicting weather reports that would affect tomorrow's schedules. Then he sat and considered the news from Central Ferry Control that in the coming months there was to be a steady build-up of transfers of new Spits from factory to pools throughout the country. The figure would soon reach a level just short of 2,500 planes, which suggested to Douglas that something big was afoot in the not too distant future. He missed elevenses and by noon was in need of a breather so he left his desk and was heading for the canteen when it struck him that Jean was thirty minutes late flying in the Spit that she'd been scheduled to pick up from a maintenance unit in Sunderland. It should have been a straightforward hop from A to B. Douglas paused on the lawn, thought hard for a few seconds then returned to his office. He picked up the phone and asked the operator in the switch room to put him through to the Sunderland base.

'Hello, this is First Officer Thornton here. I'm calling from Rixley,' he began as soon as a line was free. 'What's the latest information on First Officer Dobson's departure? Did it go ahead as planned?'

There was a pause while the morning's file was checked then a brief reply: 'Yes, sir; as planned.'

Douglas felt a flicker of worry inside his chest. 'How's the weather up there?'

'No adverse conditions according to the met boys.'

'You're sure?'

'Quite sure, sir. Your First Officer Dobson took off on time and in ideal conditions.'

'Thank you.' Douglas replaced the handset then stared out of the window. If it wasn't the weather causing Jean's delay then it must be something mechanical. There was no radio contact with the Spit, which meant that in the unlikely event of engine failure she was completely on her own. She would know the drill, of course – trim the aircraft's nose down, unclip oxygen tube if any, jettison canopy, release harness, roll aircraft upside down and good luck! The motto – 'If in doubt, bail out!' – would be at the very forefront of her mind.

'Something wrong?' Hilary asked as he entered the office.

'Yes; Jean Dobson should have landed her Spit Mark IX on Runway Two thirty-five minutes ago.'

'Damn,' Hilary muttered. 'What's gone wrong, do we know?'

'No, sir, we don't.'

'So all we can do is sit tight and try not to think the worst.' As always, Hilary kept a lid on his feelings. 'If there's trouble, Jean will know what to do.'

Douglas nodded then sat down heavily in his swivel chair. He turned to face the window, searching in vain for the speck in the sky that would materialize into Jean's Mark IX. His hands were clenched and he hardly dared to breathe.

Ten minutes out of Sunderland and at a height of 4,000 feet, Jean encountered an unexpected, weather-related problem. It wasn't cloud that affected her flight but rather the absence of it, for it meant that the late-September air was exceptionally cold. Sharp fingers of ice had begun to form on the Spit's windscreen, cutting down visibility to practically zero. Soon the side sections in the bubble canopy were also affected and she noticed a white layer of frost on the aircraft's wings.

The only possible remedy was to reduce height, so Jean quickly eased back the throttle. She felt her stomach lurch as she went into a steep dive but to her relief at 1,000 feet her solution seemed to be working: the ice had started to melt, allowing her to peer through small patches of Perspex and see that there was no immediate danger in the shape of hills up ahead. Visibility was still limited, however, so to be extra sure that the topography wouldn't be against her at this height, she used her compass to track a new course, away from land and over the North Sea, keeping the coast in sight and preparing to turn inland again when she drew closer to her destination.

It took five minutes, but once clear of the coast and flying low over the water, Jean breathed a sigh of relief and eased off the rudder pedals. She knew that the unplanned detour would make her late and that she had no way of letting Rixley know what had caused the delay. In an attempt to make up time, she upped her speed and was going along nicely at 800 feet when she felt rather than saw another aircraft approach from behind. A glance over her shoulder gave her a glimpse of fuselage that told her the day's troubles had only just begun – she'd spotted a black cross on the port side and a swastika on the tail fin: *Luftwaffe*! A fully armed Focke-Wulf Fw 190, no less.

Jean didn't hesitate. Her only hope, once spotted, was to outmanoeuvre the German plane. She knew that the one advantage she had over her opponent was her superior turn radius so she increased her revs to 2,500 and rammed her left pedal to the floor. She climbed steeply, banked then veered sharply out to sea with the Fw 190 in hot pursuit. Any moment now the pilot would fire his guns. She prepared herself for an explosion of bullets tearing through wings and fuselage, a giant force lifting her and tilting her wildly off balance as the bullets hit their target. *Don't let it happen. Change course again, dive low, use your speed to stay out of range.* A voice inside her head issued urgent orders, which she followed instinctively.

Putting distance between herself and her pursuer, Jean experienced living proof that the handling of the 190 was inferior to the updated Spit and was grateful for it. Jerry seemed clumsy in comparison but he still came after her, close enough to fire if he wanted to and driving her further out to sea.

Let's hope he's alone. Jean scanned the empty sky for other planes. *Yes, thank goodness. One against one – a fair contest – and if she used all her skill there was a good chance of coming out of this in one piece.* She clenched her jaw tight in grim determination to out-fly her opponent.

Without warning she went into a steep dive, plummeting until she was almost at sea level then levelling out underneath the 190 and speeding towards the shoreline, tricking her opponent by turning at the last second and gaining speed and height again. This manoeuvre gave her a fleeting glimpse of the burly German pilot in his cockpit. For a split second their gazes locked. She saw his eyes widen in amazement.

All of a sudden and without warning he raised his arm in salute then altered course and fell away. The chase was over.

Jean watched him climb steadily, heard his engines fade into the distance.

He saw that I was a woman! she realized with astonishment. There was such a thing as gallantry left in this war-tattered world after all. Jean had mixed feelings: she'd been intent on beating the enemy fair and square but the German pilot's reaction when he saw her had been born out of a deep-seated courtesy that she was bound to acknowledge.

However, now that the emergency was over, Jean wanted to get home fast. How much fuel did she have in her tank? She checked the gauge: maybe just enough. She would head inland, pick out a series of landmarks and hope for the best. Relaxing a little, Jean flew low along the shoreline until she recognized the small village of Maltby Bay then the distinctive layered cliffs to the north of her home town of Highcliff. She spotted fishing boats bobbing in the blue water and the untidy cluster of cottages and pubs with red-tiled roofs that formed the hub of the town. From here she would need to follow the railway line directly west for the final twenty miles to Rixley.

A glance at her watch told her that it was coming up to half past twelve. She noticed the needle on the fuel gauge hover over empty and gave a grim smile. Oh, the irony of being forced to ditch the poor Spit and bail out at the very last minute if she ran out of fuel! *Let's hope not*, she thought as she flew on at 600 feet, longing for a sight of Burton Wood and the three runways just beyond.

Two miles short of Rixley Jean saw the needle flicker then stop. She heard the Merlin begin to stutter. She wasn't going to make it after all.

The engine stalled suddenly and the Spit juddered. The tank was empty. There was an eerie silence. Surely there must be an open area where Jean could make an emergency landing. She looked down at a patchwork of small fields bordered by barns and farm buildings then considered bringing the Spit down on a straight stretch of road. But she shook her head at the thought of giving some poor motorist the fright of his life. She had a better idea. Frantically pressing the rudder pedals and riding on wind currents, she steered the now silent plane towards Burton Grange, gliding low over the village, lowering the landing gear as she aimed for the vast lawn in front of the house.

The grounds were deserted. Jean felt an almighty bump as she hit terra firma. She sat tight and slammed on the brakes, praying that she would avoid the deep holes left by the bombs. *Such a pity to wreck the crate at this point*, she reflected with wry humour.

The Spit's wheels churned up the grass, digging deep, black furrows as it squealed to a halt fifty yards from the front entrance. Unseen by any witnesses, Jean raised the canopy then unstrapped her harness. She climbed down from her plane.

Time to phone the ops room and report my location, she thought calmly as she mounted the broad steps on to the front terrace. *Apologies and so forth; you'll have to send an Amazon lorry to tow her in.*

CHAPTER SEVEN

The venue chosen for Bobbie's birthday celebration was the humble Fox and Hounds in Rixley. A small back room had been set aside for a dozen guests and Bobbie, Angela and Jean had arrived early to deck it out with balloons and a hand-made Happy Birthday banner painted by Angela on to a square of old parachute silk.

'I didn't want anything too lavish,' Bobbie explained as the three women stepped back to admire their amateurish efforts. 'It doesn't seem right to splash out when there's strict rationing everywhere one looks.'

Jean agreed. 'Even so, it's nice to have something to celebrate, for a change.' She'd taken care to look her best by lifting her long hair into a stylish pleat and wearing her smart cream jersey-knit dress with cap sleeves and a sweetheart neckline. She'd judged rightly that anything dressier would have seemed out of place in the homely surroundings.

The village pub, like many others in Yorkshire, hadn't seen a lick of paint for decades. Its ceilings sloped this way and that and the rooms were still lit by gaslight, which produced a low, constant hiss in the background. Spotting a cobweb draped across one corner of the ceiling Angela stepped on to a chair and used a handy window pole to whisk it free, dislodging a red balloon in the process. The balloon drifted down towards a burning gas mantel and burst with a loud pop, making Bobbie and Jean jump.

'That scared the living daylights . . . !' Bobbie gasped.

The landlady, Florrie Loxley, poked her head around the door. 'Was that a gun going off?'

'No; relax, Mrs Loxley.' Bobbie scooped up the remains of the balloon from the flagged floor. 'When the guests arrive, would you mind sending them straight through, please?'

Florrie nodded curtly and disappeared. She wondered if it had been a good idea to rent out the room. It might have been better from her point of view to have held the party in the Snug. That way, guests could have more easily bought drinks at the bar and upped her profits for the night. Still, the little Scottish Atta girl liked to have things her own way and a private room with their own supply of beer and whisky was what she wanted.

'Nervous?' Angela asked Bobbie as she jumped down from the chair. She too had chosen a dressed-down look, simply running a comb through her freshly washed hair and throwing on her daytime favourite: a raspberry-pink woollen dress nipped in at the waist and flaring out to mid-calf length, with contrasting white collar and belt. She wore peep-toed shoes to match.

'As a kitten,' Bobbie confessed. During the run-up to her twenty-second birthday she'd tried in vain to play it down. 'It's hardly worth celebrating,' she'd protested on the Monday as a parcel from home had arrived in the post. The package had contained a silk petticoat and a large Dundee cake, which Angela had insisted on icing with the number twenty-two picked out in blue. To Bobbie's chagrin she'd brought it along to the Fox. 'Must everyone know how old I am?' she'd said with a sigh.

'But you're not exactly ancient. In any case, you look delightful.' Angela made one last effort to cheer up her friend as the clock on the wall ticked towards half past seven. She knew that Bobbie had been feeling rather down after realizing that there was no way that she could hit her five-hundred-hour target before the big day. 'Believe me, you put us all in the shade.'

Bobbie fluffed up her hair and straightened the collar of her jade-green blouse. She'd matched it with her favourite black trousers and sophisticated heeled shoes. Guests would start arriving any time now; glasses were lined up on a trestle table next to bottles of spirits and there was a full keg of beer in the corner. Everything was ready. 'It's a shame that Lionel couldn't wangle another twenty-four-hour shore leave,' she mentioned to Angela as Jean slipped away to powder her nose. 'Is his ship still in dry dock?'

Angela shook her head. 'Last reported off the southern tip of Spain, heading for the Dodecanese.'

'You don't say.' Bobbie gave her a sharp look. 'How do you feel about that?'

'Sorry, of course.'

'I've been wondering: did Lionel have the all-important talk with your papa?'

'Hush!' Angela warned as footsteps approached. 'Yes,' she said under her breath as Jean returned. The family approved of the engagement. The deed was done.

'Marvellous!' Bobbie was on the point of sharing the good news with Jean when Angela stepped between them.

'I say, Jean, I hear you're in line for promotion to flight captain after your recent heroics.'

'Am I?' It was the first Jean had heard of it and she blushed furiously. 'Who have you been talking to?'

'Hilary. He's made sure that the top brass got to hear of your exploits. It's only a matter of time, believe me.'

Bobbie went off to greet the first arrivals, Cameron and Douglas – the former fashionably dressed in a tweed sports jacket and open-necked shirt, the latter more conservative in a double-breasted navy blue suit. 'Help yourselves to drinks,' she told them as she stationed herself by the door.

Angela towed Jean in her wake to say hello to Cameron. 'Where's Hilary?' she demanded.

'On his way.' Cameron scanned the room, which was quickly filling with guests. 'There's no Lionel, I take it?'

'Sadly, no. I was just saying to Jean: Hilary has put her name forward for promotion, and quite right too.' There was a nervous energy in Angela's voice as she skipped between subjects in her usual animated style. Her cheeks were flushed. 'I wish I'd seen Jerry's face when he caught sight of his opponent. Imagine the shock of realizing that a mere woman had outflown him!'

'It's no more than we've come to expect of you, Jean.' Anticipating a relaxed evening, Cameron poured himself a whisky. 'But I see we're embarrassing you. And you don't have a drink. What would you like?'

'Hilary, hello.' Over by the door, Bobbie's welcoming smile was broad as she stood on tiptoe and accepted a peck on the cheek. 'I was afraid you wouldn't make it.'

'Happy birthday, Bobbie – I wouldn't miss it for the world.' Though Hilary was no lover of these occasions and his desk was piled high with unanswered correspondence, he deemed it necessary to show his face. 'I may have to leave early,' he warned her. 'Please don't be offended.' He smiled and nodded hello to Cameron and Douglas then wove his way between ATA pilot Horace Jackson, Fred Rowe from the met room, Third Officer Agnes Wright and several other junior-ranking officers from the ferry pool. He'd almost reached the table where drinks and a large cake with candles were set out when Angela intercepted him.

'Hilary, at last. Did you walk here or come in the car?' Her voice rose above the hum of conversation as she linked arms with him. 'Never mind; it doesn't matter. The important thing is that you're here.'

Accustomed to her vivacious manner, Hilary didn't notice anything unusual. Angela was Angela: flitting from person to person, alighting on one then fluttering off like a bright butterfly. Truth to tell, she'd always been too frivolous for censorious Hilary's liking but Lionel had been smitten early on by her raven locks, delicate features and striking deep blue eyes – each to his own, of course. There; she was off again – sliding her arm free and floating towards the door to greet Teddy.

'Happy birthday,' Teddy told Bobbie as Angela approached. He inclined his head towards the birthday girl – a gesture that fell between a formal bow and a more intimate recognition. His eyes locked with hers for a brief moment and then Angela whisked him away.

Bobbie's heartbeat quickened. Was it because of the special look she'd exchanged with Teddy or because Angela's interruption had unnerved her? It was difficult to decide. In any case, Bobbie's duties as hostess pushed her on; more smiling and greeting followed by assigning gramophone duty. 'Who'll take charge of changing the records?' she asked the group, which included Fred, Agnes and Horace. 'The gramophone is tucked away behind the drinks table. Do I have any volunteers?'

Two hands shot up and Bobbie chose Agnes.

'Watch out; she'll be at the sherry all night,' Horace complained. A late recruit into the ATA, having failed the eyesight test for the RAF, he made up for his slight stature and already-receding hairline with a keen wit, usually directed against his female colleagues.

'Ha ha, very funny!' Teetotaller Agnes shook her head and departed.

The strain of playing hostess weighed heavily with Bobbie. She felt that the evening was off to a slow start but hoped that music would improve the atmosphere. Not that there was much room for dancing, she realized. Oh, why in the world had she chosen the Fox? Wouldn't it have been better to have held the party at the Grange, where there was more space?

'Here.' Teddy sidled up with a glass of Dubonnet. 'We can't have the birthday girl standing all alone without a drink in her hand, can we?'

Gratefully, Bobbie took the glass and felt her heart race once more. The music had started: a Glenn Miller big-band number that swung along nicely. She looked up at Teddy and thanked him.

'I'm sorry you missed your target,' he told her. 'I know it means a lot to you.'

'It does,' she admitted. Everything in Bobbie's life prior to joining the ATA had come easily; she'd never had to strive or prove herself, had simply sailed on a wave of affluence and affection into whichever harbour she chose. Ever since she could remember she'd been surrounded by family who loved her and by any number of governesses, tutors, school teachers, dressmakers, milliners, house maids, stable lads and gamekeepers whose support and encouragement she took for granted. Gaining promotion to first officer had been her first real challenge: a test of her independence as well as proof of her skill as a pilot. 'Still, there's always tomorrow,' she said to Teddy with a determined tilt of her head.

'That's the spirit.' He cast an eye around the crowded room then turned his full attention back to her. 'We can't let Jean take all the glory, can we?'

'Oh, I would never put myself in the same league as Jean,' Bobbie said quickly.

'Uh-oh, Miss Modesty! Don't let Squadron Leader Stevens hear you say that.'

'It's true. Jean is far and away the best pilot on the base. You know that she won a scholarship to the Women's Air Reserve, which makes her very bright indeed.'

'Well, I have noticed that she always has her head stuck in a book.' Teddy's attention drifted again. He saw Angela flit from Hilary to Cameron then back to Hilary. No doubt the trio were reminiscing about the good old days, a conversation that would automatically exclude him so he decided to stay where he was for the time being. A new record had begun: a cheerful song by Gracie Fields that set his teeth on edge. *Wish me luck as you wave me goodbye, Cheerio, here I go, on my way.*

'Do you fancy a stroll in the fresh air?' he suggested to Bobbie as he took her by the arm.

'Just for a few moments,' she agreed.

'Until this song is finished,' he said as he led her down the corridor and through the public bar. 'I don't know what people see in our Gracie, I really don't.'

'It's good to see Bobbie letting her hair down,' Douglas remarked. He and Jean had found a quiet corner close to the door. They'd just watched Bobbie and Teddy go outside for a breather and now sat as fly-on-the-wall observers as festivities got properly under way. Horace and Fred had stationed themselves close to the keg of beer and were imbibing freely, while Angela, Cameron and Hilary shared a joke in the centre of the room.

Jean agreed. 'It's funny, though; she was dreading reaching the grand old age of twenty-two.'

'It beats the alternative any day of the week.'

'Yes, of course.' Jean's response was quick, though she was slightly taken aback by the flash of gallows humour from Douglas.

'How old are you, Jean?' He looked intently at her as he waited for her answer.

'I'm twenty; it's on my file.'

'Yes, of course. When I was your age, back in the olden days, we never imagined events would take this turn for the worse. My father's generation had just fought the war to end all wars. No one in their wildest dreams envisaged Herr Hitler storming to power and setting up the Third Reich, taking over half of Europe.'

Jean registered the regret in his voice. 'My father thought the same way. He never fought in the Great War, though; fishing was a protected occupation.'

'Mine did.' Douglas could remember standing with his mother on the station platform in 1917, waving his father off to war. The Union Jacks fluttering in the sunshine and the men in uniform leaning out of the train windows had made it seem jolly to his ten-year-old self. His mother had dabbed her cheeks with her handkerchief then they'd gone home and had scones for tea. That had been the last time Douglas had seen his father. 'That was why I was one of the first to volunteer for the RAF this time around – so that their sacrifice shouldn't be in vain.'

The sombre subject sat uneasily beside the chirruping voice of Gracie Fields so he steered Jean in a new direction. 'You've no idea how relieved I was to receive that phone call from you last Wednesday. In my mind's eye I had you ditching your crate into the North Sea at the very least.'

'I'm sorry you had to tow her back from the Grange.' Jean's apology was sincere. 'I was hoping to save you the trouble.'

Douglas shook his head. 'I wasn't talking about the Spit; it was you I was worried about.'

Her forehead creased then she forced herself to look directly at him. The expression on his broad, square face had lost its usual guarded aspect and he stared straight at her, studying her response. 'I came through without a scratch,' she reminded him, 'so you needn't have been concerned.'

'It was the not knowing.'

'Quite. Will they ever get round to providing us with a radio, I wonder? I mean, it makes no sense to send us up without some means of communication. Or is it that they think we have enough to do as it is, just mastering the art of flying? Do you suppose that's it?'

'Not knowing what had happened to you.' Douglas cast aside his reserve. He would repeat his remark and let Jean interpret it however she wanted. She would probably see it as fatherly concern, given the difference in their ages. So be it.

She frowned again, as if trying to work out a puzzle. 'As you see: all's well that ends well.'

He thought how lovely Jean was, even when she knitted her eyebrows into a frown. There was a dignity about her that he seldom saw in young women and a self-containment that put her out of reach. *There's no fool like an old fool*, he told himself as he stamped on his tender feelings until they squealed for mercy. Then he proceeded to make a superficial remark about the new tune on the gramophone.

'Thank you, though,' Jean interrupted. She reached out to rest her fingers on the back of his hand; the lightest of touches.

Douglas lowered his gaze. Even if he'd been ten years younger and in his prime, he would have stood little chance with Jean. He saw that he was in danger of making a great fool of himself. 'Not at all,' he said as he stood up and made his excuses. 'I was only doing my job; whenever a pilot fails to bring in an aircraft on schedule, it's a cause for concern. Now if you'll forgive me . . .'

'Of course,' Jean said. Douglas left somewhat abruptly. The puzzle in Jean's mind remained unsolved.

By nine o'clock the party was in full swing. Horace had shoved Agnes to one side and chosen up-tempo records that had set everyone dancing despite the crush. A few desultory drinkers from the public rooms had gatecrashed, including non-commissioned ranks from the ferry pool – Gordon was there, joining in the fun with Olive, Harry and Stan – and now Bobbie was persuaded to stand on a chair in the centre of the room, awaiting a chorus of 'Happy Birthday' when the next record ended.

'Stay right there,' Angela ordered. 'Teddy, don't let her escape!'

Teddy jumped up beside Bobbie and put his arm around her waist while all the men in the room except Hilary and Douglas knelt in a circle at her feet. Jean, Agnes, Angela and Olive stood smiling in the background.

'Look at her; there's nothing of her,' Olive whispered to Agnes.

'Yes, you wouldn't think she was twenty-two to look at her; more like fifteen or sixteen.'

Bobbie's glowing face gave off a mixture of embarrassment and childlike delight. She came no higher than Teddy's shoulder as she looked down at her assembled admirers. 'Do I really have to perch up here?' she protested.

'Yes!' the men clamoured.

As the loud hiss of static signalled the end of the record, Teddy waved one arm in the air to conduct the raucous song. 'Ready? "Hap-py birth-day to you . . ."'

Bobbie leaned against Teddy's chest and put her hands over her ears.

'". . . Happy birthday, dear Bobbie, happy birthday to you!"'

The song finished and Teddy jumped down from the chair. He lifted Bobbie and swung her to the floor.

'Cut the cake!' Harry and Gordon cried.

Teddy led her to the table and handed her a knife. She sliced through the white icing and into the dark fruit cake.

'We need plates!' Another cry went up and Olive ran to fetch Mrs Loxley, who appeared with a pile of assorted saucers and dishes.

'This is the best I can do at short notice.' The canny landlady noticed rows of empty bottles and glasses as she plonked the crockery on the table.

'There's plenty more beer on tap in the Snug,' she announced in a loud voice as she hurried back to her post.

'Regretfully, it's time for me to call it a day,' Hilary told Douglas in an undertone soon after the cake had been cut.

'Me too.' Douglas took his car key from his jacket pocket. 'I can give you a lift back if you like.'

The two officers said their goodbyes to Bobbie then took their leave, Douglas limping heavily in Hilary's wake. They were jostled in the corridor by happy party-goers and they welcomed the cold night air as they stepped outside.

'What a racket, eh?' Hilary said through clenched teeth as he got into the car. 'But a chap has to show willing.'

Douglas said nothing. He knew he'd still be kicking himself tomorrow morning when he remembered how he'd overstepped the mark with Jean. He'd seen her chatting with Horace as he and Hilary had made their exit and the sight had made him furious. *Idiot!* he told himself as he drove through the village on the short journey home. *Get back to your chits and met reports. From now on keep your head down and try not to give Jean Dobson another thought.*

By eleven o'clock Angela had danced with every available partner, including Harry, who had two left feet, and a worse-for-wear Fred Rowe from the met room, who could do little more than shuffle and grin his way through a quickstep. Thick blue cigarette smoke curled around Bobbie's makeshift birthday banner and up towards the beamed ceiling. Empty glasses were stacked on the table next to the remains of the cake.

'My poor shoes!' Angela complained to Bobbie as Horace exchanged a joke with Fred then placed the final record of the evening on the turntable with a remarkably steady hand. 'I wish I'd known Harry and Fred were such clod-hoppers; I'd have steered well clear.'

The words were hardly out of her mouth when Teddy took Angela by the hand and claimed the last dance. He held her close and they swayed rhythmically while a stranded Bobbie was quickly rescued by Cameron. Soon they too had joined the dancers in a revolving embrace.

'I trust you've had a good time?' Cameron's hold was relaxed, one hand resting lightly on Bobbie's back. Flickering gaslight reflected in the lenses of his glasses and his expression was kind.

She nodded. 'Better than expected, as a matter of fact. Thank you for asking.'

'It's not exactly the Ritz, though.' Throughout the night Cameron had kept a watchful eye on Bobbie. He'd seen how nervous she'd been at the start and how she'd gradually relaxed. But then she'd seemed embarrassed by the hoo-ha surrounding the 'Happy Birthday' song, mostly thanks to Teddy. The silly chair business had brought out a protective feeling in Cameron, though he reminded himself that Bobbie was perfectly capable of looking after herself.

'No, I was happy to keep it low-key.' Cameron's left palm was cool beneath Bobbie's fingertips, his expression hard to read behind his glasses as she looked up into his face. When a nearby couple threatened to back into them he neatly sidestepped Bobbie out of trouble. 'How about you; have you enjoyed my party?' she asked.

'Very much. It's good to have something to celebrate once in a while – a birthday or an engagement. As a matter of fact, I'm due to attend a good pal's wedding later this month. I'm looking forward to that.'

Bobbie bit her lip and nodded. It was on the tip of her tongue to share Angela's exciting news. *Now is not the right moment*, she decided. *Far better to wait for the official announcement.*

The music ended and the couples separated – all except Angela and Teddy, whose arms stayed wrapped around each other in a dark corner of the room. Horace lowered the gramophone lid and came out from behind the table as Mrs Loxley bustled in.

'Do you need a hand with the clearing up?' Jean was the first to volunteer. She'd reluctantly agreed to a last dance with Harry, who was eager as a puppy but without a musical bone in his body, and she'd been relieved when it had ended. Now she was happy to stay behind and help put the room to rights.

The landlady handed Jean a tray then pointed to the empty glasses. When Olive stepped forward to collect the ashtrays she received a grateful nod. Soon there was a small group of helpers taking down balloons, sweeping the floor and carrying away the empty beer keg and bottles of spirits.

'Who would like a lift?' Cameron called from the doorway. 'Bobbie, why not come with me? Where's Angela got to? And Jean; it's started to rain. I'll wait in the car for you.' He stepped aside for Stan, Harry and Gordon to pass.

'Goodnight,' Stan grunted. Earlier in the evening he'd offered Jean a lift home and she'd refused, saying the walk would do her good. Now it looked as though she and one or two of the other girls had accepted the flight lieutenant's offer.

'G'night,' Gordon and Harry echoed.

'Goodnight all.' The three men disappeared into the darkness while Cameron confirmed arrangements with Bobbie. 'Find Angela and pass on my message. It wouldn't do for her to walk home by herself.'

So Bobbie began the search. She tried the sparsely furnished public bar then the cosy Snug without any luck. Perhaps Angela had already left without telling anyone? On the point of admitting defeat and returning to the party room, Bobbie opened one final door leading out into a small yard at the back of the building.

There was no light. The moon was hidden behind thick rain clouds and it was several seconds before Bobbie made out a row of oak barrels and several wooden crates stacked against a high stone wall. In the middle of the wall there was a gate that stood ajar. Bobbie had a sense that someone had recently been there; the gate latch fell with a sudden click and she heard movement in the thick darkness immediately beyond the yard.

'Angela?' *No, I'm imagining things.* Bobbie shook her head.

The gate swung open in the breeze. There was a whisper then suppressed laughter.

'Angela!' Bobbie grew suddenly angry. Whoever

was out there was doing a poor job of hiding from her. 'I know you're there. Stop being silly.'

After a pause, a figure stepped into view. It was too tall to be Angela; in fact, it was a man's outline followed by a voice Bobbie recognized.

'If it isn't the birthday girl,' Teddy said jovially as he walked into the yard, one hand in his trouser pocket, the other holding a cigarette. He advanced towards Bobbie, putting his cigarette to his lips and inhaling deeply.

'What are you doing out here?' she demanded.

'Minding my own business and having a quiet smoke.'

Bobbie saw that he was smirking and his eyebrows were raised mockingly.

Teddy came closer. 'How about a birthday kiss?' he whispered in her ear, sliding his arm around her waist.

With a small gasp Bobbie pushed him away. 'Who else is out there? Is it you, Angela?' Without waiting for a reply, she brushed past Teddy and stepped out through the gate on to a rough cinder track overlooking a steep railway embankment. Sure enough, she found who she was looking for.

'Yes?' Angela's enquiry had a hard edge. 'What do you want?'

Bobbie glanced back towards the yard in time to see Teddy disappear into the pub. 'For goodness sake, Angela; what were you thinking?'

'I wasn't thinking anything, if you must know.' This was true; one moment Angela had been dancing a slow waltz with Teddy, his arms wrapped around her. The next thing she knew they'd been standing on the embankment in the rain. 'Don't look so shocked; nothing happened.'

'I don't believe you.'

Angela shrugged. 'We were both tipsy, I suppose.'

'Did he kiss you?' Bobbie demanded.

The question was met by an impatient toss of the head. 'That really is none of your business.'

'But did he?'

Angela was obliged to raise her voice above the rumble and rattle of an approaching train. 'Really, darling, I won't answer that. And I'll pretend that you never asked.' She brushed raindrops from her cheeks but couldn't control a shiver that ran through her. 'Let's try to forget this ever happened, shall we?'

Bobbie's shoulders sagged forward. The wheels of the train clicked along the tracks and steam belched from its funnel into the night air. There was no doubt in her mind that Teddy had kissed Angela and it wasn't ever to be spoken about. 'Very well,' she agreed stiffly.

The train chugged past in a blur of metal and steam, the lights in its compartment windows casting a yellow glow on the two women standing next to the embankment. Brakes squealed as it approached the station two hundred yards from where Angela and Bobbie stood.

'Cameron will give us a lift back,' Bobbie said in a flat voice.

A guard called out the name of the station. There was a short delay before doors opened then slammed shut. A whistle blew.

'Then what are we waiting for?' Angela declared. She ran ahead of Bobbie through the unlit yard and into the pub. 'Come along, darling, before we catch our deaths.'

CHAPTER EIGHT

During her two weeks at Thame, Mary had donned overalls to stand behind a work bench and examine the oily innards of a dozen aeroplane engines. She'd sat at a desk to learn a confusing variety of control configurations and settings for the aircraft she was being trained to fly. Equally important were the Aircraft Identification classes led by Flight Sergeant Rouse, whose voice was a sharp bark and whose instructions it would be fatal to ignore. The sergeant made it clear that quick and accurate recognition of an approaching aircraft – friend or foe – would mean the difference between life and death; hence the importance of studying the posters on the classroom walls and memorizing every single silhouette.

In the evenings Mary had studied her Ferry Pilots' Notes and tried to retain speeds for take-off, climbing, cruising, landing and stalling for single-engined Spits, Corsairs, Mustangs and Hurricanes. Towards the end of the fortnight, focus had switched to Classes 3 and 4 – the twin- and four-engine operational aircraft such as Lancasters and Stirlings: yet more facts and figures to cram into her already stuffed and overheated brain.

Nevertheless, the days had sped by and Mary had absorbed information like a sponge, pouring all her energy into learning the theory and largely ignoring the recreational facilities on offer at the school. As expected, she had little in common with her fellow trainees, who spoke differently and talked of a world she knew little or nothing about. So, while her cohorts played tennis in their spare time and inhabited the town's drinking haunts, Mary stayed behind in the women's dormitory, sitting cross-legged on her bed and devouring her Notes, looking forward to the day, fast approaching, when she would graduate from training in a dummy cockpit to the real thing – up in the air at last.

'This is it.' Flight Sergeant Rouse walked Mary out on to the runway early on Friday 8 October for her much anticipated 'stooge' flight. A strong breeze swept in from the east as they approached the Oxford, a twin-engine monoplane favoured by the instructors at Thame. He walked her round the aircraft to give her time to get used to its dimensions. 'Now remember; she has a tendency to swing on take-off and landing, especially in this wind. You'll have to correct that as best you can. She's a lot faster than the Tiger Moth. Try not to stall her; she'll drop like a stone if you do. But don't worry; I'll be sitting right behind you.' Rouse tapped the mouthpiece attached to her parachute harness. 'If you get into difficulty, speak into this. I'll guide you through.'

'Yes, sir.' Mary's mouth was so dry she could hardly speak. The moment had arrived. She must seem neither too anxious nor too excited. Above all, she must keep a level head.

'The Oxford has retractable wheels,' Rouse reminded her as he stepped up on to the wing and climbed into the dual cockpit. 'See this lever? Pull it back to bring up the undercarriage. Press it forward for landing. Make sure it's locked. Watch for the green lights.'

'Yes, sir.' Mary climbed in after him, aware of the snug fit of her Sidcot suit as she wriggled into the narrow seat in front of his. As Rouse lowered the canopy, she slid her goggles over her eyes and tightened the chin strap of her helmet, checked the dials in front of her then waited for the sergeant to signal chocks away to the ground crew below.

The wind buffeted the stationary plane. It scattered early autumn leaves across the runway. The sky was dull grey.

'Fire up the engines and taxi to the take-off point,' Rouse instructed.

This is a first for me but it's an everyday event for the sergeant, Mary thought as she carefully followed orders. The idea helped to slow down her racing heart.

'Did you check with the met room for visibility?' The voice behind her ran calmly through the routine.

'Yes, sir: fifteen hundred yards with twelve hundred feet of cloud clearance.' The moment was approaching; there was no turning back.

'Very good. Check your revs, keep your hand steady on the stick – off we go!'

With the roar of the twin engines in her ears, Mary hurtled down the runway. She felt the Oxford's nose tilt upwards then there was a jerk followed by a strange floating sensation as they were suddenly airborne. The pull of gravity pushed her hard against the back of her seat. With her hand on the joystick and using her rudder pedals to combat the easterly wind, she climbed steadily then levelled out at 1,000 feet. Below them the airfield was a square of bright green, the surrounding fields a patchwork of yellows and browns.

'Steady as you go,' Rouse instructed. 'Lower your revs, increase boost until you achieve maximum cruising speed; that way you keep your petrol consumption to a minimum.'

Exhilarated to her fingertips, Mary followed a westerly course. All her pre-flight nerves had vanished; her heartbeat was rapid but steady. She was flying a real plane, hearing its roar, drinking in every detail of her surroundings: the white, wispy clouds streaming past the cockpit, the grey sky above, the colours of autumn below. And there was the ancient city of Oxford, set out like a model village complete with spires and domes. She flew over miniature college greens and narrow streets, smiling to herself, remembering her fairground ride on the Moonrocket and how she'd dreamed back then of this impossible moment. She banked the plane and turned her towards the south, felt the wind batter her port side and corrected the swing.

'Nicely done,' came the comment through her headset.

Mary felt on top of the world. An indescribable thrill ran through her as the powerful plane responded to her touch – to travel at such speed, to be in control, was beyond words! Even as she followed the instruction to turn for home and began a slow descent, her spirits continued to soar.

'Lower the landing gear,' Rouse reminded her from his instructor's seat.

She pressed the lever on cue and felt the wheels lower then lock into position. Using her compass to chart her exact course and looking out for landmarks, she headed home. Throttle down without stalling the engine, hand steady on the stick, decrease speed, hit the concrete, apply brakes. The Oxford squealed to a halt with fifty yards of runway to spare. Mary turned off the engines.

As the propellers stopped whirring, the ground crew ran up with the chocks. Rouse lifted the canopy, allowing Mary to unbuckle her harness and step out ahead of him. She stood for a moment on the wing of the training plane, looking out with pride over the airfield at the service huts, administration block and mess buildings.

'Get a move on, Holland,' Rouse barked at her from behind. 'I haven't got all day.'

It didn't matter; his two words of praise – 'Nicely done' – stayed with Mary as she walked towards the canteen.

Her instructor would put in a favourable report. She would soon move on to the final stage of her training – her first solo flight in a Spitfire Mark V.

'Oh, how I hate these overnight assignments,' Angela grumbled from the back seat of the car driven by Olive Pearson. 'Especially on a Friday; they're the worst.'

Bobbie agreed. 'I blame Douglas for picking on us,' she complained. 'He knows how much we look forward to a Friday night off yet at the last minute he says we must trek all the way to Walsall to pick up two new Spits instead.'

'In the dark!' Angela sighed. They could see nothing but their own reflections in the car windows as Olive drove them mile after endless mile, through grimy mining villages and smoky pottery towns.

'When we'd far rather go out and paint the town red.'

Olive pulled up at a crossroads to let a small convoy of army supply lorries trundle by. She tried to close her ears to the grumbles from the back seat. Had Bobbie and Angela forgotten that there was a war on and bigger sacrifices than theirs had to be made? Take Olive's own case – she had to drop off the two pilots at their digs close to the factory then drive all the way back to Rixley before morning. There would be three hours' kip for her tonight, if she was lucky.

Angela stared vacantly at the back of Olive's head and shoulders, aware that her conversation with Bobbie didn't flow as usual. In fact, Bobbie had been short with her all week, ever since the silly business with Teddy after the birthday party. There'd even been one occasion when Bobbie had snubbed Angela outright: they'd both been standing in the queue to receive their chits and Angela had tried to pass the time of day by asking Bobbie if she'd heard the report on the wireless about events in Naples. Pretending that she hadn't heard, Bobbie had turned away to speak with Jean, deliberately excluding Angela from the conversation.

'Where are we now?' Angela broke the weary silence to lean forward and tap Olive's shoulder.

'We're just coming into Larchfield.' Olive didn't turn her head as she signalled right and followed the army convoy along a street of terraced houses, all with their blackout blinds in place, smoke rising from their chimneys into the cold night air. The slow crawl did nothing to improve the mood inside the car until Angela decided to tackle head-on the problem of Tuesday night.

'Bobbie – I want to talk to you about Teddy,' she began hesitantly. She crossed and uncrossed her legs with a silky swish. 'By the way, Olive, do you have a light?'

Olive took a box of matches from the glove compartment and passed it back.

'Thank you.' A match flared and lit up Angela's perfect features; blue eyes hooded, scarlet lips pouting and head tilted back as she took her first puff. 'I'm awfully sorry if you read too much into that little skirmish,' she went on.

'If you mean the incident in the yard behind the Fox and Hounds . . .' Bobbie wound down her window to disperse the smoke. Trust Angela to phrase it in such a way that shifted the blame. 'I don't want to talk about it.'

Angela glanced across to see that Bobbie was in a seriously bad temper. 'I'm sorry,' she said again. 'Things with Teddy may have got a little out of hand, but I swear that it was nothing more than harmless flirtation – very silly on both our parts.'

Bobbie turned towards her with a frown. 'Apology accepted,' she said stiffly.

Angela wasn't convinced. 'Really and truly, can we be friends again? I'll give you a blow-by-blow account if it'll help. We'd danced the last waltz together then Teddy being Teddy, he took things a step too far.'

'So it was his fault?' There Angela went again, refusing to accept any responsibility. 'Did you conveniently forget that you're engaged to be married to Lionel?'

In the driving seat Olive pricked up her ears as she turned left out of the town and on along a country road towards the Castle Bromwich factory where the Spitfires rolled off the production line. She'd arrived late at Tuesday's party but anyone with eyes in their head could see that First Officer Browne had been leading Teddy Simpson on. And surprise, surprise; she was engaged! Now, that *was* a turn-up for the books!

'Ouch!' Angela let out a groan. Then, sitting up very straight, she said, 'No, Bobbie, I did not forget. And nothing happened. You may find that hard to believe. Teddy suggested going outside for a cigarette. I agreed. Then, when we heard you calling my name, we decided to play a childish trick by hiding on the railway embankment.'

Blimey O'Reilly! Olive's hands gripped the wheel a little tighter. Was Angela to be believed or was she simply trying to talk herself out of a tight corner?

'As I said, I'd had too much to drink,' Angela went on from behind a cloud of smoke. 'And I regret it. But nothing happened.' She spoke the last sentence with emphasis on the word 'nothing'.

Slowly Bobbie's frown eased. Angela's account began to seem plausible after all. 'I'm glad to hear it,' she said primly before relaxing into a smile. 'Truly, I am.'

Uh-oh, I wouldn't believe her if I was you. Olive drove the car through a shallow ford then up a steep hill lined by oak trees. *If you want my opinion, that pair went outside for more than a quick cigarette!*

Angela was relieved that she and Bobbie had cleared the air. 'And while we're at it, I hope you know that our friendship means much more to me than Teddy Simpson ever could.'

'Of course.' Bobbie nodded and blushed. 'Now I feel such a fool,' she stammered.

'What for?'

'For even caring what you and Teddy were up to. It's not as if I have any claim on the man.' What was an embrace and a couple of kisses in the downstairs room of a bed and breakfast when all was said and done?

'But you do like him?' Angela queried. It was easy to see how someone as naive as Bobbie could be swept off her feet.

'I do, but the question is: does he like me?' Yes, Teddy had flirted and teased since the night in Harkness and he sometimes looked at Bobbie in a meaningful way, but he'd never asked her out or given any definite sign that the kisses had meant something to him.

'Teddy likes all girls.' Angela's warning was kindly meant. 'If I were you, Bobbie, I wouldn't take him too seriously.'

Bobbie pressed her lips together to consider the advice. Angela was worldly and probably saw things in a clearer light, whereas she, Bobbie, had so little experience of men. 'You're right,' she said decisively as Olive turned up a tree-lined drive with a Tudor mansion at the end of it. The silhouette of the house showed tall chimneys and steep gables and a dim light shone from an arched main entrance. Two thin dogs ran down the drive towards the car. 'Teddy is good fun; nothing more.'

'Quite.' Angela stubbed out her cigarette in the ashtray.

Bloody hell; in future, I'll take everything these two say with a pinch of salt, Olive thought as she pulled up at the door and turned to face her passengers. 'Here you are, ladies; your billet for tonight.'

The ancient floorboards at Fenton Royal creaked and groaned as Bobbie and Angela followed their hostess up a wide flight of stairs.

'I hope you girls don't mind sharing.' The equally ancient owner, Harriet Wilby, also creaked and groaned as she showed Bobbie and Angela into the Queen's Room: an extravaganza of carved plaster-work, oak panelling and a great four-poster bed draped with faded crimson brocade. Her two brindle greyhounds bounded on to the bed as she apologized for the lack of modern facilities such as running water and electric light, pointed out a basin and ewer on the washstand and candlesticks by the bed then called the dogs to heel and said goodnight.

After taking in her surroundings, Bobbie ran after their landlady down a long, sloping gallery that gave the odd impression of being at sea aboard a galleon.

'Excuse me, Mrs Wilby, where's the WC?' she asked while the greyhounds sniffed at her skirt, tails wagging.

'*Miss* Wilby,' the no-frills old lady replied. Her

outdated clothes hung from her skeletal figure and her skin sagged like worn leather. 'I thought I'd explained; there's no running water in this wing of the house. You'll find a chamber pot under the bed.'

Bobbie thanked her but her face wore a worried frown as she reported back to Angela.

'A chamber pot?' Angela lifted the counterpane and peered under the bed to see that it was true. She quickly dropped the cover and stood, hands on hips, with an expression of squeamish distaste. 'Good Lord, it's practically medieval!'

Bobbie burst out laughing. 'Think about it; that's exactly where we've landed – in a house that was probably built when Henry the Eighth was King of England!'

Angela took the point. 'And very little effort has been made to modernize it in four hundred years.'

'There might be ghosts!' Bobbie suggested with a nervous laugh. 'Ladies in Elizabethan ruffs, rebel lords executed by the King, wafting down the gallery with their heads tucked under their arms . . .'

'That's quite enough of that.' Angela repressed a shudder and brought them down to earth with a bump.

Obviously, there was nothing the girls could do about their primitive accommodation so they lit candles and decided to make the best of things.

'It's only for one night, thank heavens.' Bobbie was the first to undress. She stood in her pyjamas at the latticed window overlooking parkland.

Angela sat on the edge of the bed to test the mattress. 'Hard as a board,' she commented before springing up and flinging off her uniform then slipping into a sleeveless nightdress. 'Brr!' She shivered as she slid between the sheets. 'It's freezing in here. Which side do you prefer?'

'This one.' Bobbie chose the side of the bed closest to the window. 'The oddest thing is that in less than eight hours you and I will have closed the door on this crumbling pile and will be sitting in the cockpit of the most up-to-date aircraft in the world, checking our revs and giving the signal for chocks away.'

'A twentieth-century miracle of engineering.' Angela pulled the sheets up to her nose. 'We'll trailblaze our way into the history books yet again.'

Bobbie and Angela lay side by side in the flickering candlelight, hands behind their heads and staring up at the plaster acorns and oak leaves carved into the ceiling. The floorboards creaked though no one was there.

'I've had a letter from Lionel,' Angela confided after a long pause. 'He wrote it the night before his ship set sail for Greece.'

'You sound upset.' Raising herself on to her elbows, Bobbie looked keenly at Angela. 'Are you crying?'

Angela wiped her eyes with the back of her hand. 'It was such a heartfelt letter, telling me how much he loves me and how he thinks about me every hour of every day.'

'I don't think I've ever seen you cry before.' Bobbie slid out of bed to fetch Angela a handkerchief. 'You must miss Lionel an awful lot.'

Angela sat up in bed and dabbed at her eyes. 'That's the saddest thing,' she confessed. 'Whole days can go by without me giving him a thought. The truth is Lionel seems to love me more than I love him. That's wicked of me, I know.'

'Not wicked,' Bobbie argued. 'You can't help how you feel. And this blasted war twists everything out of shape.'

'In what way?'

'You and Lionel are forced apart, for one thing. In normal times, when a girl gets engaged, the happy couple goes ahead and makes plans for the wedding and so on. Everyone is caught up in decisions about bridesmaids and guest lists, with nothing to get in the way. It's different with Lionel sailing off in his convoy and you flying your Spits. We need to keep our wits about us, doing this job. If we don't we're likely to end up in the drink or worse. Look at Jean and her latest scrap with Jerry – she only just managed to come out in one piece and she's the best pilot we have.'

Surprised by Bobbie's mature view, Angela nodded slowly. 'That's true. But I've known Lionel for a long time. And even before the war started, I wasn't sure how I felt about him; not deep down. He'd been part of Hugh, Cameron and Hilary's crowd for as long as I can remember; always there, always opening doors for me and offering me his arm.'

'And then at some point Lionel must have made his feelings plain?'

Angela struggled to remember. 'Not really. I don't think he ever formally asked me to go out with him. We were always just part of the crowd. And then when he did spring it on me – one night at a cabaret club in the West End – it took me completely by surprise.'

'Why – what did he do?' Bobbie was seeing a side of Angela that she hadn't known existed: less self-assured and much more serious. She wrapped a cardigan around her shoulders and listened intently.

'He didn't go down on one knee exactly, but as near as damn it. We were dancing together and he came out with it: whispered in my ear that he loved me and wanted to marry me, just like that. He had to hold me up, I was so surprised.'

'That's awfully romantic,' Bobbie insisted. 'What did you say?'

'I said I was fond of him.' Angela's voice was wistful. 'But I was only nineteen and Lionel was twenty-one. He was home on leave from the Navy.'

'He proposed and you turned him down?'

'I said we should wait. Honestly, at nineteen a girl has no clue what she wants to do with the rest of her life. I said I did like him and I found him attractive. He is, isn't he?'

'Very,' Bobbie agreed. 'You don't need me to tell you that.'

'So what is wrong with me? Am I really so shallow? Lionel is handsome and very decent, so why don't I feel the way I should?'

Bobbie hugged her knees to her chin. 'You're asking the wrong person. You know I have no idea what it feels like to fall in love.'

Realizing that there were no easy answers to her questions, Angela gave a short sigh. 'Not even with Teddy Simpson?' she asked with a wry grin.

'Most definitely not with Teddy!' Bobbie exclaimed. She saw him in her mind's eye; tall (too tall for her?), slim (too slim?), smiling (mocking her?). Handsome enough to be a matinee idol, he could play the part of the gigolo in cravat and blazer who steals the heroine from her loyal but plodding husband. There; she had Teddy Simpson down to a T. 'There's no danger on that score,' she assured Angela as she got into bed and blew out the candle.

The weather was at the forefront of Jean's mind when she woke early on Saturday morning. Was the sky clear enough to fly out? Was rain in the forecast? What was the direction of the prevailing wind? Added to the usual concerns there was the increasing likelihood of fog as autumn set in.

'Good morning, Jean.' Cameron met her on the stairs at the Grange, hat tucked under his arm, greatcoat buttoned. 'You're up bright and early. Would you like a lift with me and Douglas?'

'Yes, please.' She accepted gratefully and they walked across the hall together. They were about to leave by the main entrance when Cameron remembered that he'd arranged to meet Douglas round the back and so took Jean's elbow and steered her below stairs, along a dingy corridor and through the old butler's pantry, down the back steps into the stable yard where their lift awaited.

'I received a phone call yesterday that might interest you,' Cameron mentioned to Jean as they made their way through the house. 'About Mary Holland; you know who I mean?'

'Of course. We spoke on the afternoon before she set off for Thame. How's she getting on?'

'The call was from her instructor, Flight Sergeant Rouse. He's not a chap to lavish praise, I gathered, but reading between the lines I'd say that he was pretty happy about Mary's progress to date.'

'That's good. I like Mary. She has something about her.' Jean spoke warmly and sincerely.

'I like her too,' Cameron said as he held open the back door for Jean. 'Rouse said he was ready to send her up on her first solo flight any day now. After that she hopes to be sent back to Rixley to join our team.'

'I'll look forward to that.' Jean put on her forage cap and led the way down the steps before saying hello to Douglas who was waiting for them under the stable-yard clock. He sat in the grey half-light, his coat collar turned up, with the car engine ticking over.

'All set?' Douglas asked as she and Cameron got in. He drove steadily down the drive and through the sleeping village, happy to let the others chat.

'How likely is it that Mary will come back here?' Jean enquired.

'Quite likely if I pull a few strings.' In fact, Cameron had already set things in motion with Hilary. 'I can cite family circumstances to keep her close to home.'

'Such as?'

'Mary is from the West Riding. She has a widowed father who's getting on a bit. He's not in the best of health.'

'I didn't know that.'

'It's written in her file.' Cameron saw that they were approaching the sentry box outside the ferry pool's main gates.

The sentry recognized Douglas and waved him

through. Douglas parked his car close to the administration block and while he went straight into the
operations room to write out chits for the day,
Cameron and Jean headed to the busy canteen where
there was the usual gathering of ground crew and
pilots. Music played on the wireless and half a dozen
personnel who had finished eating sat at the long
tables doing jigsaws or playing backgammon.

By chance Jean stood behind Stan in the queue.
'No Bobbie and Angela this morning?' she asked
him as she glanced quickly around the room.

'They're in Walsall.' Stan had already checked his
schedule for the day and knew that the two girl
pilots were due in at half ten. 'They're bringing in a
couple of spanking new Spits, by all accounts.'

Teddy had come into the canteen hard on the
heels of Cameron and Jean and was standing behind
them in the queue, stamping his feet and blowing
into his hands to counteract the effects of his chilly
ride over from the Grange on a Royal Enfield motorbike that he'd brought back after a twenty-four-hour
home leave. He wore a thick woollen scarf over his
pilot's jacket and his hair had a windswept look that
he hadn't bothered to smooth down. 'What's that
you say?' he asked Stan. 'Did I hear the magic words,
"new Spits"?'

'Yes, but that doesn't necessarily mean you'll get
your mucky hands on them,' Cameron warned.
Deciding to go without breakfast, he turned back
towards the door. 'The Spits won't be here long,' he
called over his shoulder. 'From what I gather, Rixley
is a temporary stop on their way over to Northern
Ireland.'

'Don't be like that.' Teddy unwound his scarf then shuffled forward with the queue. 'My hands are as good as anyone else's to fly the little beauties over the Irish Sea. Better than most, I would say.' He winked at Jean.

'That's for others to decide,' Stan said under his breath. He'd caught sight of the wink and was nettled. Standing to one side, he offered to let Jean go ahead of him. 'You get your breakfast first,' he told her. 'I'm not on duty until eight.'

She smiled and thanked him. 'I'll be over by the window. Come and join me if you like.'

Like? Of course Stan would. In fact, it would set him up for the day. So when it came to his turn at the counter he put in a quick order for toast and a mug of tea then hurried to Jean's table.

'I hope you get one of the new Mark IXs,' he told her as he sat down opposite. 'The flight lieutenant's right about them wanting to move them on pronto, though. There's every chance that Jerry will be back on a second raid, now that we're on their radar. We're pretty much a sitting target, to tell you the truth.'

'I really don't mind what I fly.' Jean meant what she said. 'Class One right through to Class Six. In fact, I enjoy the challenge of the Class Five and Six: four engines, flying boats – anything.'

'They say variety is the spice of life.' Stan was wondering how to move on from talking about work to more personal matters when Teddy interrupted their cosy tête-à-tête by sitting down next to Jean and tucking into his plate of bacon and eggs.

'I'd agree with that; the more variety the better,

especially when it comes to the ladies.' Teddy's remark, made with a full mouth, was accompanied by the annoying wink. 'Never let the grass grow, eh, Stan?'

Jean looked from one to the other. It was obvious that Teddy had riled Stan, whose normally cheerful features were knotted into a deep frown. 'Do you know what you're flying today?' she asked Teddy as casually as she could.

'Not yet. Hopalong Cassidy hasn't issued the chits.'

Jean's large, blue-grey eyes opened even wider at the off-colour remark against Douglas. Her knife and fork stayed poised over her plate.

It was the first time that Stan had seen Jean ruffled. Colour came into her cheeks. He held his breath, waiting for her retort.

Her voice was clear and slow. 'If you mean First Officer Thornton, he gave me a lift in this morning. He skipped breakfast to hurry things along.'

Cold and stiff; really angry. Stan was fascinated.

'Take it easy,' Teddy said with a grin. 'Come on, Jean, where's your sense of humour?'

'That wasn't funny. I don't know why you would think it was.'

Cool as a cucumber. A bloody knockout.

'My, someone's touchy this morning.' Passing it off with a shrug, Teddy's mind veered off on to more important things. 'I really hope I get one of those Spits, though. I can fly her over Manchester en route to Derry, put on another display for my nearest and dearest.'

'Fine, if you fancy facing a court martial,' Stan said sharply.

'Why? Who would be any the wiser?'

'I would.'

In the split second between the sudden click as the wireless cut off and the morning announcement on the Tannoy Jean let her knife and fork clatter on to her plate. She stared at Teddy, speechless.

'Will all pilots report to the operations room for their chits,' came the nasal blare over the loudspeaker. 'Repeat: all pilots report to the operations room!'

'Action stations!' The cry went up and every pilot in the room left off what they were doing and made a beeline for the ops room, Jean and Teddy among them.

'Pass on an important message to First Officer Thornton, will you?' Dorothy Kirk from the met room pushed past Jean in the doorway into the admin block. 'Tell him thick fog is forecast over the estuary. Wasn't picked up until five minutes ago.'

'Forecast for what time?' Jean called after the young assistant, who was hurrying to spend a penny.

'Later this morning – around ten. It should burn off by noon. I'll print off the official report when I'm back at my post.'

The Tannoy announcement had taken Jean by surprise. She'd had to hurry to her locker for her helmet and parachute so for once was not near the front of the queue of pilots approaching the hatch to receive their chits. As she waited patiently, she heard Teddy's voice protesting about his allocation for the day.

'Bloody hell; a PBY Catalina!' He sounded disgusted, elbowing people aside as he came down the stairs. 'Why can't the Yanks drive down from the Clyde and fetch the old crate themselves? Why do I have to drive to Highcliff harbour to pick her up and fly her all the way up there?'

There were a few laughs at his expense – 'Not fast enough for you, Teddy boy?', 'I hear it's a sunny day up in Glasgow. Fancy a dip?', and so on – for everyone knew that the American-built flying boat was slow and ungainly, an odd-looking two-engine aircraft with its wings and propellers attached to the top of the cockpit to keep them clear of the water when landing.

Managing to stay well out of Teddy's way, Jean edged towards the hatch. When she reached the front of the queue, she took her chit and read that she was to fly a nimble Hurricane to Kent then pick up a Corsair and fly it back to Rixley. Glancing through the hatchway, she saw Douglas with his back towards her, deep in conversation with his secretary, Gillian Wharton.

'Step aside,' the bad-tempered girl issuing the chits told her. 'Next, please.'

So Jean did as she was told and made a sideways move to put her head around the door. The small room buzzed with activity – there was the clickety-clack of a typewriter, the ring of a telephone and several people speaking at once. 'Excuse me, First Officer Thornton – might I have a word?'

Douglas didn't turn.

Jean took a step forward and raised her voice. 'Excuse me, Douglas . . .'

Gillian looked up from the file that she and Douglas had been discussing. She tapped her commanding officer on the shoulder and pointed to where Jean stood.

He apologized when he saw her. 'Sorry, Jean . . . we were looking at inconsistencies in this log . . . I didn't hear you.' He waved the buff-coloured folder at her. 'Now, how can I help?'

'Expect a fog warning from the met office,' she said quickly. 'They'll send it along official channels in the next few minutes. I got it by word of mouth from Dorothy Kirk.'

'That's news to me.' Douglas reached for the telephone on his desk. 'I'll get on to them right away. Thank you, Jean.'

She retreated on to the landing then made her way down the stairs. Fog was still on her mind as she stepped outside and began the long walk to Runway 3, the furthest from the control tower. The short conversation with Douglas also bothered her. Why hadn't he turned when she'd tried to attract his attention? She'd spoken above the rattle of typewriter keys, surely loud enough for him to hear. And she remembered the look of tried patience on Gillian's face – raised eyebrows and a quick shake of her head.

Jean saw Teddy striding ahead of her towards his motorbike parked outside Hangar 2 and she remembered with a fresh burst of anger his throwaway Hopalong insult against Douglas. The anger was soon replaced by concern. Might there be a grain of truth behind the younger man's callous judgement? Was Douglas's ability to carry out his duties up to scratch or not?

'Let's hope so,' she said out loud, out of earshot of

Gordon, who was carrying out the final checks on her Hurricane.

Over the months Jean had been at Rixley, she'd come to view Douglas as a good friend. He was an affable, serious-minded man whom she could trust and look up to. After all, she never overlooked the fact that she wouldn't be here now if it hadn't been for their chance meeting in the pub. And he was the polar opposite to Teddy Simpson, just now roaring off towards the main gates on his Royal Enfield Bullet. *How dare he?* Jean said to herself as Gordon finished wiping the Hurricane's windscreen then jumped down to the ground. *Douglas is worth ten of Teddy Simpson any day. And next time Teddy decides to have a go at him, I'll tell him so.*

CHAPTER NINE

At eight o'clock on Saturday morning, a car arrived at Fenton Royal to take Angela and Bobbie to the factory in Castle Bromwich: a journey of some six miles through wooded countryside into the outskirts of the town and the vast factory where Spitfires were manufactured.

They waved goodbye with undisguised relief to poor Miss Wilby and her crumbling mansion.

'She can't have two spare pennies to rub together.' Bobbie sat back for the short drive. 'What good are oak furniture and oil paintings when you can't afford to keep a place heated?'

'Unless you burn the furniture,' Angela quipped. 'I wonder where and when the "Royal" came into it. I mean, why Fenton Royal?'

'And why the Queen's Room?' The countryside was changing quickly, giving way to neat modern bungalows and after that to acres of low factory buildings made out of steel and concrete. 'I suppose we'll never know.' Bobbie had started to look ahead to the task in hand when Angela broke into her thoughts.

'I feel so much better after our talk last night,' she confided. 'It's quite remarkable.'

Bobbie smiled in response. 'In what way, better?'

'Lighter,' Angela explained. 'It was such a relief to let it all out; like going to confession. Forgive me, Father, for I have sinned.'

'Not at all similar.' Bobbie, who had been brought up a Catholic, found this amusing. 'I didn't dish out any Hail Marys, for a start. And I'm no priest – For one thing, I don't intend to stay celibate all my life.'

'Be that as it may . . .' Angela smiled warmly back. 'I mean it, darling. A problem shared . . .' She'd lain awake long after Bobbie had fallen asleep, thinking about her engagement to Lionel. Eventually she'd been able to see beyond her doubts. Lionel certainly had his good points, besides the obvious one that his family was sufficiently respectable and well off to satisfy Angela's father, which would have proved an obstacle had it been otherwise. No, the thing that really mattered was that Lionel was exceptionally kind and considerate. Beneath his reserve and recently acquired military manner there was gentleness and a true desire not to do harm – rare qualities in a man. He might not be the most garrulous and socially adept, but his actions were generous to a fault; witness the time when Hilary of all people had come a cropper over a gambling debt and Lionel had helped him out, no questions asked. Lying in bed with Bobbie's regular breathing as a backdrop, Angela had convinced herself that this was the kind of fertile soil in which the seed of love might grow.

'So you're happy now?' Bobbie asked as their driver took them along a straight, flat road bordered by a tall chain-link fence topped with barbed wire. Beyond the fence was an enormous factory built mainly of corrugated iron and beyond that an air-field with four concrete runways.

'Happ*ier*.' The qualification was important. 'Still not head over heels, but definitely more willing to make a better go of it.'

'Good for you.'

The car stopped for two sentries to check the girls' documents before they were waved through the gates.

'What a place!' Bobbie gasped as they drove past rows of brand-new Spitfires lined up by the side of the nearest runway. 'I can count twenty without even trying.'

'Most impressive,' Angela agreed. Their driver pulled up close to the Nissen hut that served as an office while Austin pickups criss-crossed the airfield, carrying engine parts and pieces of fuselage from a mountain of scrap metal in a far corner of the air-field. They took them towards the part of the factory where they reassembled aircraft out of cannibalized spare parts. Closer to where Angela and Bobbie sat, wide doors opened on to the section where the new Spits were built. Inside they caught a glimpse of engineers with clipboards and mechanics in overalls climbing up a scaffold to run final checks on a plane that was almost ready to go.

Bobbie took a deep breath to control her mount-ing excitement. 'Here I come; Second Officer Fraser reporting for duty,' she murmured to Angela.

She was first out of the car and first into the office where a manager in a brown suit with a green tie peered over the top of his glasses and gave her the usual disbelieving shake of the head. 'Blimey; are they sending you straight from school these days?' he said by way of greeting as Bobbie produced her documents for a second time.

Angela followed soon after. She glanced at the array of posters behind the manager's desk: a dog-eared one for the RAF – *Make the RAF Supreme – Only the Best Are Good Enough!* – and beside it her own smiling image on the newly published recruitment advertisement for the ATA. It was the first time she'd seen it in glorious technicolour with all the lettering in place and she thought she looked rather good.

The factory manager did a double-take. He glanced from Angela to the smiling girl on the poster and back again. Not only were recruits getting younger, now they were sending them from the Paris catwalks as well. *Wait until the blokes on the factory floor get an eyeful of these two*, he thought as he double- then triple-checked Bobbie's and Angela's paperwork. *Talk about Anything to Anywhere; that doesn't cover the half of it!*

'If ever there was a plane for a woman to fall in love with, it's this one.' Angela stood on the runway, hands on hips, admiring the newest version of her favourite fighter plane. She patted her top pocket containing the precious Blue Book. 'There are seventy different aircraft types listed in here, and not one even comes close.'

Bobbie looked down from the cockpit that she'd just climbed into. It was barely wider than her shoulders – a tight squeeze even for her – and she smiled when she remembered the looks of horror that the ground crew had exchanged when they realized that she was to take charge of their valuable war machine. 'What are you waiting for?' she yelled down to Angela. 'Your chariot awaits; over there on Runway One!'

So Angela set off at a sprint across the grass, lugging her parachute and overnight bag and watched by the mechanics who had wheeled her plane out of its hangar. Instead of ignoring their loud shouts and whistles, she stopped suddenly, turned and dipped a quick curtsy. The men cheered raucously and waved their spanners and oil-stained rags in the air. She laughed back at them then ran on, reaching her Spit just as a member of the ground crew finished his checks.

'You'll never fly anything better than this,' he told her, giving the blue fuselage an affectionate pat. 'Make sure you look after her. And remember, you have no radio – you're on your own.'

Angela tutted at him as she sprang from ground to wing and from there into the cockpit in one smooth, elegant movement. 'This isn't the first time I've done this; far from it.'

'Even so.' Joe Kerr, the mechanic, belonged to the old 'hand that rocks the cradle' school. 'She's faster and lighter than ever. And her controls only need the lightest touch. You hardly have to breathe on them and they move.'

'Thank you, Sergeant.' Angela gave Joe a disdainful stare and strapped herself in. Didn't the dullard know that she'd beaten hundreds if not thousands of other women applicants to get on to the ATA training programme? Not that she wanted to boast about it, for that would be infra dig.

Joe and a second man in overalls waited for her to give them the thumbs-up. 'Happy?' he yelled up.

'I'd be happier if I had a radio and a couple of rounds of ammunition on board, but heigh-ho!'

Angela was well aware of the official line that contact with the enemy was rare during the short hops between ferry pools. On the few occasions when ATA pilots were unlucky enough to encounter German aircraft, they would normally be flying low enough for ground defences to engage with and shoot down the marauder. So what would be the point of furnishing the aircraft with precious ammunition before the RAF boys got their hands on them? Privately, Angela blamed a clerk in the War Office for pushing through this short-sighted view. Basically, no one with any authority cared enough to have thought it through properly.

'And I'd be happier if she put her lipstick away and stuck to flying the bloody thing,' Joe muttered to his companion.

It was true; Angela had flipped open the lid of her gold compact and was freshening up her lipstick. Bobbie had been given the green light to be first to take off, so in fact there was plenty of time.

On the neighbouring runway, Bobbie opened the throttle and hurtled down the concrete strip, faster and faster until she saw the Spit's cone-shaped nose tilt and felt a surge of upwards motion as she took off. She climbed rapidly, feeling the kick of extra power in the new engine. Soon she was soaring at 2,000 feet in perfect conditions: low winds, good visibility, with her compass set and the engine purring happily. A quick glance behind told her that Angela had also taken off successfully.

Bobbie sighed happily and eased back on the throttle until she saw Angela bring her Spit up alongside. They headed north-east together, exchanging broad smiles and thumbs-ups.

Oh joy! Angela mouthed.

Loop? Bobbie queried with a grin.

Angela nodded. A second later the two pilots flipped their aircraft into perfectly synchronized acrobatic back somersaults, nose over tail and turning full circle to fly smoothly on.

Angela grinned at Bobbie. *Roll?*

An answering nod sent them banking to starboard. But the Spits were heavier to roll than expected and it took longer so that when they emerged from the manoeuvre they found that they'd flown slap-bang into unexpected cloud.

'Where did this weather front come from?' Angela spoke out loud. She checked her altitude dial then signalled to Bobbie that she was about to straighten up then let down in a shallow dive to see if she could fly beneath the cloud.

Where are we? Bobbie checked her dials. They were further east than she'd expected and between the thick clouds she caught occasional glimpses of a wide estuary below: sea stretched out to starboard and a long hook of land to port. But where was Angela? Bobbie searched all around; there was no sign of her fellow pilot and conditions were rapidly deteriorating.

Meanwhile, Angela dived until her altimeter read 700 feet. There was no land visible through the mist and the Spit was buffeted this way and that by strong turbulence that quickly disorientated Angela and forced her to consider her next move. OK, so she was below safety break-off height and dare not fly lower. Visibility was practically zero. Worse still, she'd lost all contact with Bobbie. The needle of the altimeter jerked dramatically downwards. Four hundred feet and Angela still had no sight of land. 'Ghastly pea-souper,' she muttered angrily. 'The blasted fog must have rolled in off the sea without warning, damn it.'

Bobbie found that visibility was no better straight ahead. To the west, the bank of cloud was also impenetrable, while to the east there was the faintest glimmer of sunlight. At 1,200 feet she decided to alter course and fly in the direction of the sun. But where was Angela? What decision had she come to?

Still zero visibility. The Spit's engine sang sweetly as it carried Angela into the unknown. *Head east*, she decided. East towards the North Sea, racing on at 250 miles per hour, blinded by fog.

From concrete lookout bunkers strung out along the coast, members of the ground defence forces stared up into dense fog as they heard a sole aircraft approach from the south-west: a single-engine model, identity unknown. An instant decision must be taken. A rapid, low-level approach – possible rogue enemy on a solo bombing raid. A sergeant in a bunker on sand dunes overlooking the steel-grey sea gave the order to fire.

Machine-gun bullets strafed through the cloud cover. There was no clear sight of the target – only a shadow in the fog. The roar of the engine increased. Fire again. Keep on firing until the danger was past.

Hell and damnation! Bullets hit Angela's Spit with enormous, ear-splitting force and the plane tipped over as metal struck metal and the Perspex canopy disintegrated over her head. The blast of cold air almost ripped her seat from its bracket. She stamped on her rudder pedals as her starboard wing tip was torn off and the plane wobbled erratically. Three pieces of shrapnel lodged themselves in her instrument panel and she recoiled in shock. *If in doubt, bail out*. More bullets cut into the fuselage of her perfect flying machine. The poor, precious Spit was done for, wobbling and swinging out of control, with only seconds before it spiralled downwards and crashed. Destroyed by friendly fire.

Angela released her seat harness and braced herself as she turned the plane upside down. Gravity kicked in and she fell from the shattered cockpit. She had a split second to pull her ripcord then pray that it would open in time. So Angela left the Spit to its fate and plummeted down.

Bobbie heard the gunfire. It came from ground level but she had no way of knowing if the gunner had hit his target. *Damn this foggy confusion!* She kept on flying east until at last she cleared the mist and looked down on a steel-grey sea. The gunfire ceased. Now all Bobbie could hear was the steady thrum of her Merlin engine.

What next? Should she resume her original course? Or should she circle the area and look for Angela? The last Bobbie had seen of her was when Angela had gone into a shallow dive, no doubt to see if she could fly below the cloud. What if that had proved impossible and Angela had drawn the attention of the ground forces who manned the lookout points all along the coast? It seemed more than likely that it had been friendly fire that Bobbie had heard. She felt her stomach tighten; despite the risk, she must try to find out.

So she eased back the revs and slowly turned her plane towards the coast, flying in low and feeling the heat of the sun on her back through the Perspex canopy. The mist rapidly thinned, allowing her to make out pale strips of beach and black, rocky headlands. There was still no sign of her fellow pilot and a glance at the gauge told Bobbie that she was short of fuel. Their earlier acrobatics had cost her dear, it seemed. Should she continue to search or ought she to head straight back to Rixley? *Stay and search*. With her heart pounding and with a sense of mounting foreboding, Bobbie flew on.

Angela's parachute opened over the sea. As her Spit hit the water and broke apart like a child's balsa-wood toy, she floated peacefully down, white silk canopy above her and the chilling prospect of an ice-cold dip below. No Mae West jacket. No rescue flare. She braced herself as the restless waves raced up to meet her. In feet first and fumbling to unbuckle her harness, she felt the parachute descend over her head. Free of the harness, she plunged underwater and kicked hard, leaving the parachute behind. Angela resurfaced to fill her lungs with air and discover that she was roughly a mile out to sea, surrounded by pieces of the Spit's wing and fuselage. The water was bitterly cold, her flying suit waterlogged and threatening to drag her down. A mile was a heck of a way to swim in these conditions, but what choice did she have? So she tugged off her boots then struck out towards the distant shore.

Bobbie reached the coast and flew over beaches lined with concrete bunkers. The mist had almost evaporated; surely to goodness if the ground defence gunners spotted her plane they would recognize the Spit's distinctive shape and hold their fire. The thought that Angela had fallen foul of their guns in the fog drove Bobbie on with her search. In vain she scanned the sky for a sighting of a second Spit. Then she looked out to sea. She saw a tiny fishing boat on the horizon and beneath her a headland where breaking waves threw up clouds of white spray. She glanced at two upturned rowing boats on the sand close to the headland and then again at the brown, broiling surface of the sea. That was when she spotted wreckage: a black tyre floating on the surface next to shards of blue-green metal, a propeller blade then part of a wing with the red, white and blue RAF insignia. And swimming through the waves and the debris was Angela.

A plane flew overhead. Angela looked up. The shape was unmistakeable: a Spit flying low over the water. Hit from behind by the force of a large wave as it rolled towards the shore, she swallowed sea water then raised both arms and waved frantically.

Angela! With her bird's-eye view Bobbie saw that her friend was unlikely to make it to shore unaided. She was too far out and the offshore currents were strong. Without hesitating, Bobbie knew what she must do. Ignoring the unseen occupants of the squat

159

concrete bunkers, she circled the nearest beach with the aim of bringing her plane down on a strip of firm sand close to the water's edge. With her heart in her mouth, she unlocked the undercarriage and prepared to land.

Bobbie! Seeing that rescue was at hand, Angela was struck by another breaking wave. Blinded by salt water, she was pushed towards the headland then sucked back out, arms flailing and helpless against the force of the waves. Still half a mile from shore, she struck out towards the beach where Bobbie's plane had landed. *Swim!* she told herself with angry determination. *Swim for all you're worth!*

The tyres of Bobbie's plane hit the beach and churned up the dark brown sand. With the brakes slammed on, she fought hard to keep a straight course. The last thing she wanted was for the Spit to veer into the water to her left and leave both her and Angela at the mercy of the incoming waves. She prayed for the strength to bring the plane to a halt. Meanwhile, two soldiers had emerged from the nearest bunker and were standing on top of one of the upturned boats watching her.

I did it! Bobbie was thrown forward as the Spit stopped within a few yards of their bunker. She was out of her seat and clambering from the cockpit, yelling at the men before they had decided on their course of action. 'I'm Second Officer Bobbie Fraser, heading for Rixley ferry pool! One of your boys has shot down my fellow ATA pilot, damn it!'

The two bemused men – a corporal and a private – scratched their heads as they jumped down from the boat and strode to meet her.

'She's in the drink!' Bobbie slid down from the wing of her plane and waved frantically in the direction of the sea. 'We need a boat – a pair of oars. What are you waiting for?'

To their credit, once the ground defence men took in what was happening they were quick to react. A glance out to sea showed them the plane's wreckage and a closer inspection revealed the dark head of a swimmer struggling with the currents. The head vanished beneath a giant wave then appeared again once the wave had broken on the rocks. 'Hold on!' The corporal cupped his hands to his mouth and yelled above the roaring water. 'We're coming to get you.'

The private helped Bobbie to manhandle the rowing boat. Together they heaved it the right way up and began to drag it towards the water while a third soldier ran out of the bunker with oars. Within seconds, Bobbie and two of the gunners had shoved the boat into shallow water. The third man handed them the oars and with a final push the boat was launched.

Bobbie sat in the stern, clinging on while the men rowed. The power of the waves terrified her. The boat rocked and dipped, allowing only occasional glimpses of Angela, who seemed almost to have stopped swimming and was struggling to stay afloat. 'Hang on. We're on our way!' Bobbie shouted. 'Try to grab hold of something. Angela, don't give up!'

Angela heard Bobbie's voice but couldn't make out the words. The effort to swim was too much. Her limbs felt like lead weights in the vicious cold. She doubted that she could hold herself up until rescue arrived.

'Angela, can you hear me?' Though the soldiers rowed strongly, their progress was agonizingly slow. Bobbie heard the grating of the oars in the metal rowlocks, the slap of the waves against the sides of the boat. 'Keep your head above water. Hang on!'

Angela could scarcely move her legs. She saw Bobbie in the boat then, almost within reach to her right, a piece of wreckage from her Spit. It was a section of wing bobbing on the surface. With one final effort she lunged towards it and managed to slither on to it and lay face down, her fingers gripping its edge.

Bobbie gasped with relief. 'Almost there,' she muttered to the soldiers who strained every muscle to pull the oars through the turbulent water.

Angela turned her head in the direction of the boat. The piece of flotsam barely bore her weight and she feared the waves would snatch her back at any instant. Still she clung on, her eyes fixed on Bobbie and the straining backs of the two oarsmen.

They were within arm's reach, tossed this way and that. Bobbie leaned out as far as she dared. 'Take hold of my hand!' she yelled.

Angela groaned and raised her arm. She felt a hand around her wrist as she slid from the wreckage.

Bobbie hung on desperately. If she let go, Angela would drown. But Bobbie wasn't strong enough to haul her out of the water single-handed, so the corporal edged towards the stern to help her. As he leaned over the port side, the boat tipped dangerously and sea water rushed in. The private threw his full weight to starboard, allowing Bobbie and her helper to heave Angela into the boat.

She collapsed backwards against the side, lips blue and eyelids fluttering. The soldier who had helped Bobbie to pull Angela to safety swiftly took off his jacket and placed it over her then took up his oar again. Bobbie held Angela's hand as the men turned the boat and rowed for shore.

'You've had enough excitement for one day.' In the bar at Burton Grange that evening, Hilary was unusually solicitous as he led a groggy Angela to a chair by the fire. 'There's no need to go into lengthy explanations. Just sit down there and let me fetch you a brandy. Bobbie, you too. Put your feet up, both of you. I'll be back in two ticks.'

Neither Bobbie nor Angela had the strength to argue. Almost twelve hours had passed since Bobbie had pulled Angela out of the sea, during which time Angela had been provided with a set of dry clothes by the ground defence team that had shot her down and Bobbie had telephoned Rixley to give Douglas a brief description of what had taken place. Arrangements had been made to bring the surviving Spit back to base and a doctor at the hospital in Highcliff had examined Angela and declared her none the worse for wear. Hilary himself had driven over to fetch Bobbie and Angela home.

'I reckon we owe you an apology,' the corporal from the offending team had said sheepishly as the girls got in the car in the hospital car park. He was a tall, gangly lad with a big nose and ears, accentuated by his short-back-and-sides haircut.

Angela had nodded from the depths of his over-sized khaki jacket. Her face had regained some colour and though her body still shook with cold and shock, she was starting to feel something like her old self. 'I'll tell you what you really ought to feel sorry about,' she said with a twinkle. 'I lost my powder compact when my Spit went belly-up. It fell out of my pocket into the drink. It was a twenty-first birthday present from my fiancé.'

'We'll buy you a new one,' the corporal had promised as Hilary had started the car. Relief had softened all hard feelings and the near-disaster had ended with handshakes all round.

There had been reports to write when Angela and Bobbie got back to the airfield and much sympathy from Douglas and Cameron amongst others. It hadn't been until teatime that Angela had finally been able to take off her borrowed clothes and soak in a hot bath while Bobbie had given Jean a full report of the day's events. And it was half past eight in the evening before everyone finally congregated in the bar at the Grange.

From her fireside chair Angela fretted about the loss of her Spitfire. 'Lord knows, the RAF can ill afford it,' she grumbled. Her almost-black hair was swept back from her face and she was without make-up. 'If only we hadn't run into that fog.'

'Yes, then none of this would have happened.' Exhaustion had set in and Bobbie's response was subdued. 'I blame the person who let us set off from the factory in the first place.'

Jean happened to be sitting nearby with Douglas and Cameron. 'It was the usual story – the met people didn't cotton on until it was too late,' she informed Bobbie, looking to Douglas for corroboration.

'That's right,' he confirmed in his low, comfortable voice. 'The predicted weather front now wasn't due to blow in until evening. Luckily no other flights on the schedule were affected.'

'I got down to Kent and back without any problems.' Jean's day had been long but uneventful. She'd flown the Corsair into Rixley at four o'clock, when the base was already abuzz with Angela's catastrophe and Bobbie's audacious rescue. Pilots and ground crew alike could talk about little else – 'friendly fire', 'a brand-new Spit up in smoke', 'a nearby rowing boat, thank goodness'. As Hilary returned with a brandy apiece for Bobbie and Angela, Jean smiled then took up the conversation with Douglas and Cameron where they'd left off. 'It's high time Thame taught us blind flying,' she insisted. 'Surely today shows us that if nothing else.'

'It would certainly put an end to the dangers of low flying.' Cameron sided with Jean. 'If pilots were taught how to read instruments properly, they could fly as high as they liked to avoid fog. As it is, you always have to be within sight of familiar landmarks, et cetera.'

Douglas shook his head. 'Realistically, it's not going to happen,' he pointed out.

'Even if it meant Angela could have got herself out of trouble and delivered her very costly Spit in one piece?' Exasperated by the short-sighted policy, Jean gave a loud sigh.

'Talking of Thame, how's Mary Holland getting on?' Douglas asked Cameron. 'Is she expected to pass her conversion course at her first attempt?'

Cameron knocked back the last of his pint. 'Yes, from what I hear, she's set fair. Now if you'll excuse me . . .' His face was flushed as he got up and left, hands in pockets to affect a nonchalance that he didn't feel.

'Was it something I said?' The oddly discourteous behaviour wasn't typical of Cameron, but Douglas let it pass. He had something on his mind that he wanted to investigate with Jean's help. 'Do you happen to know when Teddy brought his motorbike to Rixley?' he asked without preliminaries.

She frowned and smoothed out the wrinkles in her skirt. 'A few days ago, after his last home leave. Why not ask him yourself?'

'He's not due back from Greenock until late tomorrow. Can you be more exact about the date?' Since his early unease about Teddy, Douglas had begun to look at inconsistencies in Teddy's recent logs, tiptoeing around the vexed subject without confronting it directly. The discrepancies could possibly be down to slackness on Teddy's part, or else it might be something more deliberate.

'I'm sorry, Douglas, I don't know.' Unusually, after a few seconds of awkward silence, Jean's curiosity got the better of her. She leaned forward in her armchair and spoke quietly. 'Is it important?'

He passed a hand through his hair and returned her question with another. 'Could it have been Friday the first?'

'Yes; around then.' If something about Teddy was troubling Douglas, Jean was willing to pursue it with him. 'It was a surprise to everyone when he roared up the drive without helmet or goggles, scarf flying in the breeze. You know Teddy: he likes to make a grand entrance.'

'That fits with my theory,' Douglas said even more quietly, leaning forward until their heads and knees almost touched. 'What about petrol coupons? Has Teddy ever talked to you about how he got his hands on a book of coupons at such short notice?'

Staring at Douglas's worried face, Jean shook her head at his odd question. 'He wouldn't discuss such things with me.' Then she experienced a leap of logic that made her gasp. 'You've noticed petrol going missing from the tanker at the base? It started after Teddy showed up with his motorbike?'

'Let's just say there are discrepancies. And that's not all, Jean.' *In for a penny* . . . 'I've found out that our absent friend's record at the Initial Training Wing isn't as exemplary as he likes to make out. In fact, he only just scraped through at his second attempt – his navigation skills weren't up to scratch, apparently.'

Slowly Jean shook her head. What was there to say, without revealing her increasing dislike of her insensitive fellow pilot?

'He came up the hard way, through the ranks. He eventually achieved sergeant, also at his second attempt. Not that I'm against that per se. It's just that Teddy gives a different impression.'

'I know what you mean.' Jean looked up to see that Bobbie and Angela were casting curious glances in their direction. She quickly sat back in her seat.

'I met some show-offs in my time in the RAF.' Now that Douglas had started, there was no stopping him. 'Flying sometimes attracts brash characters – young chaps who are mad about speed, dreaming about hurtling along at four hundred miles per

167

hour. And what did Mr Churchill call us? "The means to victory", I think it was.'

'I can see that the idea of glory might attract them.' The heroics, the square-cut uniform that attracted the girls, the romantic notion that they were volunteering to join an elite few.

'But there's a difference between showing off and, shall we say, playing fast and loose with the truth.' Douglas too caught sight of Bobbie's and Angela's amused expressions. He cleared his throat then tapped the top of his thighs. 'This is all in the strictest confidence, of course,' he told Jean.

She assured him it would go no further then asked him if he would like another drink. He nodded and she went to the bar to place her order: 'A pint of Tetley's and a port and lemon, please.'

Angela and Bobbie watched her closely. Jean Dobson was a dark horse, they agreed. She and Douglas seemed to have grown very close. Never mind the age gap; any fool could see that there was a romance in the making. And very sweet it was too.

CHAPTER TEN

'Right, Holland; you're on your own.' Flight Sergeant Rouse watched Mary climb into the Spitfire Mark V's cockpit in readiness for her first solo flight. A cool drizzle had dampened her cheeks on their walk to the runway. 'Remember everything you've been taught and keep your nerve.'

'Yes, sir.' She fastened her helmet and lowered her goggles. The moment that she'd been building up to had arrived and she felt strangely serene. This time there was no flicker of nerves as she lowered the canopy and signalled chocks away.

Once the runway was clear, Mary fired up the engine then taxied into position for take-off. Apart from the light rain, conditions were perfect: scarcely any wind, with only wispy cloud cover that gave a pearly sheen to the mid-morning light. The long, straight strip of concrete ended in a hedge bordering a country lane, with a copse of beech trees beyond. There were open fields to either side and behind her the control tower and a huddle of temporary buildings that housed the classrooms and training-school offices. Mary ran through a sequence of numbers in her head: rev counts, ground speed at the point of take-off, angle of lift. With a satisfied nod, she opened the throttle and was off. Bumping along the runway, the grass to left and right became a blur. The engine began to whine, the nose to tilt upwards. She had achieved take-off.

The Spit responded to her touch. Up it soared, high above the earth. The aircraft banked when Mary asked it to then climbed again. She held a steady course over Oxford at 300 miles per hour; toy houses below, spires in the city centre and factories on the outskirts, fields and green hills rolling on for ever in every direction. Inside her canopy, Mary delighted in the kick of the engine as she carried out some standard manoeuvres; another bank to port and then, with heart in mouth, a complete starboard roll which she came out of with a laugh of triumph before adjusting her altitude to complete more manoeuvres then reluctantly turning for home. She wanted the exhilaration, the love affair, to last longer. If only she could fly on over hills and valleys and never come down to earth.

But Mary's thorough training held good. She checked her fuel gauge and then her wristwatch to see that she was within five minutes of her scheduled landing time. So she flew back over the city and the small villages strung along arterial roads until she reached the aerodrome. Pressure on the joystick put her into a smooth descent. Details of the villages grew clearer; she saw a tractor with a load of turnips enter a farmyard, a woman glanced up at her from a cottage doorway, a man rode a bicycle along a lane with his black-and-white dog running at his side.

Judge it right to bring her down gently to ground level.
Mary's wheels skimmed the hedge and she made a
perfect landing – there was only the slightest of
bounces as she hit the centre of the runway and
applied the brakes.

She had done it! Now, after it was over, she could
allow her heart to race and her head to spin as she
sat for a moment and savoured her achievement.
She – ordinary, overlooked Mary Holland, of whom
nothing much had ever been expected – had made
her first solo flight in a Spitfire no less. This shy,
often resentful girl, who had plodded along at
school until she'd left at fourteen to work as a carder
in the local woollen mill, was now a fully fledged
ATA pilot.

It was a miracle.

After a deep breath Mary raised the canopy and
clambered out of the Spit. Rouse waited for her at
the end of the runway, ready to shake her hand. *Now
I can do anything*, she told herself as she walked on
shaky legs to meet her instructor. For her the sky
was quite literally the limit. *Anything to Anywhere; just
ask me and I'm your girl!*

'A weekend off at last; lucky you.' Bobbie greeted
Angela on the almost deserted platform at Rixley
station. It was teatime on the third Friday of October. Bobbie was in uniform, returning to base after a
hop over the Yorkshire–Lancashire border to deliver
a Hurricane to a ferry pool south of Morecambe.
Angela stood resplendent in a coat of kingfisher blue
with a black fur collar and jaunty, narrow-brimmed
blue hat. She carried a small suitcase and wore a

surprisingly glum expression for someone setting off on home leave.

'Not so lucky,' she contradicted. 'I've been ordered home to Heathfield for Father to give me a grilling – for what I don't know.'

'That sounds grim,' Bobbie admitted.

'Yes, indeed; I can think of nicer ways to spend my free time.' Angela's father had been adamant when she'd spoken to him over the phone; he'd demanded to see her immediately. Was it about the engagement to Lionel? Angela had asked. No, not the engagement. What was it then? She would find out when she arrived, had been the terse reply.

Behind them, the guard banged carriage doors and the stationmaster prepared to blow his whistle.

Angela quickly grasped Bobbie's hands. 'Wish me luck,' she said hastily.

'Yes, good luck; fingers crossed it won't turn out too badly.' Bobbie had confidence in Angela's ability to charm her way out of any tight corner. 'When will you be back?' she called after her.

Angela boarded the train then leaned out of the window. 'Sunday evening, all being well.'

The train chugged forward in a cloud of steam while Bobbie set off on the short walk to the Grange. Inside Angela's carriage, which she shared with three Merchant Navy boys and a doleful young woman in a brown beret and raincoat, she fretted over where to put her luggage. The rack was crammed with the sailors' kitbags and the woman's bulky suitcase but Angela was reluctant to place her own case on the grubby floor. So she set it on her knees until one of the sailors made a great show of removing his bag from the rack and offering to put hers in its place. This opened up a lively conversation about where the men served and what recent action they'd seen in the Med. In turn Angela told them about the September raid on Rixley – bombs exploding, fire taking hold, part of the roof caving in. The sailors viewed her with new respect. Appearances were deceptive; they'd never have guessed Angela was a pilot, they said – she looked far too glamorous for that. The unsmiling woman in the corner looked sceptical. Some girls made things up to impress boys, whereas she, a recent Land Army recruit, preferred discretion – for everyone knew that careless talk costs lives.

The train rattled over the tracks, swaying at junctions and steaming on into the dusk, up hill and down dale until it arrived at Angela's station. Several willing hands reached simultaneously for her suitcase and she was given a cheery send-off. 'Atta girl!' The sailors leaned out of the window and shouted along the platform after her.

Trevor Ingelby, her father's driver, waited for Angela under the station clock. 'Welcome home, Miss,' he said as he took her case.

'Hello, Trevor.' Still the same: upright and stiff in his grey chauffeur's coat, his expression blank under the shiny peak of his cap. Though he'd worked for the Browne family since before Angela was born, she scarcely knew the first thing about the man – where he was born, whether or not he had family, his opinions about life in general. 'How are things at Heathfield?'

They reached the Bentley and he held open the back door. 'Much the same, Miss.'

The car door clicked shut. He sat in the driver's seat and edged away from the kerb. 'How's Mother?'

'The same,' he said again.

Three years earlier Angela's mother, Virginia, had taken to her bed with an undiagnosed fever, possibly rheumatic, that had affected the movement of her joints. She had more or less remained there ever since. After much wondering, Angela had judged the retreat to be strategic, for it meant that her mother no longer had to endure the stuffy mayoral functions and endless visits to the opera, theatre and races that her father had insisted upon. Instead, Virginia now sat all day amongst a sea of white bed linen, propped up on pillows, a book open but unread on her lap, her dark hair now greying at the temples, her skin as white as paper.

'And how's Father?' Angela enquired, recognizing every single house, pub, school and chapel they passed on the way.

'He's at home,' Trevor replied.

I didn't ask where, I asked how he was. Angela's niggle over the chauffeur's remark masked her mounting apprehension. They were out of the town now, climbing the hill towards the wide, black expanse of the moor, less than a mile away from Heathfield.

'Mr Browne left his office early today,' Trevor added. 'He wanted to make sure he was at home when you arrived.'

Angela's heart sank. It had been almost a year since she was last here. She'd left home under a cloud after fierce arguments with her father about her desire to join the ATA. He'd been dead set against it even though she'd pointed out that he was

174

the one who was partly responsible. 'You gave me my first flying lesson when I was thirteen years old,' she'd reminded him. 'Behind the controls of your Gypsy Moth, remember?' If he hadn't wanted her to love flying as she did, he should never have given her a taste for it in the first place. Joseph Browne had brushed aside her logic and told her she must do as she was told. 'No daughter of mine will share a billet with a bunch of half-wit casualties from the Great War,' et cetera. 'Anyway, you'll end up like Amy Johnson,' he'd warned, 'having to bail out over the Thames, never to be seen again.'

Father and daughter had quarrelled for weeks until, distracted by supply problems in several of the mills he owned, Joseph had weakened. 'Please yourself,' he'd told her in one of his great sulks. 'You always do.'

So this return to the fold filled Angela with trepidation as the limousine crested the hill and Trevor drove slowly along the twisting moor road until the dark bulk of the house hove into view. He turned down the drive and pulled up outside the front door where Molly the housekeeper hovered anxiously.

'At last!' she wheezed as Angela got out of the car. Bronchitis made Molly's chest heave as she took Angela's case from her. A stiff black uniform encased her bulky frame and her almost white hair had grown thinner in the intervening months. 'It's good to see you, Miss Angela. I hope you're well.'

'Quite well, thank you, Molly.' Angela stepped into the gloomy hall, its wood panelling adorned with motifs of lilies and vines in the Arts and Crafts style. A log fire burned brightly in the living room to the left but it was the study door to the right that opened.

'About time too,' Joseph said as he strode to meet his daughter. 'What's this I hear about you crashing your plane into the sea?' Giving Angela no time to take off her coat and hat, he took her by the elbow and marched her into the living room. 'It's turned out exactly as I said it would. Now sit down and explain yourself. I expect you to describe the event in every last detail.'

Angela's visit to her parents' house had left Bobbie at a loose end and wondering what to do with her Friday evening. She decided to write a letter home, asking after friends and relations in the neighbour-hood and saying that she hoped the dogs, Rufus and Captain, were still enjoying their rambles out on the heather moors with gamekeeper Murdo. She assured her mother and father that she was fit and well. 'Can-teen food is plain but there's plenty of it,' she wrote. 'Bad for the waistline, as a matter of fact.' Then she sat with pen poised. What else did she have to report? That she was within twenty-five hours of achieving first officer and was enjoying every minute in the air. Yes, she would write that down but she thought it would be wise to leave out the part she played in Angela's rescue from the briny.

She penned another paragraph then ground to a halt. Rereading the letter so far, she found that it seemed flat and dull. Perhaps she would stop now and resume tomorrow. *Yes!* Bobbie hurriedly screwed on the top of her Parker pen and rushed to her wardrobe to take out a pair of black trousers and a blouse she'd made from spare parachute silk. She'd dyed the silk bright purple and chosen a pattern with care. The neckline had turned out to be more plunging than expected and the style was wraparound with a tie fastening. Standing in front of the mirror and holding the new blouse up for inspection, Bobbie decided that this would be her outfit for the evening.

Fifteen minutes later, with her wavy hair swept up in a stylish chignon, she was sitting at the bar with Teddy.

'Tell me, Pa, how did you hear about the crash?' Angela moved the sofa cushions to one side and sat down with bad grace. Immediately the heat from the fire set her cheeks aflame.

'From Lionel, as a matter of fact.' Joseph stood by the long window overlooking the garden. The gold damask curtains were drawn and table lamps placed around the room gave off pools of yellow light.

'But I didn't tell him,' Angela said with a frown. 'How did he find out?'

'From Hilary, I presume.' Earlier that week Joseph had received a letter from Angela's fiancé expressing alarm about the daily dangers faced by ATA pilots. Did Mr Browne realize that Angela's plane had recently been shot down by friendly fire, for instance? Luckily Hilary Stevens had tipped Lionel the wink, which was the reason behind this letter; Lionel had passed on the information, believing that a parent had a right to know.

'Hilary wrote to Lionel?' Angela was infuriated. She got up from the sofa and strode around the room. 'He had no right.'

'I believe Hilary only mentioned it to Lionel in passing.' Joseph waited for his daughter to calm down. He was used to her moods, a trait that she had inherited from her mother. 'Naturally he assumed that you would have written and told him yourself.'

'Why should I? Do you think Lionel writes to me every time a U-boat launches a torpedo at his ship or the *Luftwaffe* drops bombs on his convoy? This is a war, Father. We all face danger, like it or not.'

'Stop pacing the floor and sit down. Your fiancé is concerned about you. He did the right thing.'

'He did not.' Angela resolved to write to Lionel and tell him so. 'In any case, why all the fuss? I'm still in one piece, as you see.'

'Sit down, Angela, and listen to me.' Joseph waited until she obeyed. Six feet tall with a large, balding head and a heavy grey moustache, his authoritative presence dominated the room. 'The way you've chosen to help the war effort may be laudable in some people's eyes, but to me and your mother it has always seemed foolhardy.'

'Father, please . . .' Angela took off her hat and flung it aside in frustration.

'Listen to me. Your mother is not well. Worrying about you makes her worse.'

'Which you knew all along; so why tell her about this latest mishap?'

'Virginia is at her wits' end,' Joseph continued in his heavy way, steamrollering flat all Angela's objections. He would have his say then make his pronouncement on the matter. 'You're her only daughter and in my opinion she's always given you far too much leeway to do as you pleased.'

178

Angela stared up at her father. There was a greyness about him, from his well-made worsted suit with its buttoned-up waistcoat to his grainy, lined complexion and outmoded Edwardian moustache. It struck her that she rarely saw him out of his suit, collar and tie; in other words, he'd always been the businessman, never the loving father who took off his jacket, rolled up his shirtsleeves and played with the small daughter who longed to be picked up and swung around. As for a smile and a kind word; well, they were as rare as hen's teeth.

Joseph's voice rumbled on. 'The result of your mother's laxity is plain for all to see. Instead of turning out to be a refined, obliging young woman with every advantage with which to boost her standing in society, you have proved hot-headed, flighty and rash.'

The words hit like hammer blows to the solar plexus. Oddly, 'flighty' was the one that hurt Angela the most. Still her father wasn't finished.

'It's true that I must shoulder part of the blame. I encouraged your rebellious spirit by allowing you to learn to fly instead of following more decorous pursuits, something that I now regret.'

Enough! Angela sprang to her feet again. 'What do you see when you look at me, Father? Am I a creature to be tamed and trained to do as I'm bidden – no better than a dog taught to sit and stay, to run and fetch? Or am I a person in my own right, at a stage in my life when I'm entitled to make my own decisions and do what I think is best?'

'In your own right?' Joseph echoed incredulously. He strode up to her and tugged roughly at the collar of her coat. 'Who paid for this, I wonder, and all of the rest – the gowns, the necklaces, the perfumes? Yes, what do you have to say about that?'

Angela gasped under the sharpness of his attack and the threat behind it, then pulled free. She put her hand to her throat in sudden panic.

'Nothing to say for yourself now, eh?'

'Plenty,' she contradicted. 'You call me flighty and perhaps I am, because how am I to know where and on whom to settle my affections? Hugh and I had no lead to follow in this house, I can assure you! The best I could do when I was growing up was to make use of what I know I have, which is a quick wit teamed with a halfway decent appearance. I find it serves me well enough on the whole.'

'Which proves the point I'm trying to make.' Joseph's anger rose to boiling point. Patches of vivid red appeared on his lined cheeks. 'Blame me and your mother as much as you wish, but we all know that you lack the character to hold a steady course; specifically the self-discipline needed to make a success as a pilot for the Air Transport Auxiliary.'

'That's not true,' Angela protested as an arrow of fear darted towards her heart. 'How can you say such a thing?'

'Easily. Look at what you've just cost the war effort with your recklessness: a brand-new Spitfire, the very latest model.'

'I was not reckless!' She closed her eyes and swallowed hard, trying in vain to frame a coherent sentence about an unexpected weather front blowing in off the North Sea and the mistaken friendly fire. 'Oh, what's the point?'

'Lionel and Hilary will agree with me, I'm sure.'

Angela recognized the streak in her father's personality that was hard as granite, forbidding as the high stone walls and barred windows of the mills he owned. Her fighting spirit almost failed her.

'I will write to Hilary,' Joseph concluded. 'I will tell him that I no longer wish you to continue in your present situation.'

'He won't listen . . .' Angela backed away towards the door.

'He will when I point out to him the flaws in your nature and the detrimental effect this is having on your mother's health.' Joseph rubbed his palms together to produce a dry, grating sound. 'So prepare yourself, Angela. Take the train back to Rixley first thing tomorrow morning, pack your bags there and say your goodbyes. No arguments; I want you back home in Heathfield by next Wednesday at the very latest.'

After a couple of drinks at the bar in the Grange Teddy declared that he found the atmosphere there somewhat stale. 'Same old faces in the same old chairs,' he complained to Bobbie. 'All Douglas, Cameron and their cronies do is jaw endlessly about chits and schedules. What do you say to a change of scene?'

'Why not?' Bobbie, too, felt that it would be good to liven up their evening. 'Where shall we go?'

Teddy cocked his head to one side. 'Go upstairs and fetch your leather jacket,' he said mysteriously. 'Oh, and bring a headscarf. I'll meet you by the main door.'

She smiled and rushed from the room, ran upstairs to put on her flying jacket then dashed down again. When she stepped outside into a dark, damp night she found Teddy outside the door sitting astride his gleaming Royal Enfield.

'Hop on,' he said, indicating the pillion seat with a jerk of his head.

Bobbie quickly did as he said.

'Arms around my waist,' he instructed. 'Hold tight.'

Then off they roared up the drive, wind on their faces and cold nipping at their fingertips. Once on the road, Teddy picked up speed. He zoomed through the village without stopping, following the road to the coast, now and then patting Bobbie's hand to remind her to keep tight hold.

This was thrilling, she told herself; her first time riding pillion on a motorbike, swaying with it around bends, everything happening in a dark rush – flashing past trees and farm entrances, ignoring autumn leaves that spiralled to the ground then danced and skittered under their squealing tyres, roaring across road junctions without stopping to look. Almost as exciting as flying a Mustang or a Gypsy Moth. Not a patch on getting behind the controls of a Spit, however.

She freed one hand and tapped Teddy on the shoulder. 'Where are you taking me?' she cried over the rush of wind and the engine's roar.

'Wait and see. Hold on.' They'd come to a steep hill descending into Maltby Bay, the tiny fishing village north of Highcliff. Here Teddy was forced to apply his brakes and ride slowly between dilapidated cottages, some with bomb damage, all facing straight on to the cobbled street, until they reached a small quayside stacked high with creels, nets and buoys. The air was damp and salty, with an underlying stench of rotting seaweed and fish.

Bobbie wrinkled her nose at the smell. 'Don't laugh at me,' she protested as she dismounted from the bike and watched Teddy set it upright on its rest.

'Why not? You're pulling a funny face. Anyway, what's wrong with a good, healthy whiff of sea air?' He linked arms with her then walked her a few yards back up the hill before guiding her down the narrowest of dark alleyways into a small courtyard with more tumbledown houses on three sides and an ancient sailors' inn overlooking the sea on the fourth. 'Welcome to the Anchor,' Teddy announced. 'Ye ancient haunt of smugglers and pirates.'

Propelled across the courtyard towards a creaking sign above the door, Bobbie found herself entering a dingy, smoke-filled room with a stone floor and low, beamed ceiling. At the table nearest to the door three men with dour expressions, weather-beaten faces and gnarled hands broke off from their game of cards to observe the newcomers through narrowed eyes.

'Look what the cat dragged in,' one remarked when he saw Teddy.

'It's grand to see you too, William,' Teddy replied sarcastically.

The trio hunched their shoulders and resumed play, slapping down card after card in quick succession as Teddy and Bobbie approached the bar.

'You've been here before?' A wide-eyed Bobbie drank

in her surroundings – the room was as plain and dark as could be, with three round oak tables, a dartboard on one wall and some large, chipped Toby jugs lined up on a shelf behind the bar. She soon discovered that she was the only woman amongst a dozen or so men.

'Yes, I'm quite the regular here.' Teddy ordered the drinks from the landlord without asking her what she would like. 'William over there owes me money from our last game of poker but it's like getting blood out of a stone.'

'So you're here to collect a debt. And there was I thinking you were intending to whisk me off to one of the grander hotels in Highcliff,' Bobbie teased as they found a table. She pictured gentlemanly Lionel treating Angela to an evening out at the Mount: cocktails in the lounge leading to a walk along the cliff path and a romantic marriage proposal.

'This is more interesting, don't you think?' Teddy took out a packet of cigarettes and tapped it on the table. He jiggled one foot impatiently. Like Bobbie in her purple blouse and black trousers, he looked out of place amongst the gathering of old sea dogs. He wore a good Harris tweed jacket over an open-necked white shirt and his hands when he took a cigarette from the packet were smooth and clean. 'Did you know, there's a network of secret tunnels under these streets, all leading down to the harbour?'

'Whatever for?' Bobbie was intrigued.

'To cheat the excise men. Smugglers used to unload their rum and tobacco and what have you under cover of night, straight into the caves that were linked to the tunnels and no one was any the wiser. Very enterprising, don't you think?'

'What happened if they were caught?'

Teddy put his hand to his throat then mimed the action of throttling. 'Hangman's noose, no two ways about it.'

Bobbie took a sip of her drink. Though she was disappointed by her companion's choice of venue, she determined not to let it show. Instead, she set about drawing information from him. 'I've been wondering, during your training what made you choose fighter planes over bombers?'

'That's easy; I always knew I wanted to fly Spit-fires, right from the start.'

'Even before you'd been near one?' Bobbie's eager smile indicated that the feeling was mutual. 'That was my dream, too. There's something about the Spit that makes your heart race – just her shape: so lean and easy on the eye.'

'Then there's the fact that she's lethal in a dog-fight. There's nothing to compare. But mainly I trained to fly fighters because it meant I would be up there by myself, flying solo. That's what I was cut out to do.' Teddy turned his back on the card players and relaxed into the conversation.

'Yes; that moment when your instructor says she's all yours . . .'

'No more exams and interviews, no more medical tests.' He remembered with a hollow laugh one of the questions he'd been asked before gaining entry into the Receiving Wing in Torquay. What sports did he play? He'd ticked showjumping and fox-hunting over football, though he'd never been within fifty yards of a horse. In his oral tests before a board of high-ranking officers he'd successfully smoothed out his Mancunian accent.

'Why are you always laughing?' Bobbie asked.

'Because . . .' He shrugged then changed the subject. 'You know something, Bobbie, I've had more than enough of "resting", as the RAF calls it. I can't wait to get my next posting, hopefully teaching the Yanks and doing what I've been trained to do.'

'Yes,' she acknowledged. 'You've always said that Rixley is tame by comparison.'

'It is. Originally they sent me here to help shift the backlog of Spits – which is still building up in the factories, by the way.'

'I know – Angela and I saw them in Castle Bromwich. Does it mean we're heading for a big push in Europe early next year? That's what a lot of people seem to think.'

'Who knows?' Teddy didn't look that far ahead. All he knew was that he'd towed the line long enough and was desperate to start afresh. Stubbing out his cigarette, he asked Bobbie to stay where she was while he had a word with the group of card players.

A faint frown creased her brow as he walked across the room. She watched as the men looked up and Teddy talked heatedly, singling out William and tapping the cards on the table with his forefinger. William shook his head then scraped back his stool menacingly. One of the other players put a restraining hand on William's arm then pulled a folded ten-shilling note from his own pocket and shoved it across the table at Teddy, who snatched it up and strode back to the bar.

'Time to leave, before the natives get restless,' he warned Bobbie.

He led her out to black looks from the three card players and before she had time to gather her thoughts she was riding pillion again, up the steep hill out of the village then coasting along the Rixley road.

Bobbie heard Teddy whistling cheerfully as they went. 'How was that?' he asked as he approached the Grange through the back gate and came to a stop in the stable yard. 'Did you enjoy your ride?'

'Very much, thank you.' Feeling decidedly disgruntled, Bobbie dismounted. Why had she bothered to try to look her best? Her hair was a mess and she was chilled to the bone. All she wanted to do now was to head straight for bed.

'Fancy a nightcap?' Teddy asked as he parked his bike.

'No, thanks – I . . .'

'Come on, don't be a spoilsport,' he wheedled, catching her by the hand then running up the steps. 'One more won't do any harm.'

Bobbie sighed then gave in. 'All right, just one.'

They headed for the lounge to find Cameron and Hilary standing by the bar with a large group that included Horace and Agnes. Jean and Douglas sat apart, deep in conversation as usual.

'Oh Lord!' Teddy exclaimed under his breath. 'Can you believe it? No one's moved an inch – they're like waxworks in Madame Tussauds.' He spun Bobbie around then waltzed her across the hall to the bottom of the stairs. 'Tomorrow's Saturday. Let me take you out again.'

'Tomorrow night . . . I'm not sure I can.' Tempted to turn him down flat, she hesitated instead.

Teddy leaned in and kissed her gently on the lips. 'Of course you can,' he cajoled, his hands around her waist. 'This blouse suits you, by the way; you look very pretty in it. Say yes to tomorrow?'

She turned away and started to climb the stairs. 'Yes,' she told him from the third step without looking round. 'But not the Anchor. Let's go somewhere nicer than that.'

'Much nicer,' Teddy assured her, watching her continue up the stairs. 'Wear a dress this time and do your hair. I promise to take you on another magical mystery tour.'

CHAPTER ELEVEN

'Dear Hugh, Can you spare a few moments to offer your little sister some much needed advice?' Angela reread the letter she'd begun immediately after her argument with her father. 'I'm at Heathfield and Pa and I have had the most awful row – what's new there, you may well ask.'

She'd sat at her dressing table in her room overlooking the moors, her hand shaking as she wrote. 'How we got through the evening I really don't know. Pa says I must leave the ATA. He might as well tell me to stop breathing – believe me, Hugh, I don't exaggerate. I love flying and refuse to give it up, but according to He Who Must Be Obeyed, it's too risky for me to continue.'

Angela had almost wept as she'd written. She'd put down her pen and run through the events of the evening before: the row followed by a lull and then a heartfelt appeal for her father to relent that had fallen on deaf ears. Later Angela had gone to her mother's room, hoping to enlist support, but Virginia had sighed and protested that she had no say in the matter. She'd quickly played her usual trick of taking refuge in trivialities: had Angela noticed the new Turkish rug in the hall and the Venetian mirror over the mantelpiece in the lounge? Would she please close the door properly on her way out to prevent a draught?

So Angela had retreated to her room, still fuming with Lionel and wondering where to turn for support. Hugh had been the answer. Her brother was the sole person to whom her father might listen; if she got him on side he might be able to soften the old man's opinion. But she'd only written a few lines before losing heart. After all, poor Hugh was currently slogging it out in the searing heat of the Sahara, serving under Montgomery. Although her letter might reach him eventually, Angela's latest spat with their father would seem small beer compared with what Hugh faced on a daily basis. Besides, her brother, who was not well known for his progressive views, might well take the side of their father and Lionel.

So she'd put down her pen and only after a night's sleep and a brisk walk on the moor to clear her head had she gathered the willpower to resume where she'd left off.

'Dearest Hugh, please help me to make Pa see sense. Explain to him that my being in the ATA is the main reason for getting up in the morning. I come truly alive when I'm flying; more than at any other time. The thrill of being up there among the clouds, knowing that I'm doing a jolly useful job and doing it well . . . My heart would break in two if I had to give it up. Who else can I turn to except you? Lionel is no help; in fact, he was the one who landed me in this mess.'

Angela threw down her pen with a feeling of

hopelessness. She stared at the letter for a long time until the words blurred then she picked it up and carefully and deliberately tore it in half then into quarters. Then she stuffed the scraps into a corner of her suitcase. If she were to sort out this mess, it must be through her own efforts, not by blaming others or relying on Hugh for help.

She marched purposefully along the corridor and down the stairs, willing to risk one more assault on the enemy; out of the trench and over the top into a hail of bullets, no doubt.

'Father,' she began hurriedly as she entered his study after tapping on the door. 'I understand that you and Mother are worried about me, as is every parent in the land.'

Joseph looked up from his copy of the *Yorkshire Post*. He sat behind his fortress-desk in his weekend tweed suit with his reading glasses perched on the tip of his nose. 'Good morning, Angela. Trevor is standing by, ready to drive you to the station whenever you're ready.'

'Yes, but before I go I want to explain my reasons for not doing as you wish.' She watched his expression alter from its usual settled complacency to instant and fiery irritation. 'As I said last night, I will be staying with the ATA and will not allow you to interfere with my decision. I'm over the age of twenty-one, thank heavens, so it's entirely up to me.'

Joseph clenched his hands into fists and stood up. 'You know what this will mean?' he asked quietly. 'Have you thought it through?'

'Yes, it means that I'll keep on flying for as long as my country needs me. I'm sorry, Father.' Angela found herself clenching her own hands for the verbal fisticuffs to come.

Her father turned his head towards the window. 'But do you fully understand what you're turning your back on?' he said without looking at her. 'By disobeying me you will cut yourself off from this family once and for all; no half measures. You will not come back here to Heathfield; you will no longer receive your allowance. You will have no further contact with your mother or with Hugh.'

Angela slumped forward under the cruel weight of his words. 'That's unfair,' she gasped. 'We're not living in the Dark Ages. Surely a father should have the decency to allow his daughter to make her own decisions.'

'No,' he shot back. 'A daughter should respect her father's judgement.'

The wide desk formed a barrier between them. Photographs on a shelf behind Joseph showed him shaking hands with Mr Churchill inside the Houses of Parliament and standing outside a hunting lodge with fellow Yorkshire worthies, shotguns under their arms, dogs at their feet. Other pictures were of immense mill buildings with tall chimneys – hives of industry styled after Italian palazzos on which two generations of Brownes had built their wealth. There were no pictures of his wife and children.

'You understand me, Angela: if you choose to follow your own course you will leave this house and not come back.' Joseph dragged his gaze from the window to his daughter's startled face. 'I will alter my will so that everything goes to Hugh. You will not get a penny.'

'You can't mean it,' she stammered. 'Mother won't allow it.' This feeling of helplessness was worse than finding herself at the mercy of the waves after she'd ditched the Spit. Now storm waves of anger crashed over her head and the vicious undertow of her father's implacability pulled her towards the rocks.

'Your mother has no say in the matter, as you well know. If, on the other hand, you change your mind and decide to do as you're told, I propose that we carry on as before, with me providing an allowance until the war ends and you fulfil your obligation to marry Lionel.'

'Father, please!' Angela had to lean against the desk to steady herself.

Joseph stood his ground. 'The fact is, Angela, you can do less harm here, helping to look after your mother, than you can flying aeroplanes. That's obvious, surely?'

How dare he mock her and hold her in so little esteem? Because she was a woman; because women stayed at home to nurse and run the domestic side of things; because, according to Joseph Browne, that was the way the world worked. Words failed Angela.

'And may I point out,' he went on with ruthless logic, 'without an allowance or any prospect of inheritance, it's extremely doubtful that Lionel will wish to continue with the engagement. That's something else you haven't taken into account.'

'You're wrong; Lionel loves me!' she cried. Her insides churned and her heart banged against her ribs.

'*Love*,' Joseph muttered sardonically. 'Love doesn't pay the bills. And in my experience a man is lucky if it survives the first year of marriage.'

'Because you have no heart, that's why. You're not capable of loving anyone or anything except yourself and your damned mills.' She dragged these boiling resentments from the dark corners of her soul. 'Look what you've done to Mother. You've turned her into an invalid, incapable of doing anything for herself. Your tyranny has done that to her. And your intention is to turn Hugh into a likeness of yourself; a carbon copy strutting around the place, dishing out orders, only caring about his status in society. And what a dreary society it is – men with fat wallets, broad accents and bloated faces and their simpering wives who wouldn't know their *Hamlet* from their . . . from their Buster Keaton.' Angela's voice broke down and she cried tears of exasperation.

Virginia Browne had stood in the doorway long enough to hear the whole of her daughter's outburst. Joseph had noticed his wife but had made no attempt to warn Angela.

'Your father's right,' Virginia said now, 'you should go.'

Angela spun round to see her mother: a pale, gaunt figure dressed in a green silk dressing gown, one hand at her throat, her rings sparkling in the sun's rays.

'He is right,' Virginia repeated tonelessly without making any attempt to enter the room. Her voice was deadened by a lifetime's resignation to her husband's domination. 'If you can't agree to your father's rules, you must leave Heathfield and learn to make your own way in the world.'

*

Green turned to gold, gold to russet red and then to brown before the leaves finally fluttered down to the soft black earth. The sky was blue when Jean and Douglas chose to start their Saturday afternoon by walking home together through Burton Wood.

'You don't mind going at my snail's pace?' he checked as he locked the office door and they set out past the canteen.

Jean shook her head. 'I haven't had much chance to take a close look at nature recently. I missed the blackberries and horse chestnuts this year; they were gone before I knew it.'

'Yes, these days you have to run hard just to stay on the spot.'

'As the Red Queen said to Alice.' She smiled as she recollected one of her favourite sayings from the Lewis Carroll tale. '"Now, here, you see, it takes all the running you can do, to keep in the same place."'

'"If you want to get somewhere else, you must run at least twice as fast as that!"' Douglas offered the rest of the quotation. He held the gate open for Jean and followed her into the wood. 'That's exactly what it feels like to me these days. And with this leg I'm not up to sprinting very far.'

'I feel the same way.' The pace of life at Rixley rarely slackened. 'But hopefully it'll ease the situation to have Mary Holland join us as an extra pilot.'

'Yes, Cameron's a fan of hers; he pushed Hilary hard to make that happen. She's due to arrive later today, as a matter of fact.' Douglas's leg bothered him and the pain made him limp more heavily. 'Mary will need moral support when she moves into the Grange. She'll feel like a fish out of water at first.'

'Of course.' Jean took his point. 'I remember the feeling.' She stopped and took a deep breath. 'Actually, I've had a piece of good news,' she confided. 'My promotion to flight captain came through yesterday. How about that?'

On impulse Douglas grasped her hand and squeezed it. 'That's very good news. Congratulations.'

Her hand in his felt reassuring and she was happy to leave it there as they continued on their way.

'Angela and Bobbie are bound to be envious,' Douglas warned. 'Don't be surprised if they try to outdo you with fresh acts of derring-do.'

'It ought not to be a contest.' The sun's rays shone pure gold through the leaf canopy, casting a warm light and creating a feeling of deep calm. 'We're all in this together.'

'But there's nothing wrong with a healthy dose of competition.' Douglas laced his fingers between Jean's. Her hand was warm and compared to his uneven walk she seemed to glide along. 'It never did anyone any harm.'

'I'm sure Teddy would agree with you there.'

'Ah yes; Teddy.'

Jean cast a curious glance at Douglas's face. 'Have you found out something?'

He frowned and nodded.

'Don't tell me if you'd rather not; if it's hush-hush.'

'No, I'm sure you'll keep it under your hat. It was as we thought: Teddy did cook the books and help himself to quite a few gallons of petrol on the sly. I had a word with him about it.'

'What did he say?'

'He tried to brush it off but I wouldn't let him.

Let's just say I don't think he'll pull the same trick in future.'

Jean pictured the scene of the older man dragging the young hothead over the coals. 'I don't suppose he was very happy about it?'

'You know Teddy.' Douglas had a bigger dilemma but he decided to keep that to himself for now. It had to do with an extremely serious incident that Teddy Simpson had been involved in just prior to his posting to Rixley. Hilary had left an official-looking document on his desk and Douglas had glanced at it in passing: the name 'Flight Lieutenant E. J. Simpson' had caught his eye at once. There was a box at the top of the form headed 'Account of eye-witness, Flying Officer H. W. Flynn, 8 August 1943', followed by a paragraph that he hadn't had time to read before Hilary had returned to his desk.

'But let's not talk about Teddy,' Douglas said now. 'This is your big day, Jean. We ought to celebrate your promotion tonight.'

Yes, she thought, *we ought*. 'What do you suggest?'

'Is there somewhere you'd like to go? You name it.'

'How about Northgate, or is that too far?'

'Not at all; good choice.' They walked hand in hand and talked as if it was the most natural thing in the world for Douglas to invite Jean out. And that's how it felt: perfectly easy and comfortable. Still, his heart had beat faster when she'd said yes. 'What would you like to do there?'

There was a wide choice of cinemas, a theatre and two dance halls in the elegant spa town. 'I'd like to listen to some music,' she decided.

'What type of music?'

'I don't mind; anything at all.'

They smiled at each other and stopped in a small clearing with a bench.

'Shall we sit for a while?' Jean suggested. And so they sat under the trees in the dappled sunlight, watching leaves flutter in the breeze then spiral slowly down. Hand in hand. Letting the world slow down, enjoying the sunny moment while they could.

Mary wore her new wings with pride as she walked towards the canteen at Rixley. The long train journey from Thame hadn't tired her. Instead, it had given her time to overcome her nerves about returning as Third Officer Holland instead of a lowly driver. She'd pre-planned her movements on arrival; a late-afternoon walk from the train station to the ferry pool followed by a quick cup of tea and a bite to eat. With luck there would still be enough time to walk through the wood to Burton Grange where she was to take up residence in the women's quarters. Luckily the weather had been glorious when she'd stepped off the train: all green and golden in the sunlight, with the spire of St Wilfred's piercing the clear blue sky.

But in spite of her careful preparations, Mary's nerves got the better of her as she reached the canteen door. This was an awfully big thing she'd achieved – to raise herself up through sheer grit and determination – yet she was suddenly struck by a crippling sense that she didn't deserve to be where she was now, that somehow it had all been a huge mistake and that her present happiness could be snatched away at any moment. With her hand on the door, she peered through the pane of glass at Olive and Harry doing a jigsaw together and at Gillian Wharton and two of the typists from the ops room laughing at a table close to the door.

I'll skip the cup of tea, Mary decided as she backed away, straight into Stan.

'Look who it isn't!' he cried.

Before Mary could object he'd swept her off her feet and was swinging her round. She had to hold on to her hat and beg him to put her down. 'Please, Stan; you're making me dizzy.'

Laughing, he set her down then slapped her on the back. 'Look at you, Mary! Those wings suit you, by the way. And you look different. Have you done something with your hair?'

'I had it cut shorter.' She straightened her jacket then grinned at him. 'I'm glad to see your ugly mug. I was about to give the canteen a miss until you turned up.'

'I could see that. Anyway, it's good to have you back.' Giving Mary a push from behind, Stan propelled her through the door. 'Look who's here!' he cried.

In an instant Mary was surrounded by a crowd of well-wishers and swamped by congratulations. While Stan went to fetch her tea, Gordon bet her a fiver that she would make first officer by Easter and Harry admired the changes from afar: a smart new haircut, a broad smile and a touch of rouge and mascara.

'You won't want to talk to the likes of us,' Olive kidded. 'You'll be too busy rubbing shoulders with the top brass at the Grange from now on.'

'No, it won't make any difference.' Blushing from

the praise, Mary accepted her drink from Stan then sat down with the old crowd. 'We can all still meet up at the Fox, can't we?'

'You bet we can. How was the course?' Gordon offered her the last biscuit on the plate. 'Was the theory part the worst?'

'By far,' she replied. 'I thought I'd never get the hang of control configurations and settings on all the different aircraft.'

'What about the instructors?' Olive wanted to know. 'Were they as strict as they say?'

'Ten times worse,' Mary admitted. 'I suppose it's their way of weeding out the ones who aren't going to make it.'

Stan sat opposite her, his chest puffed up with pride on her behalf. 'But you did it, Mary. I'm chuffed to bits.'

She smiled warmly. 'With a hefty kick and a shove from you,' she reminded him. Stan was her best pal at Rixley; in fact, her best friend full stop. 'What's been happening here while I've been away?'

'Angela ditched a new Spit into the drink,' Gordon reported. 'A complete write-off. Bobbie saved her life.'

'Blimey.' Taken aback, Mary looked to Stan for confirmation.

'It's true. Oh, and Teddy Simpson has taken to roaring about on a Royal Enfield hoping to impress the girls; a Bullet of all things.' It was a sore point with Stan.

'And succeeding,' Gillian assured Mary from the neighbouring table.

'Watch out, ladies – stand by your beds!' Olive

gave Mary a knowing look. 'But he's not my type,' she added. 'Now, if it was Flight Lieutenant Cameron Ainslie we were talking about . . .'

'Too serious by half,' Vivien Francis, Gillian's friend, argued. 'And you wouldn't want to get on the wrong side of him. I have and it's not pleasant.'

'Anyway, thanks everyone, but I'll love you and leave you.' Mary downed the rest of her tea then stood up. She was glad when Stan accompanied her outside.

'Did I mention: it's good to have you back?' he asked as they walked slowly across the lawn. He thrust his hands deep in his pockets and kicked at a nearby stone.

'You did. And it's good to *be* back, Stan. But I'd better get a move on if I want to get to the Grange before dark.'

'What Olive said – about you moving there . . .'

'What?' Mary prompted.

'If you ever need someone to talk to . . .'

'It'll be you, Stan.' She felt tears of gratitude well up.

'That's the ticket,' he murmured. 'But if you're ever lonely over there and I'm not around, try talking to Jean.'

'Ta, I'll remember that.' It was true: Jean was definitely the most approachable of the officers billeted at the Grange.

'She takes a bit of getting to know but she'd be a good friend to have.'

Mary nodded. 'Thanks. I appreciate it.'

'Make sure you look after yourself,' he insisted. 'And good luck.'

Good for Mary, Stan thought as he watched her walk

through the deep shadow cast by the control tower towards the wood. *She's got guts for getting this far. Now let's see how she does as a junior officer in her new surroundings; that's bound to be a challenge and a half.*

Mary had never before stepped inside a house as grand as the Grange. She'd only seen such places from a distance, during day trips to the seaside, travelling through areas where the mill owners had built their mansions. They'd seemed to her no more real than castles in fairy tales – impossibly large and ornate, surrounded by parkland where swans swam on lakes and rows of regimented bushes lined the drive. Recalling the Cinderella fairy tale of her childhood, Mary felt a flutter in her stomach and stood with a nervous smile on her lips. She gazed up the stone steps at the wide doorway.

It was the first time she'd been back to Burton Grange since the German bombing raid and she was shocked by the extent of the damage. A whole wing stood in ruins amid heaps of rubble. Many windows had been boarded up through the rest of the house and the porch over the entrance had collapsed. Chunks of masonry still littered the front terrace.

'It's a mess, isn't it?' Cameron surprised her by appearing round the side of the house. He'd spied Mary from an upstairs window then run down the back stairs into the stable yard from where he'd emerged on to the terrace. He was still in uniform after a morning spent studying met forecasts with Douglas, after which he'd been delayed by Hilary wanting to reminisce about college days.

A fidgety Cameron had escaped at last then dashed

back to the Grange. His intention was to make Mary feel welcome and he'd only recognized how important this was to him when Hilary had held him up. He'd got there just in time to see her emerge from Burton Wood and walk towards the house.

'Yes, I hadn't realized how much damage there was.' She noticed that a bomb had scored a direct hit on the lodge house at the end of the drive and that deep craters scarred the wide lawns.

Cameron came down from the terrace and offered to take her suitcase. 'We came across an unexploded incendiary last Tuesday,' he told her. 'Orders are not to walk in the grounds until the disposal team has dealt with it.'

'Thank you; that's good to know.'

'Come inside; let me show you around.' Feeling unexpectedly nervous on Mary's behalf, he led the way up the steps and through the door. 'There's a library over to your left if you ever want some peace and quiet. The lounge bar is on the right. That's where we generally congregate in the evening. Straight ahead is the corridor leading down to the kitchens and servants' rooms. The old hospital wing is out of bounds, of course.'

Mary had a vivid memory of driving up in the Tilly wagon to a scene of fire and smoke, of screams and cries for help. Hunched, coughing figures had stumbled from the smoke and a cool, calm Cameron had taken charge of transporting the injured to the hospital. 'Where am I to sleep?' she asked him now.

'Upstairs; I'll show you.'

He led her up a flight of stairs, past a torn painting of a woman in a high white wig to a half landing with an arched window overlooking the grounds.

'Congratulations, by the way. I mean it, Mary; very well done.'

'Thank you, sir.'

'Cameron,' he reminded her.

'Thank you, Cameron.' To call the second in command by his first name didn't come naturally, but he was kind and polite, and was obviously going out of his way to settle her in.

'The female quarters are up there to your left. Bathroom at the far end of the corridor. I believe your room is the first on the right, next to Jean's.'

'Thank you,' she said again.

'Men's rooms are on the second floor. I wouldn't venture up there if I were you. Not without a gas mask.'

'No?'

'Some of us are scarcely house-trained – dirty clothes strewn around all over the shop, wet towels on the bathroom floor . . .'

'I see.' Her lips twitched then expanded into a broad smile. 'I'm used to that; I grew up with two brothers.'

Cameron liked Mary's grin. It showed her white, even teeth and transformed her whole appearance. He had to resist an impulse to move closer and take her by the hand. *Perhaps too complicated. Most definitely too soon.* 'Roll-calls usually happen out in the stable yard. Would you like me to explain the drill now or later?'

'Later, if you don't mind.' She took her case and went on up the stairs. Who needed a staircase this wide and ceilings this high? she wondered. What was the point of the fancy plasterwork and who was responsible for dusting the glass chandeliers? *Not me, thank goodness*, Mary said to herself as she turned left at the top then opened the door to her room. *It's not my job to scrub floors or fetch and carry for Lord and Lady Muck; not any more.*

CHAPTER TWELVE

Teddy and Bobbie's Saturday-night mystery tour had begun with a train journey to Northgate. They'd walked out of the station into an impressive square lined with elegant clothes and jewellery shops then strolled hand in hand along a broad, steeply sloping street, past an imposing town hall to the Spa Ballroom, a large Victorian dance hall advertising twice-weekly events on a poster beside the door. There was a wide entrance where groups of young men stood and smoked, mostly in uniform and all eager to eye up the girls who ran in skittish groups up the marble stairs.

Teddy and Bobbie followed a group of such girls into a glass atrium decorated with palm trees in ornate glazed pots. There was a ticket office to one side and a cloakroom to the other. 'Don't be long,' he told her as he queued to buy tickets and she went to take off her black satin cape and powder her nose.

She reappeared in her emerald-green chiffon dress with its full skirt and an off-the-shoulder neckline. Bobbie had dithered for a long time over the dress: was it too formal for wherever it was that Teddy was taking her? But then he'd promised somewhere 'much nicer' than the dingy Anchor. Was it too revealing? She'd studied her reflection in the full-length mirror in Angela's room (what would Angela's opinion have been?) then hurried back to her own room and changed several times before deciding on the green dress after all. Now, emerging from the cloakroom and seeing Teddy's glance of approval, she was glad she had.

'Do you hear that?' Teddy nodded his head in the direction of the music floating up from a room below. He led Bobbie towards a wrought-iron balcony, looking suave and at ease in a dark blue suit teamed with a white shirt and grey silk tie. 'That's a Glenn Miller number.'

Bobbie gazed down on a crowded dance floor where sailors on leave held their sweethearts close for a romantic Viennese waltz and eager Tommies leaned in to whisper sweet nothings in the ears of girls they'd only just met. She made out a small stage at the far end of the room where musicians in dinner jackets played piano, violin, drums and saxophone. There was a bar serving drinks in a side room off to the left.

'Let's dance.' Teddy led the way down curving, pink marble stairs.

Bobbie followed in high spirits. It was ages since she'd been to a proper dance; not since she'd left home, in fact. She was immediately caught up in the lively atmosphere and had a sudden giddy sensation when Teddy took hold of her around the waist then steered her on to the floor. She soon found that he was an expert dancer, able to guide her through the crowd and move with a smooth, fluid rhythm that made him stand out from other, less skilled hoofers.

'This is better than the Anchor, I take it?' He whirled her gracefully, making her skirt flare out behind.

'Much better.' Their cheeks were so close that they almost touched and his hand on her back drew her firmly in.

Bobbie Fraser really was a slip of a girl, Teddy thought as he held her tight. He usually preferred them taller and more rounded. She was pretty, though, with a slightly turned-up nose and pointed chin that gave her an elfin look. They were attracting plenty of gratifying attention from onlookers: unshowy wallflowers in faded pink dresses and shy corporals with unflattering haircuts standing awkwardly at the side of the room. 'Where did you learn to trip the light fantastic?' he asked Bobbie as the waltz drew to a close.

There was a smattering of applause for the musicians. 'At school. We had a dance teacher called Miss McKinley. It was a girls' school so my partner was always a tall girl called Peggy Irvine. Peggy was with the WAAFs as a wireless operator the last I heard.' Teddy's amused smile made Bobbie blush. 'Why, what did I say?'

'Nothing.' He pinched her waist. *A slip of a girl and so naive.* 'What slogan do they put on the recruitment posters? "Serve in the WAAF with the men who fly." You can take that invitation in more ways than one!' Teddy winked then listened to the start of the next number: a foxtrot this time.

'"Serve" . . . Oh yes, I see. Oh no, Peggy's not like that.'

'Don't you believe it; everyone's like that in this day and age. And why not?' Teddy took advantage of the fact that the more complicated dance had put off many couples, leaving more space on the floor. 'Everyone is much more free and easy, don't you find?'

Bobbie kept up with his nimble footwork: slow-quick-quick turns as their feet skimmed the floor. 'Some people are,' she conceded. She really must try to sound more worldly. 'And you're right: why not? None of us knows where we'll be or what we'll be doing this time next month; or even if we'll still be anywhere at all.'

'Quite.' There was always something about Bobbie that amused Teddy; at the moment it was the blindingly obvious effort she was making to behave more like Angela. 'Your Miss McKinley certainly succeeded in teaching you the ropes.'

'Thank you, kind sir.' Bobbie smiled prettily as the band upped the tempo and they danced on.

'Anyway, I hope your Peggy is living for the moment with the men who fly. Most of the WAAF girls I've come across do.'

'Don't we all?' she replied gallantly.

'We do,' Teddy agreed as they went on skipping and spinning across the polished floor. 'After this dance we'll stop and have a drink. What do you say?'

Jean and Douglas had ended up in the Spa Ballroom after a leisurely stroll through the quiet streets of Low Northgate, up the hill towards the dance hall, drawn there by the faint strains of music drifting out on to the pavement.

'Shall we go inside for a drink?' Douglas had suggested. 'You won't mind just sitting and watching? I'm not up to dancing, I'm afraid.'

'A drink would be nice.' Jean had enjoyed the drive over the moors. They'd witnessed a spectacular deep red sunset above a band of dark blue clouds then watched the light fade from the wild landscape – a sight that had convinced Douglas and Jean that war couldn't destroy nature and that the old ways of life would survive all conflicts. Sheep would always graze amongst the heather. Red kites would continue to soar.

Jean had found Douglas a considerate and interesting companion as usual. She learned that his father was a tea merchant who had tried to dissuade his young son from his bookish ways by encouraging him to take up rugby and cricket, without much effect. 'I preferred my geometry theorems and my kings and queens of England,' Douglas had confessed. Jean in turn had shared her love of the Brontë sisters. *Jane Eyre* especially. I first read that book when I was eleven and I was convinced that Charlotte Brontë had written it about me!'

So they discovered more areas of common interest and both found themselves content to let the evening drift on without fixing on a particular plan.

'A drink it is.' Douglas offered Jean his arm and they went into the Spa Ballroom building, attracted by a familiar melody that had been played to death on the wireless all summer long.

Jean put a name to the tune. ' "That Old Black Magic". Johnny Mercer wrote the lyrics to this one.'

Douglas paid for entrance tickets and they went

on down the stairs. He was proud to walk with Jean, who looked cool and sophisticated in a short-sleeved dark blue dress, with her fair hair pinned up to show her beautiful long neck. 'Have you heard Frank Sinatra sing it? I think I prefer that to the Bing Crosby version.'

'I like both.'

They skirted the dance floor and made straight for the bar where they soon found empty stools and ordered drinks.

'Good; it's less hectic in here.' Douglas was relieved to sit down in the relative quiet of the bar. They could glimpse the dancers through the open doorway, but the noise didn't interfere with their conversation. 'You don't mind?' he checked with Jean again.

'No. I'd rather talk than dance. If you must know, I have two left feet.'

'I don't believe that. You're probably saying it to make me feel better.'

'It's true. I missed out learning when I was at school – there was too much to do at home, helping Mother look after my father.' Jean spoke openly and without bitterness. 'Dad never worked again after his fishing boat was lost. He was left with bad injuries to his hand and his back so we had to do everything for him; Mother took the brunt of it, of course.' The brunt had included endless carping criticism and volleys of harsh insults from her disabled father; a burden much harder for Jean's mother to bear than the physical care. The atmosphere in the house as Jean grew up had been unbearably tense; her only escape the public library in Highcliff. 'It's a funny thing,' she mused. 'Learning to fly and joining the ATA has given me a freedom I never expected to have. If it hadn't been for the war, I'd still be living at home.'

'It's a case of every cloud . . .'

'. . . has a silver lining. From a selfish point of view; yes.'

'That doesn't sound selfish to me.' Moved by her story, Douglas longed to tell her how much he admired her but he didn't want to break her thread.

'Truly? Thank you. It sounds strange again when I say that I never had much expectation that I'd be happy in life but now I find that I am.'

'Good for you. Why shouldn't you be happy?'

Jean dug deep for her answer. 'Maybe I felt I didn't deserve to be. It's hard to explain. Or perhaps it was that I expected to follow in my mother's footsteps. I hardly ever saw her happy, except on rare occasions when she and I escaped from the house to walk on the beach. I remember the crunch of the pebbles under our feet and the feel of cold sea spray on our faces. Mother wouldn't talk much but a smile would creep across her face and she would hold my hand. We'd search for fossils at the foot of the cliffs.'

'Everyone deserves to be happy.' Douglas swirled the beer in his glass, only half-believing his own observation. A sailor came up to the crowded bar and accidentally jostled Douglas's elbow, making him spill some of the glass's contents on to the floor.

'Sorry, pal,' the sailor said. He glanced from grey-haired Douglas to the blonde beauty next to him and back again with an expression of mild surprise.

'No harm done,' Douglas muttered back.

The music next door changed from a foxtrot to a jazzier, louder number.

'"Chattanooga Choo Choo",' Jean remarked over the increasing din of saxophone and drums.

Douglas didn't seem to hear her. Jean's back was to the door and his attention had been stolen by a glimpse of familiar figures amongst the dancers. 'I must be seeing things,' he muttered under his breath.

Jean turned to look but all she saw was a whirl of brightly coloured dresses and dark uniforms.

'I thought I glimpsed Teddy Simpson dancing with Bobbie Fraser,' Douglas explained. 'But I can't have done, can I?'

'Possibly, yes.' Jean had noticed something between the pair at Bobbie's birthday party but she'd imagined that any serious attraction must be on Bobbie's side since, according to gossip amongst the girls in the ops room, Teddy had already built a reputation as a ladies' man.

'How could they have got here?'

'By train, I suppose.'

'But surely Bobbie's not his type . . .'

All doubt was squashed when the couple in question appeared in the doorway. Teddy's arm was around Bobbie's waist as he led her into the bar.

'Well, look who it isn't!' Teddy exclaimed when he spotted Douglas and Jean. 'Fancy seeing you two here.'

Douglas was immediately nettled by the sly, knowing look that Teddy exchanged with Bobbie but he hid his reaction behind a typically courteous gesture. 'Bobbie, you look out of breath. Here, have my seat, let me buy you a drink. And Teddy, what'll you have?'

The two men turned towards the bar while Bobbie perched on the stool next to Jean's. 'I didn't spot you on the dance floor,' she began. Then, with an embarrassed glance at Douglas's back view, 'Oh no, of course not.' She lowered her voice to a whisper. 'For a second back there, I thought Douglas was cross with me. He gave me what I call his sour-lemon look.'

'No. He was surprised, that's all.' Jean spoke guardedly while Bobbie rattled on.

'No more than I was when I found out where Teddy was bringing me. You could have knocked me down with a feather. It's *très chic* here: all the palm trees and ornamental tiles and so on. Northgate is a genteel town, by all accounts. It's the first time I've been here. Jean, what are you drinking? Douglas, did you know that Jean's glass is empty? She needs a refill.'

'Coming up,' Douglas called as Teddy handed cocktails to the girls then stood between them. 'There's nothing to beat a spot of ballroom dancing. What's your favourite dance, Jean? Mine's the quickstep.'

'I don't usually dance,' Jean replied quietly.

'Then it's high time you did.' Teddy turned to Douglas and Bobbie. 'You two won't mind if Jean and I dance the next dance, will you?'

'No, thank you.' Jean cut in before either could shape a reply. 'I'm quite happy where I am.'

'Please yourself.' Teddy shrugged and turned away. Few women resisted his charms but it seemed Jean was one of them. 'I'm glad we bumped into you,

Douglas; it saves Bobbie and me from having to get the train back to Rixley.'

Bobbie raised her eyebrows at Jean and grimaced at Teddy's lack of consideration. *Sorry!* she mouthed.

At first Douglas was too taken aback to reply.

'You're in your jalopy, I take it?' Teddy went on. 'There's room in the back for a pair of tiddlers. You don't mind, do you?'

'Not at all,' Douglas replied through gritted teeth. He felt the evening slip away from him but decency prevented him from refusing the request.

'Good chap.' Teddy hurriedly finished his drink then grabbed Bobbie's hand to drag her back towards the dance hall. 'Give us a shout when you're ready to leave,' he told Jean over his shoulder.

Douglas shook his head with undisguised contempt. 'What on earth does Bobbie see in him?'

'Oh, Teddy has made his mark amongst the Rixley girls. Perhaps she's flattered.' Jean was sorry she hadn't had a chance to exchange many words with Bobbie, who had seemed uncomfortable during the chance meeting. Her cheeks had been flushed, her eyes downcast and she'd shown none of her trademark cheery independence.

'It's up to her, I suppose. I'm sorry, Jean; now we're tied to staying here until they're ready to leave.'

'Don't be sorry. It was nice of you to agree.' Jean knew Douglas well enough to see that it had been an effort to stay civil. There had been the flicker of a frown across his brow, a flash of anger in his hazel eyes.

'I don't know about you but I was ready for another quiet stroll before the drive home.'

She leaned over and put a hand over his. 'Some other time,' she assured him as the band struck up a fresh number and a new influx of thirsty dancers crowded into the bar.

'Home, James, and don't spare the horses!' Teddy called from the back seat of Douglas's Ford. His knees were jammed against the back of the passenger seat and he sat with his arm around Bobbie's shoulder. His fingers drummed gently against the smooth, shiny fabric of her black evening cape.

Jean felt the pressure of Teddy's knees in her back. She saw how hard Douglas gripped the wheel as he turned on the engine. The sooner they reached home the better, she thought.

The best way to get through the journey was to let Teddy prattle on. He gave his opinion on the dance band – 'A decent pianist but the saxophonist left a lot to be desired' – and the town of Northgate – 'Not a patch on Cheltenham or Leamington Spa' – before leaning forward to ask Douglas about various members of the Rixley flying crew.

'Off the record, how do you and Hilary rate Mary Holland?' he wanted to know. 'Would you let her loose on anything bigger than a Class Two, for instance?'

'Third officers are qualified to fly single-engine light aircraft. That includes plenty of Class Twos.' Douglas's bland response hardly answered the question but Teddy steamed on regardless.

'What's happened to Angela, by the way? Is she in trouble over last week's dip in the briny?'

'No. Why should she be?' Bobbie replied in a defensive tone.

Teddy leaned back and casually slid his arm around her shoulder again. 'I haven't seen her around recently, that's all. I heard a rumour that she'd been hauled over the coals for losing the brand-new Spit and taken off flying duties until further notice.'

'That's simply not true.' Bobbie was keen to clear this up. 'Angela went home on leave. She'll report for duty first thing on Monday morning as per usual.'

'Well, I hope she's having a nice time, then.' Teddy probed for more information. 'Will Lionel be spending the weekend with her?'

'Not this time. He's stuck in the Dodecanese with his convoy.' Drink and light-headedness made Bobbie's tongue run away with her. 'It's hard for poor Angela, having a fiancé involved in the thick of things. Lionel arrived soon after the Germans took Kos and I don't know how many Allied ships were lost.'

'A fiancé, you say?' Douglas didn't try to hide his surprise. 'Did you know about an engagement, Jean?'

'Oh, good Lord above!' Too late, Bobbie realized her mistake. 'I wasn't supposed to let the cat out of the bag. I promised Angela.'

Jean looked closely at Douglas, whose lips were pressed firmly together. 'If Angela doesn't want it to be common knowledge then we'll keep this between the four of us,' she said.

'But you're sure, Bobbie?' Teddy wouldn't let it drop. 'Angela and Lionel are definitely engaged?'

'Please don't say anything.' She grasped his hand.

'All right, I promise,' he muttered. He felt unaccountably peeved, like a child in a sweet shop who has been offered a sugary treat, only to have it snatched away. Angela hadn't behaved like an engaged woman at Bobbie's party; far from it. She'd been all over him after the dancing had stopped and they'd gone outside into the pub yard. It had led Teddy to believe that he was in with a real chance.

So he sat in silence digesting the news while Douglas drove the moor road. Teddy leaned back and jiggled his foot against the seat in front. Was it still worth taking a serious shot at glamour-girl Angela? Or should he look elsewhere? Here was Bobbie, for instance – sitting beside him with tears in her eyes for having broken her promise to her best friend. Sweet, pretty, gullible Bobbie: sharp as a tack when it came to anything aeronautical but clueless as far as men were concerned. He only had to go about it the right way: continuing to tease, flirt and flatter. But would it be a big enough challenge? That was the question occupying Teddy as they arrived in Rixley and Douglas turned in through the back gates of Burton Grange.

A nightcap in the deserted lounge rounded off the evening for Jean and Douglas. George, the civilian barman, was about to shut up shop as they arrived but was happy to serve them before he left.

'Your usual whisky?' George asked Douglas, who nodded.

'Make that two,' Jean decided. It felt good to be back on familiar territory, especially after the awkward silences that had punctuated the drive home.

218

George poured their drinks then wished them a polite goodnight.

'I've been thinking a good deal about what you said earlier – about not feeling that you deserved to be happy,' Douglas began as he and Jean sat close to the dying fire. 'You don't mind me being serious? Stop me if you do.'

'I don't mind,' she assured him. She'd had more than enough of Teddy's flippancy on the drive home.

'It wasn't like that for me. I'm afraid I watched too many Hollywood films in my youth; the type where boy meets girl, they overcome a few obstacles then live happily ever after. So when I reached the age you are now I was fully expecting that to happen to me.'

'And didn't it?' Jean was curious. With his square, symmetrical features and high forehead, Douglas was still a handsome man and must have had plenty of romantic opportunities when he was younger.

He stared thoughtfully at the golden liquid in his glass. 'It could have on a couple of occasions,' he began cautiously, 'but at twenty-odd I wasn't very good at making the right moves.'

'You were shy?' Jean guessed.

'That's a nice way of putting it. A more honest assessment is that I was too self-absorbed, too worried about the impression I made. It must have come across as arrogance – I was told so on more than one occasion. So, in spite of expectations, I never got the girl and lived happily ever after.'

'But surely it's not too late.' The warm glow from the dying fire and the low lighting brought down Jean's guard. 'It's never too late.'

Douglas ducked his head and smiled. 'I'd like to believe you.' When he looked up he saw that she was gazing intently at him, as if working out the way his mind worked. 'I'm sorry that our evening together got ruined.'

'Don't apologize. Nothing was ruined.'

The room was full of flickering shadows. The curtains were open, the sky was thick black and a bright moon shone in. Jean's calm presence cast its spell. Without any words spoken, they rose from their seats and embraced. He held her close, felt her softness, saw her features blur as they kissed.

She sank against him. His arms were strong. She hadn't expected to feel so safe.

'Let me put in a good word on your behalf,' Teddy told Bobbie as they strolled together on the edge of Burton Wood. They'd parted from Douglas and Jean as soon as Douglas had parked his car in the mews yard at the Grange. The walk in the wood had been Teddy's idea once the others were out of earshot.

Bobbie had just admitted her frustration at still falling short of the flying hours she needed to make first officer. She greeted Teddy's offer with a shake of the head. 'I don't need your help, thanks.'

'Why not? I could have a chat with Douglas – get him to send you on a couple of long trips – to France or Belgium, perhaps. You'd clock up the hours in no time.'

'Thanks, but no,' she said again. 'I don't want any special favours. Anyway, Douglas wouldn't bend the rules for my sake or anyone else's.'

'You're right there; he's far too strait-laced.' Teddy tempered his insult for Bobbie's benefit. Po-faced bastard was more like it. All that fuss about a few measly gallons of petrol for the Royal Enfield. And the look on Douglas's face when Teddy had had the brass neck to cadge a lift home! Well, that had been priceless. 'Anyway, you'll get your promotion soon enough then we'll go out and celebrate.'

'I'd like that.' Bobbie's feelings towards Teddy swung wildly. She'd said yes with alacrity to walking with him to round off the evening and she loved the feel of her hand in his and of his arm around her shoulder. Dancing with him had been thrilling too. Besides, the memory of their kiss in the bed and breakfast at Harkness was still very much alive. But Teddy's lack of respect towards Douglas and his senior RAF officers was troubling, as was the way he seemed to blow hot and cold towards her. 'Can I be honest with you?' she said, plucking up courage as they turned back towards the house.

'Why not? Fire away.'

'I've had a thoroughly nice time tonight, but the fact is I've been advised not to take you too seriously.'

'Who by? I bet it was Angela.'

'Never you mind. But it does make me wonder about your intentions, Teddy.'

'My intentions?' he spluttered, struggling to keep a straight face. 'Are we in a play by Oscar Wilde by any chance? "What are your intentions regarding my niece, Flight Lieutenant Simpson?" Am I about to be hit over the head with a handbag?'

'Don't!' Bobbie broke free and walked more

quickly down the path towards the stable block at the Grange.

Teddy ran to catch up. Here was the challenge he needed after all. 'I didn't mean to upset you,' he pleaded. 'Slow down, Bobbie, please!'

'No, not if you're going to make fun of me.' She stopped under the clock tower and turned to confront him. 'The question is: can I trust you? And don't you dare laugh at me again.'

Teddy spread his hands, palms upwards, and his face grew serious. 'When have I ever given you a reason not to trust me? Go ahead, tell me.'

Bobbie tried to clear her head. She'd drunk too much again and it had made her gauche and confused. 'It's just a feeling. I can never tell whether or not you mean what you say.'

Teddy took hold of her by both arms. 'That's just me. It's the way I am with everyone. I can't help it.'

'But why?' His grip was tight as she tried to pull free.

'I haven't a clue. Dr Freud would have a theory about it, I suppose. I probably joke and make light of things because I'm running away from some deep trouble in my childhood; isn't that what the psychiatrists say?'

Bobbie stopped struggling. 'What trouble?'

Teddy's brow was furrowed and he took a long time to answer. 'My father ran off when I was four and a half. After that I lived pretty much on the breadline with my mother and grandfather. That's probably reason enough.'

'I didn't know that,' she said softly. 'I'm sorry.'

'Don't be; either you sink under it or you come back

fighting. I chose to claw my way out.' None of this was a lie, Teddy reminded himself. His motive for telling Bobbie at this point might be called into question, but it seemed to be having the desired effect.

'I see.' She stood motionless, gazing up at him.

'Do you?' he murmured, placing one hand gently on the back of her head. 'All this larking around; it's a big front to help me get by. But deep down it's not really what makes me tick.'

Bobbie nodded slowly. As her head tilted back, Teddy's tentative kiss took her breath away.

The kiss deepened into a close embrace. He felt her return the increasing pressure of his lips and when they finally broke apart her eyes glistened with tears and a shiver ran through her.

'Are you feeling chilly?' Teddy took her hand and quickly led her up some stone steps to a large loft where grooms and coachmen had once slept. The bare, basic room ran the length of one side of the stable yard and in the gloom it was only possible to make out open rafters and a series of skylights letting in shafts of moonlight. Teddy, however, had been here before.

'There's a stove in the corner.' He crouched to open the door and took out a lighter. 'I come here once in a while for some peace and quiet.'

The lighter flared and Bobbie made out disused furniture stacked against a wall: a table, a few armchairs, an old mattress and a broken glass-fronted cabinet. She heard the wood in the stove crackle and catch light.

'Come closer,' Teddy invited. He stretched out his hand.

Bobbie crouched beside him and leaned against him. The flames flared blue and yellow and then orange. 'I never knew this room was here,' she whispered.

'Let it be our secret.' Drawing a silver hip flask from his pocket, he unscrewed the top and offered her a drink. 'To warm you up.'

Bobbie took the flask and drank without thinking. The burn in her throat made her splutter.

'More,' Teddy encouraged, watching her as she drank again. 'There, that's better. Wait here; I'll drag some chairs across.'

Bobbie tried to stand up but she was suddenly unsteady on her feet.

Teddy reached out to prop her up. 'Wait; I've had a better idea.' Instead of bringing chairs, he dragged the old mattress across the floor then set it down in front of the stove.

Bobbie heard the sound of something being dragged. There was a flop and a thud as the mattress landed.

'Sit,' he said.

Her legs gave way and she sank to her knees. 'I don't know what's wrong with me.' The warmth of the fire felt comforting and the flutter of doubt in her stomach settled. 'I'm sorry ... you must think ...'

'I don't think anything.' Teddy knelt beside her. 'Come here.' He held his arms wide open and waited for her to snuggle close.

Closing her eyes, Bobbie breathed in the smell of his cologne and felt the rise and fall of his chest.

'Another?' He offered her the flask again.

'No.' Nothing in the room would stay still. Everything tilted and slipped. 'Better not,' she tried to say but the words too slid out of control. 'Sorry,' she breathed, wiping the back of her hand across her mouth.

Teddy kept his arm around her as he tempted her to drink again. He eased her on to the mattress then lay down beside her and stroked her face. 'There now; you'll soon be nice and warm.'

Bobbie felt her cape slide from her shoulders. Teddy's face in the firelight had taken on an oddly determined quality, quite different from the soothing tone of his voice. His eyes were hooded and dark. Doubt fluttered again and rose high in her chest. 'No, Teddy . . .' As she tried to raise herself from the mattress, the straps on her dress slipped down her arms, leaving her shoulders bare.

'Don't be silly.' He pulled her back down. 'Stay here with me where it's warm.'

She fell against him and felt him kiss her neck. Falling and falling; eyes closed, head back, feeling Teddy's mouth on her shoulders, her cheek, her lips. Falling further, she started to push against him as he cupped her breasts in his hands.

He used his weight to press her against the mattress. 'Lie down. I won't hurt you. There now; lie still. That feels nice, doesn't it?'

Falling again into a vast, dark space and aware of Teddy kissing her mouth hard, his hands on her, his weight pressing her down. Bobbie twisted her head sideways. 'No.'

'Yes,' he said. He found the zip at the side of her dress and slid it down, heard her gasp and try to pull away. Her pale skin glowed golden in the fire-light and strands of hair streaked her flushed cheek. 'It's nice, it's good,' Teddy breathed into her ear. 'You'll like it, I promise. Lie still and don't put up a fight; there's a good girl.'

CHAPTER THIRTEEN

The women's quarters at the Grange seemed the lap of luxury to Mary. Her bedroom was enormous for a start, with a window from floor to ceiling overlooking the wood. The bed was a double, with a defunct servants' bell-pull to one side. Though the patterned carpet was worn, the edging tassels were frayed and moths had been at the embroidered blue counterpane, she could see how grand the furnishings and fittings must once have been.

Awake before dawn on the Sunday morning, she lay in the darkness and was slow to identify the musty smell of the carpet and hulking outlines of her mahogany wardrobe and chest of drawers. Eventually a glint of daylight was reflected in the mirror on the dressing table: a signal that it was time to get up. So, still in her nightdress, Mary carried her towel and washbag along to the bathroom at the end of the corridor, padding on bare feet and hoping that she would find it free.

The door was ajar and she breathed a sigh of relief. There was a hot-water tap for the sink (another luxury) and a bar of Palmolive soap in a dish on the washstand. Mary washed quickly then brushed her teeth. With luck, she'd be back in her room before anyone else was up.

But when she slid back the bolt and opened the bathroom door she found Angela fully dressed and hovering outside.

Angela's face fell. 'Oh, hello, Mary. I thought it was Bobbie in there.'

'As you see; it's not.' Mary waited, straight-faced, for Angela to step aside.

'She's not in her room either.' Angela peered over Mary's shoulder as if suspecting her of hiding Bobbie in the bathroom. 'She can't be far away. I need to talk to her. It's rather urgent.'

'I haven't seen her.'

'Well, if you do will you tell her that I've come back sooner than expected. I have something important to tell her.' At last Angela backed away and Mary slipped past.

'Where will you be?' Mary asked.

'Downstairs, in the breakfast room.' Angela didn't offer to wait for her and show her the ropes. Instead, she turned on her heel and marched off.

Mary swallowed hard after this blow to her already fragile confidence. She decided to avoid the breakfast room altogether and instead walk over to the base and eat her bacon and eggs in familiar surroundings.

So she went back to her room and put on a warm green jumper, a red woollen scarf and a pair of brown corduroy trousers. She threw her overcoat over the top, slid her feet into some flat shoes then hurried downstairs.

A faint clatter of cutlery from a room to her right told her the whereabouts of Angela and her fellow officers. *It'd be like Daniel entering the lions' den if I went in there*, she thought, crossing the hallway and escaping through the front door.

Halfway down the steps, Mary remembered Cameron's warning not to walk at the front of the house until the bomb disposal team had done their work so she cut along the terrace then down into the stable yard where she saw wisps of blue smoke emerging from a chimney and the clock in the tower telling her that it was half past eight. About to hurry under the archway and follow the short path towards Burton Wood, she didn't notice Cameron and Douglas deep in conversation beside Douglas's car.

Douglas spotted her first. 'Hello, Mary. Welcome to the Grange.' He limped across to shake her hand. 'Very well done, by the way.'

'Thank you,' she replied with downcast eyes.

'We'll get you up and running first thing tomorrow,' Douglas promised, as Cameron joined them. 'Do you have any preference for your first time up in the air – a Hurricane or an F4U Corsair, for instance?'

'No, thanks. I don't want special treatment; just whatever needs to be done.'

'Fair enough.' Now that Mary was qualified to fly, Douglas would have to rethink his attitude towards her. He'd always found her a little too brusque when she'd worked as a driver so had made little attempt to get to know her. This was still the case, but the girl must have hidden depths to have sailed through the conversion course the way she had. 'Cameron here has great faith in you, don't you?'

'I do,' came the reply. Rixley's second in command

cleared his throat and glanced up at the smoking chimney.

Douglas seemed unaware that he was embarrassing them both. 'He's been singing your praises every chance he gets.'

Cameron coughed and shuffled. 'Who lit a fire in the old grooms' quarters, I wonder?' Without waiting for an answer, he went off to investigate.

Mary had wanted him to stay, if only to protect her from more of Douglas's friendly but clumsy overtures. But Cameron strode off, dressed only in shirtsleeves and casual trousers, as if glad to have found an excuse to leave.

'Cameron likes everyone to think he's the strict disciplinarian but he does have a softer side if you catch him off guard,' Douglas confided. 'Mind you, it's the first time I've seen him take someone under his wing the way he has done with you, Mary. I hear from Hilary he put in a word on your behalf to get you on to the course. Not that you couldn't have done it on merit; don't get me wrong,' he added hastily.

Mary bit hard on her bottom lip. She told herself that Douglas hadn't meant to put his foot in it. 'If you don't mind . . .' She gestured towards the path that she'd been about to take.

Douglas carried on regardless. 'In any case, you've done remarkably well to impress Geoff Rouse the way you did. I know Geoff of old and he's a hard taskmaster.'

Mary was dismayed to learn that she'd been talked about behind her back. Her face flushed bright red as she saw Squadron Leader Hilary Stevens coming down the steps to join them.

'Welcome to Burton Grange, Mary.' He took her hand and gave it one stiff shake. His aquiline features, always serious, had the keen look of an eagle as he turned sideways to glance up at the smoke coming out of the chimney. 'Who's . . . ?' he began.

'Cameron's gone to find out.' Douglas guessed what he'd been about to say.

'Very well. We don't want any mishaps. That chimney hasn't been cleaned recently, as far as I'm aware.' As Hilary spoke, his mind was elsewhere. He'd bumped into Angela in the breakfast room and listened to her fresh tale of woe. Apparently she'd been summonsed home where old man Browne had cut up rough – threatened to disinherit her, no less. Serious stuff, though Angela had tried to make light of it, as was her wont. She'd reproached Hilary for letting Lionel know about her dramatic bail-out at sea, and so he decided it would be better to stay out of it this time – let her sort things out for herself. 'If you'll excuse us, Douglas and I need to have a chat,' he told Mary now as he led the way across the yard.

The squadron leader's brush-off came as a relief. Mary fled, practically running under the stone arch and down the path, into the wood where she took out her frustration by rustling through heaps of leaves underfoot, kicking and listening to their swish until her nerves settled. A startled wood pigeon clattered down from a branch and flew ahead of her, swooping upwards then banking out of sight.

Mary stopped in a clearing, hands deep in her pockets, staring up through the canopy and trying to calm herself. She must take no notice of what people said and how they said it. Never mind if men

231

like Douglas and Hilary patronized her and girls like Angela looked straight through her. She, Mary Holland, knew she was as good as them. She'd proved it at Thame. What did it matter if she didn't fit in at the Grange? It wouldn't make her a worse pilot. And if she needed company, she would do as Stan had suggested and pal up with Jean or stick with her old friends. In any case, she usually preferred to keep to herself.

So Mary walked on towards the airbase, kicking through the leaves and disturbing more woodland creatures. A bushy-tailed squirrel shot vertically up the trunk of a beech tree; a blackbird searching for worms amongst the leaf litter sent out an alarm call to its mate. She took no notice. *I have done the right thing*, she reminded herself firmly as she reached the Nissen huts at the edge of the airfield. *What's more, once I'm in the cockpit of a Spit and flying high, I'll prove I'm their equal, whether they like it or not.*

Harry sat on a stool outside the door of the men's billet. He was dressed in singlet and trousers, braces dangling, and had set a small mirror on the card table he'd carried from inside the hut. He got out his shaving gear and was happily lathering up when he happened to glance towards the wood. He paused, shaving brush in hand.

'Blimey O'Flipping Reilly!' Harry looked again. Sure enough, there was Bobbie Fraser, standing stock-still under a big old oak tree. He almost fell off his stool. 'Stan, come and take a look at this!' he yelled.

Hearing the young lad's call, Stan sauntered down

the central aisle, between dimly lit rows of beds, tugging Gordon's blanket off him as he passed by. 'Wakey-wakey!'

Gordon swore and pulled the blanket back up over his head.

'What is it, Harry?' Stan emerged, blinking into the daylight.

'Look – over there.' Harry pointed to the small figure under the tree. 'It's Bobbie Fraser; she's got next to nothing on!'

'Bloody hell, Harry; don't just sit there!' In a flash Stan ran back into the hut and grabbed the nearest blanket. He came out again and made a bee-line for Bobbie. As he drew near he slowed down then stopped two or three paces from where she stood.

'Next to nothing' was right. Bobbie was turned away from him, dressed only in a short pink petticoat with a lacy edge. Her arms, legs and feet were bare.

'Bobbie, it's me.' Stan ventured one step closer.

She didn't turn at the sound of his voice.

He advanced again and carefully wrapped the rough grey blanket around her shoulders. 'For God's sake, girl; you'll catch your death,' he murmured.

Bobbie clutched at the warm covering and shook her head as if to ward Stan off. What on earth had happened to her? Stan gestured for Harry to come closer. 'Fetch one of the girls,' he said quickly. Then, as Harry ran off again, Stan tried to get through to Bobbie. 'You must be freezing. Why not come with me? We'll find you a nice cup of tea.'

Bobbie shook her head again. 'Did I . . . ? Have I

walked here?' Her feet were cold and sore, her fingers were numb as she tried to keep the blanket from slipping.

Bloody hell! Stan rarely found himself out of his depth but this was one of those times. Had Bobbie been sleepwalking? Or had she been drinking all night and ended up out for the count? Her face was a white mask, her sandy-coloured hair tangled and knotted.

'I have to go,' she whimpered, staggering a few steps into the wood.

Stan blocked her way. 'No, stay here,' he pleaded. A glance over his shoulder told him that Olive and Harry were on their way. 'Get a move on!' he yelled.

Overtaking Harry, Olive thrust a bundle of clothes into Stan's arms. 'Give her these before she freezes to death,' she mumbled ungraciously.

Stan thrust them back at her. 'You do it. But go carefully.'

Olive approached Bobbie. She thought she could guess what had happened here. It reminded her of the case of Lilian Watkins, the driver whom Olive had replaced. By all accounts, Lilian had been out drinking in Highcliff with a sailor boy she'd met at the fair. Things had got out of hand as they sometimes did and Lilian had turned up at the base the next morning looking the worse for wear. She'd still had most of her clothes on, mind you. 'You need to put these on before anybody else catches sight of you,' Olive advised in the same unsympathetic undertone, holding out a pair of slacks. 'Come on, it's time to pull yourself together. There's a jumper here too.'

'Gently,' Stan reminded Olive.

Shaking all over, Bobbie struggled into the jumper and trousers. Olive helped her to tuck her lacy petticoat inside the waistband.

'There, that's better.' Stan stepped between Olive and Bobbie before Olive had a chance to blurt out awkward questions. 'Now for that cup of tea and a slice of toast. And while we're doing that, you can fill us in. No rush. Olive, fetch Bobbie some shoes and socks. Easy now – gently does it.'

Angela wondered if Bobbie had been away overnight. Perhaps Douglas had handed her a chit yesterday that had sent her winging her way up north of the border again; in which case, that would have meant an overnight stop in a B & B.

That must be it, a frustrated Angela decided. Her journey back from Heathfield had involved delays and diversions and she'd arrived at the Grange after midnight, too late to speak to anyone. As dawn broke, after hardly any sleep and badly in need of a sympathetic ear, she'd discovered that Bobbie didn't seem to be around. So Angela polished off her Sunday breakfast then dashed back to her room to write a letter to Lionel. *Make it good*, she told herself. *Don't beat about the bush. Tell him the whole truth and nothing but the truth.*

'Dear Lionel,' she began before tearing the sheet from the pad and screwing it up then starting a fresh one. 'My dearest Lionel, I have to tell you about a terrible row that your last letter to Pa has caused. I'm sure you didn't intend for it to have the consequences it did, but my dear boy, you shouldn't have written and told him about my having to ditch the Spit. Knowing Father as I do, I would never have let you put pen to paper.'

Angela's stomach churned and she put down her pen. This was true, but really what good did recriminations do now that the worst had happened? She tore a second sheet from the pad and it joined the first in the waste-paper basket.

'Dearest Lionel, Pa and I have fallen out for good. The reasons why aren't important; suffice it to say that he has ordered me out of the house and will have no further contact with me unless I bend to his will and give up flying for the ATA.

'I can't agree to do that. The work is too important and besides, the request is unreasonable. So I refused point-blank.'

Misery threatened to swamp Angela so she stood up and paced the floor. In reality, the argument went far beyond the matter of her continuing to fly. If it hadn't been this, the break with her father would have happened over something else: perhaps his tyrannical treatment of her mother or of women in general, or some other important issue where he would have sought to override Angela and bully her into submission. Exercise of power was the only thing that mattered to Joseph Browne. Defiance led down a one-way street ending in exile and penury.

On the verge of tears, Angela sat down again and took up her pen. 'I make this sound simpler and more clear-cut than it was. By deciding to stay in the ATA I know without a shadow of a doubt that Pa will carry out his threat to disown me. I'll be written out of his will and won't be allowed back to Heathfield to see Mother. Father will also try to influence Hugh against me, which will hurt a great deal if it comes to pass. And worst of all, dear Lionel, it will affect us badly – you and me. For I am penniless now and not the good catch you thought I was when you proposed marriage.

'I imagine you reading this and springing to your feet to declare that it makes no difference; you will marry me in any case, because that is the good, kind-hearted soul that you are. However, I can't let you do that. I thought about it long and hard during the night and know that it won't do. Unless we continue as equals, there's no hope for our future together. I *need* to be equal, Lionel.' Angela underlined the word 'need' twice. 'Not because people would think badly of me for marrying into money without a penny to my name (which they would), but because I would think badly of *myself.*' She underscored 'myself' once. 'I would be unhappy and that would make you unhappy, don't you see?

'No doubt you will read this letter and feel for a while that your heart is broken. But the Navy has given you many responsibilities and your mind will be taken up with fighting the enemy. In time I hope the broken pieces will heal.

'I say this from my heart, dear Lionel; I truly wish you to be happy in your life. In years to come I hope we can meet as friends; me finding my feet in the commercial aviation field, perhaps, and you following your father into the highest ranks of the civil service. All will turn out for the best, my dear; believe me.'

The words came slowly and caused Angela much

heartache. She signed it simply, with her name and one kiss.

Sighing, she blotted the page then reread the letter in its entirety. She'd done her best to express herself honestly but the words and phrases seemed flat and lacking in emotion. Why couldn't she be softer? What was missing in her make-up that made even breaking her engagement sound formal and coldly thought out? Was it because, as she'd originally suspected, she was incapable of fully loving Lionel? Of loving anyone with her whole heart, for that matter?

Enough of that! Angela folded the letter and put it in an envelope. She would slip it in the village post box on her way to the ferry pool in the morning. The deed would be done.

Stan had second thoughts about taking a bewildered Bobbie to the canteen. It would be too noisy and crowded, he decided. Perhaps the women's billet would be better. There again, it didn't feel right to hand her over to an unsympathetic Olive.

'Silly little fool,' Olive had murmured behind Bobbie's back when she'd brought back shoes and socks. 'What's the betting she's had too much to drink and ended up doing what a nice girl oughtn't.'

'That's not Bobbie's style,' Stan had objected. Then again, what did he really know about what went on at the Grange? 'Ta for the clothes and the shoes,' he said to Olive as he led Bobbie towards the control tower.

'Tell her I want them back – when she comes to her senses.'

'Will do.' Stan noticed that Harry still hovered in the background, his chin covered in white shaving foam. 'Thanks, I can manage now,' he told him. Hoping that the squadron leader's office would be deserted at this time on a Sunday morning, Stan steered Bobbie down the side of the building towards a back entrance but she pulled back from the shadowy alley and he decided not to force her to go on.

'Fair enough,' he murmured. Perhaps it would have to be the canteen after all.

They'd turned around and were heading in that direction when Mary turned up out of the blue. She emerged from the wood wearing an overcoat and a red scarf, her face flushed from a brisk walk. When she saw Stan she waved.

'Come here, quick!' He beckoned her across.

'Stan, what's wrong?' One look at Bobbie standing in jumper and trousers that swamped her small frame told Mary that something was badly amiss.

'I don't know; I can't get a word out of her. Why don't you have a go?'

Mary frowned doubtfully. She'd never spoken to Bobbie except to ask for destinations and drop-off points. 'Shouldn't I run and fetch Angela?'

At the sound of the name Bobbie breathed in sharply and shook her head in agitation. 'No! I'm all right. I don't need Angela.'

'You're not all right,' Stan insisted. He led Bobbie to a bench at the front of the building and sat her down. 'Wait here with her while I fetch a hot drink,' he told Mary.

He was gone before she could object so she sat down nervously next to Bobbie.

'Don't tell her.' Bobbie clutched at Mary's sleeve with a frantic look. 'Don't say a word to Angela.'

'We won't,' Mary promised. *Tell her what?* she wondered.

'I don't want anyone to know.'

'Don't worry, I won't say anything.' Mary tried to piece things together. Why was Bobbie in borrowed clothes? And why did she look like death warmed up?

Bobbie's breath was ragged and she shivered in spite of the warm clothes. The gaps in her memory terrified her; one minute she and Teddy had been riding back to the Grange in Douglas's car, the next they were together in some kind of barn or loft. It had been very dark. Then there were flames and the sound of logs crackling. She remembered the firelight reflected in Teddy's eyes.

Mary sat quietly. Was this a bad hangover or something more?

Teddy's voice. *I won't hurt you . . . Lie still.* His lips, his hands on her. Bobbie shot to her feet and looked round wildly. 'How did I get here?' she begged.

'I have no idea.' Definitely worse than a hangover, Mary concluded. Bobbie's face looked haunted. It reminded her of the dazed expressions of the people she'd seen wandering the corridors of the hospital at Highcliff on the night of the air raid: relatives of the dead and injured, the old man calling out his wife's name and getting no response. She put her arm around Bobbie's shoulder. 'It's all right; you're not in any danger.'

Teddy's voice and his cruel face and the sensation of falling out of control, of being helpless, of blacking

240

out completely. Then a memory of coming round and it still being night and Bobbie remembered lying on a mattress, alone and undressed. Then there was another black, blank gap and the cold wind and sigh of leaves in trees. A maze of oaks and ash, beech and sycamores. Sharp thorns underfoot. Icy cold.

'There, there,' Mary said, holding Bobbie tight. 'Here's Stan with a hot drink. Sit down again; here, next to me. Let me hold the cup for you. Now sip this carefully in case it scalds your tongue.'

Before Douglas and Jean had parted the night before, he'd warned her of a busy week ahead. 'Make the most of your day off tomorrow. We're expecting another big push of the new Spits – out to Belgium and parts of northern France, as well as Scotland and Scandinavia. I might even have to fly the odd crate myself if we run short of pilots.'

But their evening had ended strangely after that first kiss; they'd left the lounge hand in hand and had reached the bottom of the stairs but then they'd stepped apart at the sound of someone moving along the landing on the first floor. Though no one had materialized, the interruption had broken the mood and an awkward exchange had followed.

'Thank you for a lovely evening,' Jean had said.

'My pleasure,' he'd replied. 'We must do it again.'

'Yes, we must.' She'd waited for him to kiss her a second time but it hadn't happened. 'Thanks again,' she'd whispered, one foot on the bottom step.

She was too lovely, too perfect, too young. Douglas remembered with a sharp stab of shame the look of scorn on Teddy's face when he'd spotted them together in the bar at the Spa Ballroom. *Don't be such a bloody fool*, he told himself. On Monday he would sit at his desk and write out the chits. Jean would fly her plane. That summed them up: he the desk-bound crock, Jean soaring through the air in a magnificent flying machine. *Leave it at that.*

Though disappointed, Jean had followed Douglas's lead. She got up the next day determined to have breakfast then set out on a bicycle ride along the lanes around Rixley. It was a cold morning so she wrapped up well in her sheepskin jacket, scarf and gloves then went down to the yard to borrow one of the Grange bikes stored in an empty stable next to the boot room adjoining the main house. There she ran into Teddy, similarly wrapped up and about to set out on his motorbike.

'Good morning, Jean; did you sleep well?' he called as he sat astride the bike and rocked it back off its stand.

'Very well, thanks.' Choosing a push-bike, she wheeled it under the arch, hearing Teddy start his engine then follow her.

He slowed almost to a stop as she mounted her bicycle. 'Are you going far?'

'No, not far. How about you?'

'Maybe to the coast and back. Not much petrol since Douglas clamped down.' He patted the tank then opened the throttle. 'See you later, Jean.'

Relieved as always to see the back of Teddy, she watched him roar off around the back of the house then made her way out on to the lane. She chose a route that skirted the village and came out beside St

Wilfred's where a steady stream of churchgoers in Sunday best entered the church. From there Jean cycled on past the ferry pool; an easy, flat ride that allowed her to enjoy from a distance the autumn colours of Burton Wood. The sky above the bank of orange and gold was clear blue. A dog at a farmyard gate barked and strained at its chain. Further along, two little girls played hopscotch on the pavement outside their house and a lad perched on a low tree branch whistled cheekily at Jean as she rode by.

When she came to an unmarked crossroads at the top of a long hill she stopped. The wind had picked up and nipped her cheeks. Reckoning that she was about an hour from home, she was ready to turn around when Dorothy Kirk, the met-room typist, climbed a nearby stile and jumped down on to the grass verge. Dorothy was soon followed by Viv Francis from the ops room and Douglas's secretary Gillian Wharton.

'Hello, Jean, what are you up to?' Dorothy was the first to greet her. 'Silly question; you're out on a bike ride.'

'Keeping trim,' Viv added. 'Not that you need to.' She was envious of Jean's slim figure and gave her own stomach a quick pat. 'Not like some of us.'

Dressed in walking gear of corduroy slacks and windcheater and carrying a rucksack, Gillian was the last to jump down from the stile. She approached Jean with a smile. 'We've covered seven miles this morning; around the reservoir then on past the ruins of the old monastery. Do you know it?'

'Yes, it's a good long hike.' Their three cheerful faces boosted Jean's mood.

Dorothy's nickname was Dotty and it suited her scatterbrained nature. She did everything in a rush and said whatever came into her head but she was funny with it and her jokey style made her popular with the boys in the met room. Viv was her opposite: easy-going and steady, with thick, straw-coloured hair that she wore in an unflattering short bob. She was the first to admit that her aim in life was to slip under the radar and escape the notice of her bosses. The way to do this was to work quietly and efficiently and to get on with everyone. This left Gillian to take the energetic lead whenever the trio went out on jaunts together. Today Viv was map-reader-in-chief.

'We'll ask you to join us next time,' Gillian told Jean, 'if you fancy it.'

'Count me in,' Jean agreed. 'Or else we could all set out on a bike ride.'

'No, thanks; that's not for me,' Dotty protested. 'I'm not safe on two wheels. I collide with lamp-posts.'

The others laughed.

'And I don't have enough puff to get up these hills.' Viv too was happier to walk.

'Then it looks like it's just you and me, Jean.' Gillian slipped her rucksack from her shoulders then took out a vacuum flask and offered her a drink of tea. The tea was poured and the autumnal splendour of the valley below admired, after which the talk turned to recent goings-on at the ferry pool.

'My boss had a proper dressing-down this week,' Dotty reported gleefully. She was often in trouble with Fred Richards, the head of the met room, and couldn't resist the chance to gloat. 'Squadron Leader

Stevens blamed him for not picking up sooner on the met report from Central Control last week.'

'About the weather front rolling in off the North Sea?' Gillian asked. The incident in which the new Spitfire had been lost was still a major talking point among office staff.

'Yes. Fred was accused of not acting on the information soon enough.'

Jean was curious. 'How long did he hang on to it for?'

'Ten or fifteen minutes, that's all. But, as the squadron leader was quick to point out, every minute is vital when Douglas is sending planes out.' Dotty kicked her heels against the wall that they'd perched on to drink their tea. 'Talking of which . . .' She jerked her elbow into Gillian's ribs.

'What?' Gillian pushed her short red hair back from her forehead so that it stood straight up in the wind.

'Tell Jean what you were telling us – you know, about First Officer Thornton.'

Jean's attention was sharpened further.

Gillian wrinkled her nose. 'Maybe it'd be better to keep schtum about that.'

'Go on, tell her,' Dorothy urged. 'Jean's not the type to spread it around.'

Viv followed her usual course of saying nothing, but she listened and observed.

'The thing is,' Gillian quickly overcame her scruples, 'you must have noticed this yourself, Jean – Douglas sometimes doesn't listen to what people say.'

'Or doesn't *hear*,' Dotty added pointedly.

'He doesn't listen or he doesn't hear; which is it?'

Gillian confessed that she couldn't decide and welcomed Jean's opinion.

'I don't know. He hasn't said anything to me.' Jean's chest tightened. Obviously, no one except Teddy and Bobbie knew about her and Douglas (if indeed there was anything to know) so she had to be careful what she said.

'But you remember when you popped into our office on the day of Angela's crash?'

'Yes; to pass on Dotty's message.'

Gillian nodded then hurried on. 'You spoke and Douglas didn't hear you? You had to raise your voice.'

'I remember.'

'That happens a lot with him, especially when there's background noise. Believe me, I can count a dozen times in the last week alone.'

'So what are you saying?'

'That he's going deaf.' Dotty interrupted with her usual bluntness. She turned from Jean to Gillian. 'But First Officer Thornton is too proud to admit it. That's what you think, isn't it?'

'I'm not sure. I'm just posing the question.'

'What's your opinion, Jean?' Viv spoke for the first time. 'You know him better than we do. Is Douglas fit to carry out his job?'

With a frown Jean handed her cup to Gillian. 'Don't ask me; I'm no expert,' she said quietly. While the talk drifted on she firmly reknotted her scarf.

'Who else might have a view?' Dotty asked. 'I suppose we could take it higher up, to Flight Lieutenant Ainslie, for example.'

'Or Jean could take the bull by the horns and

tackle it with Douglas himself.' Gillian came down on the side of a direct approach.

'Right, I'll be off.' Jean ignored the last suggestion. The conversation had rattled her and she resolved to be on her way. 'Thanks for the tea.'

Viv, Gillian and Dotty watched her get back on her bike.

'Don't crash into any lamp-posts!' Dotty called as Jean set off.

'We'll see you in the morning,' Gillian added.

'Bright and early.' Jean waved and cycled on over the brow of the hill. She hoped that the tightness in her chest would fade but instead it got worse as she coasted down into the next valley. *They're right; Douglas can't hear properly*, she thought with another dull thud of certainty. *But if anyone mentions it, he'll deny it*. She sped on, past five-barred gates and sheep grazing in fields. *He's proud. He won't own up to any weakness*.

But what if she and the three other girls kept their doubts to themselves? What then?

Jean approached a bend and braked. A tractor trundled towards her, almost forcing her off the narrow road. She swerved on to the grass verge then eased the bike down again on to the tarmac.

Ought she to warn Douglas that people had started to notice that he missed a lot of what was being said to him? Might he then blame her and end their friendship altogether? That would be his pride talking, of course. But what on earth would Douglas do if he was forced out of his job because of it, rejected by the RAF and then by the ATA?

Jean braked again then turned left at the junction

leading to Rixley. At the gate to St Wilfred's she stopped and gazed in at the rows of moss-covered graves. The church door was closed after the morning service. All was quiet and still.

She was sure of only one thing: if increasing deafness meant that Douglas was unable to hear the decrease in the rev count of a plane's engine in time to prevent it stalling and going into a fatal tailspin then he ought not to be behind the controls of an aircraft. 'Douglas mustn't put himself or anyone else in danger,' she said out loud. 'Really and truly, he ought not to fly.'

CHAPTER FOURTEEN

Hilary's expression was grim as, first thing on Monday morning, he tapped the table with the end of his fork to claim the attention of his officers sitting down to breakfast at the Grange. When the clatter of cutlery and the general chatter didn't subside, he tapped again.

Jean broke off from her conversation with Agnes and Mary and looked towards the table at the far end of the room. She and the other early risers sensed bad news.

Their commanding officer waved a piece of paper in the air and spoke briskly. 'I have here a report of an overnight bombing raid on Northgate,' he announced without preliminaries. 'Between the hours of nine thirty and eleven fifteen p.m. there were six direct hits in all. Extensive damage is reported to buildings in the town centre and on the outskirts of town, namely the areas of Foxborough and Welbeck. There are as yet no firm reports of casualties but the information I have here lists two of our ground personnel as currently missing.'

An audible gasp ran around the room, followed

by a tense silence. Mary held her breath and waited for the squadron leader to name names.

'Private Mechanic Harry Wood and Corporal Mechanic Gordon Mason did not return to Rixley last night. It is known that they were visiting North-gate for personal reasons. Any further information will be posted on the ferry pool board.' Hilary sat down between Cameron and Douglas, clasping his hands and resting them on the table. He remained silent as the news gradually sank in.

'Harry and Gordon?' Agnes whispered in disbelief. 'I saw them cycling through the village yesterday teatime, large as life. They must have been setting out for Northgate by bike.'

Mary recalled her last sighting of Harry hovering by the control tower at the ferry pool, his jaw covered in shaving foam, watching uncertainly as she and Stan had taken care of Bobbie. She heaved a sigh of relief that Stan hadn't been mentioned in Hilary's report then prayed that neither Harry nor Gordon was badly injured.

'Why is Jerry dropping bombs on Northgate?' Jean wondered aloud. The spa town seemed an unlikely target. 'Unless they mistook it for one of the mill towns further west.'

'There's an RAF training camp in Foxborough,' Agnes reminded her.

'Anyway, Jerry's not particular.' Teddy's voice broke in. He'd come into the room in time to hear the tail end of Hilary's announcement and didn't seem unduly upset by it. 'He'll bomb any old target rather than fly back with a full load. I've seen him blow up a field full of cows for want of something better.'

Jean, Agnes and Mary chose to ignore Teddy and were relieved when he sat down with Cameron, Douglas and Hilary.

Meanwhile, people slowly digested the bad news along with their toast and jam. 'Listed as missing' was a phrase that held out hopes for Gordon and Harry's safe return. Perhaps the plucky pair had stayed behind to help air raid wardens with the aftermath and would turn up at the ferry pool later today, battered and bruised but otherwise none the worse for wear. But surely they would have telephoned to say they were safe? Not if they were up to their necks in clearing rubble, they wouldn't. Wait and see; it was all their friends and colleagues could do.

'It's a good job Jerry chose Sunday and not Saturday to bomb the blazes out of Northgate.' Teddy leaned across the table to speak to Douglas. 'Otherwise you and I might not be sitting here now.'

Cameron looked uncertainly from one to the other: Teddy smiling and winking, Douglas clearly irritated to the point of rapping his spoon down into his empty bowl and getting up to leave.

'I said, it's a good job—' Teddy repeated.

'I heard what you said,' Douglas snapped back. 'I'm running late,' he explained. 'Cameron, would you like a lift?'

Cameron nodded. 'Excuse us, gentlemen . . .' He scraped back his chair and followed Douglas.

Hilary's eyes narrowed as he studied their back views. 'You and Douglas were in Northgate on Saturday?' he asked Teddy.

'Yes; with Bobbie and Jean, as a matter of fact.'

251

Teddy spoke breezily. 'We made quite a night of it before Douglas drove us all back home.'

'Bobbie and Jean,' Hilary echoed. 'I see.'

'Oh, I say; no! Don't read too much into it,' Teddy protested good-humouredly. 'We're all just good pals – nothing more.'

'Flying is my life.' Angela had come to Bobbie's room just before dawn to explain at last her reasons for writing the letter to Lionel. 'I'll never give it up, even if Father carries out his threat to cut me off.'

'Surely he wasn't serious.' Bobbie summoned every ounce of willpower to carry on as normal: she took her uniform from the wardrobe then placed it carefully on the bed. 'He couldn't mean what he said.'

'You don't know my pa; he meant every word, which is why I've written to Lionel to break off our engagement.'

'You never did!' Bobbie tried to make out Angela's expression in the dim light. The news drew her out of the fog of confusion that she'd been in since Saturday night.

'I have and I intend to send it to him this morning, before I change my mind.' Angela's voice faltered then she gave herself a shake and went on with renewed determination. 'The thing is, I need the excitement that flying brings. Yes, we run an enormous risk every time we take off, but there's nothing in life to compare with the thrill of being behind the controls inside that cockpit. You understand me, don't you, Bobbie?'

'I do. And besides, why throw away the training and experience?' Bobbie was in no doubt that Angela should stay with the ATA but she thought it would be rash to send the break-up letter to Lionel straight away. 'But my advice is to hold fire and wait.'

'What for?' Angela dipped her hand into her inside jacket pocket for her packet of cigarettes. She felt the smoothness of the scarlet silk lining that she'd requested from the Savile Row tailor who had customized her uniform, remembering the eager-beaver enthusiasm she'd experienced on being accepted into the service. Forgetting about the cigarette, she stood up and paced the room as Bobbie stated her case.

'Wait for the dust to settle. Give your father time to reflect before you even think of giving up Lionel.' Bobbie began to get dressed, slipping into her underthings while Angela's back was turned.

Angela disagreed. 'You're not paying attention – once that man has made up his mind he never backs down. I'm not kidding; my pa has a heart of stone. In any case, I felt a sense of relief when I finished the letter and sealed the envelope. That sounds awful, I know.'

Bobbie zipped up her trousers then buttoned her pale blue shirt. She went to the dressing table to run a brush through her hair, catching sight of Angela's reflection in the mirror. 'In what way, relieved?'

'It brought a breath of freedom back into my life.' Angela tapped the envelope against her thigh. 'This decision may land me firmly on the shelf for the rest of my life but, if that turns out to be the case, at least I'll never have to put a husband and family before flying.'

'Poor Lionel; that's a shocking thing to say.' Bobbie gazed at Angela's face in the mirror.

'I know, but it's true.' Angela decided to smoke after all.

The click of the cigarette lighter took Bobbie back to the moment when Teddy had crouched by the stove to light a fire and the memory made her drop the hairbrush on to the floor with a sudden clatter.

Angela inhaled deeply. 'The truth is I'd never excelled at anything before I learned to fly. I was extremely average at school despite the money that Father poured into my education. I simply wasn't interested in geometry theorems or the life cycle of the fruit fly. As for algebra . . .' Angela stooped to pick up the hairbrush and hand it back. 'But flying a Spit is the one thing I know I'm good at. My dream is to keep on doing it, getting better and better until the point where I know that no one – woman or man – can beat me. I want to be the best aviator in the country.'

'I do understand.' Bobbie's hand shook as she took the brush.

'Oh, dear girl, are you sickening for something?' Angela stared over Bobbie's shoulder at their reflections. Neither looked as if they'd slept and Bobbie's eyes were swollen and red. 'Have you been crying?' she demanded.

Bobbie quickly shook her head. 'It's a sniffle, that's all.'

'A sniffle, my backside! You've been upset. And I was so busy pouring out my woes I failed to notice. What's happened while I've been away?'

'Nothing,' Bobbie said faintly, brushing her hair fiercely and refusing to look Angela in the eye.

Angela thought back over the weekend. 'Where were you on Saturday night, by the way?'

'Nowhere.'

Angela stubbed out her cigarette in the heavy, cut-glass ashtray on Bobbie's bedside table. 'You weren't in your room when I put my head around the door. I assumed at first that Douglas had sent you to some God-forsaken corner of the frozen north.'

'No, I was here at the Grange all weekend.'

'So why weren't you in your room?'

Letting out a long sigh, Bobbie kept her back turned as she searched in a drawer for her tie. 'I must have popped out for some reason.'

'I looked in again next morning: your bed hadn't been slept in. And when I checked later in the day, there you were, dead to the world.'

Bobbie found the black tie and slammed the drawer shut. 'Good Lord above, Angela, will you please stop asking questions!' She turned to face her, eyes blazing.

'Aha.' A different, unexpected picture presented itself – of young Bobbie painting the town red on her night off. 'You were otherwise engaged?'

'Please leave me alone,' Bobbie begged as she fumbled with the tie. 'At this rate I'll never get to the ferry pool in time to report in and receive my chit.'

Slowly Angela backed towards the door. Obviously Bobbie was not about to elaborate. 'I'm sorry,' she murmured. 'I'll go down and order breakfast for you, shall I? What'll it be: the full works or just porridge?'

'Porridge, please.' At last Bobbie managed to knot her tie. She calmed her voice to answer normally. 'I'll follow you down as soon as I've made the bed.'

'As long as you're sure you're all right,' Angela said as she left the room.

'I'm fine, thank you.' *Leave me alone. Don't ask me questions that I can't answer.* The blanks in Bobbie's memory yawned like the deep, dark craters on the lawn in front of the Grange. The sensation of falling into blackness came back with a vengeance so she sat on the edge of the bed, gripping its iron frame until the dizziness stopped and she was fit to go downstairs to breakfast.

The falling sensation slowly passed. It left Bobbie disorientated, uncertain of either time or place until another knock on the door brought her round.

'Bobbie, are you there?'

It was Mary's low, quiet voice. Bobbie went to the door and opened it.

'I've just had breakfast and now I'm setting off for Rixley. Do you fancy walking with me?' After the previous day's mysterious episode at the base, Mary wanted to find out how Bobbie was coping. 'I thought you might appreciate some company,' she added gently.

'That's sweet, but no thanks.' Bobbie had a hazy memory of being walked back to the Grange in clothes that didn't belong to her. Then Mary had run a bath for her and Bobbie had rubbed and scrubbed herself all over with flannel and nailbrush, scrubbed again and wept. Mary had fetched Bobbie's clothes and taken away the others. She'd persuaded her to go to bed and rest, asked no questions and shown Bobbie more kindness than she felt she deserved. 'Angela has ordered breakfast for me downstairs.'

'Champion. I'll see you at the base then.'

'It's your first day,' Bobbie remembered suddenly.

'That's right; it is.'

'Good luck, Mary. And thank you.'

Mary smiled and nodded. Bobbie still didn't seem right – her voice was not much more than a whisper and her delicately freckled face had regained none of its colour. Her eyes were still red from crying. And she seemed a million miles away from what was going on around her. 'Ta-ta for now,' Mary said as she put on her hat and zipped up her jacket. She breathed in its new, leathery smell and ran through the morning's procedure as she descended the stairs: first stop the locker room and a quick check of items in her locker – her goggles, helmet, map and parachute pack – then on to the ops room to pick up her chit for the day. *I can hardly wait*, she said to herself as she left by the back door and crossed the stable yard. Her spirits rose and her stride lengthened as she entered the wood. *Third Officer Mary Holland reporting for duty, Monday October the eighteenth, 1943, at eight o'clock sharp.*

Bobbie stood on the landing watching Mary leave. She knew she ought to force herself to eat and drink but her throat was tight as she went down the stairs. She felt frightened, like a child who fears monsters hiding in dark corners even though the child has been told again and again that monsters are not real. Afraid of what or of whom? The click of a cigarette lighter, flames, Teddy's face, his voice, his weight pressing down. Bobbie paused in the hall. She'd woken up alone in a dark room without her clothes. Then, after that, all she could remember was a cold wind, branches overhead, Harry calling for Stan. Olive's contemptuous look.

What did I do? Bobbie asked herself. There was enormous shame in it, whatever it was – sharp shame that pierced her again as she remembered swallowing whisky from Teddy's flask. And then black guilt. And shame again that Stan and the others knew something that Bobbie did not and she would have to face them today, aware that they would greet her with guarded expressions then whisper behind her back. She closed her eyes in an attempt to blank it all out then opened the door into the busy breakfast room.

'Bobbie, over here!' Angela sat with Teddy and Hilary, pointing to the empty chair next to her.

Teddy glanced up from his plate of eggs and bacon. He smiled fleetingly at Bobbie then went on talking to Hilary.

Bobbie's slight frame shook from head to toe. It seemed impossible to walk between tables, smiling and saying good morning, to sit between Angela and Teddy as if nothing had happened. But perhaps nothing *had* happened? Had it or hadn't it?

Was Saturday night a hysterical episode of her own making, brought on by drinking too much and passing out? *What did I do?* At the table Teddy laughed and talked as usual while Angela pointed to Bobbie's tray. *What did I do?*

The clamour of voices, crockery and cutlery, of chairs scraping over linoleum and the glimpse of kitchen activity through swing doors proved too much for Bobbie. As Angela called her name again, she shook her head then turned and rushed from the house, following the route that Mary had taken through Burton Wood.

*

Anything to Anywhere. Douglas sat at his desk rapidly writing out chits. The met report was good: clear weather over the north of England, some cloud to the south. This meant he could get all of his planes safely off the ground before ten o'clock. Agnes Wright to Ulster, Angela to Walsall in a Spit that was going in for repair. Bobbie to Bristol in a Miles Magister. Teddy to Hatfield in a Dauntless A-24 (knowing that Teddy would hate the old workhorse), Jean in a Spit to Reading.

Douglas paused before signing off Jean's chit. Despite his decision to stay away from her in future, he couldn't get her out of his thoughts. He'd kept busy on mundane chores all through Sunday morning: splitting logs for the woodpile alongside the Grange handyman, Ernest Poulter, then washing and polishing his car until it gleamed. But one glimpse of Jean returning from a bike ride had thrown him.

Dazzling was how Douglas would describe her: upright on her bike, her long legs pedalling with ease, her hair blown back from her beautiful face. The sight had stayed with him through an afternoon of letter writing followed by room tidying – hanging clean shirts on hangers, stuffing dirty washing in a canvas bag ready to go down to the laundry room – then dinner and the challenge of being merely chatty with the woman he adored. How was the bike ride? How lovely the trees were at this time of year.

Douglas went on making out chits. Jean in a Spit Mark V to Reading. Mary in a brand-new Spit in a hop across the Lancashire border to the ferry pool near Lancaster – giving her the very best, most up-to-date machine for her first flight.

Cameron looked over Douglas's shoulder to read Mary's chit. 'No need to send anyone to fetch Third Officer Holland,' he remarked. 'I'll be in that neck of the woods later this morning. I can easily drive her back.'

'Right you are.' Cameron's offer released a driver for other duties so Douglas took him up on it. He pushed a pile of chits across his desk towards Gillian. 'These are signed off,' he told her. 'You can go ahead and make the announcement.'

Over in the canteen, the sound of the Tannoy whistle startled Mary and made her spill tea into her saucer.

'Steady on,' Stan said with a reassuring smile. Not surprisingly, Mary had been jumpy all through breakfast. He too was on edge, worrying over Gordon and Harry's failure to return to base.

'Will all pilots report to the operations room for their chits!'

Gillian's crisp voice was the signal to scramble so Mary reached for her forage cap and joined the other pilots in a rush for the door. 'Wish me luck,' she said to Stan as she hurried away.

'You won't need it,' he called after her. 'You'll be fine.'

She paused and turned to look him in the eye. 'Thanks,' she whispered for the umpteenth time as others barged past. 'I mean it, Stan. Thank you.'

Then she was out of the canteen and hurrying towards the control tower to collect her chit; no time to think or get too nervous as she was jostled towards the head of the queue and the sign over the hatch saying 'All Pilots Report Here'. She took the slip of paper that Gillian slid towards her.

Spit Mark IX! Mary read the information. Brand new. A short hop to ease her in.

'Happy?' Gillian asked through the glass partition.

Mary grinned and nodded.

'Hang on to the chit. It has to be signed off at the other end,' Douglas's secretary reminded her. 'You're next off the runway so you'd better get a move on.'

Mary slid the paper into her top pocket and ran downstairs to collect her helmet, map and goggles. Then she set off towards the hangar, clutching her parachute pack to her chest, arriving breathless as Stan towed her plane into position. He jumped down from the Amazon lorry to unhitch the Spit.

'She's a little beauty,' he reported as he prepared to drive the lorry clear.

Standing at the end of the runway, Mary's heart beat so fast that she couldn't speak. She gazed up at the Spit's smooth, polished, perfect lines; beautiful and deadly.

'Don't be nervous.' Stan had parked the Amazon and strode back towards her.

'I'm not.'

'Fibber. Everyone is, no matter how many hours they've clocked up.'

'All right, a bit,' she admitted as she fastened her helmet and lowered her goggles. Then, with a boost from Stan she stepped on to the wing and into the cockpit where she strapped herself in and began the start-up checks. First, secure the hood; second, open up the throttle before checking the instrument panel. She heard the engine begin to turn and then sing. The glorious sound filled the cockpit. Mary looked left and right, above and behind. The coast was clear. At a thumbs-up from Stan, she watched him take away the chocks.

As the oil temperature gauge rose to fifty degrees, Mary returned the thumbs-up. The propellers blurred in front of her, the Merlin engine roared. Her grip tightened on the stick and she taxied along the runway, gathering speed until she felt the small bump and jerk that signalled lift-off.

'Very good,' Stan said, standing next to the Amazon. After a textbook take-off Mary was airborne, with sun reflecting off the wings; no tricks, no loops, no rolls, just a steady rise into the blue sky. 'Little beauty,' he murmured again.

So light, Mary thought; *so easy to manoeuvre*. Up she soared, with green fields below and the engine's song in her heart.

Angela caught up with Bobbie in the queue to receive their chits. They stood directly behind Jean, with Teddy some way ahead of them.

'Why did you skip breakfast?' Angela asked, concern written all over her face.

'I wasn't hungry.' Bobbie dreaded catching Teddy's attention so she kept her answer short.

'But you're fit to fly?'

Bobbie drew a deep breath. She had a bad headache and a queasy stomach but she was determined to carry on as normal. 'Fit as a fiddle, thanks.'

The queue shuffled forward until Teddy received his orders for the day. 'What's this?' he complained to Gillian as he read the chit. 'A bloody Dauntless? You must be joking.'

Gillian shrugged at him. 'If that's what First Officer Thornton has written down . . .'

Teddy shook his head in disgust. 'Where is he? Let me have a word.'

'Sorry; no can do.' Gillian knew that Douglas had left the office to talk with Fred Richards about a new met report forecasting rain later in the day. 'Step aside, please.'

But Teddy didn't budge. Instead, he listed the reasons why giving him the Dauntless was a waste of his time. 'Any idiot can fly that old crate. Give it to someone with fewer hours. There's Mary Holland, for a start. Let her cut her teeth on it.' He glanced over his shoulder. 'Or Jean here. Jean doesn't mind what she flies, do you, Jean?'

'I fly what I'm told to fly,' she answered in a steely tone while a flustered Gillian repeated her request for Teddy to step to one side.

'Here, Angela; you'll take the Dauntless off my hands, won't you?' Teddy thrust the chit at her with little hope of her agreeing. Then he noticed Bobbie next in line. 'All right then; Bobbie, how about you?' he wheedled.

Anger flared up out of nowhere. Bobbie forced herself to raise her head and look directly at him. She shook as she spoke. 'I don't take orders from you and nor does anyone else.'

Teddy breathed down his nose with a snorting sound. 'Bloody hell. It's coming to something when a bunch of women can order a bloke around.'

'What's the problem?' Douglas came out of the

met room into an atmosphere that he could have cut with a knife. Within seconds he'd assessed the situation and pinpointed Teddy as the cause. Angela quickly confirmed his suspicions.

'Flight Lieutenant Simpson isn't happy with the Dauntless,' she reported with a knowing look as Jean received her chit from Gillian.

'It's an insult,' Teddy muttered, waving his slip of paper in Douglas's face. 'I can handle any bloody plane the RAF asks me to – Lancasters, Stirlings, Liberators; you name it.'

'I don't want to hear it.' Douglas didn't flinch under Teddy's irate gaze. 'If you have a complaint, you'd better come into the office and put it in writing.'

'Oh, sod it!' If the old crock wanted to make a sodding point, then let him. So Teddy shoved the chit into his trouser pocket and stormed off.

By this time, Angela and Bobbie had received their orders for the day. 'Bristol and Walsall; oh, joy!' Angela declared as they went downstairs. Once at their lockers, she took out a small paper bag and handed it to Bobbie. 'Fox's Glacier Mints,' she explained. 'Suck a few on your way to Bristol. Keep up your energy.'

Bobbie thanked her. 'Did you post the letter?' she remembered to ask.

A single nod was the answer. 'Who's driving you home?' Angela enquired as they walked together towards Runway 2.

Bobbie checked the details on her form. 'Olive.'

'Same here. I expect she'll drive you from Bristol to Walsall then pick me up there.' Angela was pleased with the arrangement. 'You'll find me tucked away in a corner of the factory canteen, reading the latest Agatha Christie. Then we'll enjoy the drive home together.'

They parted with smiles: Angela to her damaged Spit, Bobbie to her Miles Magister. Meanwhile, Jean had lingered outside the ops room, waiting for a chance to speak with Douglas.

'There's no alternative,' he said to Gillian as he emerged from his office. 'Someone has to fly to Reading to pick Jean up to get her back in time to hop a Corsair over to Foxborough later today. No one else is available.' He noticed Jean at the top of the concrete stairs. 'You're stuck with me, I'm afraid.'

Jean glanced sideways through the glass hatch. A worried Gillian spread her palms and mouthed the words, *Say something*.

It nudged Jean towards the subject that she'd been fretting over. 'Do I gather you're planning to fly me back?' she asked Douglas.

'That's right. Look out for the Anson around midday.' A glance at Jean's face told him that something was amiss. 'What's the matter?' he asked more briskly than he'd intended.

With a slight shake of her head she led the way downstairs and out on to the lawn. 'Couldn't you send a driver instead?'

'I need you back quicker than that. Anyway, we don't have anyone.' He coughed to clear his throat. 'Jean, have I offended you? Please tell me if I have.'

'No,' she insisted. 'Believe me, you never would. It's just that I thought you'd be too busy.' At the last moment her courage failed her and she sidestepped the issue of Douglas's poor hearing.

'Never too busy for you,' he told her as he walked with her towards the runway. 'I hope you know that.'

'Yes.' This was obviously Douglas's way of breaking down the awkward barrier that had been raised between them. 'I appreciate that.'

'Until midday then.' He parted from her with one of his characteristic slight bows; a mixture of chivalry and military correctness.

It struck Jean like a lightning bolt as she stood at the edge of the runway that what was struggling to emerge between her and Douglas was love. All of a sudden, as she watched him walk away, taking in his broad shoulders and the curve of his head, she recognized what she felt. She thought of the green and red RAF dog tags that Douglas carried everywhere; his life story engraved on them. Then there was his low voice, his reticence, his bookish nature. Everything drew Jean to him and melted her heart.

How had this happened without her knowing? She'd imagined herself immune to romance, certainly when she'd mixed with callow recruits during training. But her feelings for Douglas had crept up on her and until this moment she hadn't seen them for what they were: a combination of respect and tenderness, a longing to know him better – all rolled together in what could only be described in the one word, 'love'.

With a fluttering heart Jean climbed with her parachute pack into her Spit. She'd settled into the cockpit and strapped herself in when Stan sprinted towards her.

'News from Northgate!' he yelled up at her before

the Merlin engine had time to build up enough revs to move forward. 'Gordon's ended up with two broken ribs. Young Harry wasn't so lucky. They dug the poor blighter out and rushed him off in an ambulance. He died before they got him to hospital.'

CHAPTER FIFTEEN

Mary's maiden flight over the Pennines went without
a hitch. The nerves that she'd experienced at take-
off soon vanished and she opened her mind to the
marvellous sights below: huge expanses of heather
moorland broken by rocky outcrops, with mill towns
nestling in green valleys, their tall chimneys visible
even at 2,000 feet, their steep rows of terraced
houses partly hidden beneath skeins of thick factory
smoke. Careful to pick out the triple landmark hills
of Pen-y-ghent, Ingleborough and Whernside, she
flew on in clear skies over the Lancashire border
past Pendle Hill and on towards her destination –
an RAF base outside the ancient county town of
Lancaster.

This was the only way to live, Mary decided: in
the moment and flying free as a bird, blissfully cut
off from the rest of the world. The powerful little
Spit was a demon of speed and manoeuvrability, the
most thrilling aircraft in the world, and she enjoyed
every second in the air, wanting it to last for ever.
But all too soon the end was in sight – three rough
airstrips running parallel on flat land close to the
coast, surrounded by the usual array of camouflaged

Nissen huts, single-storey military buildings and a prominent control tower. So Mary prepared for landing with a light touch on the joystick and an easing of the throttle as she pressed the overhead switch to bring down the undercarriage. The Spit's wings shuddered at her final approach but Mary held a steady course and touched down with scarcely a jolt; no last-minute drama, no slewing to the side on the smooth runway, no unnecessary burning of tyres on tarmac.

Two members of the RAF ground crew waited with the chocks as a smiling Mary cut off the engines, unstrapped her harness then raised the canopy. When she stepped out on to the wing and took off her helmet, the two men on the ground looked at her in amazement.

'Where's the pilot?' the older one asked, as if expecting a second person to emerge from the tiny cockpit.

Mary approached them, grinning broadly. 'It's me; I'm the pilot.'

'Blimey!' The sergeant mechanic still couldn't believe his eyes. 'Did you just land that crate by yourself?'

'Bloody brilliant.' The younger one ran up to congratulate her. 'You handled her just right.'

'Not bad for a woman,' the sergeant added grudgingly.

'Take no notice of the sarge – he still lives in the Dark Ages. I'm Archie, by the way.'

'Hello, Archie.' With his arm hooked through hers, Mary let herself be guided towards the control tower by her new friend. Her confidence soared to fresh heights as she followed him into an office at the base of the tower. 'Third Officer Holland bringing in the new Spit from Rixley,' she reported to the clerk at the desk as she handed over her chit.

'Sign here.' The brisk, bespectacled operations officer shoved a form at Mary without looking up. 'And here. And here.' He jabbed with the blunt end of his pencil at the necessary boxes.

'Now, it's time for a cuppa.' Archie held the door open for her and they left the office together. 'I say, Mary; no offence, but what's a nice girl like you . . . ?'

'Doing behind the controls of the latest Spitfire?' Mary gave a good-natured laugh. She felt wonderful – the best she'd ever felt in her whole life – and for once, she decided not to let any man's opinion bother her. 'No offence taken. I just follow orders, that's all.'

'Tea!' Archie said again. He was curly-haired and bright-eyed; one of life's breezy optimists. 'When I say "nice", I mean not stuck-up like some Atta girls I come across. You look a million dollars in that uniform, but I could tell the minute you opened your mouth that you were one of us.'

'I am,' Mary agreed as she followed Archie into the canteen. 'An ex-mill girl and proud of it. I'll have two big sugars in that tea, please.'

After Cameron had finished his meeting in Lancaster with a set of high-ups in the RAF, he made his way to the base where Mary had landed her Spitfire. A thought crossed his mind that Douglas's allocation of the latest model might have been a touch too ambitious for a first flight but he dismissed the doubt by recalling Mary's excellent record at Thame. *I'm damn sure she made it through without a hitch,* he told himself as he drove up to the sentries at the gate and announced the reason for his visit. The sentry checked Cameron's documents then signalled him through.

It was a large base for RAF squadrons that carried out operations over the Irish Sea and the Atlantic, so there was all manner of aircraft lined up beside the runways – a dozen twin-engine medium bombers alongside the bigger Lancasters and Stirlings. The smaller Hurricanes, Corsairs and Spitfires were gathered beside a second runway. It was an altogether magnificent sight. Cameron felt his chest swell with patriotic pride as he pulled up beside the control tower. How long would it be before his stint of duty at Rixley ended? Not long, he hoped. Like all pilots in the RAF, he badly wanted to get back to active service and engage with the enemy, or at least be in charge of training new recruits rather than filling in endless forms and carrying out disciplinary procedures for the ATA.

Stepping out of the car, Cameron straightened his jacket and adjusted his cap before knocking on an office door. As he entered he was pleasantly surprised to see an old acquaintance manning the desk. 'Well, if it isn't Laurence Craddock! How are you, Laurie, old chap?'

'Bloody hell, Cameron Ainslie!' As Laurence took off his glasses and stood up to shake Cameron's hand, it was obvious that his left arm hung uselessly at his side. 'Not too bad, except for this.' He poked the arm with his forefinger.

'What happened?' Cameron and Laurence had been in the same squadron at the start of the war and Cameron had always looked up to ace-pilot Craddock, who had chalked up eight kills and innumerable direct hits.

'I came off worst in a spat off the Italian coast. The docs told me I was lucky to keep the arm. They awarded me a DFC then kicked me off operations for good, worse luck.'

'I sympathize; I'm itching to get back in the air myself.' Cameron spent a few minutes with his old flying pal, exchanging stories and recalling better days. Then he explained the reason for his visit. 'I'm here to pick up one of our pilots.'

'The girl who landed the Spit?' Laurence had in fact paid more attention to Mary than he'd let on. He'd been impressed by her smooth landing and then rather taken aback by her broad Yorkshire accent when she'd handed over her chit. 'I wouldn't have thought she was your type, Cameron old son.'

His visitor's fair complexion turned bright red. 'Strictly business,' Cameron retorted. 'I was at a disciplinary briefing at Lancaster HQ so it made sense for me to drop by and pick her up.'

'Pull the other one,' Laurence teased. 'Not that I blame you. Third Officer Holland is easy on the eye, to say the least.' He'd noted Mary's large, wide-apart grey eyes, her trim figure set off by close-fitting trousers and bags of what he would call spirit.

Cameron's shrug was dismissive. 'What about you, Laurie? Did you tie the knot with the Land Army girl you used to knock about with?'

Laurence shook his head. 'Marjorie decided I

wasn't such a good bet after all. She got herself hitched to an able-bodied bloke in the Merchant Navy instead.'

'I'm sorry to hear that.'

'Don't be. I reckon I had a narrow escape.'

'Plenty more fish, eh?' Despite the forced bonhomie, Cameron found his old friend's situation disheartening. 'Anyway, I'd best be off. Any idea where I'll find my passenger?'

'Try the canteen – second building on the left as you go out.'

They shook hands again then Cameron followed Laurence's directions. He found the canteen deserted except for a woman behind the counter and Mary sitting alone at a table by the door.

She glanced up from her magazine with a triumphant grin but then her habitual shyness kicked in and she quickly dropped the smile.

Cameron hesitated. He seemed to have this effect on women: their faces went from sunshine to shade as soon as they saw him – all except Angela, whom he'd known since they were kids. Mary, in particular, brought the shutters down whenever he came near. 'Are you ready?' he asked in his formal, precise way.

Mary jumped up and followed him outside. She saw Archie and his surly sergeant running engine checks on the Spit that she'd delivered and returned Archie's cheery wave. Then she got into Cameron's car, predicting a long, silent drive across the Pennines, through the Yorkshire Dales and across the Wolds to Rixley. She was surprised when, not two minutes into the journey, Cameron made a foray into everyday conversation.

'Lucky for you the weather was perfect for your first flight.'

'Yes,' she answered quietly.

'It can change quickly at this time of year.'

'It can.'

'The forecast for tomorrow is rain.' Cameron persisted despite Mary's curt replies. 'Douglas won't send anyone out until it clears; they say around noon. You'll be able to have a lie-in.'

'That's good.'

He drove along a narrow road between well-maintained drystone walls. The massive bulk of Pendle Hill lay ahead of them, reminding him of a local legend he'd learned about in his youth. 'According to the history books, there were witches here in the olden days; in the early sixteen hundreds.'

'The Witches of Pendle.' Mary knew the story. 'The court found them guilty of witchcraft and hanged them.'

'They were a barbaric lot back then.' Relieved to have found a topic that interested her, Cameron went into more detail. 'I think it had something to do with two feuding families, each accusing the other. There was a living to be made out of casting spells, apparently, and neither family liked the competition. So they say.'

'So nothing to do with actual witchcraft?' Mary was amused.

'No; money was at the bottom of it. The feuding ran out of control and it ended up with the whole lot being brought before a judge. They all pleaded not guilty but it was too late. Eight were hanged.' Cameron slowed down at a fork in the road. 'Listen,

274

Mary; my family used to own a country house a mile or two from here so I know this area like the back of my hand. What do you say we stop off for a drink?'

'All right,' she agreed without thinking. 'Do you know a decent pub?'

'Just up here.' He took the narrower road that led towards the famous hill. He and Mary were making progress, it seemed. Still, it would be best to tread carefully.

'A *country* house?' she echoed. 'Does that mean you had one in the town, too?'

'In Liverpool. My old man made his pile in shipping insurance. That was the business to be in before the war.'

'Two houses.' The idea was unheard of in Mary's world and she fell quiet as they wound their way up a twisting lane.

'It's not as grand as it sounds. Anyway, those days are in the past. Dad had to sell both places once the effects of the war started to bite.' Cameron glanced sideways and saw that Mary had retreated into her shell. Luckily the Red Lion lay at the top of the hill, in the small village of Ketley. He pulled up outside the door then waited for her to get out. 'I'll be back in a jiffy,' he told her as he drove into the yard beside the pub. *Tread carefully*, he repeated to himself. *Find out what makes her tick.* For Cameron was more and more fascinated by Mary's apparent contradictions; by her mixture of fierce ambition and trembling insecurity and by the vulnerability he detected beneath the sometimes hostile exterior. *Maybe I've got it wrong*, he thought as he parked the car. *Perhaps I'm just not her type. Anyhow, let's find out.*

There was quite a view for Mary to take in as she stood by the door of the Red Lion, with Pendle looming behind and a long, open sweep of farmland below. The pub itself was an old building with narrow, mullioned windows, a shallow porch and an oak door. The sign above the porch showed a lion standing on its hind legs, wearing a crown.

'Let's hope Beryl has lit the fire,' Cameron said when he returned and held the door open for her to enter. 'It's turning chilly.'

'Beryl?' Mary queried.

'She's been the landlady here for as long as I can remember.' Sure enough, a log fire greeted them. It belched smoke across the empty room as the draught from the open door reached the flames. The smoke caught in the back of Mary's throat and made her cough as Cameron chose a table near the window.

Once Cameron had taken off his cap, the elderly woman behind the bar recognized him and bustled across. 'Look who it isn't!' she declared, wiping her hands on her apron before embracing him. 'You're a sight for sore eyes.'

Cameron extricated himself from the hug. 'Beryl, how are you? You're looking in the pink, as ever.'

'Not too bad,' she conceded, her grey eyes sparkling. She was a round woman with a huge bosom and apple cheeks whose movements were surprisingly light and sprightly. 'And how are Mr and Mrs Ainslie? Both well, I hope. Did you know that the people who bought your old house lost two sons in quick succession – one in North Africa, the other in the Far East? The mother hasn't left the house since, poor thing.' Beryl paused for breath then eyed Mary. 'And who is this young lady?'

'This is Mary Holland. She's a pilot with the ATA.'

'Never!' the landlady marvelled. 'You don't look old enough. But you and Cameron make a handsome pair, I must say.'

'Oh, no . . .' Mary began.

Cameron laughed awkwardly. 'Hold on, Beryl; I'm afraid you've got the wrong end of the stick.'

'Have I?' Undeterred, Beryl pressed ahead. 'I've got eyes in my head and they're telling me something different. You've got yourself a catch in this one,' she told Mary with theatrical confidentiality. 'Good-looking and clever with it; a real brainbox, in case you didn't know.'

'Honestly and truly,' Mary protested, her face burning, 'Flight Lieutenant Ainslie is driving me back to base, that's all.'

'If you say so. Now, Cameron, will it be your usual pint of best bitter? And you, Miss Mary; what can I get you?'

'Sorry about that,' Cameron muttered as Mary ordered a shandy and the landlady sailed off. He fixed his glasses more firmly on to the bridge of his nose then sat down with a worried frown. 'Beryl has a reputation for putting her foot in it, but she's harmless enough.'

'No need to apologize.' Perhaps stopping for a drink hadn't been such a good idea after all. Mary shifted uncomfortably on her chair then suddenly saw the funny side.

'What?' Cameron asked when he saw her smile.

The smile developed into a laugh. 'Your face; you

look as if you wish the ground would swallow you up.'

'I'm glad you find it funny.' He screwed his face into an even deeper frown. This was not going at all well.

Realizing that Cameron wasn't used to being laughed at, Mary made an effort to straighten her features. 'I'm sorry.'

Beryl was still busy behind the bar. 'Would you rather skip the drink?' he offered. 'If you like, I can pay up and we'll head straight off.'

'No; I'm happy to stay.'

'To celebrate your first official flight,' he agreed. When Mary smiled, her face changed completely. The shadows fled; she looked open and relaxed. 'Have you phoned home to share your good news?'

'No, Dad doesn't have a telephone in the house. And anyway he wouldn't be that bothered.' She spoke matter-of-factly. 'I'll write to my brother Tom and tell him. He'll be pleased as Punch for me.'

'Where's Tom?'

'In Tunisia, the last I heard.'

'When was that?'

'In June this year. He's not a great letter writer,' Mary added wistfully.

'No news is good news in this day and age,' Cameron reminded her. The rapid changes in Mary's mood continued to intrigue him: one moment laughing, the next drifting off into dreamy sadness. 'You have another brother, I seem to remember?'

Mary waited for the landlady to bring their drinks before replying. 'Frank – he's the black sheep. Don't ask.'

278

'Your mother?'

'She died a while back.'

'Mary, I'm sorry. I didn't mean to pry.'

Back behind the bar, Beryl stood with a satisfied smile, watching Cameron and Mary lean forward to talk as she wiped glasses and stacked them on a shelf.

'What about you?' Mary asked. 'Do you have any brothers?'

'No, I'm an only child.'

'I'll bet your mum spoiled you rotten.'

'Guilty as charged.' It was true; Cameron had formed only a hazy idea of how easy he'd had it until the lead-up to the war, when he'd joined a long queue inside a giant aircraft hangar to swear his oath of allegiance alongside hundreds of other would-be recruits. There were lads there from the back streets of Liverpool and Manchester, desperate to become wireless operators or gunners. All were rejected for not having gone beyond elementary standard in school. They trudged off, heads hanging – some swearing, some swaggering, saying they'd only applied for the sake of the uniform and free dental care. *Sod the RAF*, they'd said, *and getting shot to smithereens for one and six a day.*

It was still hard for Mary to picture Cameron's comfortable, cushioned life before the war. 'When did you leave home?' she asked.

'At eight.' He smiled at her shocked reaction. 'To go to prep school and then on from there to Rugby, then a year at Oxford before I volunteered.'

'How old are you now?'

'Twenty-three.'

'What was it like – leaving your family?'

'Hard,' he admitted. 'I wrote dozens of letters pleading to be allowed home: "Dearest Mother, I am very unhappy here. The big boys are bullies. The food is horrid and my bed is hard." With rotten spelling and smudged with tears. I'll never forget how lonely I felt that first term.'

'But you got used to it?'

'Eventually. I can't say I actually enjoyed it, though. But then no one likes their school, do they?'

'I did,' Mary countered. 'School was better than home for me. I loved arithmetic and composition. My teacher gave me books to read that took me out of myself for a while; *Just William* and *King Solomon's Mines* were my favourites, and *Black Beauty*.'

There she went, off on one of her journeys to a destination where it was impossible for him to follow, so Cameron quietly drank his beer and waited for her to come back.

'I had to leave school when I was fourteen to get a job – working in the local mill from seven in the morning until half five at night. I carried on reading, though, whenever I found time; I prefer history now – the Tudors and Stuarts.'

What seemed normal to Mary was strange to Cameron and vice versa, yet somehow learning about the differences brought them closer. He saw her in a new, brighter light that revealed the dreams underlying her words. 'I was once engaged to be married.' Out of the blue he told her something that few of his colleagues knew. 'To a girl at Oxford.'

Mary tilted her head to one side and gave him a sharp look. 'What was her name?'

'Valerie Martin. Her mother was a suffragette fighting for votes for women and she passed on the beliefs to her daughter. That's the reason I fell for her, I suppose. Equality between the sexes has always struck me as blindingly obvious. Valerie and I were too young, of course.'

'Who broke it off?' Mary had stopped noticing the nosy landlady or the sudden, heavy patter of raindrops against the window panes. Her drink stood on the table untouched.

'She did; sensible girl. I'm no good with women in general – perhaps you've noticed.'

'Why not? I mean, why are you no good?'

'I don't know. I suppose, like a lot of men, I find it hard to say what I feel. To me it's worse than pulling teeth.'

Mary smiled at the image. 'You expect us girls to know how you feel without you having to explain?'

'Yes. Women have more intuition.'

'In general?' she teased.

Cameron gave a self-deprecating laugh. 'Drink up,' he prompted. 'Otherwise we'll be here all day.'

So Mary downed her shandy and let the conversation drift along on a less personal level – the success that Angela's poster seemed to be having in recruiting more women into the ATA, the gaps in engine theory that Mary had noted in the course at Thame, the scandal of paying women pilots twenty per cent less than the men until as recently as May.

'We're paid the same now, thank goodness.' Mary stood up first and reached for her cap. 'It's just a pity that they still won't let women fly for your lot,' she concluded.

'For the RAF?' Cameron considered this one step too far. 'Personally I'm not for it,' he admitted with a swift wave of farewell to Beryl as they left the pub and hurried out to the car. 'I can't see women being prepared to drop bombs and fire machine guns willy-nilly. It doesn't seem natural.'

So much for equality between the sexes. Mary made a mental note. 'But it's all right to send us up without weapons or even a radio to our names,' she pointed out, turning up her collar against the rain. 'To make us sitting ducks.'

'Touché!' Always the gentleman, Cameron held open the door.

She had one foot inside the car and one hand on top of the door to steady herself when she paused and glanced at his face – smooth, unmarked skin, grey eyes with hazel specks, fair hair lifting straight back from his forehead.

Catching the moment, Cameron leaned forward and kissed her.

It was a brief, soft touch of lips but it changed everything.

'I hope you don't mind?' he murmured as he drew back.

She shook her head and kissed him again in the deep shadow of Pendle Hill, haunt of witches and their black magic spells. Mary and Cameron cast caution to the wind that gusted down from the high ridge and kissed a third time, arms locked around waist and neck, lips wet from the rain.

Bobbie had flown Magisters many times before. They were slow, two-seater trainer aircraft: monoplanes with a fixed undercarriage and an open cockpit, lumbering old crates made out of spruce and plywood that were to be avoided if possible. Today, however, Bobbie scarcely cared what she flew.

Open to the elements, she sat at the controls hoping that it wouldn't rain. The wind was bad enough, gusting in from the north-west and doing its best to push the Maggie off course. Her destination was the ferry pool at Whitchurch and she observed the various landmarks with a weary familiarity, only paying proper attention when the glistening waters of the Bristol Channel and her journey's end finally came into view. 'Thank the Lord!' she said with a sigh as she began her descent. 'The sooner this is over the better.' She'd lowered her revs and was keeping an eye on the altimeter when, out of nowhere, an aircraft sporting the RAF insignia shot at high speed at right angles across her bow with a single Jerry in hot pursuit.

Suddenly Bobbie was fully alert. She recognized the two outlines at once: a DH80 Mosquito and a Focke-Wulf, one of the best piston fighters that the Germans had. She watched in horror as the Focke pilot released a hail of bullets at the Mosquito, which banked then increased height steeply before performing a rapid loop and coming back at Jerry, his own guns blazing.

The action was too close for comfort, Bobbie realized, and the Maggie was notoriously slow to respond. At this rate, she was in danger of being caught in the crossfire. So she descended more steeply and felt a sudden lurch in the pit of her stomach. Again the two fighter planes crossed her path, guns going at full blast and bullets strafing through the air as they dipped below her. To her horror, the Focke gained on the Mosquito and scored a direct hit on the RAF man's tail fin and fuselage. Bobbie watched the Mosquito stall then struggle on in the direction of the coast while the German pilot eased off, seemingly content to observe his stricken enemy rapidly lose height. There was no choice for the RAF man: as his Mosquito plummeted in a plume of blue smoke, he was forced to eject. She prayed that he would make a clean exit and sure enough, his parachute opened – pure white against the bright blue sky – which left Bobbie and her Maggie at Jerry's mercy.

The Focke pilot turned. He came at full speed directly towards her, reserving his fire until he was close enough for Bobbie to see the head and shoulders of the helmeted figure at the controls. He fired wide then, with split-second timing, he banked to starboard, the wing tips of the two planes almost touching.

Jerry was toying with her – and enjoying it. As he gained height, Bobbie followed her only course of action, which was to continue her descent, hoping that he wouldn't come at her again once she flew within range of ground-defence gunners. Gripping the joystick and with the ferry pool runway now clearly visible, she fought to hold her nerve.

The gunners on the ground reacted as she'd hoped. They let rip at the Focke, holding him off as she approached the airstrip. But he made one last attempt; roaring at her from above and behind and firing furiously before overtaking her and ascending almost vertically out of reach of British fire. Bobbie heard his bullets rip through her port wing. The tip of the plywood frame splintered with a loud crack, throwing her off balance as she went in for landing. She stamped on the rudder pedals. At 300 feet she was still in control. The green landing strip blurred beneath her, and she skimmed the tree tops then landed with a thud and a strong thrust backwards in her seat, squealing to a halt.

Bobbie slumped against her harness, head spinning, unable to believe that she'd survived the attack. Ground crew came running but she stayed in the cockpit. Her fingers refused to cooperate as she fumbled with buckles and when she did release the harness, her head fell forward and hit the control panel. For a few seconds she was knocked unconscious and when she came round she felt hands helping her and saw two faces at close quarters, too blurred for her to make out.

'Take it easy,' a voice said as Bobbie tried to fight the men off.

'She's taken a knock to the head,' someone else said as he pulled Bobbie upright. 'Blimey, she's light as a feather.'

'Careful; she's bleeding. Steady now; we'll lift you out.'

Bobbie was too weak to push them away. She felt herself being raised from the cockpit then lowered and placed gently on the ground. The sun blinded her when she tried to open her eyes.

'What's your name, love?' one of the blurred faces asked as he attempted to unzip her suit.

She tried to answer but could only groan.

'Someone, fetch a medic.'

'Does anyone know first aid? Don't move her.'

'That was a damned close shave.'

A babble of voices surrounded Bobbie. Only dimly aware that she'd managed to land her plane, she lay on the ground without moving. Blood trickled from her temple and she wondered why she couldn't raise her head or move her hands. She groaned again and gave in. What would be would be.

Olive sat in her car at Whitchurch watching planes come and go. She'd parked by the control tower to wait for Bobbie and was busy filling in a cross-word puzzle when the action started. She heard the sudden rattle of gunfire and looked up to witness a fierce dogfight between a lone Focke and a Mosquito, going at it hammer and tongs while an unarmed, yellow Magister was caught helplessly in the crossfire. At first Olive concentrated on the two fighter planes but then it occurred to her that the unlucky third pilot might, in fact, be Bobbie.

With a knot forming in her stomach, Olive opened her door and stepped out of the car for a better view. As the fighters banked and looped the loop, firing furiously, she saw the Mosquito come off worst. The pilot bailed safely, thank heavens, but that left the Maggie at Jerry's mercy. Olive crossed her fingers, hardly daring to breathe but relieved to see the gunners in two bunkers at the edge of the airfield spring into action to drive the Focke away. The end result: one lost plane and a damaged Magister. Could the pilot bring it limping in? Olive set off at a run towards the runway where it aimed to land.

'Take it easy,' a mechanic said to the pilot as Olive

reached the scene and saw in a moment that her fears were realized. It was indeed Bobbie who lay semi-conscious on the ground, a small figure with her sandy hair fanned out around her head.

'She's taken a knock to the forehead.'

'Steady now; we'll lift you out.'

Four men had climbed on to the wing and raised Bobbie out of the Maggie's cockpit as Olive pushed her way through.

'What's your name, love?' someone was asking the injured pilot.

'Her name's Bobbie Fraser,' Olive said as she came to Bobbie's side. First aid was called for. 'I know first aid,' Olive said. 'That's the way; try not to move her in case she's broken something. Bobbie, it's me – Olive. Can you hear me?'

Bobbie sucked in a long, jagged breath and tried to raise her hand while Olive took out a clean cotton handkerchief, folded it into a pad and pressed it against the gash on Bobbie's forehead. 'Someone, fetch water,' she instructed. 'Grasp my hand,' she told Bobbie as she tested her reactions. 'That's good; now the other one.'

Slowly Bobbie opened her eyes. When she was able to focus she recognized Olive and gripped her hand more firmly.

'Good. Do you think you can sit up?'

'I'll try,' Bobbie breathed. Her head hurt like billy-o and she felt terribly weak.

By this time a second woman was on the scene, working with Olive to raise the patient. 'Third Officer Betty Cooper,' she muttered by way of introduction. 'I qualified as a nurse before I joined the ATA.'

Together Betty and Olive sat Bobbie up. Betty quickly replaced the blood-soaked hankie with a thick pad of lint, which she secured with a sticking plaster.

'Will it need stitches?' Olive wondered.

'Probably not,' Betty replied. 'The cut's not deep. It's the concussion we have to worry about.'

'I'm all right,' Bobbie said faintly as she made an effort to stand up but her legs failed to cooperate.

'Says you,' Olive remarked.

'Here; we'll carry her.' Two of the men who had been first on the scene gently lifted Bobbie under instruction from Betty and carried her off the runway.

'What time is it?' Bobbie whispered to Olive as she slowly made sense of what was happening. 'Are we in time to drive to Walsall?'

'Never mind about that.' As the panic subsided, Olive began to plan ahead. 'Let's get you sorted out first.'

The men took Bobbie to the first-aid station then hung around outside the door with Olive while Betty cleaned the wound and applied a dressing.

'She was bloody lucky, excuse my French.' One of the men offered Olive a cigarette, which she refused. 'I thought she was going to crash into those trees.'

'Luck had nothing to do with it; Bobbie is one of our best pilots,' Olive argued. 'I'm proud of her, if you must know.'

In the short time that Olive had been at Rixley she'd got a fly-on-the-wall measure of most of the female ATA pilots. She'd liked Jean from the start and just lately Mary had earned her grudging

288

respect. But it had taken her longer to warm to Angela and Bobbie. Olive and Angela were obviously chalk and cheese – worlds apart in every way – while Bobbie had seemed wet behind the ears, with an annoying childlike quality when it came to men. Despite that, Olive had to take her hat off to both women: they were daredevils in the air and willing to face any risk to get their planes from one ferry pool to the next.

Before long, Betty and Bobbie emerged from the first-aid room. 'No broken bones,' Betty reported briskly. 'Still some dizziness but no nausea, and the bleeding has stopped. I'd say she was fit to carry on.'

'I'll keep an eye on her,' Olive promised. Walsall was three hours away so it would be dark before they got there.

'Don't do anything strenuous for the next day or two,' Betty instructed Bobbie as she handed her over to Olive.

'I'm fine,' Bobbie asserted. 'Honestly, I don't want any fuss.' She thanked everyone who'd rushed to her rescue then refused Olive's help into the front passenger seat. With a backward glance at the Maggie listing to portside on the runway, she sighed then looked straight ahead.

'Sit back and take it easy.' Olive started the engine then eased the car towards the exit. 'By the way, I'm sorry I was offhand with you the other morning.'

'Were you?' Bobbie couldn't remember.

'Yes, when you borrowed my clothes. I was a bit hasty: too quick to judge.'

'Apology accepted.' Bobbie looked down at her hands. Her head throbbed and she wasn't fine, not really. Her chest was tight and her pulse raced. She could have died up there; been snuffed out like a candle. And what would it all have been for? *For King and country*, she tried to remind herself. *That's what I'm meant to think.*

Only it hadn't felt like that when she'd come face to face with the Focke pilot. Beneath his helmet and behind his goggles there was a young man more or less the same age as Bobbie, with a mother and father to mourn him if his plane went down – a boy-killer with death in his heart. *It shouldn't be this way,* Bobbie thought as she rested her head against the seat. *War is madness when all's said and done.*

CHAPTER SIXTEEN

Jean reached Reading without incident. She'd spent much of the short flight coming to terms with the news of Harry Wood's death, picturing the grief that his parents must suffer and reflecting on how everyone at Rixley would miss him. Such loss was sewn into the fabric of warfare, along with heroic feats on the ground, at sea and in the air. All families in the kingdom were affected, all friends and colleagues left saddened and diminished by these events.

No doubt the Rixley crew would eventually hear from Gordon details of the bombing raid on Northgate. Jean hoped that Harry hadn't suffered too much, had perhaps been knocked unconscious at the time of the blast and had never come round. Tears welled up when she remembered his unmarked, eager, nineteen-year-old face.

Having made her usual textbook landing and handed over her Spit without fuss to the ground crew, Jean's mood was subdued as she walked to the canteen to wait for Douglas. *Ah, Douglas!* The name was enough to conjure up the storm of emotions that she'd kept at bay until the moment earlier that day when she'd stood with him by the pilots' hatch and he'd said in his halting way that he would never do anything to offend her. She remembered their earlier kiss in the lounge at Burton Grange and the leap of joy in her heart then the uncertainty afterwards, when Douglas had acted so coolly towards her. *Have I got this right?* she asked herself as she sat and stared out at the usual ferry pool activity – Amazons towing aircraft into position on runways, ground crew running hither and thither, pilots reporting in and signing off at the ops room. *I know I care for Douglas, but does he care for me?*

Doubt was a state of mind that Jean hadn't had much practice in dealing with. She liked to be in control, to plan a course through life and stick to it. It seemed that love scuppered such resolve; threw you off balance in a situation where there were no rudder pedals or joystick to correct the steering or adjust the altitude. It was like blind flying without instruments to guide you.

Does he care for me? she wondered again. *And how shall I find out?*

She studied the sky for signs of Douglas's Anson. A Lancaster roared down the runway and took off, followed by two Hurricanes. A plane circled high overhead, waiting for the approach to clear. Could this be her taxi-plane?

Another doubt darted into her head: shouldn't she have tackled the thorny topic of Douglas's poor hearing as Gillian had suggested? *Yes, I should,* she told herself firmly. Then, *Yes, I will – soon!*

Once the sky was clear, the circling plane made its approach. As Jean had suspected, it was the Anson, with Douglas at the controls. She watched anxiously and was relieved to see the pilot crank down the undercarriage and land his aircraft smoothly and without a hitch. Perhaps Gillian had been wrong, after all.

As the propellers of the old reconnaissance aircraft slowed, Douglas unstrapped his harness and peered out through the square windshield. No wonder the damned thing was mostly used as a training aircraft these days. It had taken almost 150 cranks of the handle to lower the undercarriage – an exhausting process that had left him out of breath. The aircraft had been all right in its day, with space for a bomb-aimer to lie prone in the nose section, with the pilot in his cockpit behind and two folding canvas seats to the rear for a wireless operator and a navigator. But these days the RAF demanded more speed and manoeuvrability of its front-line bombers. 'You're like me, old girl,' Douglas muttered as he hitched his lame leg towards the exit door. 'Practically on the scrap heap.'

'Stay where you are,' Jean called from the runway. She'd left the canteen as soon as she'd been sure that it was Douglas's plane. 'I've already signed us out to save you the bother. We can head straight off.'

So Douglas resumed his seat, restarted the engines and waited for Jean to climb aboard. She chose a fold-up seat directly behind him.

Hitching her parachute pack on to a hook beside her seat, she leaned forward to tap him on the shoulder.

He turned to find her face close to his.

She smiled and kissed him on the cheek. 'I'm glad to see you,' she whispered.

He gasped at the touch of her warm lips on his cold skin. Then he smiled back. 'You're wonderful, Jean; did you know that?'

'You're not so bad yourself.' She settled into her seat then strapped herself in. 'Go right ahead, First Officer Thornton; we're cleared for take-off.'

'Harry Wood was a grand lad.' Inside Number 1 hangar at Rixley, Stan tossed a spanner towards the replacement mechanic, a seventeen-year-old cadet named Bob Cross from the Air Training Corps. 'You'll have all-on to fill his shoes.'

Bob reached out to catch the spanner like a cricketer fielding a difficult catch. He'd arrived at Rixley on the Tuesday following the Northgate raid. Despite a raw enthusiasm and an eagerness to prove himself, the sallow-faced, dark-haired lad found that he hadn't exactly been welcomed with open arms. 'I'll do my best, sir,' he assured Stan on the Thursday following his arrival.

'Your best might not be good enough,' Stan growled. 'Pass me that wrench.'

The newcomer stared at a bewildering row of tools set out on Stan's workbench. 'Which one?'

Stan continued to lean over the nose cone of the Hurricane that was in for repair. Seemingly he had eyes in the back of his head. 'Not that one; the big one next to it,' he muttered impatiently.

Bob rushed to oblige in a pair of overalls hanging at half-mast from his lanky frame.

'Poor sod.' Mary stood with Jean at the entrance to the hangar, looking out at a downpour as they listened in on the bad-tempered exchanges between

Stan and his hapless new apprentice. The two women were at ease, arms folded and leaning against the hangar door.

'Stan's still upset about Harry and who can blame him?' It was half past eight and Jean and the other pilots had just learned that low cloud would prevent them from flying until after eleven. 'We all are. What happened in Northgate has put everyone on edge.'

'Have you heard the rumours that are doing the rounds?' Mary went on. She was especially disappointed by the delay on this, her fourth day of flying. 'They say that Jerry has Rixley in his sights again.'

'They always say that.' The drumming of rain on the metal roof of the hangar was a depressing sound but Jean tried to make the best of things.

'Yes, but that doesn't mean it's not true. Cameron mentioned that Hilary is taking the threat seriously this time.' *Ah, Cameron!* Since Monday Mary had spent three evenings on the trot with him, either walking in the grounds of the Grange or sitting quietly in the Fox and Hounds. He'd been quite open about their blossoming romance whilst Mary, true to form, had felt it was wise to be more circumspect. *Wait and see*, she'd told herself. *If it all goes wrong between us, the fewer people who know about it the better.* 'Of course, fingers crossed the rumours could still be wrong.'

'Yes; let's hope so.' Jean glanced up and saw no break in the clouds. 'I'm thinking of making a run for it,' she decided. 'Are you coming?'

So they sprinted for the canteen where they found Angela also at a loose end.

'How's Bobbie's head?' Mary asked as she pushed wet strands of hair back from her face and noticed that the room was full of disgruntled, thwarted crew. The windows were steamed up and once more the rain pelted loudly on the roof.

'Mending slowly but surely.' All week Angela had taken meals to Bobbie's room and run around doing her laundry and other chores while the patient recovered. Only that morning she'd changed the dressing on Bobbie's forehead and seen for herself that the cut was healing well. But Bobbie's mood was still low and Angela had been unable to coax her out of her room. 'Jean, you are such a dark horse,' she began on a different tack.

The accusation startled Jean into thinking of Douglas. 'Why? What have I done now?'

'You're wearing your new flight captain stripes.' Angela patted the three shiny gold stripes on Jean's sleeve. 'Why didn't you share the good news?'

'Congratulations!' Mary cried as Jean blushed.

'Actually, a little bird did inform me.' Angela was in one of her teasing moods; her way of overcoming the boredom of not being allowed to fly. 'A little bird who happens to be sweet on you, as a matter of fact.'

'Angela, please!' Desperate for her to keep her voice down before she named Douglas, Jean tried to slide away from the counter with her mug of tea.

'A little bird whose name begins with S.'

'S?' Jean stopped short.

'Yes; don't look so surprised. I mean Stan Green; who else?' Realizing by the look of puzzlement then dismay on Jean's face that she'd overstepped the mark, Angela quickly backed down. 'Darling, it's none of my business. I'm sorry.'

Mary's eyes opened wide. Could it be true that Stan was keen on Jean? He'd never mentioned anything, but now that Mary considered the possibility she thought there might be something in it. It was a nice enough idea if it turned out to be correct.

'You're quite wrong.' Jean gathered her dignity and prepared to walk away. 'That's all I have to say on the matter.'

'Drat!' Angela grimaced at Jean's elegant back view then cast a sideways glance at Mary. 'Me and my big mouth!'

That evening, after a frustrating afternoon of trying to get as many planes as possible off the ground, Douglas joined Jean in the officers' mess at the Grange.

'You look tired,' she commiserated. 'Let me get you a drink.'

'No need; George will bring one across, and one for you too.' He settled in the easy chair opposite, making the most of the new, relaxed atmosphere between himself and Jean. One kiss of greeting had been all it took to break his resolution to step back. 'I took the liberty; I hope you don't mind.'

'Not at all.' Jean stifled the urge to lean over and hug him; that would have to wait until the next time they found themselves alone – hopefully tomorrow evening when they planned to visit Gordon in the military hospital in Foxborough. 'Tired and worried,' she added.

'I am, a little,' Douglas admitted.

'What about?'

'The usual.' Their whiskys arrived and the room began to fill up. Horace had just come in with Agnes and Fred and the trio went to join Angela and Teddy at the bar.

Angela's choice of a simple but striking white blouse and wide black slacks teamed with a red gypsy bandana made her the centre of attention as usual, Jean noticed.

Douglas followed the direction of Jean's gaze. 'Angela puts on a good show; I'll say that for her.'

'How do you mean?'

'You'd never guess that she's recently had a bad row with her father over staying with the ATA.' Douglas preferred not to go into too many details, though he'd heard them from Hilary. 'I admire her for standing up to the old man. She has integrity, whatever else people say.' The whisky warmed him as it slid down his gullet. 'Which is more than can be said for our friend over there.'

Jean picked out Teddy from the group. He was casually dressed in an open-necked shirt and cravat, with a tweed jacket, brown trousers and brogues. 'Has he been up to his old tricks again?'

'No; I put a permanent stop to that. You remember I hinted that there was something more serious?' Their renewed intimacy prompted Douglas to take Jean into his confidence. 'Hilary has an official file on his desk dated August this year. It has Teddy's name on the front. The form inside had the look of a court martial document, though I can't be sure.'

'Good Lord! Can an RAF pilot be court martialled for stealing petrol?' Jean took a guess at what the file might contain.

'No, that would bring a simple reprimand from his squadron leader, unless he put someone else in danger or harmed someone by it. That's a possibility, I suppose.'

They sat in silence, gazing across at Teddy who entertained the others with a tall story. He had one hand around Agnes's shoulder but was paying more attention to gorgeous, vivacious Angela, while Horace and Fred stayed quietly in the background. There was much smiling and laughter as Teddy rounded off the tale and more drinks were ordered.

When Teddy noticed that Jean and Douglas were staring at him, he broke away and sauntered across with his glass. 'Now then, you two – mind if I join you?' he queried jauntily.

'Come again?' Douglas failed to catch what Teddy said.

Teddy grinned and took a swig from his glass. 'Never mind; I can see that three's a crowd.' With a wink at Jean he wandered on through the door and into the hall.

'Did you see that?' Jean was incensed. 'Teddy Simpson just winked at me. What a cheek!'

'Ignore him,' Douglas said. Jean when angry was quite something. He was fascinated by the colour rising in her cheeks and the flash of fire in her grey eyes. 'Let's talk about something more pleasant. 'What do you say we make a night of it tomorrow after we've visited Gordon in the hospital?'

Teddy continued to smile as he went up two flights of stairs to his attic room. *High time to pay Bobbie a little visit*, he thought.

After Saturday night he'd deliberately played things cool and the tactic seemed to have paid off. People's memories were mercifully short, so that Bobbie's appearance half-naked at the edge of Burton Wood was already almost forgotten. There'd been a temporary setback for Teddy when Cameron had investigated the mystery of who had lit the log fire in the grooms' quarters, but that fuss had also soon died away. Then a major reprieve had come about on Monday after Bobbie's close encounter with the Focke. The head wound that she'd sustained had kept her in her room ever since.

Teddy whistled as he rummaged in his bottom drawer and found a slim square packet wrapped in cellophane. He tucked it in his jacket pocket, checked his reflection in his shaving mirror, adjusted a stray lock of hair then descended the stairs.

'Knock-knock!' He stood outside Bobbie's room and tapped on the door. Without waiting for an answer, he went in. 'How's the patient?' he asked cheerily.

Sitting in a cane chair by the window, Bobbie gasped. She was dressed in pink silk pyjamas and sat curled up with her feet tucked under her and a book on her lap. Her wavy hair was tied back by a white ribbon to keep it clear of the large dressing on her forehead.

'I've brought you a present to cheer you up.' As Teddy strolled across the room, he pulled out the cellophane packet and placed it on her open book. 'A pair of stockings,' he explained. 'I guessed your shoe size at four and a half; I hope that's near enough.'

Bobbie stared at the shiny wrapping. With a shaking hand she whisked the slim packet on to the floor. 'Get out,' she hissed.

'Don't be like that.' Teddy stooped to pick it up. 'I came to find out how you were, that's all.'

'I said, get out!' He leaned over her, close enough for her to smell the whisky on his breath; the same smell as when he'd kissed her and pressed her down on to the mattress. 'Get out or else I'll call for help.'

Teddy ignored her, perching on the low window sill and stretching out his legs. He tossed the nylons on to Bobbie's dressing table then, folding his arms, he leaned back against the cold window pane. 'Everyone's downstairs in the bar. No one will hear you.'

Bobbie leapt up and ran frantically for the door, only to find that Teddy had beaten her to it.

He gripped the door knob. 'Calm down, Bobbie. I thought you'd be pleased to see me.'

She groaned, tried to prise his fingers from the knob then gave up and retreated to the window. 'What do you want?'

'I told you: to see how you are and to give you a present. What could possibly be wrong with that?'

'I don't want you here. Please leave.' She stared at him with a mixture of fury and fear.

'Bobbie,' he crooned, still standing between her and the door but advancing slowly towards her, 'whatever is the matter? What is it that I'm supposed to have done wrong?'

'Don't come any nearer,' she warned.

Teddy stopped in the middle of the worn Axminster rug, taking his time to gaze around the room at Bobbie's hairbrush on the dressing table, next to a

301

gold powder compact and a tube of lipstick. 'This is the after-effect of Monday's near miss,' he surmised. 'Believe me; shock can do this to a person. It's made you jumpy for no reason.'

'Believe you!' Bobbie echoed. Her whole body was shaking with anger now; how dare Teddy come in without being invited? How dare he look at her things and judge her?

'Yes,' he insisted in a low voice. 'Just hear me out.'

She backed away until she reached the window. 'No; why should I?'

'Listen to me,' he pleaded. 'About Saturday night; I gather you may have got the wrong end of the stick.'

Bobbie groaned again then put her hands over her ears.

'We were having such a good time at the Spa Ballroom, remember? Come on now; you can't deny it.'

Bobbie let her hands drop to her side. Palm trees and a piano, a crush of twirling bodies, Teddy's hand on her back as they waltzed. Smiling, laughing.

'There; you see. And after the first few dances, we bumped into Jean and Douglas, which threw a dampener on things for a while but at least we wangled a lift home out of it.'

Drinks at the bar, a band playing. A ride home on the back seat of Douglas's Ford – Bobbie had no trouble remembering this. Still she kept herself pressed against the window, watching Teddy warily.

'Douglas drives like an old-age pensioner, so we didn't reach home until after midnight. We both breathed a sigh of relief when we said goodnight and watched him and Jean disappear into the house.'

A dark night with thick cloud covering the moon. The cobbled stable yard. Tottering in high heels up stone steps. Where? Why?

'It was late but neither of us was ready to turn in.' Teddy took two cautious steps forward. 'We went for a walk. You were cold.'

A black sky. Tottering and shaking. A silver flask with a drink that burned her throat. Flames flickering. Teddy's voice, his face, with eyes that didn't reflect what his voice was telling her. 'No.' Bobbie warned him not to come any closer.

'Right you are. I promise I won't lay a finger on you. I only want to find out why you're so on edge.'

'I don't . . . I didn't . . .' Particles of memory collapsed like soot falling down a chimney, blackening everything in the hearth below.

'You were cold so I lit a fire,' Teddy reminded her. 'You never gave me any sign that you weren't willing.' He went carefully, studying her reaction, watching her eyelids flicker, hearing her broken intake of breath. 'If you had, I would have stopped straight away.'

Bobbie shook her head. 'I don't . . .' *Remember*.

'I would never hurt you; you know that?'

Slowly she nodded.

'I took care of you, Bobbie. It's obviously a bit of a blur to you at the moment but afterwards I made sure you got safely back to your room and so on.'

A black layer of guilt covered events that could never be washed away. No memory of her room but of trees, wind and wandering barefoot until dawn.

'You believe me, don't you?' Teddy waited and when Bobbie didn't reply, he decided to take a calculated risk. 'Ask Douglas if you can't recall the exact details. He was here when we came back to the house; he definitely saw me take you up to your room.'

'Douglas saw us?' She closed her eyes and slumped forward, wilting under the burden of fresh shame.

'Don't worry; Douglas is unshockable. He's seen it all before.'

'Go away – please!' Bobbie breathed. She felt for the chair and sank down.

Teddy judged that he'd done enough for the time being. 'I can see you're tired,' he sympathized. 'Can I get you anything?'

'No. Please just go.'

He smiled and nodded. 'I'll leave your stockings there on the dressing table.'

Bobbie didn't reply. She closed her eyes and felt she would be sick. Opening them again at the click of the closing door, she gulped in air, forced back tears and then leaned sideways to press her burning cheek against the smooth, black window pane. In all her life she had never felt so alone.

CHAPTER SEVENTEEN

'It's a poor show, Angela.' Hilary spoke his mind on the Friday evening as they walked home together through Burton Wood. (Later, as he sat by the library fire quietly nursing a brandy and reflecting on their conversation, he saw that he'd gone about things the wrong way.) 'Lionel says in his last letter to me that you've broken off with him without waiting to hear his opinion on the row between you and your father.'

Angela whisked a hazel wand through some bushes to the side of the path. 'It's true; I've released him from our engagement,' she confirmed.

'Without hearing what the poor chap has to say,' Hilary repeated. 'That was rather heartless of you.'

Angela's heart jumped and skipped. 'Oh, you know me,' she quipped, 'I'm like the Tin Man in *The Wizard of Oz*: the girl who has no heart.'

Hilary ignored the flippant remark. 'Lionel is a thoroughly decent fellow. There's no doubt in my mind that he would have stood by you.' He wished that Angela would throw the stick away. The sound of it whistling through the air and rattling through the bushes irritated him.

'That wasn't the point. The truth is that Lionel would have been made a pariah in our set if he'd married beneath him. You know that as well as I do.'

'You're wrong,' Hilary insisted, taking her hand and pulling her to a halt. 'Times are changing. People no longer care who marries whom.'

'Lionel's parents would care; my father would make sure of that.' Angela hid her anger behind a loud sigh. 'I know you mean well, Hilary, and you care a great deal about Lionel. But you must trust me in this; how would we have managed if Lionel's family had followed suit?'

'You mean, if they'd disowned him too?' Hilary silently questioned this version of events. He thought Angela exaggerated as usual.

She tugged free then walked ahead. 'At least now you acknowledge what Pa has done – cast me off and so forth.'

'I know; he wrote to me to tell me as much.' Hilary had received a short letter from Joseph Browne that had condemned Angela for disobedience and had blackened her character, using words such as hotheaded, undisciplined and unfit to serve.

Hilary had been sickened by it and had written a brief reply explaining that he could bring no influence to bear on Angela's decision to remain with the ATA and that in fact she was one of his best officers and could in no way be criticized over her ability as a pilot. He was sorry that Mr Browne held such a low opinion of his daughter and hoped that time would improve the situation – *Yours most sincerely*, et cetera.

'So now you see what I'm up against.' Angela slowed down then walked in step with Hilary. 'People say that Pa and I are too alike: both stubborn as mules and unable to see the other's point of view. That used to infuriate me but now I suspect there may be something in it.'

'No.' Hilary sprang loyally to her defence. 'You lack his ruthless streak. You mostly think well of people and have a kind heart. That's why your break with Lionel has surprised me.'

Angela stopped at the edge of the woods. 'You think I was cruel?' The word brought tears to her eyes.

'Yes, you've left the poor chap heartbroken.'

She nodded. 'For a while, yes. And I'm desperately sorry for that. But, Hilary, you don't know everything that went on between Lionel and me.'

Hilary stared down at the sodden leaves underfoot. It was perfectly true: he'd dedicated himself one hundred per cent to his career at the expense of any meaningful relationship with a member of the fairer sex. 'Go ahead – enlighten me.'

'For a start, I suspect that Lionel only loved me for the way I look and not for the way I think and act. I would soon have proved a disappointment to him as a wife and – God forbid – as a mother. Worst of all, I suspect that I said yes on an impulse because I didn't want to hurt him.'

'I see.' Hilary raised his gaze and looked across the grounds at the bomb-damaged Grange.

'What would you have done in my place?' she murmured as they both stared straight ahead.

'The same,' he acknowledged after a long pause. Walls crumbled, roofs collapsed, the world turned on its head. 'To be completely honest with you, Angela, from what you've just told me, I may well have done exactly what you have decided to do.'

'Spoilsport!' Horace called after Angela who was making an early departure from the Grange bar that same evening. He sat at the card table with Agnes and Fred. 'We need our fourth player.'

Angela paused at the door. 'Sorry, darling – I can't stop yawning. It's time for me to hit the hay.'

Truth to tell, she was bored without Bobbie. The mess had been unusually quiet all evening – no Hilary or Cameron, and no sign of Douglas, Jean or Mary either. As for Teddy: he'd pestered her to hop on the back of his blessed motorbike and ride to Highcliff with him, an invitation that she'd turned down flat. So now, at ten o'clock on what should have been a fun-filled Friday night, Angela was heading for bed.

However, as she passed Bobbie's door, she had second thoughts. A cup of Horlicks and a chat with her best pal might be just the ticket. So she knocked and waited. There was silence from inside so Angela knocked again. Eventually the door opened.

'Angela,' Bobbie said in a small, flat voice. She had removed her lint dressing and the inch-long gash on her forehead stood out darkly against her pale skin. She wore pyjamas under a white candlewick dressing-gown.

'Yes, it's me. Were you expecting someone else; a gentleman caller, perhaps?'

'No.' Colour crept into Bobbie's cheeks.

'I'm teasing, silly. Will you come down to the kitchen with me for a mug of Horlicks?' Expecting a yes, Angela was already on her way to collect the jar from her room when Bobbie called her back.

'I can't,' she told her. 'I'm not dressed.'

'Who cares? Anyway, we can easily sneak down the back stairs.' Angela sensed a deeper reason behind Bobbie's reluctance. 'We can skip the Horlicks if you'd rather. Let's settle down here for a cosy chat instead.' Slipping past Bobbie, she crossed the room and settled into the cane chair by the window. 'Ooh, nylons!' she exclaimed when she saw the packet on the dressing table. 'Lucky you – I've used up all my clothing coupons and don't have a single pair to my name.'

'Take them,' Bobbie said tensely.

'Darling, I couldn't possibly. Don't you need them yourself?' Angela sprang up and fingered the smooth cellophane wrapping. 'American Tan,' she said with an envious sigh.

'Take them,' Bobbie repeated. She hadn't been able to touch the damned things since Teddy had left them there.

'If you're sure? I'll take them with me after we've had our chat.' Angela sat Bobbie down in the chair she'd vacated then drew up the dressing-table stool to sit facing her. 'I have some good news,' she went on, leaning forward to touch Bobbie's knee. 'Hilary has written a letter of support to Pa, backing my decision to carry on flying. That was decent of him, don't you think?'

'Yes, and you deserve it,' Bobbie told her. 'Have you heard back from Lionel?'

'Not yet. You know how things are – he may have written but his letter could be held up in a sorting office in Athens or Gib or Timbuctoo – anywhere at all. I'll be lucky if it arrives before Christmas.' Angela gave a wistful smile. 'But then, Lionel might never write to me again, and who could blame him?' There was a pause before she steered the conversation in a new direction. 'So tell me, Bobbie dear, when are you going to stop hibernating and come out and have some fun with your chum?'

'Soon,' Bobbie promised unconvincingly.

'On Sunday, then? I have the day off. We could brush away the cobwebs with a walk around the reservoir if you feel up to it.'

Bobbie stared down at her hands. The idea of running into Teddy made them start to shake. And worse; she would also have to face Douglas, Jean and Mary, not to mention Olive and Stan once she was well enough to return to duty. She swallowed hard and shook her head.

'Hmm.' Angela paused to consider her next move. 'Darling, I'm worried about you. Are you putting things off for a reason? Is it the close shave with Jerry – has it put you into a blue funk?'

Bobbie remembered all over again the sound of wood splintering, the stomach-churning lurch of the Magister as it keeled over to starboard, the fight to bring it in to land. 'None of it makes sense,' she murmured. 'Do you happen to know, did our RAF man make it home all right?'

'I believe he did.' Angela grasped Bobbie's shaking hands and looked into her eyes. 'You'll come through this, you know. You've done it before.'

Bobbie fought back tears. 'Don't be kind to me,' she pleaded. 'It'll make me cry.'

Angela dug into her pocket for a handkerchief. 'Feel free. And remember what an enormous help you were to me at Fenton Royal and how much lighter I felt after we'd had our talk. Now it's my turn; why not let me be the shoulder for you to cry on?'

'It's not the dogfight,' Bobbie confessed as she took the handkerchief and twisted it between her fingers. 'I'm not bothered about that.'

'What then?'

'It's Teddy.' Saying his name created a hole in the dam that Bobbie had built up during the past week. Her feelings flooded through in a murky, foaming wave. Guilt, shame and self-loathing broke over her head.

'Oh dear, what's he done now? Woe betide him if he's upset you.'

'He gave me the stockings.' Bobbie dropped the handkerchief and covered her face with her hands.

'Bobbie, I don't understand. Why should a gift make you cry?'

'He came into my room without being invited.'

Angela tutted. 'That's not on for a start. Would you like me to have a stern word on your behalf?'

'No!' Panic clutched at Bobbie's throat as she struggled to her feet. Her hands began to tingle as her chest tightened and her heart beat at an alarming speed. 'Don't say anything – please!'

'Dear girl, what is it?' This didn't add up. Why should such a small thing send Bobbie into a tail spin? 'There's more, isn't there?'

'I can't tell you – I'm trying my best but I can't.' Struggling to breathe and to stand upright, Bobbie collapsed again into the chair.

Angela knelt beside her. 'What did Teddy do to you?' she asked calmly. This was something grave that needed careful handling.

'I don't know.' Bobbie's wail floated up into the carved cornices, into every frayed and faded corner of the room. Her heart carried on racing. 'That's just it; I can't remember.'

'Dear, dear girl.' Placing her hands over Bobbie's, Angela waited.

'It's a blur.' Sobs shook Bobbie's slight frame. 'I went to Northgate with him.'

'That must have been last Saturday,' Angela guessed. 'Take a few deep breaths. There's no need to hurry.'

'We danced. I wore my green dress. I was happy he'd asked me.'

'Hush; I know that you liked him because you told me so.' Angela patted Bobbie's hands and felt anxiety form a tight knot in her stomach. 'But, dearest girl, I did warn you that Teddy Simpson wasn't for you; don't you remember?'

'He kissed me.' Bobbie went on as if she hadn't heard. 'One night when our trains were delayed; where was it?'

'Harkness,' Angela remembered.

'Yes. I thought he cared for me. He made me think so.' Hunching her shoulders, Bobbie snatched her hands away then folded her arms around her stomach.

'On Saturday, you danced with Teddy and then what happened?' Angela was still set on a steady course to find out exactly what had happened.

'Douglas brought us home.' *Home, James, and don't spare the horses.* A starless sky, thick night, head swimming as the car eased round bends in the road, Teddy's arm around her shoulder. A dark gap of lost time. Can I trust you? More blackness. The flare of a lighter flame, the burn of strong drink in her throat. Blackness again. Bobbie wept as she tried to explain.

'Where?' Angela asked tenderly. 'Where were you when something bad happened?'

Bobbie shook her head helplessly. 'I came round when it was light. Harry found me at the edge of Burton Wood without my clothes. Mary brought me home. I washed and scrubbed my skin until it was red raw. What must they think?' she wailed again.

A dreadful picture formed in Angela's mind. 'Listen to me; this is important. Did Teddy give you a lot to drink?'

Bobbie nodded mutely.

'Did you pass out?'

'Perhaps; I don't know.'

'Listen again; did Teddy force you into doing something that you didn't want to do?'

Bobbie glanced up at Angela with a look of dark despair. 'I think he did,' she whispered in a broken voice before the wave of guilt and shame struck again.

With mounting fury Angela went back over what she'd heard. 'Bobbie, think hard. Do you know what became of your clothes?'

A shake of the head was all the answer Bobbie gave. Then she clutched Angela's arm. 'Don't tell anyone,' she pleaded. 'You won't, will you? I couldn't bear it if people knew what I'd done.'

'You didn't do anything,' Angela insisted in a bid to lift the guilt from Bobbie's shoulders. 'Teddy did.'

'But he'll deny it.' He'd knocked on her door and come swaggering into her room as if nothing bad had happened. 'And people will believe him.'

'Who?' Angela demanded. She stood up and paced the room in exasperation. 'Who would believe Teddy Simpson over you?'

'There would be gossip.' Bobbie sighed. 'They'd say there was no smoke without fire. And for all I know they'd be right.' The gaps in Bobbie's memory were dark holes down which she repeatedly tumbled. 'And what proof do I have? It's simply his version against mine.'

'That's the reason I asked you about your clothes.' Angela came to a halt by the dressing table. 'They might provide us with the proof – if your dress were torn or . . .' Bobbie's shudder prevented Angela from finishing her sentence. 'What exactly were you wearing?' she asked instead.

'My black cape and my green chiffon dress.'

'I know the one. Which shoes?' Angela went to Bobbie's wardrobe to find out for herself. 'Was it your black patent pair?'

Drying her tears, Bobbie pulled herself back from the brink. 'What difference does it make?'

Angela turned to her with a frown. 'Your clothes can't have vanished into thin air,' she insisted. 'If we can track them down it might be a first step towards proving what Teddy did to you that night.'

'No.' For the first time Bobbie's head was up and her voice was stronger. 'I'd rather we didn't. I don't want you to rummage around looking for so-called proof or say a word to anyone. You must promise.'

'But if we don't do something, Teddy will get off scot-free.' Angela spoke through gritted teeth.

'I know but you have to promise,' Bobbie said again. She'd worn her most revealing dress for Teddy and danced with him cheek to cheek.

No. Lie still, don't put up a fight. No. You'll like it. Lie still.

She'd led him on.

'All right.' Angela muttered her agreement.

She sat with Bobbie until midnight, talking not of Teddy or of the dogfight in the air or of her own split from Lionel. They spoke of Jean's progress up the ranks and clever Mary's skill in the air. Angela told Bobbie about Stan's soft spot for Jean (don't say a word) and Cameron's for Mary (who would have seen that coming?) until fear slowly dissolved from the room.

As the clock on Bobbie's dressing table ticked on towards half past the hour, Angela at last felt it was safe to leave. 'You'll come down to breakfast tomorrow?' she asked gently as she stood by the open door.

'I'll try.'

'And on Sunday, perhaps we'll take that walk by the reservoir?'

'Perhaps.' The door closed. Bobbie spotted the untouched packet of nylons. 'Angela, you forgot the . . .' Her voice faded and she stayed where she was, in the chair by the window.

Angela strode on into her room then flung herself down on her bed. She stared up at the ceiling, feeling anger boil inside her. How dare Teddy take advantage – of Bobbie of all people? Angela longed to slap the smug smile off his face and make him pay. But her hands were tied because a promise was a promise.

She lay awake and fully dressed, finding patterns in the cracks in the ceiling – the shape of a bear's head, a fork of lightning. There must be another way to bring Bobbie's persecutor to account. What about playing Teddy at his own game – how would that work? Angela thought for a long time until the glimmer of an idea appeared.

'It's decent of you to drop by.' Gordon lay flat on his back in his hospital bed. He smiled wanly at Douglas and Jean as they drew chairs up to his bedside. 'The doc won't let me out until Monday, then he says I'll have to take it easy for a week or two.'

Jean took a small bar of milk chocolate from her handbag and placed it on his locker. 'Make it last,' she told him with mock sternness. 'And don't go giving it all away.'

The Foxborough hospital ward contained a dozen injured servicemen; six beds to either side, all occupied by patients sporting bandages or plaster casts, some attached to drips, one whose face had been badly burned. As Douglas chatted with Gordon, Jean tried not to stare at the casualty directly opposite: a lad of seventeen or eighteen, barely conscious, whose legs were protected by a wire cage that raised the blankets to form a hutch-shaped hump. She was shocked when she caught a glimpse of the boy's face: the blood-stained gauze dressing had slipped to reveal two damaged eye sockets and deep gashes across forehead and cheeks.

'We're missing you at Rixley,' Douglas told Gordon.

'Aye; how's Stan coping?' Gordon's ribs hurt when he moved. The pain made him wince as he shifted position.

'He's doing his best. There's a new lad called Bob Cross to help him.'

'I don't envy him; I bet Stan's giving him a hard time?'

'He is,' Douglas acknowledged with a smile. 'He says he's not a patch on poor Harry.'

Gordon nodded then pressed his lips together. When he spoke again he made an effort to seem philosophical. 'Harry was in the wrong place at the wrong time,' he told them without prompting. 'It was quick – over in a flash. He never knew what hit him.'

'That's a blessing,' Jean said softly.

'It is. We were walking through Low Northgate, minding our own business. Harry's mother lives on Valley Crescent. That's where we were headed – to visit her. There's a park at the bottom of the hill – so nowhere to take shelter when Jerry dropped his bombs – in the dark, out of nowhere; boom!'

Douglas listened quietly as Jean tried in vain to control the shiver that ran through her.

'I stayed rooted to the spot. Harry made a run for it towards the White Deer Hotel. Mine was the right decision as it turns out. Poor kid; he didn't make it out of the park.'

Douglas shook his head sadly. 'What a waste.'

'His mother came to see me yesterday. I told her the truth; Harry wouldn't have suffered, thank God.' Gordon leaned his head wearily against his pillow. 'She was grateful for that. It does make you wonder what it's all for, though.'

'But you have to ask yourself: what's the alternative?' Douglas's voice was firm and steady. 'If we hadn't made a stand when Hitler went into Poland, where would we all be?'

There was no answer to this and a gloomy silence descended until a nurse bustled into the ward. 'Time's up,' she announced to Douglas and Jean who were the only visitors. The nurse was starched in appearance and professional in manner; pristine white cap and apron, black stockings and shoes, with neat, dark brown hair beneath the cap. 'I'm sorry; you'll have to leave,' she said in her high, prim voice.

So they said their goodbyes in sober mood. 'Ta very much for coming,' Gordon murmured as Douglas shook his hand.

Jean glanced again at the blinded boy. She shuddered a second time and was glad when Douglas took her hand to walk down the long corridor, out into a clear, starry night. Then, instead of driving straight back to the Grange, he suggested finding a quiet corner where they could sit and have a drink.

'Unless you're too tired?' he asked hesitantly.

'No; I'd like that. But not here in Northgate.' With her nerves already stretched to breaking point by the hospital visit, she knew that seeing the bomb damage in the town centre would prove a final straw.

So Douglas drove her out of town and they soon found themselves surrounded by rolling farmland – a patchwork of small fields visible in the moonlight, rising to high, open moorland broken by outcrops of dark rock. Eventually they came to a village with a stone cross at its centre and rows of cottages facing on to the cobbled marketplace. Douglas drew up under an inn sign showing the silhouette of a black horse against a white background. 'Will this do?' he said.

Jean nodded. With Harry still at the forefront of her mind, she waited in the entrance to the pub while Douglas parked the car then joined her. 'Let me buy the drinks,' she offered then, without waiting for a reply, she went up to the bar and ordered two whiskys. With a determined expression she took them to the small table by the fire that Douglas had chosen and sat down opposite.

He watched her warily, leaving his drink untouched. 'What are you up to, Flight Captain Dobson?'

'What do you mean? Can't a girl buy the drinks if she feels like it?'

Douglas frowned. 'I don't mean that. But why do I get the idea that you're about to give me a good talking-to?'

'Well spotted,' she replied, leaning across to rest her hand on his. It was now or never but she must tread gingerly. 'Douglas, you must know by now that I care a great deal about you.'

He felt his stomach churn. *You must know that I care about you, but you must also see that we make a very odd couple. You're much too old for me for a start ...* 'Stop.' He withdrew his hand. 'I can guess what you're about to say.'

She reached out again. 'No, you can't. Just listen for a moment. It struck me the other day that I care about you more than I've ever cared for any man.'

'Honestly?' How could he believe her? There was the age difference and his hopelessness with women and his damned limp, all conspiring against him.

'Yes, it's true.'

'How can it be?' The patched-up leg and the loss of face when they'd chucked him out of the RAF, the self-conscious, awkward schoolboy still lurking deep in his psyche, manifesting in everything he said and did. 'The world's your oyster, Jean. You're wonderful. Why ever would you choose me?'

'Because I did.' The fire had brought a flush to Jean's pale cheeks and its light glowed in her fair hair. 'It crept up on me without me realizing. No, that's not quite right. I looked up to you from the start.'

The hammering of Douglas's heart made him short of breath. Admiration wasn't love. There was still room for her to backtrack. *We can't be lovers but I hope we can be friends.*

Seeing the uncertainty in his eyes, Jean paused. Then she thought again of Harry and the fickleness of Fate. '"Care" isn't a big enough word,' she went on slowly. 'I knew that when we first kissed – in the lounge at the Grange. Since then you've always been in my mind. Even when I'm flying or when I'm sitting quietly trying to read, it turns out that it's you I'm thinking of.'

Douglas shook his head in disbelief. 'My dear girl.'

'Don't shake your head,' she pleaded. 'You don't even have to tell me that you feel the same way; just let me get through this and say what I have to say.'

'I love you.' Suddenly he grasped her hand. 'I do.'

'And I love you,' she whispered slowly, against the crackle and spit of logs burning in the grate and the hum of conversation in the background.

Douglas saw the movement of her lips, only half-hearing what she said. Jean was to be his after all.

Her hair glowed gold, one half of her face was in shadow.

'To us,' she said, lifting her glass with the warmest of smiles. They chinked glasses then drank their whisky. 'And now you must make me a promise,' Jean went on.

'Anything.' He would climb a mountain, give up everything he owned, cross an ocean, defend her to his last breath – now that he was certain that she loved him.

'Before you take up another plane, please go and see a doctor about your hearing.' She saw his eyes narrow and his head jerk backwards. 'I know that's the last thing you expected. But I'm serious. I want an expert to examine you.'

'There's no need,' he began. Then he stopped. 'What makes you say that?'

'Because it's not safe for you to fly if you can't hear the plane's engines.'

'And why do you think I'm having trouble hearing?'

'I've watched you. It's obvious; to me and to other people as well. Oh, Douglas – please don't be angry.'

'I'm not.' Settling back in his chair, he sat with a furrowed brow. 'I just don't acknowledge that it should be a problem. These old Ansons and Maggies; I've flown them for years. I can practically do it in my sleep.'

Jean waited. She'd said enough and now it was up to him.

'I keep a careful eye on the rev counter and if the engines do stall and I begin to lose height, my reactions are still quick enough to get me out of trouble.'

Picking up his drink, Douglas swirled the dregs around the bottom of the glass. 'Anyway, it's only once in a blue moon.'

Jean looked steadily at him and said nothing.

'I do get a ringing and a clicking in my ears,' he admitted at last. 'Tinnitus; a lot of RAF chaps I know get it. The docs tell them it's something you have to try to ignore. And you soon learn to lip-read – that helps.'

'Douglas,' she breathed, 'see a doctor. Do it for me.'

He thought hard then nodded slowly. 'I will; when I can find the time.'

'Soon.' Jean sighed with relief. She loved this man for trusting her and for not being angry. Her heart swelled with tenderness as she gazed at his face, vulnerable in the firelight. 'And please keep both feet firmly on the ground until you do.'

CHAPTER EIGHTEEN

'All credit to Mr Churchill,' Jean declared as she and Mary set off briskly on Sunday morning to walk around the reservoir. Their friendship was developing nicely, each gravitating towards the other once they realized how much they had in common. They were warmly dressed in thick socks, scarves, berets and jumpers and had set off straight after breakfast at Jean's suggestion. 'I hear on the wireless that he's pressing for General Chiang to sign up to fight against the Japs.'

Mary too had listened to the report. 'The prime minister and Mr Roosevelt will manage it between them,' she agreed. 'We're due some good news in amongst our ships being sunk off Brittany and what with the dockers deciding to go on strike.'

Jean was determined to look at the positives. 'We've got the Italians with us now, don't forget. And I'm sure we're building up to something very big – if not this year, then next. Douglas and Hilary say we're likely to be busier than ever, coming up to Christmas.'

Mary didn't see how she and her fellow ATA pilots could work any harder. She herself had moved three planes out of Rixley in a single day – short hops admittedly but they'd left her hardly knowing whether she was coming or going. On each occasion she'd again impressed the ground crews at the airfields where she'd landed and her confidence was soaring. She'd even thought of volunteering to work today if Douglas needed her but Stan had wagged his finger and advised Mary to take a day off while she had the chance. 'No one will thank you for spreading yourself too thin,' he'd told her. 'It's Sunday tomorrow; have a lie-in, write a few letters and do a spot of ironing . . .'

Mary had laughed and told him that she'd rather be behind the controls of an aircraft any day. But she'd taken his advice and now here she was, striding out with Jean, with the grey, glassy reservoir stretching before them. Ducks flew low and landed on the water with a splash, while leaves fell and mud squelched underfoot.

'Talking of First Officer Douglas Thornton . . . I didn't know what to make of him for long enough,' Mary admitted as they reached a fork in the footpath. The water was to their right and to their left there was an ancient, ivy-covered manor house – apparently still lived in to judge by a goat tethered to a post in the overgrown front garden and by three or four red hens pecking at the gravel by a side door. 'I considered him stand-offish.'

'Douglas?' Jean's face coloured up and she blustered her way through. 'Oh, he's fine once you get to know him.'

Mary reacted to Jean's blushes. 'Oh, crikey! Did I put my foot in it?' Choosing the path close to the water's edge, she forged ahead.

'Not at all. And yes, Douglas is a good friend, in case you were wondering.' Jean followed in single file, looking out across the reservoir to the hills beyond and discovering the freedom to be frank with Mary. 'More than a good friend, as a matter of fact.'

'You don't say?' Mary stopped and turned, causing Jean to almost bump into her.

'Yes; what's wrong with that?'

'Nothing. Nothing at all.' A smile creased Mary's smooth features. Jean and Douglas made a fine if unexpected couple. But then she spared a thought for poor, lovelorn Stan and her face grew more serious. 'I'm happy for you,' she said with an effort. 'Does anyone else know?'

'I don't think so. I wasn't sure myself until Friday. You're the first person I've told.'

'Ah, then I'm honoured.' Mary turned and walked on, swishing through wet ferns to either side of the narrow path. After a while she spoke again. 'Jean, do you mind if I ask your advice?'

'Fire away. But if it's about revs per minute and maximum altitudes, I doubt that you need any. I'm sure you know as much as I do about engines and so forth.'

'It's about Cameron.' Mary walked steadily on. The wind off the water and the spiralling leaves gave her a similar willingness to share confidences. 'I don't know why but he's taken me under his wing.'

Jean suppressed a smile. 'Yes, I had noticed, along with everyone else at the Grange.'

It was Mary's turn to blush. 'We're chalk and cheese, though.'

'In what way?'

'Our families and such like.'

'That's true.' Though Jean didn't know much about Mary's background, she'd assumed that there hadn't been a penny to spare when she'd been growing up.

'I'm not ashamed of where I come from,' Mary insisted untruthfully. 'But the thing is, Cameron wouldn't have a clue about what my life was like.' She thought of the shared privy in the back courtyard, the sound of clogs traipsing down the street at seven in the morning, of her father coming home drunk from the pub.

'Does it matter?' Jean got straight to the point. 'Cameron is no snob, I can guarantee.'

Mary slowed down to clamber over a fallen tree. 'It's caught me by surprise, that's all. I'm wondering what to do about it.'

'Do you have to do anything, if Cameron has been making the running?'

'That's true,' Mary said slowly. Evening drinks with fellow officers at the Grange had ended in moonlit walks – just the two of them. Professional exchanges about flying routes had led to arrangements to meet whenever possible – for a snatched cup of tea in the canteen or when Cameron had gone out of his way to pick Mary up from a destination ferry pool. 'You don't have to put yourself out,' Mary had protested. 'I can easily get the train back.' 'I don't have to but I want to,' Cameron had insisted. Events were moving swiftly and Mary felt swept along.

'But I hope I'm not giving him the wrong impression,' she said now.

'In what way?' Jean was quick to compare Mary's situation with her own. 'No, no need to explain; I think I know what you mean. But honestly, you don't strike me as the type to play games.'

'Thank you.' Mary felt reassured. 'I do like Cameron, but it's early days and I'm not sure where it's leading – or where I want it to go.'

'Then tell him that.' Jean swung one leg over the fallen tree and sat astride it. 'Say exactly what you've said to me. He'll understand.'

'It won't put him off?'

'I doubt it.' Jean slung the other leg over the smooth grey trunk. 'I've seen the way he looks at you, Mary. Cameron is smitten, believe you me.'

'Look who it isn't!' Teddy ran down the steps into the stable yard to intercept Angela and Bobbie. 'Where are you two girls off to this fine morning?'

Instinctively Angela stepped between him and Bobbie. Her face gave nothing away as she answered him. 'We fancied a breath of fresh air, didn't we, Bobbie? How about you? Are you going for a spin?'

'Sadly, no. Hilary collared me over breakfast. He wants me to check through some paperwork with him, worse luck.' Teddy's words gave the smug impression that he'd become indispensable to Rixley's commanding officer. He side-stepped Angela and stood face to face with Bobbie. 'Hello there. It's good to see you out and about at long last.'

She blinked and took a step back.

'I've been worried about you,' Teddy insisted as he took in Bobbie's waiflike appearance. Despite several layers of thick woollen clothing, it looked as if the slightest breeze would blow her clean away. 'We all have: me, Hilary, Douglas – everyone's wondering how soon you'll be able to report for duty; not too long now, by the look of things.'

Bobbie summoned the presence of mind to return his gaze. Here he was, smiling at her, standing hands in pockets, pretending he cared. 'I've asked Douglas to put me back on tomorrow's rota,' she said with a nervous frown.

'Champion. And I hope that means we'll see more of you in the evenings in the weeks to come. Life has been dull without you.'

Bobbie threw Angela a panicky look.

'Give the girl a chance.' Giving Bobbie a quick, meaningful glance, Angela shouldered her way between them again. 'Anyway, consider my feelings well and truly hurt, Flight Lieutenant Simpson.'

He responded with a careless laugh. 'Why? What did I say?'

What did the look mean? Bobbie wondered. Why was Angela flirting with Teddy in spite of Bobbie's revelation?

Angela would explain later. Meanwhile, she went ahead with the charade. 'That life has been dull without Bobbie. I've been trying my very best to keep you entertained, and all the while you were secretly pining away.'

Raising his hands in surrender and grinning, Teddy backed away. 'Ladies, please; no squabbling over me.'

'Don't flatter yourself.' With an arch look and a sudden switch of mood, Angela whirled Bobbie away, linking arms and guiding her out under the clock tower. 'Hush,' she whispered. 'Don't look back. Let Teddy Simpson draw whatever conclusion he wishes.'

By coincidence, Bobbie and Angela's planned route took them in Mary and Jean's footsteps around the reservoir. They walked slowly between the bare trees, stopping for Bobbie to catch her breath by the rusty iron gate that led to the crumbling manor house. From here they gazed out over the flat expanse of water towards a long, straight dam at the far side.

'Let's hope Jerry never scores a direct hit on yonder dam,' Angela remarked. Despite her light-hearted manner, war was seldom far from her thoughts, however peaceful the scene. Feeling a sudden, hard shove against her back, she turned in alarm to see a black goat with curved horns and green eyes peering over the garden wall and thrusting its nose at her. The creature had apparently broken free from its tether and was preparing to cause mayhem. 'Oh, no you don't!' she cried as it gripped one corner of her red silk scarf between its teeth. She tugged hard but the goat refused to yield.

'Satan, let go!' An old woman came out of the door and hobbled towards them, stout walking stick in hand. She thwacked the stick against the goat's bony hind quarters, which only served to infuriate it and make it tighten its grip.

Bobbie flashed a look of astonishment at Angela. The old woman could have stepped straight out of *Hansel and Gretel*, with her hooked nose and hunched shoulders, wispy white hair and long, checked skirt. A second thwack missed its mark and the stick whistled close to Angela's ear.

Time to beat a hasty retreat. In danger of being strangled, Angela loosened the scarf from around her neck and watched Satan bound off across the garden with it in its mouth. 'That scarf came from Harrods,' she complained.

'The goat doesn't care where you bought it,' the old woman observed phlegmatically, 'as long as it tastes good.'

Which it obviously did. Angela and Bobbie watched the goat drop the scarf to the ground then gobble it up.

'Is its name really Satan?' Bobbie's eyes were wide.

'Aye – devil by name, devil by nature.' Resting on her stick, the goat's owner wondered aloud how she would recapture the miscreant. 'I'll never catch him by myself.'

'Why not let us . . . ?' Bobbie began.

'Absolutely not!' Angela hissed from behind her hand.

'It'll have to wait until Jeremiah gets home.' Unbothered by the prospect, the old woman shuffled off towards the door through which she'd emerged.

'Jeremiah?' Bobbie's jaw dropped. 'What mother would name her baby after the weeping prophet from the Old Testament?'

'Yes; I expect this one's a bundle of joy, too.' Angela chuckled then shivered as she set off along the path through the wood. 'Brrr; I'm feeling a wee bit chilly.'

Are you feeling chilly? Totally without warning Teddy's voice filled Bobbie's head and the dread came rushing back. *Chilly.*

There's a stove in the corner, he'd said. The room had been dark, cold and empty, with furniture stacked to one side. There had been stone steps leading up to it and skylights in the roof.

'Angela,' Bobbie whispered.

'What is it?' Angela turned to wait.

'I've remembered where Teddy and I were when it happened.'

Mary and Jean had followed the footpath across the top of the dam and were completing their circuit of the reservoir when they came across Angela and Bobbie.

Bobbie was sitting on the ground with her head in her hands while Angela crouched beside her.

Jean was the first to react. 'What's happened?' she asked as she ran towards them. 'Did Bobbie fall?'

Angela put up a warning hand. 'No, no. Stand back; she'll be all right in a minute or two.'

Seconds later Mary arrived to hear Bobbie sobbing her heart out.

'She's all right,' Angela insisted for a second time.

Mary refused to be fobbed off. 'Why is Bobbie crying?'

'It's private, darling. Please don't make a fuss.'

Ignoring Angela, Mary squatted down and put her arm around Bobbie's heaving shoulders. 'Carry on,' she encouraged softly. 'Don't mind us.'

Recognizing Mary's voice, Bobbie rested her weight against her. Shafts of light filtered between her fingers. Darkness slowly lifted. *Are you feeling chilly?* Teddy had lit a fire and dragged a mattress across the room. Bobbie had sunk to her knees.

As Bobbie remembered more details, Jean led Angela to a safe distance. 'What's going on? Who's upset her?' she demanded.

'I promised not to say.' Through Bobbie's sobs, before Jean and Mary had turned up, Angela had learned some vital new facts. The assault had happened in the grooms' quarters above the stables. Teddy had used force. The haunted look on Bobbie's face as she'd revealed these things would stay with Angela for a long time.

'I understand.' Jean knew not to press for more and turned her attention to the practical problem of getting Bobbie safely home. 'She's not injured?'

'No, but I doubt that she has the energy to walk.'

'Then we'll carry her,' Jean decided. But then again; the old house was nearby. Perhaps they could ask there for help.

Angela guessed by the direction of Jean's gaze what she was thinking and shook her head. 'We'll wait a while,' she insisted. 'There are only so many tears a girl can cry.'

Kneeling beside Bobbie and hugging her tight, Mary thought back to last Sunday morning when Bobbie had materialized at the edge of Burton Wood in only her petticoat. No one knew what had led to this; all they knew was that Bobbie had been in a daze and had to be given clothes and taken back to the Grange. Mary remembered standing at the bathroom door and hearing Bobbie cry, scrub and cry, scrub again. 'Hush,' she said now. 'We're all here. No one's going to hurt you.'

'I can't break my promise.' Angela's voice was strained as she and Jean continued to talk in rapid whispers. Anger against Teddy surged through her veins. 'But Bobbie has told me all I need to know and I swear the person responsible will not get away with this.'

'Hush.' Mary rocked Bobbie backwards and forwards. 'You're safe now.'

The darkness lifted and Bobbie saw once again Teddy's face, heard his voice, tasted his whisky, felt herself trying to push him away. She looked up at Mary through her tears. 'Safe?'

'Yes. Tell me all about it if you can.'

Bobbie lowered her head and hid her face behind her hands. 'I thought I'd dreamed it but I hadn't. It was real and it was partly my fault.'

'How could it be?' Mary pictured Bobbie standing in her underthings at the edge of the wood, her face as pale as death, with not a clue as to how she'd got there.

'I let myself down, I did things . . . He said I let him.'

'Men say that.' Take Frank, Mary's black-sheep brother; that was exactly what he'd said about fifteen-year-old Molly Carson: 'She let me. She wanted to.' 'Where are your witnesses?' the constable had asked Molly's father when he'd stormed to the police station to accuse his feckless, ne'er-do-well neighbour. No witness, so no trial before a jury, the constable had said. But the next day Arthur Carson and his two sons had cornered Frank in a dark alleyway and thrashed him. They'd warned him never to show his face in the town again. It was rough justice, but justice nevertheless. 'Who are we talking about?' she asked Bobbie. 'Who's "he"?'

'This is Teddy Simpson's fault!' Jean spoke angrily and broke away from Angela. She saw it all in an instant: how Teddy had romanced Bobbie by whirling her around the dance floor in Northgate then sitting with her in the back seat of Douglas's car, how he'd whisked her off from the stable yard for a moonlit walk in Burton Wood. 'Bobbie, why didn't you say something?'

Angela hurried after Jean and pulled her away. 'It's worse than you think,' she began to explain. 'Teddy plied her with drink.'

Mary helped Bobbie to her feet. 'Teddy said you let him but that's not true,' she continued softly. 'He never gave you any choice.'

Jean looked in alarm at Angela. The word for what Teddy had done to Bobbie stuck in her throat and almost made her choke. 'He forced himself on her?'

Angela nodded in acknowledgement. 'I'm afraid that's right.'

'This is not your fault.' Mary spelt it out slowly for Bobbie. 'You didn't imagine it. Teddy planned to do it all along.'

'He got you drunk on purpose,' Angela added. 'My poor dear girl; do you understand?'

Bobbie struggled to breathe. She tilted her head and stared up through the branches of the beech trees, saw black rooks sail across white clouds. On the morning after, she'd come to her senses and found herself alone and without her clothes. Teddy had vanished. The last thing she'd been aware of before she'd passed out the night before had been his weight on her, pressing her down and the word 'no' on her lips. 'I had to run away,' she whispered.

Mary, Angela and Jean gathered round to shield her from the wind. There were more tears, friends' hands holding her up, soft words spoken.

'I didn't know what else to do so I ran away,' Bobbie repeated. 'I was scared that Teddy would come back and find me – that's why.'

Douglas waited until all the chits were issued before he called in a favour from Harold Inman, an old friend currently working as a consultant at the King Edward Hospital in Highcliff. 'Can the test be arranged on the q.t.?' he asked over the phone. 'Wednesday afternoon, you say? Thank you, old son; I'm much obliged.' Douglas carefully replaced the receiver in its cradle.

'Happy now?' he asked Jean who stood in the office with her chit in her hand.

'Wednesday,' she repeated. 'Will your friend carry out the test himself?'

'No, I expect it'll be his registrar. Harold will look at the results then give me the bad news in person.' Shuffling his papers into a tidy pile, Douglas cleared his throat as the door behind Jean clicked open and Gillian entered the room.

When Douglas's secretary exchanged glances with Jean, she understood that Jean had done the dreaded deed. 'Stan said to tell you that your Spit is ready and waiting for you on Runway Two,' she reported with a sympathetic smile as she took her seat behind her desk. 'And, sir, the met-room boys are right this minute heading to the canteen for a cuppa if you care to join them.'

Jean ran down the steps with a sense of relief. The

news from the doctors might not be all bad, she told herself. Perhaps the damage was temporary, or if not, perhaps wearing hearing aids would allow Douglas to carry on flying. *Hope for the best*, she told herself. Picking up her parachute pack from the bench beneath the control tower, she sprinted towards her plane – the last pilot to take off on this clear-sky Monday morning.

'Better late than never,' Stan grumbled as he and Bob kicked away the chocks. The youngster didn't look where he was going so backed straight into Jean as she was about to vault up on to the Spit's wing.

'Ouch; my foot!' She wiggled her squashed toes inside her fur-lined boot.

'Sorry . . . I didn't mean . . . sorry!' The lanky lad offered garbled apologies before scurrying off towards the nearest hangar.

Stan offered Jean a hand to get up into the cockpit. 'Nitwit,' he muttered about his assistant.

Jean shook her head. 'Don't blame Bob – I was in too much of a hurry.' With one foot on the wing, she hesitated. 'Douglas and I went to see Gordon on Friday,' she mentioned as casually as she could. Ever since Angela had teased her about an admirer whose name began with an 'S', Jean had been keen to clear the air between herself and Stan but hadn't been sure how to go about it. Now, however, she realized that she'd much rather Stan heard the news from the horse's mouth.

'I know you did,' Stan said grudgingly, looking down at the runway instead of at Jean. 'I visited him yesterday. Gordon mentioned that you two had beaten me to it.'

Where did Jean go from here? How to break it to Stan gently?

Slowly he tilted his head back to meet her worried gaze. 'You and Douglas – congratulations,' he said awkwardly. 'I wish you all the best.'

Jean blinked in surprise before clambering into the cockpit with less than her usual grace. 'You knew?'

'I've got eyes in my head, haven't I?' *Chin up, best foot forward – time to move on.*

'Thank you, Stan. I mean it.' Jean turned on the engine, surprised when Stan jumped up on to the wing then leaned in to peer at the control panel.

'Just checking the oil warning light,' he explained. 'I topped her up last night so she should be fine. Away you go.'

Jean smiled at him then lowered her goggles. Her hand was already on the joystick, the revs mounting as Stan slid to the ground.

'We'll have to go out for a drink some time; you and Douglas, me and Gillian,' he yelled above the engine's throaty roar.

'You and Gillian?' Jean echoed. Had she heard that right?

'Yes,' Stan shouted, giving Jean the thumbs-up as the wind from the propellers tugged at his clothes. 'She's good fun, is Gillian. I took her to a darts match at the Fox on Saturday night. We got on like a house on fire.'

Chin up. Angela's last words before Bobbie had climbed into her cockpit still rang in Bobbie's ears. Now she flew at 3,000 feet over the moors of the

North Riding, with Richmond below and the coast ahead. The day was crystal clear. She could see for miles.

'Will you be all right?' Jean had been full of concern at breakfast. 'You don't think it's too soon?'

'No, I'll give it a go,' Bobbie had replied. 'I want to prove to myself that I can still fly. *Aetheris Avidi*, and all that.'

'Good for you.' Mary had been the only one who hadn't fussed or questioned. She'd walked quietly with Bobbie through Burton Wood then queued with her to receive her chit.

'A Spit to Lossiemouth,' she'd announced. 'Hurrah; I can do that in my sleep.' Her destination was ferry pool unit number 10. She would hug the east coast as she headed north, take in Holy Island before crossing the Scottish border then on over the empty, mostly featureless Lowlands with their mile after endless mile of farmland. All would be calm and straightforward. Bobbie would be able to leave everything behind and breathe easily.

'How will you get home?' Jean had wanted to know as she too walked out to the runway.

'I'll fly back in a Corsair, weather permitting.' Bobbie had her orders for the day written on her chit and her Pilots' Notes tucked firmly in the breast pocket of her Sidcot suit.

Jean, Angela and Mary had gathered to wish Bobbie luck and she'd been first off the ground – increasing revs and gathering speed, hand on the stick, feeling the tilt of lift-off, the rapid climb. Bobbie had relaxed, airborne at last.

*

On the Wednesday afternoon of that week Cameron drove Douglas to Highcliff and dropped him off at the harbour side. Each had been lost in their own thoughts so the journey had been mostly silent until their destination came into view.

'Give my regards to Harold,' Cameron said as he steered down the narrow main street. 'Tell him long time no see. We'll have to put that right.'

'I'll tell him.' Douglas had given Cameron the deliberate impression that this was a social call. He'd asked Cameron to drop him off some distance from the hospital and told him that a lift back to Rixley was already organized. After Cameron pulled up beside a stack of fishermen's paraphernalia, close to a moored fishing boat, Douglas got out then rested one arm on the roof of the car and leaned back in. 'What time will your hearing finish?'

Cameron was to be part of another disciplinary panel, meeting at an RAF station ten miles up the coast. A wireless operator had been caught dead drunk while on duty. The lad had been incapable of climbing unaided into his aircraft, let alone carrying out his reconnaissance duties. His pilot had reported him and now he was up before a four-man panel, including his squadron leader and Cameron. 'With luck we'll be through by three. I hope so; I've arranged to pick Mary up. She's due to fly in to Richmond at four.'

'What a coincidence.' Douglas winked then patted the roof of the car with the flat of his hand, a signal for Cameron to turn then set off back up the hill as Douglas made his way to the hospital. It amused Douglas that Cameron, normally such a stickler for

339

the rules, would turn a situation to his advantage when it suited him. And who could blame him when it came to his protégée? Mary Holland had come back from Thame transformed, emerging like a bright blue butterfly from her dowdy cocoon. Of all the Atta girls Douglas had come across, he had never seen anyone so downright proud of gaining her wings.

Driving up the hill, Cameron glanced at Douglas in his overhead mirror. It was common knowledge among their crowd that Harold Inman had been invalided out of the Royal Navy and had ended up in charge of the Ear, Nose and Throat Department at King Edward's. *Social call, my foot!* Douglas's meeting with him today was beyond doubt a medical matter. 'Fingers crossed it's nothing serious,' Cameron said out loud as he came to a junction and turned on to the Richmond road.

Mary flew in early and had to wait three-quarters of an hour for Cameron's car to appear. He seemed thoughtful as he opened the boot for her and waited for her to stash away her belongings.

'How was the hearing?' she asked once they were under way.

'Simple enough.' Cameron looked straight ahead as he worked his way through the gears. Despite the warm day, he still wore his hat and gloves. He sat upright behind the wheel, the stresses of the day apparent in deep frown lines between his eyebrows. 'A young wireless operator was found drunk and incapable when reporting for duty; an open-and-shut case.'

The dismissive tone made Mary mirror his frown.

It kept her at a distance and reminded her of the old, stiff-upper-lip Cameron, before she'd got to know him better. 'You're quiet,' she observed tentatively. 'Are you sure there's nothing the matter?'

'Quite sure.'

'That's all right then.' Abandoning the staccato exchange, Mary lapsed into silence. Cameron's smile of greeting had been lukewarm, she remembered. There'd been no kiss on the cheek and none of the usual lively questioning – how was your flight, what did you fly, have you had a good day? *Ah*, she thought with a sudden sinking feeling, *someone has had a word in his ear since I last saw him, along the lines of, 'Don't get too familiar with the lower ranks.' Hilary perhaps.*

Cameron felt Mary shift nervously in her seat. He glanced sideways to see her sitting slightly forward with a glum expression, clutching her gloves and staring out of the side window at the setting sun. Perhaps she was upset because she'd had to wait. Better make amends. 'I'm sorry I was late,' he said. 'The hearing went on longer than expected.'

'These things happen. I didn't mind waiting.' They'd reached the junction with the Great North Road, where a convoy of army lorries meant that Cameron had to pull up while Mary's thoughts followed a miserable route. *If Hilary has issued a warning not to fraternize, please tell me. Better to say outright that you and I are not meant to be rather than leave me in suspense.*

The lorries trundled by, followed by two Austin pickups packed with squaddies then by a farm tractor and a motorbike.

'Today was a preliminary hearing. It turned out it wasn't a first offence. The alcohol was for Dutch courage, according to the lad's pilot. Without it he was a gibbering wreck every time he climbed into a plane.'

Mary turned to look at Cameron. 'What'll happen to him now?'

'Court martial and automatic discharge. Maybe even a prison sentence.' He checked that the main road was clear then pulled out. 'Some might count themselves lucky to be out of the fray, but not this lad. He swore to the panel that he would never touch another drop, that he would turn teetotal and never let us down. I wanted to believe him.'

'But?'

Cameron shook his head. 'He was too far gone along that path, drinking five or six pints every night, hiding bottles of spirits under his mattress. He wouldn't have been able to keep his word.' There was another matter bothering Cameron that he and the lad's squadron leader had talked through, but he would keep quiet about that for now. 'It's a fine line between having a couple of drinks with your pals just to take the edge off things, which most of us do, and drinking yourself senseless, as in this case.'

'I wouldn't like to be the judge of that,' Mary said quietly.

Having waited for an open stretch of road, Cameron signalled to overtake the army convoy then his face relaxed a little. He put his foot down hard on the accelerator. 'I'm sorry if I've been off with you. I've got a lot on my mind.'

Mary gave a long sigh of relief. It seemed their way ahead was clear after all.

'Incidentally, did I say how glad I was to see you?'

'You did not,' she fired back, blunt and to the point. 'As a matter of fact, I thought that you'd gone off me. Don't look at me like that, Cameron; keep your eyes on the road!'

'Gone off you?' he echoed as Mary grabbed the steering wheel to keep him from mounting the grass verge. 'Good Lord, woman – you're not serious!' He steered off the road into a layby and squealed to a halt. Ignoring derisive yells from the squaddies as they rode by, he took Mary's gloves and placed them carefully on top of the dashboard. Then he held both of her hands in his. 'Why would I do that?'

'Because,' she said with a shrug. For the reasons she'd talked to Jean about: two families that were chalk and cheese, a father and a brother whom she would gladly disown. But now, as she gazed at Cameron's face, his eyes began to tell her a different truth. Without a word spoken, she understood exactly where the relationship was leading and where she wanted it to go.

Dismissing her doubts and fears, Mary leaned forward to kiss this complicated, clever and compassionate man. Oh, and handsome too; never forget that.

'You see,' Cameron breathed as their lips touched. 'No one could ever compare with you, Mary; not in a million years.'

CHAPTER NINETEEN

'Did Bobbie get back safely?' That night Teddy made a beeline for Angela in the bar at the Grange. He was still in uniform, with his tie loosened and the top button of his shirt undone.

Angela tilted her head and viewed him through half-closed eyes. 'Yes, she did, since you ask.'

'Good for her. Three days back in the aviation saddle; this calls for a celebration. Is she in her room?' About to dash off and fetch Bobbie, Teddy was prevented by Angela's restraining hand.

'She's having an early night. It's been a long day; the poor darling is done in.'

'And no wonder, after what she's been through.' Jean had been buying drinks for herself and Mary but now she butted into the conversation.

Teddy found himself uncomfortably sandwiched between Angela and Jean, with Angela's hand still on his arm. He sensed a build-up of tension as he reached across the bar for an ashtray for Angela.

'Yes, Bobbie took a nasty bump to the head,' Angela drawled through pouting red lips and a spiral of blue cigarette smoke.

'But she hasn't let that little incident in the Maggie

344

dampen her enthusiasm.' Jean fixed Teddy with her coolest stare. 'Bobbie's made of sterner stuff.'

'That's good to hear. A whisky for me, please, George. Ladies, in her absence, why not raise a glass to our little Scottish Atta girl? Long may she live to fight another day!'

How dare he? Cutting Teddy dead without a word or a smile, Jean stalked off with her drinks, leaving him to Angela's tender mercies.

'What's got into the Ice Maiden all of a sudden?' he muttered. He'd never taken to Jean and naturally assumed that Angela shared his low opinion. After all, he and Angela were cut from the same stylish, extrovert cloth. 'Never mind about Miss Misery-guts over there; what would you say if I were to let you in on a little secret?'

'It depends what it is.' Flicking ash into the ash-tray with her long, tapered fingers, Angela prepared to play the role of her life. While every nerve ending screamed for her to move as far out of Teddy's orbit as possible, she kept an outward calm, smiling and raising the cigarette to her lips. 'Well?' she murmured, head to one side.

Teddy put a finger to his lips. 'It's still hush-hush.'

'I won't tell a soul, I promise.'

'No one else knows.'

'Yes, darling; there's no need to tell me what hush-hush means.' Tilting her head to the other side and inhaling smoke with a quiet pop of her lips, a smile played at the corners of Angela's mouth.

Bloody hell; did this girl realize the effect she had? Those deep blue eyes set against her pale, smooth skin, the long neck, one shoulder thrust provocatively towards him. 'I'm in line for a new posting at last. It's a big step up.'

'You don't say,' Angela said slowly. 'When exactly?'

'In ten days from now.' He watched her face carefully for her reaction.

'Where to? Will it be over the pond as expected?'

'Not quite. The Yanks will have to wait. It turns out I'm needed closer to home; if I said exactly where and who for I'd be in real trouble.'

'Uh-oh, top secret?' *Hell and damnation!* Angela's fingers itched to wipe the smirk off Teddy's smug face. 'Well, congratulations. I'm sure your aviation skills are much in demand.'

He slid his empty glass across the bar. 'Another whisky please, George. Make it a double. Oh, and the same for Angela too.'

'Does Bobbie know about this mysterious promotion?' she asked with another flick of her cigarette.

'No; why?'

'I thought you might have taken her into your confidence, that's all.'

'Listen, Angela, Bobbie's a sweet girl but she wouldn't be able to keep the news under her hat – not like you.'

'Sweet?'

'Yes, your typical girl next door, bless her.' A chap could drown in the depth of those come-hither blue eyes. As if magnetized, Teddy drew his stool a little closer.

'I got the impression that Bobbie meant more to you than that,' Angela said without blinking.

'Why? What's she been saying?' Teddy's guard shot up. What new game was this?

346

Angela continued with a conspiratorial smile. 'It's not what Bobbie says – it's more what I observe for myself. There was that pair of nylons for a start.'

'Oh, she told you about them, did she?'

'Naturally; we two are thick as thieves. It was a kind thought, darling; a gift any girl would be glad to receive. And I'm sure it helped speed Bobbie on her road to recovery. Then before that there was the night out to the Spa Ballroom – she told me all about that little escapade.'

Hearing Angela's heavy emphasis on the word 'all', Teddy sieved his drink through his teeth then rapped down his glass. 'Did she say that she had a good time?'

Slowly and deliberately Angela stubbed out her cigarette. 'She had a marvellous time, darling. Those were her very words.'

'Good; glad to hear it. Poor Bobbie ended up a wee bit tipsy; did she say?'

'Yes.' Angela leaned closer so that their shoulders touched. 'Between you and me, she's not a great imbiber – due to a serious lack of practice in her youth. A couple of drinks and Bobbie is flat on her back.' She finished speaking and stared him down.

Teddy dropped his gaze. 'Thanks for the tip. I'll remember that. Luckily Douglas was there that night to offer us a lift home then I made sure it was straight up to bed for Bobbie, to sleep it off.'

Angela smiled through her revulsion. 'You're a true gent, Flight Lieutenant Simpson.'

'You're very welcome, First Officer Browne.' Teddy took a deep breath. It seemed Angela had bought his version of events; he was still off the hook.

'I only wish I'd been there to keep an eye on her.' Angela leaned back on her stool and ended her performance with a flourish. 'Unfortunately that was the very night when my pa cast me off without a penny, so I was otherwise engaged.'

'Teddy lied through his teeth.' Angela got together with Mary, Jean and Bobbie over breakfast the next morning. 'And bloody good he was too.'

The four women had chosen to eat at the ferry pool rather than the Grange, specifically to stay out of Teddy's way. A wireless played Mantovani tunes over the loudspeaker as they talked through their next tactic and there was a hum of voices and the rattle of crockery and cutlery in the background as ground crew and drivers prepared for the day ahead.

'Far from admitting what he'd done, he made out that he'd looked after you,' she explained to Bobbie. 'Honestly, you'd have thought that butter wouldn't melt.'

'That's Teddy for you.' Jean gave Bobbie a sympathetic smile. 'You never know; perhaps he even believes what he's saying. People can convince themselves that black is white if they really want to.'

Angela shook her head. 'Teddy's clever; he knew what he was doing. There's a cool brain at work there, covering his tracks.'

'There's a hell of a lot at stake,' Mary pointed out. 'Teddy's career – his whole life, in fact – goes up in smoke if only we can find proof of what he did.'

'Talking of which.' Angela gulped down the last of her tea. 'He claims to have got a new posting – supposedly top secret and all that.'

'When?' Jean was surprised by the news.

'In a couple of weeks – don't worry, there's still time for us to get our man.'

'If you say so.' Jean didn't put much faith in Angela's plan, which evidently involved a complicated deception and an ongoing battle of wits. She, like Mary, had been more in favour of tackling Teddy head-on but they'd been overruled by Angela who'd pointed out the fatal flaw in their argument: in the absence of any evidence it would be Bobbie's word against his. 'But what if he cottons on? What then?'

'He won't.' Angela glanced at a worried-looking Bobbie. 'It comes down to me being an even better play-actor than he is. Trust me; I'm sure I can pull it off.'

Bobbie listened in silence. She'd struggled to swallow even one slice of toast and marmalade. The knot of anxiety in her stomach grew tighter and she was glad when the voice on the Tannoy called for all pilots. She was the first to jump up from the table then first in line to receive her chit.

Meanwhile, Angela went to her locker to pick up her parachute pack before going upstairs. Though she'd sounded confident, there was plenty for her to think through. As her next move she decided to seek out Douglas, deliberately putting herself at the back of the queue directly behind Agnes and Horace.

Teddy stood well ahead, joining in the usual conversation about weather conditions and destinations. He smiled at Bobbie as she squeezed past, chit in hand. 'Hello there; what's Douglas got in store for our wee lassie today?'

'A Hurricane to Wolverhampton.' Sickened by his

proximity and false bonhomie, Bobbie answered abruptly then hurried on down the stairs.

The queue shuffled forward until Angela at last reached the front and spotted Douglas at his desk. She ducked to speak through the gap under the glass screen. 'A quick word?'

He nodded reluctantly and beckoned her into the office. 'Hello, Angela. What can I do for you?'

'In private,' she said pointedly.

Gillian rose swiftly from her seat and departed, saying she would leave them to it.

'Well?' Douglas made it clear that by rights Angela should already be halfway to her runway.

She refused to be hurried. 'It's about Teddy Simpson. A little bird tells me that he's moving on.'

Douglas motioned for her to shut the door. 'Who told you that?'

'He did. Teddy made out it was a step up the ladder. I wondered what you knew – off the record, so to speak.'

With a shake of his head Douglas dashed Angela's hopes. 'You know I can't say. I'd have thought promotion was unlikely, though.'

'Is that because you dislike the man or is it based on something more solid?'

'I make no comment,' he said stiffly.

Angela tutted then persevered. 'Oh come on, Douglas – we know each other pretty well.'

'So you know me well enough not to ask.' Tapping the end of his pencil against the desk, he was, however, on the point of saying to heck with rules and regulations when there was a knock on the door and Hilary came in.

He glanced with surprise at Angela. 'Is something the matter with your chit?'

'No, nothing at all.' Honesty struck her as the best policy on this occasion. 'The fact is, I'm trying to prise information out of Douglas but it's like getting blood out of a stone.'

Irritated, Hilary glanced at his watch.

'Oh, darling, don't be boring,' Angela went on. 'I can easily make up time once I'm in the air. My question to Douglas was about Teddy and his imminent promotion to squadron leader.'

'Come again?' Hilary cocked his head to one side.

'Aha!' It was rare to take Hilary by surprise so Angela forged ahead. 'No, Douglas and I didn't think that promotion was on the cards either. But squadron leader would be the next step up from flight lieutenant when Teddy starts his new posting.'

Hilary chose his words carefully. 'Angela, I've told you before: take everything Teddy Simpson says with a big pinch of salt.'

'So the promotion part is a fib?'

Hilary slapped the gloves he was carrying against his thigh.

'I take that as a yes. But Teddy is definitely leaving Rixley?'

'As yet nothing is set in stone.'

'He *may* leave?' Looking from Hilary to Douglas and back again, Angela was sure that both men knew more than they were prepared or allowed to say.

Hilary cleared his throat then, seemingly changing the subject, he spoke slowly to Douglas, one eye still on Angela. 'About this file.' He tapped a buff-coloured folder on the desk. 'Have you had a chance to take a look?'

'I have.' Douglas pushed the file to the edge of the desk, into a position where Angela could easily read Teddy's name, service number and current rank on the cover under an official black stamp showing the King's Crown.

'What do you make of Flying Officer Flynn's eye-witness account? Will it stand up to scrutiny in court?'

Angela caught her breath. A jumble of fresh ideas crowded in. For a few seconds she assumed that Hilary and Douglas must be several steps ahead of her over the Bobbie affair. But then who was Flying Officer Flynn and what was the nature of the offence that Teddy was charged with? Was this, in fact, something entirely different?

'The prosecutor ought to have a back-up statement,' Douglas replied, 'to be on the safe side. At the moment I'd say it's fifty-fifty: Flynn's word against Teddy's.'

'Thanks; I'll pass that on.' Hilary grunted and tucked the folder under his arm. 'Not a word, First Officer Browne,' he muttered under his breath. 'Understood?'

'Yes, sir.' Teddy was under investigation, for goodness sake! A court case was pending; that much was certain. 'Thank you, sir. Now if you don't mind, I have a plane waiting for me on the runway and it's not going to fly itself.'

Jean had changed out of her uniform into jumper and slacks and was in two minds as she stood at her window, looking out over the front lawn at a bomb disposal team still at work under floodlights. They'd been called back earlier in the day by handyman Ernest Poulter when he'd spotted a suspicious object half-buried in a ditch close to the main gate.

Should Jean seek out Douglas and ask him about the results of yesterday's hearing test? Or should she wait for him to tell her in his own good time?

Her dilemma was solved by a knock on her door. She answered it to find the man himself standing outside.

'I've just finished work for the day; do you fancy a drink?' he asked tentatively. He looked pale and worn out.

Jean nodded and as they walked down the stairs, Douglas offered to bring the drinks to her in the library. 'Where it's quiet,' he added.

So Jean knew that the talk would be serious. Surrounded by leather-bound tomes stacked on shelves from floor to ceiling, she pulled down the blackout blind then settled into a shabby chesterfield chair and prepared herself.

'I've been on the blower to Harold,' Douglas confirmed when he carried in two whiskys and a jug of water then pulled up a chair. 'He's taken a look at my test results and decided that my eardrums have taken a bashing from flying more than my share of four-engine bombers. There's some hearing loss that can't be reversed – mainly in the left ear. On top of that there's the tinnitus.'

'What does that sound like?' Jean controlled her reaction as she studied Douglas's woebegone expression.

'It's more of a ticking than the usual ringing,' he said in a flat voice. 'Apparently the dratted thing might improve, provided I stay away from loud noises. Only time will tell.'

'That's something to hang on to, I suppose.' Oh, but the poor man looked miserable and defeated!

'But any future flying is out of the question.' Resting his head back against his chair, Douglas sighed heavily at this, the worst of verdicts. 'Good God, Jean; all I feel fit for is the knacker's yard. The kindest thing would be to take me out and shoot me.'

'I'm so sorry,' she breathed, her heart racing beneath her calm exterior. She thought guiltily that perhaps it would have been better for him not to have known.

Douglas jerked forward to try to snap himself out of self-pity. 'Hark at me, going on as if it's the end of the world.'

'It's bad enough,' she commiserated. 'I am sorry – truly.'

Dear Jean; her concern was obviously heartfelt. 'It's not your fault. And I won't blame you if—'

'Stop!' She slipped from her chair to kneel on the rug at his feet and rest her arms across his lap. She looked up earnestly at him. 'I won't let you think such a thing, let alone say it.'

Douglas nodded slowly. 'You're sure?'

'Quite sure.' Jean brought to mind an image in an old painting. She remembered the name 'Amy' carved into a tree. There was an anguished-looking couple standing next to it and ivy partly obscuring the name. The painting was called *The Long Engagement* and Jean knew with complete certainty that she did not want to be that sad Victorian girl in the purple cloak. 'I love you,' she whispered, putting her arms around Douglas's neck. For better or worse. For ever and ever. 'We should get married as soon as possible. What do you think?'

'For me, this is the place where it all started.' Cameron sat behind the wheel of his car, staring out into blackness. Mary sat beside him in her green coat and matching hat. Her collar was turned up and the narrow-brimmed hat sat at an angle that concealed the upper part of her profile.

So this was the end of Saturday night's mystery jaunt: the clifftop at Highcliff, in the grounds of the old church. Mary smiled and turned expectantly towards him.

'Do you remember the night of the bombing? This is where we came after we'd taken the wounded men to hospital.'

'Of course I remember.'

'That was when you first worked your magic on me.' Cameron gazed out at the moon and stars.

'A peculiar sort of magic: me hardly saying a word after falling down in a dead faint. And by the way, running out of petrol and us being stranded overnight wasn't my idea.'

He laughed. 'Not your normal romantic tryst, I agree. You were an enigma, Mary – a fascinating one. And my, did you keep me at arm's length for long enough.'

She shook her head. 'Not on purpose. It never entered my mind that you could be interested in me.' Parked twenty yards from the cliff edge, Mary was able to make out the outline of the ruined walls. She heard a distant sound of waves pounding against rocks below.

'So when did you realize?'

Mary thought hard then answered earnestly. 'On my first night at the Grange – when I called you "sir" and you said for me to call you Cameron. You gave me such a kind look; that's when I had my first inkling. But my mind was taken up with everything to do with flying. I was so excited to have won my wings that I put the notion to the back of my mind.'

'You're still an enigma,' Cameron decided. 'I've never met anyone like you before.'

'And that's a good thing?' Here they were, perched on the top of the cliff, talking and not touching or kissing, trying to feel their way forward.

'It's wonderful,' he assured her. 'To have found someone who doesn't follow the crowd – that's the thing I love most about you.'

Mary savoured the sensation of standing at the threshold of a completely new life. The wild darkness of the weather only added to her excitement. 'My father made me think it was wrong to stand out,' she admitted. '"Don't make a fuss, Mary", "Cheer up, Mary", "Only speak when you're spoken to". That was the message all the time I was growing up.'

'Things are not so very different now,' Cameron pointed out. 'We're all supposed to keep our heads down and do as we're told – "yes, sir; no, sir; three bags full, sir" – at least until the war ends and we're demobbed.' This brought him to the verge of sharing a piece of news that he'd been sitting on for days. Now was the time to do it, he decided. 'There's something you need to know,' he began. 'I've been afraid to tell you but it wouldn't be fair to keep it from you any longer.'

'You've been given a new posting,' Mary said before he could continue. She felt certain in her heart that this was what Cameron had been about to tell her.

'To an RAF station outside Aireby,' he confirmed. 'I'll be back in harness, working with Bomber Command.'

Mary's chest tightened and her heart raced. His two final words terrified her.

'It's what I always wanted and expected to happen,' he went on quickly. 'After all, it's what I was trained for. It was hard for me to leave my squadron and come to Rixley for a so-called rest – I felt I was letting the other lads down.'

'You don't have to explain.' Bomber Command suggested nightly raids, fresh missions, new tours of duty. And each time Cameron flew his Lancaster or Stirling out of the Aireby base to intercept Heinkels and Messerschmitts over the English Channel or the Irish Sea, each time he flew in formation over the Netherlands, on over France and into Germany to destroy enemy airfields, dams and munitions factories, the chances of him not returning rose higher and higher. 'I understand.'

Cameron drew a deep breath. 'You don't have to worry, Mary – I'll mostly be training new recruits, not flying out on missions.'

'I see.' His reassurance comforted her, but the reality remained that he was being torn from her and thrust into the unknown. Mary stared out at the starry sky, at pinpricks of light against vast darkness. 'When will you leave?' she asked.

'A week from today.'

Seven days. She shook her head in despair.

'I know,' he murmured as he felt for her hand and squeezed it. 'I feel it too. But we have a whole week before then. Let's make the most of it.'

Yes, of course Cameron had to go; there was no choice. Mary knew she must be brave. 'What shall we do now?' she asked with a fluttering heart.

'What do you want to do?' Turning the ignition key in the lock, he started the engine. 'You choose; anything you like.'

'I'd like to go to the best hotel in Highcliff.'

'Good idea. I know a nice place with a lounge bar where they still serve cocktails.' Cameron turned the car towards the gate.

'To find a room and stay there overnight,' Mary said in a clear voice.

'Together?'

'Yes, together.'

He glanced at her as she sat quietly beside him, staring straight ahead – chin up, steadfast and beautiful as they drove out of the shadow of the ruined walls.

Mary took in very little about the outside of the sea-front hotel that Cameron had chosen. The smart, middle-aged receptionist assured them that they would wake up to a sea view and that breakfast in bed could be provided if they so wished. A young girl in a black dress and waitress's apron and cap appeared from a back room to show them up to their suite on the first floor.

'We're right behind you,' Cameron told the girl in his businesslike way.

She met his gaze unabashed and smiled at Mary in friendly fashion as she led the way to the lift. 'It's our best double room,' she promised. 'Everything is en suite. You'll find clean towels and everything else you need in the bathroom. There's a telephone by the bed for you to ring down to Reception if you need anything.'

'We'll be fine,' Cameron assured her as he and Mary stepped out of the lift. 'We'll find our own way from here, thank you.'

To the sound of the lift doors sliding shut Mary walked with him along a carpeted corridor. She stood to one side while he turned the key in the lock.

He stepped aside to let her walk ahead of him. 'You're sure?'

She walked into the room. It was spacious and modern, not stuffy and crammed with fussy ornaments. The walls were pale green, the bed the biggest she'd ever seen, with gleaming, shell-shaped lamps on small tables to either side. Mary nodded as she focused on her surroundings.

Cameron hung his jacket over the back of a chair by the window. 'Can this really be happening?'

She took off her hat and coat. 'I certainly hope so. Otherwise I'm going to wake up in the morning and find it was all a dream.'

'Come here,' he said, smiling. He needed to have his arms around Mary's waist, to touch her and breathe her in. 'Seriously, I can hardly believe it – you here with me.'

She stood on tiptoe to kiss him. 'It is a kind of

magic. Then again, it feels like the most natural thing in the world.'

Cameron lifted her off her feet and swung her towards the bed. She felt light and soft and the skin on her neck was warm when he kissed it. He lowered her on to the emerald satin eiderdown then lay beside her and propped himself on one elbow. 'What would you wish for – if you really had magical powers?'

'For you not to go away.' Mary's reply was instant. 'For time to stand still and for us to stay right where we are.'

With their limbs intertwined and Cameron's face caught in the lamplight, they shared a sense of sinking into a sublime, surprising happiness.

They were at ease. There was no urgency as kisses lingered and caresses comforted the hurts that the world had dealt them. The harsh words of Mary's childhood lost their grip under Cameron's gentle fingertips, the pain of his broken engagement eased.

'Shall I turn off the lights?' he asked as Mary's fingers undid the buttons of his shirt.

'No, I like to look at you.' She traced the line of his collarbone then laid her head against his bare chest.

Her hair fanned out against his skin as she nestled against him. He would love her and look after her for as long as she would let him; of that Cameron was certain. She would surprise and amaze him. New ways that they learned together, hour by hour and day by day, would lead to open horizons.

'Aireby is not so very far away,' Mary murmured.

'No. And I have my car.'

'We'll carry on seeing each other.'

'Often.' He held on to her and kissed her. 'And when you're not with me in the flesh and I'm feeling blue, remembering this moment will make me happy again.'

Mary cried at this.

'Please don't.'

'I can't help it.' She kissed him again. 'These are not sad tears,' she whispered.

She was wondrous. The curves of her body were new and exciting and she was open with him. They belonged together.

Mary lay beneath him. Cameron would take the lead and she would trust him not to hurt her or do her harm. It was strange and at the same time the most natural and thrilling thing – to love this man who adored her, who would go away and come back again, please God, whose eyes would come alive at the sight of her, whose kisses made her life complete.

CHAPTER TWENTY

'Angela, wake up!' Bobbie knocked hard on the door. 'Can you hear me?'

'What is it?' Angela crawled out of bed and struggled into her dressing gown. 'Bobbie; is that you? I look dreadful – can you give me five minutes?'

'No, Angela – I need to speak to you now.'

Angela staggered to the door. 'What's happened? Has Teddy been bothering you again?'

'No; Lionel's here.' Bobbie was all of a dither. 'He's downstairs. Come quickly.'

Angela grasped the edge of the door. 'Lionel?' she echoed.

'Yes. He's on shore leave – in the library, waiting for you.' Bobbie had been making her way down to breakfast and had bumped into Lionel in the entrance hall.

'Tell him I can't see him,' Angela gasped. Her hand flew up to smooth her hair. 'Why is he here? Didn't he get my letter?'

'I have no idea.' Bobbie only knew what she'd already told Angela. 'I asked him to wait in the library where it's quiet. You can't send the poor man

362

away without seeing him. Shall I run back down and tell him to wait while you get dressed?'

Angela groaned then nodded. 'I'll be five minutes.'

As Bobbie delivered the message, Angela flung on some clothes and ran a comb through her hair. *Lionel; here at the Grange!* Of all the things she might have expected from her day of rest – ironing, mending, hiking or writing letters – her ex-fiancé's arrival was nowhere on the list. Fully dressed, she ran to the bathroom and splashed water on her face, patted it dry with a towel then checked her reflection in the mirror. *Ghastly!*

Outside in the corridor she ran into Jean.

'Lionel is downstairs,' Jean began.

'I know!' Angela wailed. The sooner this encounter was over the better. So she ran full tilt down the stairs and into the library.

Lionel stood in uniform with his back to the empty fire grate, hands clasped behind him. His thick brown hair had been flattened by his cap, which lay on the window sill with his gloves and scarf. Despite his tanned skin, he looked drawn and anxious.

'Darling!' Angela began. 'Why didn't you warn me?'

'Hello, Angela.' He took an eager step towards her then read her dismayed expression and stopped. 'It's early; I hope you don't mind.'

'No, of course not.' Good manners took over. 'Can I get you something to eat; some tea at least?'

'No, thank you.' He patted his jacket pocket. 'I got your letter.'

Angela stayed by the door. An avalanche of emotions threatened to overwhelm her. 'I'm most awfully sorry if you're upset.'

'I was at first,' Lionel conceded. 'It came as quite a shock.'

'I know and I am desperately sorry.' The truth was that a face-to-face break-up was different; it was much more complicated and difficult than simply writing a letter. For a moment Angela resented the intrusion. 'Are you sure I can't get you some tea?'

'Forget about the tea,' he said brusquely. 'I haven't got long – I have to be back in Hull by midday.'

'I see. Well, sit down at least.' Angela drew up two chairs by the window. 'Where's your car?'

'Hilary told me to drive in the back way. The car's parked in the stable yard.'

'Good; there may still be unexploded bombs out front.'

'I told him I'd come to see you.' Lionel sat awkwardly on the edge of his seat.

'Really?' Angela's hackles rose. 'And what advice did our mutual friend offer?'

'I didn't ask him for any. This is between you and me.' Since Lionel had received Angela's letter he'd rehearsed a dozen times what he wanted to say – where to begin and how to go on, how he wanted the conversation to end. But in the event the prepared lines fled and he was left tongue-tied. So he sat and frowned, gazing out through the window at Burton Wood and waiting for Angela to speak.

'I was right, wasn't I? Pa left me with no alternative.'

'Right to carry on flying for the ATA or right to break off with me?'

'Both.' Crossing her legs, she tapped the arms of her chair and let a silence develop.

'Correct on the first count, wrong on the second.' Lionel averted his gaze and waited in silence for her reaction.

Angela gave a short, exasperated sigh. 'I did try to explain. How could we have gone on under the circumstances? I'm poor as a church mouse now – I have to make my own way in life.'

'I thought you said you'd prefer that.'

'I do. I'd far rather stand on my own two feet than rely on Pa's allowance.'

'Yes, I see.' Lionel mirrored Angela's actions by crossing his legs and tapping both armrests. 'I'm sad on your mother's behalf, however.'

She nodded in acknowledgement. 'But Ma has a choice too, if only she would see it.'

'She hasn't been educated to think like that,' he pointed out. 'She was brought up in an age where a wife was expected to accept her lot – like my own mother when the worst befell her. Come now; don't look so surprised.'

Angela's mouth fell open as she envisaged the house in Dorset and Lionel's seemingly contented, refined and delicate mother surrounded by her books and watercolour paints like a character from a novel by E. M. Forster. What exactly did Lionel mean?

'Mother made the best of things, even after she'd learned the name and circumstances of the woman with whom Father was carrying on,' Lionel went on calmly. 'Of course, she withdrew from London. It would have been too humiliating to have stayed.'

'I'm sorry; I wasn't aware.'

'Quite.' Lionel stood up suddenly and took his silver cigarette case from his pocket. 'A lot goes on that isn't spoken about. I've learned from Mother to keep my emotions well hidden, which means that I'm afraid I come across as rather a stuffed shirt.'

'No, I never thought that.' Angela followed him across the room.

Tapping the end of a cigarette against the case, he regarded her through narrowed eyes. 'What *did* you think of me – steady, reliable Lionel but not very exciting?'

'Reliable; yes, and a true friend.'

'But boring.'

'No,' Angela insisted. 'You were always kind and generous. And I'm *not*, you see. I'm a superficial girl except when I'm flying a plane and doing my job; that's the only part of my life that I take seriously. Otherwise it's been one long party.'

Lionel flicked his lighter into action and shook his head.

'Yes,' she argued. 'I love nothing better than to go out and have fun. You've seen how I've been over the years: the dresses, the make-up, the music. And deep down you must know that these are not the best qualities to look for in a wife. Believe me, darling, you're much better off—'

'Angela, don't.' Putting the lighter away then inhaling deeply, he stopped her with another shake of his head. 'I don't care how many parties you attend or how much money you have or haven't got. It's irrelevant to me. All I care about is that your father has been cruel to you and has hurt you desperately but you haven't let him crush your spirit; instead, you've fought free of him. It's made me love you more than ever, if that were humanly possible.'

Taking a sharp breath, she turned away. 'Lionel, you're not being practical.'

'What's practicality got to do with how I feel?'

'How you feel?' She looked puzzled, as if the depth of Lionel's emotions wasn't something that she'd taken into account. 'Listen, you may hurt for a little while but it will soon wear off—'

He stepped in front of her. 'Damn it, woman; what are you saying – that I'm as shallow as you claim to be? That love can be washed away without a trace, like words written in sand when the waves come in? It's just not true.'

'With time,' she insisted. 'You will forget about me; honestly you will.'

'I don't want to forget about you. Would I have come here if I did? It cost me a lot, you know. And I'm not here to grovel. If you tell me to my face that it really is over between us, then I will go away and you won't hear from me again. But I won't ever forget you.'

'Give me that cigarette, would you, darling?' Angela accepted it with a deep frown. Lionel's words had thrown her off balance and she needed time to recover. 'Never mind my father; what about yours? Shouldn't he mind dreadfully if we were to continue?'

'To hell with my father. It's my life, not his.'

'Fine words don't pay the bills,' Angela muttered through a cloud of smoke. But the sand shifted beneath her feet; everything she'd thought of as certain was sliding from under her. 'I was sure I'd done the right thing,' she murmured.

'To throw away our chance of happiness?' Lionel raised his eyebrows and spoke with a touch of sarcasm. 'How can that be right?'

'It seemed so when I wrote the letter.'

'But now?'

'I'm not so sure.' In fact, she was not certain at all; not when she looked closely at Lionel's face and saw passion burn in his brown eyes and heard it in his voice. What she'd judged to be his steadiness had suddenly become unshakeable strength and his presence exerted an unexpected power over her.

'And if I tell you that I still love you?' he asked quietly.

'Then I believe you.'

'That I will always love you?' Lionel didn't move towards her but stayed on the spot, watching her closely.

Angela nodded once and was about to speak.

'No, don't say anything.' Lionel advanced and took away her half-smoked cigarette then stubbed it out in the fire grate. Then he stroked strands of hair from her cheek with the back of his hand. 'Not until you've had time to work out whether or not my visit changes things.'

'It does,' she acknowledged in a whisper.

'Hush; I know it's taken you by surprise. And I may not have succeeded in winning you back; I am prepared for that.'

Angela inclined her head towards his hand then held it there, against her cheek. 'Thank you.'

'For what?' His full heart almost burst. He simply wanted to hold her and help her to believe in herself.

'For coming here. For being kind and true.'

He bent his head to kiss her softly on her cheek. 'Write to me, once you've had time to think.'

'Give me one week.'

'A week,' he agreed. Taking up his hat and gloves, Lionel backed towards the door. 'I'll wait to hear.'

Then he was gone and there was the sound of his footsteps crossing the hall, of Douglas saying a surprised hello, of their voices fading as they walked out on to the front terrace together, exchanging news.

Up at 2,000 feet, behind the controls of her Spit, Bobbie breathed easily. On the ground she would still jump at her own shadow, dreading a chance meeting with Teddy and anxious to avoid the curious glances of everyone around her. During the weekend just past she'd even had to steel herself to accept the sympathy of Angela, Mary and Jean without breaking down, their kind words and actions serving as reminders of the awful event that she longed to wipe from her brain.

So she'd kept to herself and had arrived at the ferry pool early this Monday morning; had been first in line to accept her chit then had dashed off to collect her parachute pack, helmet and goggles before a queue could form.

Bobbie discovered that her job for the day was to deliver a brand-new Spit to a ferry pool in the Scottish Borders; it was her favourite route and one she knew by heart.

'Atta girl!' Stan had said in his friendly way as she'd climbed into the cockpit on Runway 3. 'You'll enjoy this one.' He'd removed the chocks and given her the thumbs-up then waved her off with a grin – for all the world as if she were the carefree Bobbie of old.

She'd waved back and now, heading north at 300 miles per hour, she had a clear sky ahead and untamed moors below and she was that girl again. She had space and speed; complete control.

Bobbie sat in the tiny cockpit looking down on the world. She observed the coast to the east and beyond that the glittering sea, where a small convoy of ships were dark oblongs trailing their thin wakes through the brown water. The coastline was sharply indented and marked by a rim of white waves. Onwards, upwards; she flew the precious new Spit to its destination.

With soaring spirits she lived in the glorious moment until, out of the blue, a fellow pilot flew up from behind. The P-51 Mustang came level with her on her port side, its wings almost touching the Spit's. Gripping the stick with a sickening feeling of certainty and dread, Bobbie glanced sideways.

Teddy waved at her from his cockpit then banked his plane steeply. She held her breath. He came at her again from behind; this time to starboard. He grinned and waved again, banked away and increased his speed, challenging her to keep up.

Hold a steady course, don't increase the revs; ignore him.

Directly ahead of her, he flipped the Mustang into a spectacular backward roll, inviting Bobbie to join in and not to be a spoilsport, behaving as if they were performers in a flying circus, not part of the war effort at all.

Bobbie refused to react. *Let him play the fool. Don't be intimidated.* She watched the trail of vapour from the Mustang disperse and waited tensely for Teddy's next move.

He turned then came straight at her in a blatant game of dare, sunlight reflecting off his wings and fuselage. Who would give way first?

I know your game! Bobbie held her nerve. *You don't scare me!*

Teddy flew level and straight, threatening a head-on crash until at the last, terrifying moment he thrust the stick forward to drop out of sight.

Bobbie gasped and flew on.

Below her, Teddy sat grinning at the controls of the Mustang. He was taken aback by Bobbie's nerve but he wasn't done with her yet; not until he'd forced a reaction out of her. He'd planned this little game before take-off, as soon as he'd noticed Bobbie's name and number on the destination chart behind Gillian's desk and found out that he too was heading north. A cocky game of dare would provide an unwelcome reminder of the balance of power between him and Bobbie; Teddy would easily prove himself the stronger of the two, both on the ground and in the air. 'Just in case she gets a different idea into her head,' he said out loud as he gained altitude and approached the Spit from behind.

You mean to break me but I won't let you! Gritting her teeth, Bobbie glanced over her shoulder. As the Mustang approached at high speed she saw Teddy for what he really was: a bragging playground bully who relied on lying and cheating to make his way to the top. With a supreme effort of will she held her course.

Teddy flew up on the port side as close as he dared. He pointed at her then at his own chest before tilting his head back and miming the action of drinking from a glass. *You and me; tomorrow night?* he mouthed with a confident grin.

Bobbie didn't stoop to reply. She resisted the strong temptation to use the Spit's manoeuvrability to outfly him. *Sit tight. Don't play him at his own game.*

He flew closer still, attempting to force her to veer to starboard. If Bobbie's foot on the rudder pedal faltered even for a moment, their wing tips would touch, sending one or both planes off course and out of control. But her nerve didn't fail as she stared straight ahead.

Give way, damn it! Teddy thought. They were approaching the Scottish border and his destination was directly west, into Cumberland. He didn't have enough petrol to fly further north. The smile slowly vanished.

The Spit responded to every touch and Bobbie continued to hold her course. She saw that Teddy's expression had hardened and she sensed anger in his movements. *I'm stronger, I'm better than you!* A new realization coursed through Bobbie's veins as Teddy's plane fell away and she carried on flying north, straight and true.

'Fly safely,' Cameron said to Mary as she collected her chit.

'I always do,' she assured him. She'd learned that she was to take a damaged Corsair to Wolverhampton then meet up there with Angela and Jean before all three pilots were driven back to Rixley by Olive.

Cameron stood two steps below her on the stairs. 'I know you do,' he said fondly.

From the top step of the painted concrete stairs Horace called down to Agnes about her day's activities. 'What did you get?'

'A Mosquito, worse luck.'

'Where to?' Horace barged past Cameron and Mary to join Agnes.

'All the way to Thame,' she informed him. 'What about you?'

'Same as you, but in a Maggie.'

Horace and Agnes began discussing the peculiarities of the two old workhorses as they strode off towards their runway.

Cameron spoke softly to Mary. 'I'll hope to see you later.' His on-duty manner was on the point of breaking down and it was only the appearance of Hilary at the bottom of the stairs that prevented him from embracing Mary before she left.

'Yes, sir,' she said with a bright smile. They both waded minute by minute through the agonies of counting the days leading to Cameron's departure, each trying to put on a brave face for the other's benefit.

'Get a move on, Third Officer Holland,' Hilary said sharply as he mounted the stairs and squeezed past.

'It was my fault.' Cameron offered his apologies. 'I held her up.'

Hilary grunted then disappeared into the ops room while Cameron winked reassuringly at Mary

373

who ran off to find her aircraft, hard on the heels of Jean and Angela. The three pilots exchanged cheerful waves as they climbed into their cockpits then waited for chocks away.

Before long they were airborne and flying in loose formation towards the Midlands factory – south-west over coalfields and steelworks, over vast, pot-bellied cooling towers that churned out smoke and steam and on towards their shared destination. They landed safely on adjacent runways and were soon surrounded by the usual gang of eager, smiling ground crews to whom they handed over their aircraft.

'Blimey!' A corporal mechanic examined Mary's damaged Corsair, putting his finger straight through a hastily patched area in the belly of the fuselage. 'It's a wonder you made it here in one piece.'

Meanwhile, another mechanic quickly examined Angela's papers. 'This Hurricane came all the way from a Maintenance Unit in Aberdeen, it says here. It needs a new propeller shaft, by all accounts.'

'Don't ask me,' Angela replied airily as she went to join Mary. 'I just fly the thing.'

The girls took off their helmets and unzipped their flying suits as they waited for Jean at the end of the runway.

'Can you see our car?' Jean greeted them then led the way into the nearby office where they would officially sign off. Like Mary and Angela, she was keen to set off for home as soon as possible.

'No, there's no sign as yet of the lovely Olive.' Angela looked out of the window at a scene of high activity. Two planes flew out as a third flew in while Tillies and pickups criss-crossed the airfield. Ground crew clustered around the latest arrivals, ready with chocks and toolkits.

'Your driver telephoned to say she's been held up,' a girl behind a desk informed them with thinly disguised satisfaction. These racy women pilots had a tendency to look down their noses at ordinary mortals so she felt it did them no harm to have to twiddle their thumbs once in a while. 'She said she had no idea how long she'll be.'

'The canteen's open,' a more obliging male clerk informed Mary, Jean and Angela.

So they signed their papers then made their way to a low, flat-roofed concrete building where tea and food were served. Settled at a table close to a window overlooking the main gate from where they could keep an eye out for Olive, talk soon turned towards affairs of the heart.

'Mary Holland, you're a sly one.' Angela adopted her usual teasing tone as she flipped open her brand-new powder compact (courtesy of the ground defence boys at Highcliff) and used the small round mirror to refresh her lipstick.

Mary rose to the bait. 'What do you mean?' she asked with a guarded expression.

'I mean you and Cameron, of course. Oh, come along; don't try to deny it. It's as plain as the nose on my face that he follows you around the Grange like a little puppy dog.'

'Tell her to mind her own bloody business,' Jean told Mary with unusual animation as she aimed a kick at Angela's shins.

'Mind your own bloody business,' Mary said with an embarrassed grin.

'Ouch, Jean; that hurt,' Angela complained. 'Anyway, Cameron *is* my business,' she said primly. 'He's been like a big brother to me over the years. And before either of you says anything, I deny all charges.'

Jean was also in the mood to tease. 'Really? I'm willing to bet that there was a time when you viewed Flight Lieutenant Ainslie with more than sisterly interest.'

'Not guilty,' Angela insisted. 'Yes; Cameron fits the suitor bill – tall, fair and handsome, so to speak. But I practically grew up with the dear boy. Hugh and he used to press-gang me into playing cricket with them. I was always the wicket-keeper, worst luck.'

'So I'm safe,' Mary said wryly.

'You'd have been safe anyway.' Angela had moved on from lipstick to powder puff, with which she briskly dabbed her nose and cheeks. 'Cameron is smitten with you, darling. You're much more his type than I am – silent and enigmatic, with hidden depths like the adorable Greta Garbo. You remember – "I vant to be alone!"'

'Tell her to shut up,' Jean urged again.

'No, I don't mind,' Mary admitted. 'It's a relief to have it out in the open, especially since Cameron has to leave Rixley soon. After that I'll be on tenterhooks, watching out for the postman, waiting to hear from him. He's been posted to the RAF base at Aireby,' she explained to a puzzled Angela and Jean.

'Oh, you poor thing!' they chorused as one.

'Life is cruel for star-crossed lovers.' Angela sighed. 'Romeo, Romeo, wherefore art thou . . . ?'

'Shut up, Angela. But Aireby is close by,' Jean commiserated with Mary. 'And while we're at it with the confessions, I have some news of my own.'

'Do tell.' Angela's deep-blue eyes sparkled. 'No; let me consult my crystal ball.' Her hands hovered over the small metal teapot on the table in front of them. 'The mist is clearing; Jean, I see you walking arm in arm with a distinguished older man. He's in uniform. You're deeply in love. His name begins with a . . . "D". Yes; Douglas Thornton is his name!'

Jean took Angela's joshing with good grace. 'It's perfectly true; Douglas and I are engaged.'

'No!' Mary leaned across the table and grasped Jean's wrist. 'You two will tie the knot?'

'I was right,' Angela crowed. 'He went down on bended knee without consulting yours truly?'

'Actually, it was me,' Jean said, loud and clear. 'I was the one who proposed.'

'Congratulations.' Mary beamed at Jean as Angela gave a delighted squeal. 'He said yes? Of course he did; you're engaged. That's marvellous.'

Jean recalled how fast her heart had raced as she'd knelt beside Douglas in the library at the Grange. *We should get married as soon as possible. What do you think?*

He'd gazed down at her for a long time. 'Are you sure?' he'd said at last.

'Never more certain,' she'd murmured. She'd held her breath and he'd taken her hand in his. His whispered words had fallen like a blessing on her head.

'Yes, we'll be married. Name the day.'

Soon after Christmas – in the register office in Northgate. They would find two witnesses and do it without fuss on the first Saturday in January. There would be a wedding ring and a short civil ceremony. All would be perfect.

'How did you manage to keep that under your hat?' Angela demanded.

'It only happened last Thursday.'

'Today's Monday – that's four whole days!' Angela was almost speechless with excitement.

'You know me.' Jean basked in a quiet, golden glow of happiness. 'I'm not one to make a fuss. And Douglas is the same. We want to get married quietly. In any case, Angela, you have no room to talk; you've been playing your cards close to your chest.'

'What does she mean?' Mary demanded.

'I expect Jean is talking about Lionel's visit.' Angela assumed a careless air that fooled no one.

'Aha!' Mary pounced on the opportunity to turn the tables. 'How did he pull that off? Did he get shore leave? Where did he take you? Come along, Angela, I'm all ears.'

'Really, I'd rather not talk about it.' Angela pretended that she was busy looking out of the window for Olive. 'Some other time, perhaps.'

'No, you can't fob us off that easily,' Mary insisted. 'Has Lionel bought your engagement ring? Is that why he came?'

Angela settled back into her seat. 'There is no engagement,' she said in a dull voice. 'There; now you know.'

Jean and Mary stared quizzically at her. 'Oh dear; that's a shame,' Jean murmured.

'I'm really sorry.' Mary supposed that it was Lionel who had broken it off – hence the reason for his visit.

'Don't be, darling.' Angela made as if to pull her packet of cigarettes out of her pocket then thought better of it. 'I wrote Lionel a letter soon after Pa disinherited me, doing the decent thing by releasing him and so forth. Bobbie knows the full story. It was a weight off my mind, to tell you the truth.'

'But . . . ?' From Angela's tone and unusually thoughtful expression, Jean sensed that there was more to come.

'But Lionel, bless his heart, refused to see things my way. He came all the way to the Grange to tell me that he still loves me.'

'Oh, poor Lionel.' Though she didn't know the man, Mary's heart went out to Angela's rejected fiancé. 'All for nothing.'

'Who said it was for nothing?' Angela tapped the table nervously. Beneath the newly applied make-up her face looked careworn. There were dark circles under her eyes and a knotted frown creased her usually smooth forehead. 'I did listen to what Lionel had to say.'

'And?' Jean prompted.

'I promised I would think it over.'

'And?' This time it was Mary who pressed for more information.

Angela shrugged. 'I don't know.'

'What do you mean, you don't know?' To Mary it seemed obvious; either Angela still loved Lionel or she didn't.

'It's complicated.' Angela sighed. 'How can it work between us now that I have no money, no station in life? Lionel's family is filthy rich, you see.'

'So?' Mary raised her eyebrows and glanced at Jean, who remained silent.

'His father won't allow me to drag his son into the gutter – not without a fight.'

'Oh, for goodness sake!' Mary couldn't help herself. Slapping the table with both palms, she rose to her feet with an indignant snort. 'That would be the end, wouldn't it – for you and Lionel to land up in the so-called gutter? Somehow I can't see that happening; can you, Jean?' Really and truly, Angela was talking a load of rubbish. 'Try getting a job as a weaver or a spinner in one of the mills I used to work in, being paid a pittance and getting laid off when the orders stop coming in – then you'd know what you were talking about.'

'You're right, Mary; I'm awfully sorry.' A sudden, acute awareness of her family's textile empire pushed Angela into a profuse apology.

Jean looked from the privileged mill-owner's daughter to the erstwhile wool carder. 'Oddly enough, you are both in the same boat,' she pointed out with calm logic. 'It turns out you're both in love with men who are much wealthier than you and in your minds you regard it as a problem.'

Mary nodded. 'That's true. I thought in the beginning that I wasn't good enough for Cameron, that I didn't belong in his world.' Now, however, Mary had only to be with him for a few seconds, to listen to his voice and feel his soft touch, to know that their love was real and enduring. 'It's different now, though.'

'Naturally, darling,' Angela said wearily. 'Anyone with eyes to see knows that you're the best thing that's happened to Cameron in a very long time.'

'Exactly.' Jean pursued her argument, aware that at any moment Olive might arrive and put an end to the conversation. 'These obstacles are inside our own heads; take the difference in ages between me and Douglas as another example.'

'Talking of whom . . .' Angela was reminded of the file that had lain on Douglas's desk and she was glad to change the subject. She rushed ahead without thinking. 'Jean, has Douglas mentioned to you that Teddy may be about to be hauled before a military court?'

There was a stunned silence. 'You're not serious?' Mary asked.

'Hand on heart,' Angela swore. 'I've seen the file. I understand there's at least one witness – a man called Wynne or Flynn.' Oh dear; she'd promised Hilary she would keep schtum and now here she was, putting her clod-hopping, great big foot in it.

'Douglas hinted at it but I wouldn't expect him to break confidentiality,' Jean said primly after she'd gathered her thoughts.

'What's Teddy done now?' Mary wanted to know. 'Is it to do with Bobbie?'

Angela backtracked frantically. 'Please forget it; I ought not to have said anything.'

'But you did,' Mary persisted. 'If it's not what Teddy did to Bobbie, then why is he in trouble?'

'I don't know – truly, I don't.' Angela reached for her cigarettes and this time she went ahead, lighting up then inhaling deeply as she thought things through. 'Perhaps I should try to winkle it out of him.'

'Are you sure?' Not for the first time, Jean cast doubt over Angela's tactics. 'If Teddy really is in line for a court martial, oughtn't we just to sit back and let events take their course?'

'Jean's right,' Mary agreed, after weighing up the pros and cons. 'Let's concentrate on looking after Bobbie and leave Teddy to his fate.'

Angela ground her partially smoked cigarette into the ashtray. 'Absolutely not,' she decreed. 'For a start, he refuses to leave Bobbie alone. Haven't you noticed how he torments her with gifts and insinuations to throw us off the scent? I for one refuse to let him carry on punishing her in that way.'

'There's something else to take into account,' Jean pointed out. The more she thought it through, the more clearly she saw that the risk Angela proposed to take was too high. 'It'll come to an end soon enough; Teddy has already announced that he's leaving Rixley.'

'For a promotion,' Mary added.

'Promotion, my foot!' Angela exclaimed. 'That's another lie – to hide the fact that he's going up before the beak. If necessary Teddy intends to go out in a blaze of false glory.'

'You may be right,' Jean admitted. 'But either way Bobbie will be rid of him.'

'But without getting the justice she deserves.' It remained crystal clear to Angela that Teddy must be made to pay. 'Bobbie would have to live with that fact for the rest of her life.'

'Yes, I see that.' Mary poured the last of the tea and milk into her cup. 'But if Teddy is as dangerous as we think then you need to be very careful.'

'I will be,' Angela promised. 'As I've said before, it's a question of playing a role, of getting him to trust me.'

Jean gasped as she gained a clear grasp of

Angela's goal. 'Are you saying that you intend to make Teddy confess?'

Without answering, Angela reached for her helmet and parachute pack. 'Here comes Olive,' she announced airily as a black car swept through the main gate with their driver at the wheel.

'Angela!' Jean stood in her way. 'Why would Teddy do that? He has far too much to lose.'

'Jean's right.' Mary added her opinion. 'You'll never manage it.'

'Oh ye of little faith!' Angela retorted as she slipped past Jean then hurried outside. 'Just watch me. If there's one thing I'm good at besides flying the latest Spit, it's twisting an unsuspecting admirer around my little finger.'

CHAPTER TWENTY-ONE

'How's my favourite poster girl?' Teddy intercepted Angela at the base of the control tower at Rixley. He was fresh off the train from Whitehaven, with his parachute pack slung over his shoulder, his sheepskin flying jacket unzipped and a red and blue striped scarf wrapped casually around his neck.

'I'm tickety-boo, thank you. How's your fine self?'

'All the better for running into the best-looking pilot in Yorkshire.' Teddy's banter concealed the bad mood he'd been in all day, ever since he'd come off worst in his mid-air battle of nerves with Bobbie.

'You're very sweet, considering the journey I've just endured – all the way back from Wolverhampton, squashed like a sardine in the back seat of Olive's Ford with Jean and Mary. A chump up front was being taught the basics of the four-speed gearbox. I must look a complete mess.'

'Impossible.' A grinning Teddy linked arms with Angela and guided her towards the canteen. 'What do you say we refresh ourselves with a cuppa, reinforced with something a little stronger?' He drew his flask from his pocket and waved it temptingly in front of her face.

'Just the ticket,' she murmured as she flashed him a brilliant smile and fell into step beside him.

They entered the busy canteen with a flourish: Teddy gallantly holding the door while Angela sashayed ahead. Stan sat at a nearby table with Bob, earnestly discussing outstanding repair jobs; in the far corner of the room, Hilary, Douglas and Cameron compared notes for the next day's schedule. There was a general bustle and much chatter.

'Find us a nice quiet seat while I fetch the teas,' Teddy suggested to Angela.

So she chose a spot in a shallow recess beyond the counter, smiling briefly at Hilary as she passed his table.

'Two teas coming up!' Unable to do anything in a low-key way, Teddy swaggered as he threaded his way towards her. 'I assumed you don't take sugar,' he said as he sat down next to her. 'You're sweet enough . . .'

'Oh, please – not that old chestnut!' she said with a pout, pretending to be put out.

'My apologies; I'll try to be more original in future.'

'I should hope so, darling.' Angela took her first sip of scalding tea then pointedly slid her cup towards him.

Teddy winked and drew out the flask then poured a generous measure into both cups. 'Just the job, eh?'

'At the end of a long day,' she agreed, sipping again. 'Chin-chin.'

'Yes; bottoms up.'

'After this, it's a hot bath and an early night for me – unless you happen to come up with a more entertaining alternative.'

Teddy leaned closer. 'Such as?'

'Such as a Clark Gable or Cary Grant flick at High-cliff Odeon.' She looked him in the eye and feigned surprise. 'Why, Teddy Simpson, surely you didn't think I was suggesting something less wholesome?'

'As if I would!'

Angela let an innuendo-laden pause develop. Teddy's shoulder touched hers and his face was so close that she couldn't make out his features. 'Knowing you – yes, you would,' she drawled.

'And?' he prompted eagerly. Not for the first time he felt he was in with a real chance with Angela.

She paused again then leaned away. 'It's a no from me, darling. I'm actually much too tired – for a film or for anything else.'

Teddy felt a thud of disappointment. Why lead him on in the first place? Still, he must not let Angela see that she'd got to him. 'And here was I, getting my hopes up . . .'

'Another time, perhaps.' Leaving her tea unfinished, she stood up.

'You'd better make the most of me while you can; I depart these shores next week,' Teddy reminded her as he too stood up from the table.

'Oh, boo!' Angela simpered, swishing past the table where Hilary sat with Douglas and Cameron. 'Rixley without Flight Lieutenant Simpson – whatever shall we do?'

She didn't look back as she left the canteen and when she felt a tap on her shoulder as she made her way along the path, she expected it to be Teddy refusing to take no for an answer.

'Angela, can I have a word?' Hilary's question

came across as an order that must be obeyed. 'In my office, please.'

'Now?' she asked once she'd overcome her surprise. 'I'm awfully tired. Won't it keep?'

'Not too tired to lead Teddy by the nose,' Hilary muttered without breaking his stride. 'Of all people!'

Angela followed Hilary into his room, which was stacked with files and papers on every available surface. There were two telephones and a typewriter on his desk; every inch of wall was covered in maps and charts.

'Sit down.' He pointed to a chair made of canvas and tubular steel.

Angela's stomach fluttered. Had it somehow got back to Hilary that she'd blabbed about Teddy's court martial? *If so, better to sit tight and let Hilary do the talking.*

'How's Lionel?' He took up position behind his desk, standing with hands clasped behind his back. His sharp features gave nothing away.

Her eyes widened. This was not what she'd been expecting. 'He's well, so far as I know.'

'And have you given him a final answer?'

'I have not.' Her clipped reply indicated that this was none of her commanding officer's business.

Hilary unclasped his hands and leaned forward. 'About Teddy Simpson . . .'

Ah, now for the nitty-gritty.

'Is Lionel aware that he has a rival?' Hilary watched Angela closely as his urbane question hit its mark. 'No; don't answer that. I'm merely pointing out your responsibility towards somebody who happens to be a close friend of mine. Frankly, Angela, it would be my duty to inform Lionel if I found out anything untoward.'

'Teddy is not Lionel's rival,' she replied as calmly as she could, though her heart hammered against her ribs and her breath came short.

'Then why?'

'Why what?'

'Why carry on with the fellow the way you do?' Hilary's voice rose and a flush appeared on his neck and cheeks. 'Back there in the canteen for all to see. And not only there; I've watched you in the bar at the Grange, openly vying with Bobbie for Teddy's attention, and before that, at Bobbie's birthday party. To put it bluntly, Angela, I expected better.'

'I'm sorry to hear you say that,' she whispered.

'You don't deny it?'

'No, but I have my reasons.'

'Don't be ridiculous. What possible excuse could there be for throwing yourself at Teddy Simpson, in spite of being engaged to Lionel and given the trouble I took to warn you off?' Hilary tapped the file sitting on top of the blotting pad in the centre of his desk.

Recognizing the official stamp and reading Teddy's name at the top of the folder, Angela couldn't contain herself a moment longer. 'You have no right to criticize me without knowing the full story,' she began, before making a lunge for the file. Hilary snatched it away. 'In any case, what I choose to do in my own time has nothing to do with you.'

'Unless it undermines discipline on the base – as I've said before.' Hilary held the file at a safe distance then went on with his attack. 'The men are beginning to gossip about your association with Flight Lieutenant Simpson. You're losing their respect.'

'Which men?' She almost howled with indignation.

'The ground crew and some of the other pilots. I make a point of keeping my ear to the ground.'

'Does anyone accuse me of not doing my job?'

'No,' he conceded. 'Nevertheless, Cameron and Douglas agree that your behaviour off-duty gives rise to concern.'

'How dare they – how dare *you*!' She paused to draw breath. 'If I was a man, you'd never talk to me in this way. It would simply be a case of "boys will be boys" and there's no point trying to deny it. Well, I don't accept that, Hilary – not any more. We're all equal in wartime and men and women must be given the same freedoms.'

'The freedom to behave as badly as Teddy? The freedom to ruin yourself?' Hilary challenged. 'I mean it – if you're not careful and you carry on as you are, he will drag your name through the mud.'

Angela rushed forward to try to snatch the file from Hilary but he pushed her away. 'Why? What has Teddy done that makes you so adamant?'

He held the folder to his chest. 'If what's in this file is true, it's bad; very bad.'

'Hilary, please!'

There seemed only one way to resolve the impasse. 'Very well; if it will bring you to your senses.' Without opening the file and clicking into a professional tone, Hilary slowly revealed its contents. 'In March this year Teddy's squadron was scrambled to intercept German planes off the Lincolnshire coast.'

Angela held her breath and took in every detail.

'His orders were to come up from behind the targets and open fire. But the first report from the ground was mistaken: the only aircraft in the sky were British. Teddy ignored a subsequent radio order to cease fire. He hit his target with deadly accuracy and shot Spitfire pilot Murray Henderson through the head. Henderson died instantly.'

Angela's heart almost stopped. 'He shot down one of our own?'

'Teddy denies it, of course. He's adamant that he never received the second order to hold his fire.'

'And until it's proved one way or the other, no official action can be taken?'

Hilary nodded. 'Yes, but that's why he was posted to Rixley: to fly unarmoured planes for the ATA. It was thought that here he couldn't present a danger to his fellow pilots.'

Thinking of Bobbie, Angela gave a hollow laugh. 'You've known this all along?'

'Yes.'

'And not said a word? No, of course not – Teddy is presumed innocent until proven guilty.'

'Quite.' Hilary laid the file on his desk. 'What a bloody awful mess,' he murmured. 'If it was anyone else, I'd be prepared to give him the benefit of the doubt – but with Teddy, I'm not so sure.'

'He's a slippery customer,' Angela conceded.

'Some of what he says rings true.' Hilary spoke his mind with rare frankness. 'I've gone into his record and discovered that he was an exceptionally able pupil at his grammar school in Manchester, and a fine athlete to boot. But a tutor at the Initial

Training Wing was the first to notice Teddy's tendency to exaggerate his achievements. Nevertheless, the pressure was on to prepare as many pilots as possible for active service so any doubts were overlooked.'

Never in the field of human conflict ... The prime minister's voice infiltrated Angela's whirling thoughts ... *was so much owed by so many to so few.* Since Dunkirk, young men of varying abilities had been snatched fresh from school and crammed with facts about signalling, navigation and aircraft types. They were issued with ill-fitting uniforms and cursorily tested for colour-blindness and tunnel vision, for dexterity and reaction time. Then, before these boys knew it, they were awarded their dog tags and were up in Tiger Moths at 1,000 feet, completing their training before finding themselves behind the controls of Blenheims and Wellingtons – lethal machines that they had little experience of flying. If they were lucky they survived six missions; a fact that was glossed over during their training programme.

'It's madness,' Angela whispered, 'when you stop to think.'

'It doesn't pay to dwell,' Hilary countered swiftly. 'But now at least you see why it's essential for both you and Bobbie to give Teddy Simpson a wide berth. The circumstances of the court martial would be bound to play on a man's mind and make his behaviour unpredictable, to say the least.'

'Yes, I do see.' Angela looked back over Teddy's many lies and deceptions. 'He comes out with absolute balderdash for much of the time.' She knew she ought to steer clear, but ... but there was the unbreakable, binding promise that Angela had made to Bobbie and a simmering anger against Teddy that refused to go away. 'Thank you, Hilary; I appreciate your giving me the low-down.'

'Unofficially,' he reminded her. 'This goes no further.'

'Understood.' Angela stooped to pick up her belongings. 'You can rely on me.'

'And write to Lionel,' Hilary added with heavy emphasis. 'Put the poor fellow's mind at rest.'

'I will,' she promised. One way or the other she must make up her mind about their future. 'This weekend if not before.'

Bobbie fell asleep as the railway carriage clicked and swayed along steel tracks, across the Scottish border, heading south to York where she would have to change trains for Rixley. She'd spent an uncomfortable night in a B & B close to the ferry pool where she'd delivered the Spit, kept awake by well-founded worries about bed bugs and by the sounds of rowdy drunkards roaming the streets long after midnight. Glad to move on, she'd got up early and caught the first train south.

'The next station is York.' The announcement woke her with a start, leaving her little time to gather her overnight bag. 'Change here for Northgate, Highcliff and Rixley.'

Still scarcely awake, Bobbie shuffled off the train. The station clock told her that it was half past one and she gleaned information from a porter that the Rixley train was due to depart in five minutes from Platform 3, which gave her just enough time to hurry across the bridge and squeeze into the carriage immediately behind the hissing steam engine.

'Here, love; have my seat.' A middle-aged man leaned out from his compartment and tapped Bobbie on the arm. Taking her bag, he slung it on to the luggage rack as she sank down. 'I've got a daughter in the ATA,' he informed her. 'Vera; my eldest girl.'

'Ta very much.' It was a thirty-minute hop but Bobbie was grateful nevertheless. Ten minutes into the journey she was asleep again and it was the same passenger who woke her to tell her that they'd reached their journey's end.

'Good luck to you,' he said as he helped her to disembark. 'I don't know where the country would be without girls like you and my Vera.'

She thanked him again, said goodbye then emerged from the small station on to the pavement where, to her dismay, she bumped into Teddy and Horace.

'Fancy that!' Teddy exclaimed. 'We were all on the same train without realizing.'

Before trusting herself to reply, Bobbie pressed her lips firmly together and took a deep breath. 'Hello, Teddy; hello, Horace.'

'Here, let me carry your bag,' Teddy offered.

'No thanks, I can manage. Where did Douglas send you today, Horace?'

'Only over to Foxborough with Teddy here, to deliver two Corsairs. It's an early finish for us, thank goodness.' Anyone more opposite to Teddy than Horace was hard to imagine, with his slight, short stature and receding hairline. He spoke quietly, with a shy smile.

'Hey-up,' Teddy interrupted. Hearing a low rumble of aeroplane engines, he glanced up at four Lancasters and two Stirlings flying low overhead. 'It looks like our chaps mean business later on tonight.'

The rumble rose to a roar that seemed to run through Bobbie's whole body as the planes flew from west to east, through low grey cloud.

'Talking of business, how about letting me buy you the drink I mentioned yesterday?' Teddy jostled Bobbie's elbow as they walked past the Fox and Hounds. He winked knowingly at Horace. 'Bobbie likes to play hard to get,' he explained, 'but really she can't resist.'

'When did you mention it?' she demanded with a sudden flash of anger mixed with scorn. 'Ah yes, I remember – when you were playing silly devils in mid-air and I was busy trying to avoid a head-on crash.'

'Just a bit of fun.' He shrugged. His sideways glance at Horace was meant to indicate that Bobbie suffered from the typical female complaint of vivid imagination. 'No need to lay it on so thick.'

Bobbie walked quickly ahead. When Teddy ran to catch her up, she stopped in her tracks. 'Get this clear,' she said to him, slowly and deliberately so that Horace could hear and there could be no mistake. 'I do not want you to buy me a drink. In fact, I want nothing to do with you; is that understood?'

With the entrance to the Grange in sight, Teddy glanced uneasily at Horace then gave a shallow laugh. 'Women, eh? One minute they're all over you, the next it's claws-out.'

The gorge rose in Bobbie's throat but she managed to push down the sickening memories – the stone steps, the dark room, the smell of whisky on Teddy's breath. At last she was able to look him in the eye. 'Don't come near me again,' she said clearly. 'Ever. Don't even talk to me.'

Teddy put up his hands in mock surrender. 'Uh-oh; I can see that someone didn't get much sleep last night. What or who kept you awake, I wonder?'

'Hang on, old chap.' Mild-mannered Horace considered Teddy's last insinuation a step too far. 'A joke is all well and good but there is a limit, you know.'

'Ta, Horace, but I can stand up for myself.' And Bobbie found to her amazement that it was true: Teddy Simpson's hold over her was slipping. She could now look at him and detect with satisfaction the uncertainty and insecurity that lurked behind his bravado.

'Please yourself,' Teddy muttered as they entered the grounds to the Grange. 'It doesn't bother me; there are plenty more fish in the sea.'

Teddy had felt the power shift. For a minute it had unnerved him but then he'd reassured himself that he'd already done enough to ensure that any charge that Bobbie might bring against him would come unstuck. For a start he'd made sure that she'd had too much to drink on the night in question – always a good ploy – and afterwards he'd cleared up after himself by stuffing her cape, shoes and dress into the stove. And time had passed – enough to make people wonder why Bobbie had waited so long to accuse him. He would be able to claim that she was not as naive as she seemed; that in fact she was the one who had led him on.

Nothing to worry about, he thought as they went their separate ways: Horace and Bobbie to their rooms and Teddy to the stable yard to tinker with the engine of his Royal Enfield. He'd taken off his jacket and rolled up his sleeves ready to begin when Olive drove Angela, Jean and Mary into the yard.

They clambered out of the Ford with evident relief.

'Here we are: the Three Musketeers!' Angela declared. 'Fresh from Cheshire and all points west.'

'Lucky you.' Teddy picked out the spanner he needed to take off the engine cover. 'Douglas dug out another Maggie for me to fly after I'd delivered the Corsair. I didn't stagger much further than Northgate with her. Still, the good news is we've all got a free evening.'

'Yes; to do laundry and write letters.' Mary was the first to leave the yard, followed by Jean, who had arranged to have tea with Douglas.

Teddy paused, spanner in hand. 'How about you, Angela? I don't suppose you fancy a quick spin?'

'Where to?'

'Wherever you like.'

'Later on; to the Odeon in Highcliff,' she decided without hesitation. 'You're luck's in: I scanned the newspaper advertisements; they're reshowing *Casablanca* tonight with Humphrey Bogart and Ingrid Bergman.'

Teddy leapt at the chance. 'Right you are. What time does it start?'

'Half past seven. That means we should leave here at half six – still plenty of time to spruce ourselves up.'

The arrangements were smoothly made; Angela and Teddy would meet under the stable-yard clock at the appointed time.

It was only when Jean went up to her room after sharing tea and sandwiches with Douglas in the Grange bar that she bumped into Angela on the landing. Angela was dressed to kill in high heels, nylons and a pale blue jersey-knit dress, carrying her coat over one arm. She wore a poppy-red lipstick and her glossy dark hair was brushed and styled to perfection. 'Goodness; you must be going somewhere special,' Jean remarked brightly. 'Has Lionel been in touch?'

'Lionel is back with his ship.' Angela's reply was offhand and she hurried on.

Jean walked along the landing with an uneasy feeling. Surely, after all the doubts that she and Mary had expressed, Angela would have told them about any assignation with Teddy? She knocked lightly on Mary's door. 'Angela's on her way out. Did she say where she was going?' she asked.

Mary shook her head. 'I haven't seen her since we got back. Shall we see if Bobbie knows?'

They hurried to Bobbie's room. It turned out that Bobbie knew no more than Jean and Mary did.

'Ought we to be worried?' Mary stood by Bobbie's window overlooking the crater-strewn front lawn. 'Perhaps we ought to come clean?'

'Who with?' Bobbie grew aware of more planes flying over: the third group of RAF bombers to be seen heading east that evening. The sight seemed ominous in the gathering dusk.

'With you, for a start.' Jean followed Mary's train of thought. 'Angela is certain that she can wangle a confession out of you-know-who.'

'She's going about it in her own inimitable way,' Mary explained. 'Jean and I aren't too happy about it, but Angela has promised us that she'll be all right.'

'We couldn't go to Douglas or Cameron with our worries – not after you swore us to secrecy.' Jean wished it had been otherwise, but a promise was a promise.

'Yes, but this wasn't meant to happen!' Bobbie's distress was plain to see.

'That's Angela for you.' Mary paced the room. At this rate there'd be no chance of catching up with their hot-headed friend.

'Angela stayed behind in the yard to talk to Teddy,' Jean remembered.

'Perhaps we should go down . . .' Mary began.

'. . . and check.' Bobbie was the first to act. She ran ahead of Jean and Mary, down the stairs and out through the servants' quarters on to the back steps just in time to see Angela in her teal blue coat and hat climbing on to the back of Teddy's motorbike.

They were too late to stop her. With his collar turned up and wearing his flying jacket and gauntlets, Teddy kicked the bike into action. Angela put both arms around his waist and held tight. Jean, Mary and Bobbie stood and watched helplessly as Teddy and Angela disappeared under the archway, along the narrow path and out through the back gate.

*

'"Play it, Sam. Play 'As Time Goes By'."' Angela imitated Ingrid Bergman's rich voice with its intriguing Swedish accent.

She and Teddy walked arm in arm through the brightly lit foyer of the Highcliff cinema then out through a revolving door and on to the dark street.

'"Of all the gin joints in all the towns in all the world . . ."' Teddy managed a decent impression of Bogart's drawl.

'". . . she walks into mine."' Angela concluded.

They laughed and chose their favourite scenes – Rick furious with Sam for disobeying his order never to perform the 'As Time Goes By' song, Rick in the final scene making Ilsa board the Lisbon plane with Laszlo.

'Would you have done the sensible thing and got on that plane with your husband?' Teddy asked Angela as they reached the spot where he'd parked his motorbike.

'No, darling; I'd have stayed in Casablanca with Rick. No regrets – not a single one.'

They chatted on as they got on the bike and wove through the narrow streets of the fishing port. They soon left the town behind and Teddy was able to pick up speed. Angela crouched behind him, her head turned sideways and her cheek pressed against the cold, smooth leather of Teddy's jacket. There was an extraordinary orange moon in a sky that had grown clear during their time in the cinema. It was large, full and round – suspended like a bright bronze disc against a background of midnight blue. The road ahead was empty as they crested the hill on to the open moors, the only sound a faint thrum of aeroplane engines flying east but too high to be seen.

As they approached Rixley, Teddy slowed down. He coasted through the village and was about to turn into the main entrance of the Grange when Angela tapped him on the shoulder. 'Use the back gate,' she reminded him. Though it added a couple of minutes to their journey, it was better to be safe than sorry.

'Brrr, my poor fingers and tootsies are frozen!' she complained when at last they reached the gate. It was shut so she quickly hopped off and opened it. Teddy, meanwhile, killed the engine and quietly walked the bike into the grounds.

'Shh!' He held a finger to his mouth then pointed to the unlit downstairs windows of the house. 'It's late. They've all gone to beddy-byes!'

So he wheeled the Enfield along the path and Angela walked alongside him, clapping her gloved hands together to try to restore feeling. Their feet crunched on the gravel until they came to the clock tower and passed under it into the cobbled stable yard, where Teddy stopped and heaved the bike on to its metal stand.

He turned to Angela and took her hands in his, raising them to his lips before blowing into her cupped palms. 'Better?'

She shook her head then shot him a conspiratorial glance. 'A spot of whisky might do the trick, though.'

'Good thinking.' *The girl wants to have fun!* With a satisfied nudge, he drew his flask from his pocket and unscrewed the lid then handed it to her. '"Here's looking at you, kid,"' he said with a wink and the Bogart drawl.

Angela sipped and swallowed. *For much needed courage*, she thought. She sipped again then handed Teddy the flask and tipped her head back to glimpse the vivid orange moon. It seemed smaller now and was about to disappear behind the clock tower. A shiver ran through her in spite of the whisky.

'Here; let me warm you up.' With the flask in one hand, Teddy put both arms around her waist and held her close. 'How about that?' he murmured. 'No; wait!' Another idea seemed to have occurred to him. 'Come this way.'

'What's happening? Where are you taking me?' Angela resisted. Yes, her goal of the evening was to soften Teddy up and trick him into making his confession, but on the other hand she knew she couldn't trust him or his motives. In fact, she foresaw with heart-stopping certainty where this particular game was leading.

'Somewhere nice and warm,' he promised, one arm still around her waist.

Reluctantly she let him guide her across the yard. 'Why not the house?'

'Because the walls there have ears and we don't want Bobbie and the other busybodies to know what we're up to, do we?' Soft and persuasive, Teddy guided her on towards the stone steps leading to the grooms' quarters.

'Darling, aren't you assuming rather a lot?' Angela made a show of demure protest.

Teddy's answer was to offer her the flask again and then redouble his persuasion. 'Drink some more of this. Come up here with me and let me light a fire. You'll soon be cosy and warm.' *Yes; she'll co-operate. A girl like Angela knows what she's letting herself in for; she's trodden this road a dozen times before.*

Angela let the whisky touch her lips and tongue but didn't swallow. 'A fire, eh? That's certainly tempting.'

'And the night is still young. If we went into the house we'd have to go our separate ways – you to your lonely room and me to mine.'

'Which would be a pity,' she agreed. 'Somehow I'm not in the mood for sleeping.'

Teddy put one foot on the bottom step. 'That's more like it. We think along the same lines, you and me.'

'In what way?' *Keep a clear head and give the performance of your life.*

'We both like to throw caution to the wind once in a while.' There was no need to say more; Angela knew what he meant.

'Yes, and who cares what time we get back and what other people say afterwards?'

'Not me,' Teddy said with a grin. This was going very well indeed, even if it had meant sitting all night watching Bergman make eyes at Bogart. Still; if it kept the girl happy . . .

'Me neither!' Angela cocked her head to one side and joined him on the steps. 'You know me, Teddy: always game.'

'Come up,' he cajoled. 'There's firewood next to the stove and I have a lighter. I'll lend you my jacket. We'll have you warm in no time.'

CHAPTER TWENTY-TWO

'Angela's not back yet.' Bobbie's face was worried when she knocked on Jean's door dressed in her pale blue shirt and navy trousers. 'It's gone eleven and she's not in her room.'

Jean was in pyjamas and dressing-gown and her hair hung loose around her shoulders. She'd been sitting in bed reading the closing chapters of Thackeray's *Vanity Fair* when Bobbie's knock had interrupted her. 'What can we do?' she wondered as she came out on to the landing.

'We could go downstairs and check if she's there,' Bobbie suggested.

Their voices drew Mary out of her room. She was still fully dressed after parting from Cameron only half an hour earlier. 'What's up?' she asked.

'There's no sign of Angela.' Bobbie turned on the light and descended the stairs.

Jean and Mary followed but before they'd had a chance to begin their search, Hilary rushed down from the top floor, taking the stairs two at a time. He looked as if he'd flung on his uniform and appeared in the hallway minus his tie, his jacket hanging open.

'Why, Hilary, what's the matter?' Bobbie's first thought was for Angela. Perhaps he'd received a telephone message that had alarmed him.

'Rixley – a German attack is imminent,' he reported abruptly. '*Luftwaffe* sighted over Highcliff, apparently heading in this direction. It could be a follow-up to their last raid – an attempt to put us out of action for good.'

The words were hardly out of his mouth when Cameron, Horace and Douglas raced down the stairs. Agnes and several other pilots in various states of undress had also been roused by the clatter of footsteps and the sound of voices.

'Cameron, come to the base with me,' Hilary ordered. 'Everyone else, stay here on high alert. Lights off, observe total blackout. You all know the drill.'

Jean sought out Douglas, who was now in charge at the Grange.

'Roll-call,' he decided as he turned off all the lights. 'Make it snappy.'

'Where?' Horace wanted to know.

'Here, in the front hall.' Douglas made a quick mental check of who might still be in their rooms. 'Jean, go and fetch Angela. Horace, find out where Teddy is.'

'Angela isn't in her room,' Jean informed him. 'She and Teddy went out.' This was very bad, she told herself. Suppose Angela was still with Teddy, on their way back from wherever they'd spent the evening. They might be caught out in the open if and when the bombs started to drop.

With an impatient shake of his head, Douglas dismissed Angela from his mind. 'Everyone, assemble here in the hall! Jean, fetch the list from Hilary's office.'

Bobbie caught hold of Mary's arm. 'What now?'

Mary fought to stay calm as she pictured Cameron arriving at the base with Hilary to raise the alarm. 'We follow orders,' she gasped. What else could they do?

So Mary and Bobbie joined the crush to silently assemble inside the main entrance, eyes and ears wide open and expecting the worst. Jean arrived with clipboard and pencil. The roll-call began.

'Is there a light switch?' Angela asked Teddy as they entered the loft. She took off her hat as she stood in the doorway then felt with her fingertips along the rough stone, dislodging some gardening tools that were propped against the wall but failing to find a switch.

'We're in the dark, I'm afraid,' Teddy said with a chuckle. 'In the old days servants and grooms had to make do with candles and oil lamps, I suppose.'

No electricity. As Angela's eyes got used to the gloom, she was able to make out the long room with open rafters and a pile of disused furniture stacked at one end with an old mattress laid flat on the bare boards next to a stove – all as Bobbie had eventually related. The only light came from the moon through small panes of glass inserted into the roof. 'The places you bring me to, Flight Lieutenant Simpson!' Angela declared with a loud, theatrical sigh.

'This was how the other half used to live.' Before

Teddy got busy with firewood, he drew Angela further into the room. Then he took off his jacket and wrapped it around her shoulders. His hand stroked her cheek and he kissed her on the forehead then on the lips. 'More whisky?' he murmured as he drew back.

She nodded. 'How did you know what was in here?' she asked as he crouched to open the stove door. 'I take it you've been here before?'

Teddy rested on his haunches and glanced up at her. 'Once or twice, whenever I need some peace and quiet. Why do you ask?'

'No reason – just curious.' Angela risked a sip from the flask. She must stay calm and not arouse his suspicions. 'You're quite the romantic, aren't you?'

'In what way?' Leaning sideways, he reached for kindling for the stove.

'Finding us a cosy love-nest in which to end a perfect evening.' She went up to him and pulled him to his feet. 'I'm still awfully cold,' she said with a shiver.

So he wrapped his arms around her and kissed her again. 'I'm a very lucky chap,' he whispered in her ear. 'Every red-blooded male on this base would give their eye teeth to be here with you.'

'Of course they would, darling, but it's not them I'm interested in.' Angela stood with her arms around Teddy's neck, pressing her body against him.

'So why me?' Vanity led him to ask the question. The fire could wait a while.

She smiled and leaned away, hands still clasped at the nape of his neck and swaying from one hip to the other. 'Where to begin? Let's start with the dashing figure you cut when you first arrived. All the girls were ready to fall at your feet, but I expect you're used to that.'

'Steady on,' he protested, aroused by the swing of her hips. Did Angela mean it or was she mocking him? It was difficult to be sure. But she was here with her arms around his neck and he could smell her perfume and feel the smooth perfection of her cheek and lips, the curve of her breasts as she pressed against him, so what did it matter what mood she was in?

'I'm serious, darling. First impressions are so important. And of course it turns out that you have a fascinating history – grammar school boy made good, and so forth. I find that intriguing.'

'Carry on,' he urged as he stroked her hair. 'Don't stop now.'

Angela had known all along that flattery was the way to bring down Teddy's guard. 'I'm curious to find out more. Where did the ambition come from? What drives you on?'

Mockery or sincere praise? Again the doubt flitted across Teddy's consciousness. Once more he chose to ignore it. 'The fact is, I wanted to prove to myself that I was as good as the kid born with a silver spoon in his mouth,' he answered. 'I mean, why should they have everything handed to them on a plate and I have nothing? That didn't seem fair.'

'And prove it you did, Teddy dear.' There was another kiss and another shiver from her. 'You chalked up three kills with your last squadron and now it seems there's a big promotion in the offing. That can't be bad.'

He drew away and set about laying kindling inside the stove. 'Your turn; now you have to tell me something that you normally keep close to your chest.'

With a soft swish of knitted fabric, Angela sat down on the mattress and drew her legs under her. 'Of course, darling; what would you like to know?'

'What happened to poor old Lionel? Is he permanently off the scene?'

'Oh, Teddy; your powers of observation seem to have deserted you.' She pouted as she held up her left hand and waggled her fingers. 'Do you see an engagement ring?'

'No,' he conceded.

'No, because I called it off. I'm currently free as a bird. In any case, you're hardly in a position to talk. Your name has been linked with dear little Bobbie.'

With his lighter at the ready, Teddy paused. 'I've told you before: Bobbie and I were never serious. I hope she doesn't still give you the wrong impression about the two of us.'

Angela smiled. 'Don't flatter yourself, darling – she and I have better things to talk about.'

'That's all right then. Because we both know that Bobbie has a tendency to get hold of the wrong end of the stick.' An urge to justify himself pushed Teddy into dangerous territory. 'She wasn't too happy when I finally set her straight.'

'Was that before or after you gave her the stockings?' Angela made a point of asking.

Teddy blinked then flicked his lighter to produce a flame. 'Long before,' he insisted. 'The stockings were a small get-well present after she took the knock on the head.'

'Ah, yes; Bobbie's near miss.' Angela watched carefully as he held the long, slim flame to the kindling. Her eyes widened as she spotted a fragment of vivid green fabric lying in the old ashes. The pile of sticks sparked and caught fire. Without stopping to think, she jumped to her feet, leaned forward and quickly scooped the charred scrap out of the flames.

Hilary reached the ferry pool in record time. He screeched to a halt and jumped out of the car. 'You raised the alarm?' he demanded of the sentry.

'Yes, sir!' The corporal ran from his box to lift the barrier. 'I set off the siren. All personnel are aware.'

'Good man.' Returning to the car, Hilary drove on to the base. He parked next to the control tower then ordered Cameron to double-check that a roll-call was under way. Meanwhile, he ran up to the ops room to pick up the telephone. He dialled the coastal watch operator and asked to be put through to the Highcliff unit. 'I don't care if the line is busy,' he barked into the receiver. 'This is Squadron Leader Hilary Stevens calling from Rixley on a matter of utmost importance.'

Outside, Cameron sprinted towards a large group gathered on the lawn close to the canteen. He passed one or two stragglers emerging half-asleep from their billets. 'Shift your backsides, get in line!' he yelled. '*Luftwaffe* attack imminent!'

'How close are they, sir?' Stan had put himself in charge of the roll-call. He left off counting when Cameron arrived.

All eyes turned from the dark, empty sky to the ferry pool's second in command.

'I can't tell you that. The squadron leader's on the blower trying to find out. They can't be far away, though.'

Voices murmured uneasily. Someone at the end of the line struck a match to light a cigarette, only to have it knocked from his trembling hand. 'Daft bugger!' Olive muttered in the pitch darkness. 'Does he want to advertise our whereabouts?'

'How many planes?' Stan wanted to know.

'Can't tell you that either.' Cameron looked beyond the dark mass of Burton Wood, up at the full moon. Apart from the sound of wind whistling through the branches there was an eerie silence.

'How long do we have to stand here?' a peevish voice asked.

'We're sitting ducks if we hang around much longer,' another remarked.

'We wait for an order from the squadron leader,' Cameron said firmly.

'Sod that, sir!' It was Stan who objected. 'There're two Spits out there on Runway Two, plain as the nose on your face. If Jerry spots them, we're done for.'

Cameron nodded. 'You're right, Corporal. Drive two trucks out on to the runway and tow the aircraft out of sight, quick as you can.'

Glad to be doing something useful, Stan took Bob with him while the others waited with mounting unease for news from their squadron leader.

Back in the control tower, Hilary listened intently to the latest information supplied by ground defence. 'RAF, you say?' He felt the tension drain from his body. 'On their way back from a mission over Denmark?'

'Correct, sir,' the soldier in charge replied. 'There was a second sighting twenty miles north-west of here. They say it's not Jerry after all; it's definitely our boys.'

Hilary let out a long sigh of relief. 'Thank you, Sergeant. We'll stand down at this end.'

He replaced the receiver into its cradle. Buttoning up his jacket, he tugged it straight then proceeded down the stairs and cupped both hands to his mouth. 'Stand down,' he yelled across the grass. 'It turns out to be much ado about nothing. As you were and back to bed, everyone.'

'Give me that!' Teddy had moved too slowly to prevent Angela from snatching the piece of green fabric from the cold ashes.

She crumpled it in the palm of her hand and formed a fist then she stepped away from the unlit fire. 'Give you what?'

'That – whatever it is!'

A remnant of Bobbie's dress: concrete proof that Teddy had destroyed evidence after the attack. It was easy for Angela to picture the scene: Bobbie unconscious and almost naked on the mattress, her torn dress and jacket cast aside. Having finished with her, Teddy must have decided to cover his tracks. He'd opened the door of the stove and thrown the ruined clothes on to the flames. In the morning Bobbie could say whatever she liked but he would insist she'd been too drunk to remember anything. If accusations flew his way he could say that she'd made the whole thing up and there would be no evidence to the contrary. His plan had almost worked.

'I said, give it to me.' Teddy lunged at Angela.

'Tut-tut; such a fuss.' Angela side-stepped then wagged her finger at him. 'All over nothing.'

'If it's nothing, then show me what you found.' His anger rising, he circled around her to see what she was hiding.

'Certainly not.' With her hand behind her back and with Teddy's jacket slipping from her shoulders, Angela continued to back away. The jacket fell and wrapped itself around her legs, making her stumble sideways. She put out her hands to break her fall.

Teddy swooped. He wrested the scrap of chiffon from her grasp.

Angela felt a sharp pain in her ankle. She'd twisted it and, worse still, Teddy would recognize the fabric. He would see how she'd snatched the proof from under his eyes.

It took him only a second or two. He looked from the green remnant to the stove then at Angela struggling to raise herself from the floor.

'Don't look at me like that, darling.' She reached out her hand as she made one last attempt to continue the charade. 'Help me up.'

Teddy rushed at her and thrust her back down. 'Nice try,' he said. 'But I see what you're up to and it won't wash.'

'Teddy – my ankle!'

He bent down and jerked his jacket from under her then he seized her by the wrist. Angela would be no more of a match than Bobbie had been if it came to a physical fight.

'I thought . . . but I must have made a mistake.'

Angela switched tactics. 'I'm sorry; in future I'll mind my own business.'

'Sorry for what?' Teddy knelt beside her and thrust his face into hers. 'For trying to make a fool of me? Or for believing what your pathetic little friend told you? Either way, it's too late – apology not accepted.'

With her free hand Angela wiped away the spray of Teddy's saliva from her face. Instinct kept her silent and she watched him warily as he stuffed the green fragment into the fire. Everything about the man was repulsive – his spitting, snarling insults; the beastliness of his actions; the cocky assumption that he would win in the end.

'It's a pity, though,' he went on more calmly.

'Let go – please!'

Despite her plea, he held on to her and smiled nastily. 'It's a pity because we could have had such a fine time up here, you and I – a nice warm fire, plenty more to drink. What would have been wrong with that?'

'Everything,' she said with a shudder as she tried to pull free. 'Teddy Simpson, you have no conscience and you *are* a fool if you imagine that you can get away with rape. There; I've said it. What you did to Bobbie was unforgivable and soon everyone will know it.'

Teddy was unmoved. As far as he was concerned, nothing had changed. 'Do you think so? Why will anyone believe you and Bobbie rather than me?'

'Because it's the truth.'

'That's naively touching – you sound more like Bobbie than the hard-boiled Angela that I know and love.'

'And people aren't stupid,' she went on angrily. 'Hilary for one is under no illusion; he sees you for what you are.'

'Is that right?' Mention of their squadron leader threw a different light on things; Teddy saw that he needed to think this one through. He raised Angela to her feet, dragged her across the room then trapped her against the wall. 'Explain what you mean.'

As her back thudded against the wall, a fresh pain shot down her spine and she struggled to draw breath.

'Explain!' He slammed her against the rough stone a second time.

'Stop – you're hurting me,' she gasped. 'Hilary knows about your court martial. He has a copy of the file. You ignored orders and shot down one of our own.'

Teddy's forearm pressed against her throat as she finished speaking. He was too strong for her; there was no way to escape.

'Lies,' he said calmly as he kept up the pressure. 'I followed orders to the letter: "Come up from behind and shoot Jerry down."'

'But it wasn't Jerry – any fool can tell one of our planes from theirs. You learn the difference in your first week of training.'

'Not if it's pitch black and you're flying through low cloud. How was I supposed to know?' Teddy had rehearsed his version of events many times. 'The court will take one look at the circumstances and throw out the charge.'

Angela pushed against him with all her might. Then, ignoring the pain in her ankle, she brought her knee up sharply to catch him in the groin. He bent double, allowing her to break free. 'There's a witness, you idiot!' She scrambled for the door but Teddy was quick to recover and he rushed at her and knocked her forwards on to the floor. He fell full-length on top of her.

'You still don't get it, do you?' he said savagely.

His breath felt hot on the back of her neck as, filled with disgust, she lay unable to move.

'Witness or no witness, all I need to say is that my head-set wasn't working. I never received the second order to cease fire – simple as that.'

Still Angela fought to wriggle free. The door was six feet from where they lay.

'Oh Angela, it's useless to fight me.' Teddy's voice grew almost tender and he pressed his lips against the top of her head. 'The big question right now is: how do I deal with you?'

'Don't!' She felt him mumble the words into her hair as his weight shifted and he ran his hand down her side and across the curve of her buttock. It didn't stop there – he reached down to raise her skirt then felt for the bare flesh above her stocking top. Her skin crawled as he stroked the back of her thigh with his thumb.

'Come to think of it, I don't see why we shouldn't finish what we began.' Teddy grunted then shifted again – just enough to roll Angela on to her back then trap her once more. 'What do you say?'

She wrenched one hand free and slapped him hard on the cheek. He jerked back then grunted again and sank on to her, tugging at the top of her dress and ripping the bodice.

'Yes; one way or the other we'll finish it.'

His lips pressed against Angela's neck as she went on struggling. She retaliated with fists and knees but his weight was too much for her.

He reached down again and pulled her skirt and petticoat up round her waist. 'If this is the way you want it . . .'

'Don't!' she pleaded. She glimpsed the high rafters then turned her head to the side and strained away from him to avoid his lips. 'Teddy, don't!'

'False alarm!' Douglas addressed the officers assembled in the entrance hall. 'That was Squadron Leader Stevens on the phone with the latest intelligence. Jerry won't be bothering us tonight after all.'

Jean broke ranks and ran towards him for an explanation, barging past Agnes and Horace whose ripe language turned the air blue. 'How did that happen?' she demanded.

'It was our boys, not theirs.' Relief had an unexpected effect on Douglas, who had been geared up for action. The sudden reversal had left him feeling strangely adrift. 'Now I suppose we might as well get some shut-eye.'

'Whose mistake was it?' Jean wondered as she walked with him towards the stairs.

'Who cares?' Agnes said with a shrug. She too was heading upstairs.

'Bloody idiot, whoever it was.' Horace gave the base of the newel post a vicious kick before following the others.

Mary and Bobbie brought up the rear. 'Thank goodness for that,' Mary muttered. 'I didn't fancy a

416

night camped out in the cellars while the bombs rained down.'

'Same here,' Bobbie agreed. 'Remember last time, when it was the real thing?'

'How could I forget?' Mary decided she would wait up for Cameron to get back from the ferry pool. 'I'm heading for the kitchen to make a cuppa. Would you like one?'

Bobbie shook her head. 'I still wonder where on earth Angela's got to.'

'And Teddy.' Mary had second thoughts about the tea. 'You don't think they've been holed up in his room all this time, ignoring the roll-call? Shall I get Horace to go up and investigate?' She hurried off without waiting for an answer.

'No, they would have heard . . .' Bobbie's sentence tailed off. *Doors opening, footsteps running along corridors*, she thought with mounting unease. Nevertheless, it was very late so where were they? Had Teddy's bike broken down and left them stranded? Or might Mary have been on the right track after all? There was one quick way to find out.

Bobbie went out through the main door, then strode along the terrace and round the side of the house to see if Teddy's motorbike was parked in the stable yard. Yes; there it was – close to the stone steps leading up to the grooms' quarters. 'Oh!' she said out loud and was about to retrace her steps. 'Oh!' again.

The moon shone high and bright in the clear sky. The minute hand of the clock jerked forward. *Angela isn't in Teddy's room*. Bobbie's heart missed a beat as the truth struck her. She stood stock-still, studying

417

the row of stables and the grooms' loft above. *I know exactly where they are.*

Against her will Bobbie relived the sickening flop and thud of the mattress on to the bare, dusty floor. *Lie still and don't put up a fight; there's a good girl.*

She fought the nightmare: *I am safe. Angela isn't.*

Teddy's lips and hands all over her. *Lie still.* Flickering flames. Lips and hands.

Do something, Bobbie told herself.

After Teddy had forced himself on her she'd feared that she would fall for ever, that there would be no end. Black oaks and ash trees, beech and sycamore crowded her memory. Sharp thorns underfoot.

I came through it; I survived. Now Angela needs me.

Hoping against hope that she was wrong, Bobbie forced herself to walk slowly towards the steps. Every sound in the silent yard was magnified – the rustle of fallen leaves, a door banging in the main house. A car approached along the back lane. More planes flew in from the east.

She reached the door and listened.

'Don't! Teddy, don't!'

Bobbie flung open the door. There were two people on the floor in the dark – Teddy and Angela. He was on top of her, tearing at her clothes. There was a tangle of pale limbs. Angela cried out for Teddy to stop.

Tools leaned against the wall – a gardener's fork, a hoe and two spades. Bobbie grabbed one of the spades and ran at them. Teddy's back was arched over Angela, Angela's face was turned away, her hands trying in vain to push him off. Bobbie raised the flat blade of the spade and swiped it sideways with all her might. She caught Teddy in the ribs and knocked him clear. Then she took hold of Angela's arm and dragged her to her feet. Teddy's hand grasped at Bobbie's ankle and she struck him with the spade a second time. He fell back and Angela and Bobbie fled from the room.

CHAPTER TWENTY-THREE

'I don't know about you but I could certainly do with a drink,' Hilary told Cameron. He drove under the clock tower and pulled up in the stable yard next to Teddy's motorbike.

'You're on.' Cameron got out and slammed the car door. He paused to glance up at three Stirlings flying low over Burton Wood. The drone of their powerful engines filled the air. 'Denmark,' he muttered. 'All safely out and safely back, touch wood.'

'Yes – let me check with Douglas to see if he cares to join us.' Hilary jumped out and overtook Cameron to run up the steps leading to the front terrace.

'I'll see you both in the bar in five minutes,' Cameron called after him. He stood for a few moments reflecting on the night's false alarm with a mixture of anger and relief. Visibility had been nigh perfect so how come the ground defence people had made such a rudimentary error? All done in the heat of the moment, Cameron supposed. And those chaps in the coastal lookout bunkers worked under a great strain, knowing that one moment's lapse of concentration on their part could lead to disaster. 'We're all living on our nerves,' he muttered to himself as he followed Hilary up the steps. He walked along the terrace, across the hall and into the lounge where he opened a bottle of whisky and lined up three glasses, ready to pour.

Hilary paused on the first landing. 'Have you seen Douglas?' he asked Jean, who waited outside the bathroom door, washbag and towel in hand.

'He's gone up to bed,' she reported. 'You'll catch him if you're quick.' As Hilary hurried on, Jean tapped on the bathroom door. 'Everything all right in there?' she queried.

A second later Bobbie flung open the door. 'Come in!' She dragged Jean into the room and gestured towards Angela who sat on the edge of the bath with her head in her hands. 'Teddy – he . . .'

Jean took in the scene. Steam rose from the water running into the old-fashioned, claw-foot bath and condensation had formed on the green and white tiles. The orange and white striped towel around Angela's shoulders didn't hide the fact that her dress was badly torn. She sat barefoot and sobbing silently, her body heaving. 'Good God!' Horrified, Jean closed the door behind her. 'When? Where?'

'During roll-call. The same place as before – grooms' room above the stables. He would've . . .'

'But you stopped him?'

'Yes. I got there just in time.'

Jean knelt beside Angela. 'Did Teddy hurt you?' she whispered.

Angela shook her head without looking up.

'She was limping,' Bobbie explained. 'I knocked him for six then brought her to the house.'

'Here; let me help you.' Turning off the tap, Jean

421

raised Angela to her feet. Then she slid the towel from her shoulders and eased her out of her dress. 'Where's Teddy now?'

Bobbie carried a wooden chair from under the window and made Angela sit again so that they could help her off with her stockings. 'I laid him out flat,' she told Jean. 'He's probably still there.'

Sitting in her satin petticoat, Angela looked up. 'I'm sorry,' she breathed. 'Such a fool. So much trouble.'

Bobbie hugged her. 'Listen to me; we're going to get you into this bath and look after you. Then we're going to get you to bed.'

'Can you manage that by yourself?' Jean checked with Bobbie. 'There's nothing else for it – Hilary needs to know about this, the sooner the better.' Without waiting for Bobbie's response, she hurried away.

'There, there,' Bobbie murmured as she slipped Angela's petticoat over her head. 'Jean will sort everything out for us. The bath is ready for you. Come on now; easy does it.'

Jean had reached the bottom of the stairs when she ran into Mary who had failed in her mission to track down Teddy and Angela in the men's quarters. 'Come with me,' she insisted.

'Where to?' Mary sensed another emergency – surely not another air raid warning? 'What's wrong, Jean? Where are we going?'

'It's Angela; I'll explain later.' Jean rushed out of the front door ahead of Mary. They ran along the terrace, down the steps then into the stable yard where several cars and Teddy's motorbike were parked.

'It's pitch black – I can't see a thing,' Mary complained.

'Quickly,' Jean urged. As her eyes grew used to the dark, she made out that the door to the grooms' quarters stood open. 'We have to find Teddy.'

Angela . . . Teddy. Mary connected the two names and feared the worst as she followed Jean up the steps. 'What did he do to Angela?'

'He attacked her – tried to rape her.' The second Jean stepped inside the room she sensed they were too late. The loft was empty. She picked up a garden fork lying near the door to use as a weapon if necessary. Then she checked to make sure – treading cautiously past the stove and an old mattress to the far end where broken furniture was stacked then returning again. 'He's got away,' she reported back to Mary.

'Are you sure?'

'Yes, certain.' Jean threw down the fork with a clatter then stepped outside. 'We really do need to find Hilary.'

So she and Mary retraced their steps, across the yard, up the side steps and along the terrace.

'Knock-knock.' Up on the attic floor, Hilary tapped on Douglas's door. 'Are you awake, old chap? Do you fancy joining Cameron and me for a nightcap?'

'No, I won't; ta.' Douglas was already in his pyjamas, ready for bed. He opened his door with an apologetic grin. 'It's been a long day.'

'Right you are.' Hilary was about to go back downstairs when Douglas spoke again.

'By the way, Teddy was missing from roll-call. So was Angela. I thought you ought to know.'

Hilary nodded. Something had to be done about those two, but it would wait until tomorrow morning. On second thoughts, he might as well knock on Teddy's door and tackle him straight away.

No sooner said . . . Floorboards creaking, Hilary strode along the dark corridor and rapped on Teddy's door.

No answer.

Hilary paused to consider his next move then cautiously opened the door to a chaotic scene – clothes and magazines strewn everywhere, sheets pulled from the bed, a wall mirror smashed and a wooden chair lying broken on the floor. Someone had gone berserk in here. He swore and pulled the door to then strode back to Douglas's room. 'Get dressed!' he yelled through the door. 'Come downstairs double-quick. Join me and Cameron in the bar.'

'More planes,' Mary remarked. She and Jean paused on the terrace to observe two RAF bombers approach from the east, their engines stuttering as the planes lost height.

'Those two will be lucky if they make it home.' Jean watched with a worried frown. 'They sound as if they're low on petrol,' Mary agreed.

But they had no time to waste so they hurried on into the house where they found Cameron and Hilary hovering at the foot of the stairs.

'Has anyone seen Teddy?' Jean asked.

'I was about to ask you the same thing.' Hilary had

just brought Cameron up to speed and now they waited impatiently for Douglas to join them.

'He attacked Angela,' Jean told him hastily. 'Don't worry; Bobbie's looking after her. Mary and I have searched the stable yard – he's not there.'

'How long ago?' Hilary looked at his watch and saw that it was almost one o'clock.

'Just now. Teddy's motorbike is still there.'

'Which means he's on foot – he can't have got far,' Mary reasoned.

As Douglas hurried down the stairs, Jean pulled him to one side to describe the new emergency.

'Teddy wrecked his room,' Hilary informed the others. He envisaged Teddy losing control and lashing out at whoever stood in his way. 'He sees that the game is up.'

'So what now?' Cameron wanted to know.

'We'll search the ruined east wing and the grounds.' Hilary decided that he and Douglas would take the former while Cameron checked the front lawns. 'Jean and Mary, you stay inside. Search the servants' quarters, attics, cellars – anywhere you can think of. Stick together. If you corner Teddy, don't take risks. Report back to me.'

The group was about to disperse, each person grimly determined to hunt Teddy down. Mary reminded Cameron about the dangers: 'Don't forget about the incendiaries – the bomb disposal boys might not have found them all.'

He kissed her briefly. 'I'll be careful,' he promised as he went off.

Douglas said the same to Jean as he followed

Hilary. Together the two men clambered over piles of rubble then disappeared into the deserted hospital wing.

Soon Mary and Jean were left alone. 'Cellars first?' Mary suggested.

Jean shook her head. 'I wouldn't choose to hide there if I were Teddy; far too easy for us to trap him.'

'Likewise the attics.' Mary put herself in Teddy's position. 'What would I do if I were him?'

'I wouldn't stick around; I would run.' Jean decided that the chances of finding Teddy in the immediate vicinity were low.

Mary agreed. 'Not on foot, though. I'd use my motorbike.'

Without saying another word the two women sprinted along the terrace and rounded the corner in time to see the fugitive creep cautiously from the boot room at the back of the house. He carried a haversack over one shoulder and looked in every direction as he inched towards the nearest parked car. Jean and Mary stayed in the shadows then, as soon as Teddy's back was turned, they ran down the steps into the stable yard, aiming to cut off his exit.

Without noticing the girls, Teddy reached his bike. He seized hold of the handlebars and rocked it off its stand then sat astride it. He kicked hard to start the engine – once, twice, three times. The machine spluttered into life.

Mary and Jean reached the archway. They heard the roar of Teddy's motorbike and saw him manoeuvre it between the cars. He turned it to face them then saw in his headlight beam that they meant to block his escape. He set off towards them.

With Mary beside her, Jean put up a warning hand. The bottom half of Teddy's face was hidden by a scarf, his head was bare and he was wearing his leather gauntlets and pilot's jacket with its collar turned up. He glared and rode straight at them.

Mary felt Teddy land a kick on her thigh and she staggered sideways against Hilary's parked car. At the last second Jean jumped clear. Teddy was through the arch and roaring up the gravel path towards Burton Wood.

'We can't let him,' Mary gasped. A quick glance at Hilary's dashboard told her that he'd left his ignition key in the lock. 'Quick; get in!' she yelled at Jean, who was beside her in a flash. Before Teddy had reached the gate, Mary had started the engine and driven under the archway in hot pursuit.

Hearing them coming after him and seeing that the gate ahead was closed, Teddy decided there was nothing for it but to ride his bike straight through. Picking up speed, he lowered his head and hunched his shoulders to prepare for impact. With scarcely a judder the flimsy latch gave way and the gates swung open. Now there was nothing to prevent his escape.

Mary's heart was in her mouth. 'Hold tight,' she said to Jean through gritted teeth. The gates swung on their hinges back towards the car but she didn't slow down. There was a splintering noise as they bulldozed through.

'Ouch!' Jean grimaced at the damage done to bumper and front wings.

Then they were out on the lane and Teddy was ahead of them, careering along the back lane towards the churchyard, leaning into the first sharp bend, taking it at speed.

Jean grasped the door strap. She heard the squeal of the car's tyres as Mary took the bend on two wheels. There was a distance of a hundred yards between them and Teddy. When he reached the junction with the main road he turned left towards Highcliff. 'He'll be faster than us on the open road,' she predicted with a sinking heart.

Mary scarcely slowed for the junction. There was another squeal of tyres. The chase was still on – Teddy gained a little but not much as they sped through the village.

He glanced behind with nothing in his mind except getting away. He didn't care where to or what he would do next; he was only aware that the glamorous, successful life that he'd worked towards over the last few years had blown up in his face – and all over a scrap of green fabric and bloody Angela. Bloody Angela and bloody Bobbie: brainless bitches the pair of them. Teddy increased his revs and built up more speed.

'Faster!' Jean held tight.

Mary grasped the steering wheel with both hands as she drove through deep shadows cast by trees out on to open road. Here the moon shone bright and she too picked up speed. She knew the stretch of road well: every farmhouse and barn, every stone wall and hedge.

Teddy gained again. He ignored the drone of a plane's engines coming up from behind – no doubt another RAF boy flying low, decreasing its revs in preparation for landing.

Jean glanced up as Mary pressed the accelerator to the floor. She gasped then looked again. The shape was unmistakeable – a Ju 88!

'What?' Mary asked.

'Junker – overhead; coming in low!'

For a split second Mary took her eyes off the road. She saw a black swastika against a white background on each wing tip. The plane was low enough for her to read the German airman's *Luftwaffe* number stencilled on to the grey fuselage as he flew overhead at less than 100 hundred feet.

What was the pilot playing at? He was much too low to bomb them; had he even seen them? Jean could make no sense of what was happening until the bomber's engine suddenly cut out and there was deathly silence.

'He's run out of fuel!' Mary realized. A giant shadow passed over the car. In the moonlight Mary and Jean made out every nut and bolt of the lowered undercarriage.

The Junker glided over them.

'He's going to make an emergency landing,' Jean cried. 'Brake, Mary; brake!'

Teddy looked up and saw the enemy plane falling from the sky.

'Brake!' Jean cried again.

Mary slammed her foot on the pedal, just in time.

As the Junker kept on falling, Teddy upped his revs in the belief that he would pull safely away. *I can beat the Jerry bastard*, he thought. But then no – his Enfield didn't have enough power and the aircraft overtook him. It dropped to the tarmac ahead of him. Its wings tore up the hedges; its tyres burned a black trail on to the tarmac. Oil poured from its damaged engines as it veered into the steeply sloping stubble field to the left.

Teddy braked hard. His bike hit the oil slick and skidded. He put his foot out in an attempt to stay upright but the bare metal of the stand scraped the tarmac and sent up sparks. Instantly flames engulfed both bike and rider. The fire roared. The unharmed German pilot and his gunner climbed out of their crumpled plane and raised their arms in surrender.

Mary brought Hilary's car safely to a halt fifty yards short of a wall of greedy orange flames and black smoke – an inferno. She and Jean sat in silence, knowing there was nothing to be done. Teddy could not be saved.

'I'll write to you as soon as I'm settled.' Cameron's bag was packed. It was time for him to leave Rixley and move on to his next posting with Training Command. The imminent separation from Mary tore at his heart.

She stood with him on the terrace at the Grange. The sky was grey, the trees almost bare. 'Make sure you do,' she murmured.

'And I'll speak to you on the phone whenever I have a free evening.'

They held hands and gazed straight ahead at rooks gathered high in the branches of the sycamore trees.

'I'll let you know when I get notice of my first leave,' he promised. 'I'll be over here like a shot.'

Mary nodded. Cameron would teach signalling and navigation to raw recruits. He would train them in dummy cockpits – these are your five dials, this is your joystick, your radio. Then he would send them up on their first solo flights. They would learn formation flying and go out on bombing exercises, drink too much beer and carry out their first missions with deadly hangovers – these boys of eighteen and nineteen. She grasped his hand and sighed.

'Don't be sad.'

'But I am – I can't help it.'

'Even though I love you more than I can put into words?'

Mary risked turning her head towards him, trying not to cry. 'That's why.'

Cameron smiled and wiped away her tears. 'Enjoy flying your Spits,' he encouraged gently. 'Spare me a thought when you're up there in the pale blue yonder.'

'Always,' she promised. November mists would shroud the moors, winds would blow. She would fly wherever Douglas sent her. And she would think of the man she loved.

'I have to go.' Cameron held her and kissed her. 'I love you, Mary Holland – I hope you know that.'

She kissed him back. 'I do, Flight Lieutenant Ainslie. Truly, I do.'

Sitting in the ops room at Rixley, Douglas pulled his two RAF dog tags from his pocket and placed them on the desk – one red, one green, hexagonal in shape, each inscribed with his name and pilot number. He slid the green one towards Jean. 'Take it – it's yours,' he told her.

'Douglas, I can't.' Jean stood with her chit in her

hand, her forage cap tucked under her arm. Destination, Firth of Forth and all points north. She shook her head. 'These tags mean the world to you.'

He gazed up at her. 'So do you, Jean – the absolute world. I want you to have it.'

So she picked up the disc and turned it between her fingers. *Thornton, D W, 43792.* 'I'll wear it around my neck. It'll bring me luck.' She looped the cord over her head then lowered the zip of her flying suit and tucked the tag out of sight.

'You don't need luck, Jean; not with your ability.' Douglas stood up to walk her down the stairs out on to the runway. 'You'll have no problems with the weather until you reach Holy Island. Then you'll run into thirty-mile-an-hour winds blowing in from Scandinavia, so be prepared.'

'I will.' Jean stopped at the end of the runway to watch Stan tow her P-51 Mustang into position.

'You've checked your Notes?' Douglas asked.

She tapped her top pocket and nodded. 'You're not to worry about me, you hear?'

He smiled and nodded unconvincingly.

'I mean it; I'll be back before you know it.' She would drop off the Mustang and catch the overnight train home. 'It's Sunday tomorrow. Perhaps we could go for a spin to Northgate in the afternoon – just you and me.'

'You're on,' Douglas said. Jean took half of his heart with her when she walked across the runway – so beautiful and brave.

Stan gave Jean a leg-up on to the wing and she turned to wave at Douglas. Then she blew him a kiss.

She wore his green tag around her neck and in

January they would be married. With one final wave, Jean climbed into the cockpit of the Mustang, fastened her harness and set the controls ready for take-off.

'Darling Lionel, My answer is yes.' Angela started her letter by jumping in with both feet. Yes to the engagement. Yes to his kind, kind heart.

'We will get married, you and I, if you can forgive me for all that has gone before – my foolishness and my doubts.'

She sat in her room, pen in hand and looking out of the window at planes taking off from the ferry pool. A Mustang rose effortlessly above the trees then a Lancaster followed by a lean, sleek Spit Mark V. Angela's spirits rose with it. *Lucky devils*, she thought. *And here I am, grounded by the doc, trying not to dwell on the Teddy Simpson fiasco.* Easier said than done, of course.

'Sleep,' Bobbie had told her straight after the event. 'Tomorrow you'll feel better. And the day after – gradually, one step at a time.'

The shock of Teddy's death had ricocheted around the ferry pool – not in the air scrapping with the enemy but on his blessed motorbike; an unlucky accident that no one could have foretold.

To disappear in an instant and leave nothing behind – that took some getting used to. But life went on, Stan had reminded everyone. On the Friday he'd met up with Gillian in the Fox where Dotty Kirk had been chatting ten to the dozen with Gordon and Olive had amused herself by teasing young Bob Cross.

'I'd have had Teddy's flying jacket if he hadn't

been wearing it,' she'd joked. 'Don't look so shocked – Teddy wouldn't have needed it any more, would he?' It didn't pay to get too close to the people you worked with, she'd advised the lad. You got the rug pulled from under you if you did.

At the Grange, Angela had been forced to lie low to nurse her injuries. On the day following Teddy's death, Hilary had approached her and Bobbie and asked what they wanted to do about Teddy's savage assaults. 'Nothing,' they'd said in the same moment. What would be gained by pursuing a dead man? Hilary had been relieved; they must all look forward and not back.

Only one question had remained unanswered. 'Was Teddy guilty as charged in the court martial documents?' Angela had wanted to know. 'Or did he really not receive the order to cease fire? Did he believe that he had Jerry in his sights when he fired his guns?'

Hilary had shrugged. 'We'll never know for certain – only that Teddy's gunner was on the scene and was willing to give evidence against him.'

'And one of our boys died,' Bobbie had added. That was the saddest thing. And in Angela and Bobbie's book, the fact that Teddy had never expressed any remorse over the fatal error counted hugely against him.

Pen still poised and gazing into the far distance, Angela felt sure that at some point she would describe to Lionel what had taken place in the room above the stables – without fuss; simply an account. Then in her mind Teddy Simpson would truly be laid to rest.

434

She went on with her letter. 'We will get along nicely without Pa's consent – I see that now. Because, with a fair wind behind us, love will carry us through the rest of this war and afterwards in peace time – you on dry land, me in the air still following my dream.

'Jean and Mary told me recently that I'm a slow learner in matters of the heart. "Hah!" I said. "That's the pot calling the kettle black. Ha-ha-ha!" But they're dear girls and you will like them when you meet them properly. Bobbie has agreed to be my chief bridesmaid when we marry. So you see: we Spitfire girls stick together.

'Too much chatter from me, my darling, but everything I write comes from the heart. I love you, my dear, and want to send this letter off without delay. Until I have time to write more – Your loving Angie.'

Bobbie sat at the controls of the Spit, waiting for take-off. It was a specially adapted reconnaissance model, complete with cameras bolted to each wing. Visibility was 1,500 yards, with 1,000 feet of cloud clearance – perfect conditions for her flight to Brize Norton, where the ageing Spit would henceforth be put to use in the RAF training programme for air gunners and pilots.

'She's seen plenty of action,' Stan had informed her as he'd finished his inspection of the oil filter and propeller spinner. He'd pointed to the victory tally stencilled on the aircraft's flank – six small white swastikas – and given her the thumbs-up. 'Up the revs,' he'd instructed before joining Gordon at the back end. Then two ground crewmen had thrown their weight on the tail fins to act as human ballast while Bobbie had checked the prop speed then returned the thumbs-up.

'Chocks away!' Gordon yelled as he and Stan pulled them clear.

Bobbie's hand hovered over the stick. The engine sang sweet and smooth as it reached full throttle and she released the brake and rolled forward. She swiftly built up speed. Objects on the ground rushed by in a blur – control tower and office block to one side, Nissen huts and Burton Wood to the other. A touch on the stick was all she needed to rise from the ground.

Oh, the power of it and the glory! Bobbie glanced down at Rixley village and the grey roof of Burton Grange. She gained height, snug in her narrow seat, safely strapped in as she banked to starboard and prepared to head south. The Spit tilted, its wings glinting in the sunlight. *Beautiful, thrilling – Brize Norton, here I come!*

Bobbie hadn't mentioned it to anyone but today's flight was special. It would bring her up to five hundred hours and the rank of first officer, alongside Angela and not far behind Jean – a milestone if ever there was one.

But for now she sat back and soared, lost in the glorious moment, hurtling through the clear air, mistress of all she surveyed.

AUTHOR'S NOTE

As with many readers of this fictionalized account of
the wonderful Spitfire girls, my direct family links
with those who served during the Second World War
are now sadly broken. But I'm sure that memories of
our parents' and grandparents' wartime experiences
retain a strong hold over all our imaginations.

Though I can no longer listen to my father Jim
Lyne's sadly infrequent anecdotes about serving as a
chief petty officer with the Royal Navy – the free
cigarettes and rum rations, the camaraderie, the
occasional shore leave spent with his musician uncle
in Glasgow – in my head I do still hear his voice
recounting the terrifying moments after his ship,
HMS *Tanimbar*, was torpedoed off Malta in June
1942. Happily, I also have his crystal-clear written
account of this event, penned some sixty years
afterwards:

> The *Tanimbar*, with its cargo of aviation fuel,
> blew up. Protected by a steel wall formed by
> the captain's bridge, I was one of very few sur-
> vivors of the blast. The vessel sank fast . . .
> Along with two other lads (one of whom

couldn't swim), I floated around amongst the flotsam and eventually finished up sitting astride an upturned lifeboat . . . All watches stopped at twelve noon when we hit the water.

When I first heard this story as a child, it had a huge impact. I saw and heard in my mind's eye the sea aflame, the non-swimmer crying out for help, the encounter with a Dutch survivor on the upturned boat asking Dad for, of all things, a light for his cigar. Then there was the secret escape from Malta that conjured up yet more dramatic images – the cramped, nine-day journey to Gibraltar by river-class submarine which crawled along the seabed and only surfaced at night for fear of further U-boat attacks.

Dad was twenty-one years old at the time; a similar age to many of the young women who feature in this story of the female pilots who delivered fighter planes and bombers to the RAF.

As for the ATA pilots themselves, after the war many had no option but to leave behind the perils and thrills of flying the iconic Spitfire and settle for marriage and quiet domesticity. These remarkable women can no longer tell their own stories but their names deserve to live on – Margot Duhalde from Chile, Maureen Dunlop from Buenos Aires, Jackie Sorour from Cape Town, Jackie Cochran from California, and the home-grown Joan Hughes, Freydis Leaf, Mary de Bunsen, Anne Blackwell, Diana Barnato Walker, Mary Ellis . . . the list goes on.

How, I wonder, did these fiercely independent, courageous and often eccentric women survivors deal with post-war rationing on butter, sugar and eggs, or with the everyday chores (and delights) connected with child rearing? For what could possibly compare with that moment when our fearless Atta girl climbed into that cockpit and ran those checks on hydraulics, trimmers ... flaps, gills, gauges; the indescribable adrenaline rush of taking to the sky in a Spit, alone and free?

Jim Lyne in his Royal Navy uniform.

ACKNOWLEDGEMENTS

Francesca Best, my editor at Transworld, has steered this project with the steadiest of hands. Thank you, Francesca, for your unflagging enthusiasm and belief.

At the very start of this journey Kim Read at the Yorkshire Air Museum in Elvington near York helped set me on the right road; Kim, I sincerely hope that you don't spot too many factual errors here.

Finally, it turns out that many of my friends share my admiration for these amazingly bold and brave ATA women, so special thanks are due to Paul and Carol Withey for chewing the fat with me and providing invaluable pointers in the right direction.

And as ever, thank you Caroline Sheldon for reasons too many to mention.

If you loved The Spitfire Girls *don't miss . . .*

The Land Girls at Christmas

'Calling All Women!'

It's 1941 and as the Second World War rages on, girls from all over the country are signing up to the Women's Land Army. Renowned for their camaraderie and spirit, it is these brave women who step in to take on the gruelling farm work from the men conscripted into the armed forces.

When Yorkshire mill girl Una joins the cause, she wonders how she'll adapt to country life. Luckily she's quickly befriended by more experienced Land Girls Brenda and Grace. But as Christmas draws ever near, the girls' resolve is tested as scandals and secrets are revealed, lovers risk being torn apart, and even patriotic loyalties are called into question . . .

With only a week to go until the festivities, can the strain of wartime still allow for the magic of Christmas?

Available now . . .